HIS WICKED KISS

The moment he inclined his head, Emma rose on tiptoes. Her arms went around his neck with enough force to bring her body flush to his. His hands at the small of her back held her there. She lifted her face and the distance that separated their mouths ceased to exist. When he whispered her name, it was as if she could taste the sound of it on her lips.

She was delighted to learn her name tasted like warm brandy.

Restell edged Emma backward against the pianoforte, and her hip brushed the keys. Neither of them noticed the oddly discordant accompaniment to their kiss, nor would they have done anything differently if they had.

This kiss would suffer no trivial interruption.

There was little that was gentle in the press of their mouths. Need did not make much allowance for tenderness. There was heat here, and passion. Nothing about the movement of his lips across hers was hurried. He drank slowly, tempered by the knowledge that he had been thirsting for just this end for a very long time and desiring that the end should not come too quickly. Emma's desire matched his own.

Her fingertips brushed the damp, curling ends of his hair just above his collar. The color and texture of it was so light she might have been threading sunshine. She felt him shiver, then knew a like response in herself. His tongue swept across the ridge of her teeth. She opened her mouth wider and her own tongue tangled with his . . .

Books by Jo Goodman

The Captain's Lady
Crystal Passion
Seaswept Abandon
Velvet Night
Violet Fire
Scarlet Lies
Tempting Torment
Midnight Princess
Passion's Sweet Revenge
Sweet Fire
Wild Sweet Ecstasy
Rogue's Mistress
Forever in My Heart
Always in My Dreams
Only in My Arms
My Steadfast Heart
My Reckless Heart
With All My Heart
More Than You Know
More Than You Wished
Let Me Be the One
Everything I Ever Wanted
All I Ever Needed
Beyond a Wicked Kiss
A Season to Be Sinful
One Forbidden Evening
If His Kiss Is Wicked

Published by Zebra Books

IF HIS KISS
IS WICKED

Jo Goodman

ZEBRA BOOKS
Kensington Publishing Corp.
www.kensingtonbooks.com

ZEBRA BOOKS are published by

Kensington Publishing Corp.
850 Third Avenue
New York, NY 10022

All Kensington titles, imprints, and distributed lines are available at special quantity discounts for bulk purchases for sales
promotion, premiums, fund-raising, educational, or institu-
tional use.

Special book excerpts or customized printings can also be created to fit specific needs. For details, write or phone the office
of the Kensington Special Sales Manager: Attn. Special Sales
Department. Kensington Publishing Corp., 850 Third Avenue,
New York, NY 10022. Phone: 1-800-221-2647.

Zebra and the Z logo Reg. U.S. Pat. & TM Off.

ISBN-13: 978-0-8217-7777-0
ISBN-10: 0-8217-7777-7

First Printing: September 2007
10 9 8 7 6 5 4 3 2 1

Printed in the United States of America

For Mark Irvin and the Vilgas
Terrific neighbors
Flamingo commandos
I surrender

Prologue

June 1822
London

"Be a dear, won't you, and fetch my bonnet?" Marisol looked past her reflection to where her cousin was standing at the foot of the bed. "You look at sixes and sevens, Emma-lyn. It is not at all becoming. Dithering never is. You might at least occupy yourself with some small task."

Emma knew that she had never dithered in her life, but she offered no rejoinder to refute Marisol's observation. Experience taught her that a denial would not serve. Marisol remained firm in her views and such evidence that could be mounted to sway a less rigid mind was regarded as a nuisance.

Emma glanced at the window. The damask drapes were drawn back so they framed a rapidly graying sky above the rooftops. "You realize it is going to rain, don't you?"

"That is of no consequence to me." Marisol shifted her chair closer to the vanity and examined the pearl earbobs she had chosen. "Are these all the thing, do you think? I cannot decide if I prefer the studs or the ones that dangle."

Emma did not offer an opinion. Marisol's discourse was not truly intended to elicit a comment. Her cousin was merely speaking to herself. "Will you want the black leghorn bonnet?"

"What?" Distracted from her fashion dilemma, Marisol

frowned. Her perfect bow of a mouth disappeared as she pursed her lips. She regarded Emma, exasperation and impatience bringing her eyebrows together until only a slender crease separated the pair. "My new leghorn? I should think not. Why the satin quilling would be ruined. You said yourself it is going to rain. And the feathers? They will droop to comical effect. That is not done, Emmalyn, even by you."

At this inkling that it would be she, not Marisol, who would be stepping out in the rain, the fine, dark hairs at the back of Emma's neck rose slightly. She touched her nape with her fingertips, gently massaging her hackles. "The satin straw bonnet, then."

"Yes." Marisol's frown eased. "I confess I had been thinking of something else, but the satin straw is the best choice. You are so clever to think of it." She turned away from the mirror entirely and looked up at Emma. "You are always so good to me, Emmalyn. I do not tell you often enough, I'm quite certain of it. I am resolved that I must tell you at least once a day how very dear you are. You'll remind me, won't you?"

"If you like," Emma said, her features perfectly schooled. She hurried into Marisol's dressing room before she surrendered to the almost violent urge to laugh.

The satin straw bonnet was several years out of fashion, although only the most slavish devotees of the Paris style would know. Marisol recently purchased a striped Barcelona handkerchief, which she used to replace the bonnet's original blue satin ribbon. Emma had to admit it was a fetching confection—on Marisol. For herself, Emma preferred something less likely to draw eyes and comments.

Marisol had settled on the delicate, dangling pearl earrings and was admiring their effect when Emma returned with the bonnet. The pearls lightly brushed the slim stem of her neck as she twisted her head to one side, then the other. "It is the most delicious sensation to feel them touch my skin." A small shiver accompanied this observation and she looked immediately to Emma for her reaction. When Emma merely regarded her without expression, Marisol was moved to add, "It puts me in mind of a kiss, you know, just there, against my neck. Do you know such a feeling, Emmalyn?"

"I dare say I do." She held out the bonnet to her cousin, then drew it back as Marisol swiveled on her stool and lifted lambent blue eyes in her direction. The expression was at once sly and curious, and Emma was made wary. A tendril of silky ebon hair fell against Marisol's temple, and the curl lay there unmoving as though painted by a fine hand. The effect relieved the symmetry of Marisol's countenance, but immediately made Emma more aware of the features that lent her cousin an almost doll-like perfection. Marisol's complexion was without blemish and fashionably pale. This porcelain canvas made the pink hue in her cheeks all the more startling, and the rose blush softened or deepened with such charming results that it was as though Marisol had the knack of willing it so.

"Have you been kissed then?" asked Marisol. Her full bottom lip was thrust forward in the first stage of a pretty pout. "Why is it that you have never told me? I will have his name. I *must*. We are agreed there shall be no secrets between us."

Emma could not recall that she had ever entered into such an agreement with her cousin. It would be such an uncharacteristic lapse in good judgment that it could mean only that she'd been kicked in the head by a horse. "His name was Fitzroy. Are you quite happy that you have it from me?"

"Fitzroy? What sort of name is that?"

"A fine one, I suspect. He was comfortable with it, at least it always seemed so to me." Emma held out the bonnet again as Marisol sucked in her bottom lip. "Here. Shall I help you arrange it?"

Marisol took the bonnet, but placed it in her lap. She continued to regard Emma with some misgivings while her fingers fiddled with the bonnet's trim. "Fitzroy. Was that his Christian name or his surname?"

Emma pretended to be much struck by the question. "Do you know, I don't believe I ever inquired," she said at last. "I only ever knew him to have the one name."

"But you permitted him to kiss you?"

"Yes, of course. He was most amiable and I liked him immensely." Emma noted that confusion set Marisol's perfect features slightly awry. "Have I given you cause to think ill of me?" she asked. "You are frowning in earnest."

"Then it is very bad of you to make me do so." Having admonished Emma, Marisol effortlessly smoothed her expression and presented what might be interpreted as only polite concern. "I could never think ill of you, Emma, but it is rather surprising to hear you speak so blithely on this matter of being kissed. I feel as if I should be reminding you that it is a dangerous practice to engage in flirtation with a man to whom you have not been properly introduced."

Emma watched as Marisol paused, blinked slowly and widely, then finally framed a perfect O with her lips. Such was her cousin's look of dawning comprehension. The physicality of the effort never failed to fascinate Emma. "Yes, dearest," Emma said kindly. "You heard yourself say it, now what is to be done?"

"But I was speaking of you," Marisol protested. "You cannot hold me to the same standard that I hold you."

"What an absurd thing to say. Why ever not?"

"The simple answer is that you are four years my senior. Still, I do not account that twenty-two is such a great age, nor eighteen an age of no consequence. The truth is that you are an infinitely better person than I am."

Now it was Emma who blinked. Her eyes, more green than blue but with an unmistakable hint of the latter, were shuttered briefly by long dark lashes. When a cocoa-colored tendril of hair fell forward it did not lay prettily against her temple, but curled like a hook around one raised eyebrow, giving the impression that it not only had lifted the eyebrow to just that height but also held it in place. Emma thrust her jaw out and blew upward, causing the curl to flutter but failing to dislodge it. She was moved at last to impatiently brush it aside.

"A better person?" asked Emma. "You cannot possibly believe that. We are different, surely. That is a fair observation. But this other? No. You very much mistake the matter."

"I am vain and silly," Marisol said frankly. "Father says so, and he would know for I am like my mother in that way. Do not distress yourself, Emmalyn, casting about for some kind words to soften his remarks. Father loved Mother to absolute distraction and loves her still if the truth be known. He loves me no less, not in spite of who I am, but because of it."

"That is not the observation of a silly young woman."

"Yes, well, it is but the mood of the moment. Foolishness will return directly."

Set figuratively back on her heels by Marisol's candor, Emma pressed her lips together and wondered what more could be said.

Marisol glanced over her shoulder at her reflection, then caught Emma's gaze in the mirror. "And you yourself know that I am vain. How can I not be when I have little else beyond my beauty to recommend me? You are the fiercely clever one, Emmalyn. Father says you might well have been born a man for all your clever ways."

"I'm sure he meant that as a compliment," Emma said dryly.

"Oh, indeed. You are like a son to him; he's told me so. A son is better than a daughter, I think, for there are vastly different expectations. You are the son."

"That is not so, Marisol. Uncle's feelings for me are not what they are for you."

"Of course they are not, but I am not speaking of his feelings, only of the fact that he thinks of you as he would a son. It does not mean that he loves me less, but that he depends on you more. It's been that way since you came to live with us. How long has it been now? Two years?"

"Almost three," Emma said quietly.

Marisol turned abruptly. The bonnet spilled from her lap to the floor, and she made no move to retrieve it. When Emma would have done so, she stopped her, reaching to grasp her hand. "A less vain and silly girl would not have forgotten that next month is the anniversary of your own dear parents' death. Forgive me, Emmalyn. I spoke without thinking."

"There is nothing to forgive."

"You really are the better person." Marisol squeezed Emma's hand lightly. "Certainly more generous."

Emma waited until Marisol released her hand, then stooped to pick up the bonnet. When Marisol made no move to take it, Emma sighed, accepting the inevitable. "It's to be Mr. Kincaid, then? You have some message for him."

"Did I not say you are fiercely clever? You have read my mind."

"Hardly. I know neither where nor when, and I most assuredly do not know what."

"Madame Chabrier's is where you will be going."

"The milliner's?"

"Yes. Mr. Kincaid will meet you there."

"That is hardly one of his usual haunts. And don't you prefer Mrs. Bowman's fine hats?"

"Yes. It will seem to be a chance meeting. I did not want anyone placing a different construction upon it."

"Since you're sending me, the chance of you encountering Mr. Kincaid seems to be . . . well, there is no chance at all. No one will remark on me crossing his path."

"But I didn't know when I agreed to meet him that I would be sending you in my place. I thought that was evident."

"Perhaps you will want to revise your opinion that I am the clever one."

"Perhaps I will," Marisol said. "But not just now. It does not serve." She glanced at the clock on the mantel. "Mr. Kincaid and I agreed on one o'clock as the correct time."

"It is almost one now."

"Yes, but then I am invariably late. Mr. Kincaid knows that as I took pains to explain the nuances of being late as my fashion and being fashionably late. I am striving for the latter. He'll wait."

"And if he doesn't?"

"Then I shall be devastated."

"But why? You are not even meeting him."

"But he doesn't know that. Really, Emma, can you not keep up? He is expecting me. I am relying on you to judge his reaction when he sees that you have come in my place."

"Very well, and when I judge that his very correct manner is politely masking his own dashed hopes, what do I do?"

"You give him this." Marisol reached delicately beneath the scalloped bodice of her walking dress and pulled out a folded square of lightly scented paper. "This will explain why I cannot see him any longer."

"I see." Emma took the note in her left hand and closed her fingers around it. "And if it appears that he is relieved that I have come in your stead?"

"Then you will give him this." Marisol stood and lightly laid the flat of her hand against Emma's cheek. "But you will do it with much feeling. Recall that you are delivering the insult on my behalf and you should respond accordingly."

"I don't think I can slap Mr. Kincaid, with or without feeling." Emma watched as Marisol slowly dropped back to her stool, her knees folding under her gracefully until the deflation was complete. "Perhaps if I simply tell him that you do not wish to see him again, it will suffice." Emma offered this suggestion with no hint of the exasperation she felt. "I will allow that in this instance he does not deserve the scented note penned by your hand. He would not treasure it appropriately."

Marisol lifted her head and regarded Emma with new appreciation. "That is just my thinking on the matter. He does not merit a memento of our brief liaisons, not if he is unmoved by the withdrawal of my attentions. A slap seems just. After all, he has trifled with me."

There was an odd sort of logic to Marisol's argument that Emma was very much afraid she was beginning to follow. "I'm certain I could use great feeling when I tell him that you no longer wish to see him." Emma did not explain that the great feeling would be one of relief. Marisol's assignations with Jonathan Kincaid were no secret to her. Whether or not they could remain a secret to Marisol's father and her fiancé for much longer had been a question in Emma's mind for some time. Mayhap her cousin had begun to question the same thing. "When I have finished speaking to him, he will comprehend that he is no gentleman and has earned nothing so much as our enmity and contempt. Is that agreeable to you?"

"Very much so. You will use your most clipped accents, won't you? And I do not think it will be amiss if you stare at him just so." Marisol's light blue eyes narrowed slightly and the effect was frosty.

"I suppose I can manage that."

"Of course you can. I learned it from you."

"Oh." Surprise mixed with dismay and made the single word almost inaudible. For a moment, Emma was at a loss. "I had no idea."

Marisol's icy glance melted as she beamed. "That is because you spend no time in front of the mirror. A sharp setdown as you do it, accomplishing the thing with only your eyes, comes naturally to you. It puts me quite in awe."

Not so much in awe, Emma thought, that Marisol was ever restrained from speaking her mind. The fancies that flitted through her cousin's gray matter found immediate expression at the tip of her tongue. Emma did not point this out, nor did she comment on the singular nature of what she was certain Marisol intended as a compliment. Instead, she placed the straw bonnet on her head and tied the ribbons. "I'll get my pelisse."

"No, take mine. If I do not mistake the change in the weather, you will need it. I could not forgive myself if you took a chill. The green one, I think. It is easily my favorite, but it will look even more appealing on you."

"It is no trouble to retrieve my own."

In answer, Marisol extended her arm and pointed in the direction of her dressing room. "You'll find it in the armoire. Berry brushed it out this morning."

Emma located the pelisse, slipped it on, and belted it just under her breasts. Her thought when she caught sight of herself in the cheval glass was that the silk-lined green muslin fell in a vertical line that was not unflattering. As invariably happened, at first glance, she was struck by her resemblance to Marisol. The impression no longer lingered in her mind as it used to, but faded quickly, resolutely pushed aside by the knowledge that it was merely a trick of the shifting light and the angle of the reflecting glass.

Marisol was standing at her vanity when Emma returned to the room. She clapped her hands together, perfectly pleased with what she had been able to bring about. "I knew it would suit you," she said. "Come, make a turn and let me see you to full effect."

Emma hesitated, saw nothing for it but to oblige her cousin's whim, and did so.

"Why, Emmalyn Hathaway, you look quite lovely." She stepped forward and smoothed one of the ruffles at the cuff so that it lay smoothly against the back of Emma's hand. "I shouldn't wonder that Mr. Kincaid will mistake the matter and think I am come, at least until you close the distance between you."

"Is that part of your plan, Marisol? Are you encouraging him to mistake my identity in the hope that it will give rise to a more profound reaction?"

"Do you think it will? I confess it hadn't occurred to me, but it can only be for the best. You will have less difficulty judging the bent of his mind. You do not want to give him my note if he deserves a setdown."

"My brief acquaintance with Mr. Kincaid does not make me suppose there is any bent to his mind. He is rather more straightforward than that."

Marisol communicated her doubt. "If you say so, but in my experience men possess twists and turns of thought that make me dizzy. Do you have my note?"

Emma indicated that she had slipped it under the belt. "I won't lose it."

"Promise me that you'll come back directly."

Emma knew this was not because Marisol had any concerns for her safety but was desirous of hearing the details of the meeting sooner rather than later. "The rain will encourage me to return quickly." She went to the door, opened it, then paused on the threshold. When she looked back, Marisol was already moving toward the window. "Marisol?"

"Yes?"

"I won't do this for you again." Emma turned away but not before she saw that her cousin had the grace to blush.

Chapter 1

"You have a visitor."

Restell Gardner made no response to this announcement. He remained as stone in his bed, refusing to surrender to a single twitch that would indicate that he was not deeply asleep.

"It is no good, sir," Hobbes said as he poured water into the washbasin. "You have warned me of this very trick yourself and begged me not to be fooled by it. So we are at odds, you see, for I am armed with the knowledge of your pretense and must act accordingly, while you will continue to lie abed and favor me with an abrupt snore to put me off. When that does not have the desired effect, you will roll to your other side and compel me to hobble around the bed to address you directly. You will, of course, continue to ignore me, forcing me to take measures that may well relieve me of my employment. You will understand, sir, that such an outcome is hardly in keeping with your promise to treat me fairly."

At his first opportunity to be heard, Restell offered a weary observation. "Is it your plan, Hobbes, to speak at length on this matter?"

"Yes, sir."

Restell did not open an eye. "I don't snore."

"I can't say that I know if you do or don't, Mr. Gardner, only that you'd pretend to."

"Where did I find you, Sergeant Hobbes?"

"In the mews, sir, just behind the Blue Ruination, drinking bad gin and bemoaning the loss of my leg."

"I don't suppose you miss the mews."

"No, sir. Nor the gin. Still miss my leg, though this peg has its uses right enough."

Restell rolled onto his back and rubbed his eyes. When his hand fell away, he brought Hobbes into focus. The former regiment man was standing at his bedside—towering, really—with the water pitcher poised at a threatening angle. Restell waved him off. "You didn't mention water torture. I'm thoroughly awake, thank you very much."

"My pleasure, sir."

"I was being sardonic."

"So was I."

Grinning, Restell pushed himself upright, stuffed a pillow under the small of his back, and leaned against the bed head. He ran one hand through his pale, sun-bleached helmet of hair, leaving it furrowed and in perfect disarray. "What was the hour when I returned?"

"Gone three. It was a late night for you, sir."

Restell needed no reminder. It had been an age since he'd trolled the gaming hells. He could not recall that he had ever been made so weary by it. "And the hour now?"

"Not yet eight o'clock."

"The hell you say. And I have a visitor?" He had to restrain himself from pulling the covers over his head. "God save me, it is not my mother, is it?"

"No, sir. Nor any other of your family." Hobbes skirted the bed and went to the washbasin, his limp hardly noticeable this morning. "I understand she is female, though."

"That alone does not account for the hour of her visit. Who is she?"

"She wouldn't say. Mr. Nelson asked her for her card, but she declined to give one."

"Curious."

Hobbes nodded. "I thought the very same." He set towels

to warm at the fireplace, then began whipping lather in a cup for his employer's morning shave and ablutions. "Do you wish to bathe?"

"Above everything. I reek of the gaming hells."

Hobbes made no comment about this last, though it was true enough. "I'll see to it." He set the lathering cup down and crossed the room to ring for assistance. "Will you break your fast here or in the morning room?"

"Here." Restell swept back the covers and threw his legs over the side of the bed. He sat there for several moments, head in his hands as though to steady it, then kicked his slippers aside in favor of padding barefoot across the cold floor to the dressing room. "Do you think she'll wait?" he called to Hobbes.

"I couldn't say, sir." He picked up the warm towels and carried them to Restell. "Does it matter?"

"She is an inconvenient female. I should like the opportunity to tell her so."

"Do you think she doesn't know? They frequently do, sir."

"Then they should try harder to resist their nature," Restell said sourly. "Have you a headache powder, Hobbes? Satan's minions are doing a gleeful dance inside my skull."

Hobbes made sympathetic noises. "Right away."

Restell felt marginally better after he bathed and shaved. He was returned to human form by the time Hobbes tied his stock, brushed his jacket, and the headache powder began to work. Following a leisurely breakfast and perusal of the morning paper, he pronounced himself prepared well enough to receive his visitor in the library.

He had only just begun to seat himself in the wing chair by the fireplace when Nelson announced her. It was all rather awkwardly done—the announcement because Nelson had no name for their visitor, and Restell's rise from the chair because he unfolded in a manner reminiscent of a jack-in-the-box. Restell noted that the butler quickly exited the room, but not so fast that he missed Nelson's lips begin to twitch.

There was no reaction from his visitor, at least none that

Restell could observe. Her features were obscured by a gauzy veil secured to the brim of a leghorn bonnet. He wondered at the affectation. Clearly she was in high mourning, making it known by choosing black as the single color to drape her slim figure, but the veil was not at all in the usual mode. Did she wear it all the time? he wondered, or had she chosen it purposely for this morning call?

"Have you been offered refreshment?" he asked. Although he had yet to hear her speak, he had it in his mind that she was a woman of no more than middling years. There was no discernible hesitation in her step, and her carriage was correct but not rigid. She was not compensating for some frailty. "Tea, perhaps?"

She shook her head. The veil rippled with the movement but remained in place. She held her reticule in front of her, at the level of her waist, and made no move to set it aside.

Restell understood why Nelson had not refused her entry, even at the inopportune timing of her arrival. She was preternaturally calm, possessed of a resigned bearing and purpose that made one suppose she would not be easily turned from it.

"Will you be seated?" asked Restell.

"I have not decided."

"You have not decided if you will sit?"

"I have not decided if I will stay."

Restell shrugged. "Then you will not object if I attend to my correspondence. You may stand or sit, stay or go, as the mood is upon you." He gave her no further attention but walked to his desk and began examining the post that had arrived the previous day. He chose a letter with the recognizable seal of the Earl of Ferrin and hitched one hip on the edge of the desk as he opened it. He was peripherally aware of his visitor's study, but he ignored it in favor of the missive from his stepbrother.

He read through the greeting and far enough beyond to be assured of the good health of everyone in Ferrin's household before the visitor interrupted him.

"I did not think you would be so young," she said.

"I am six and twenty. That is not the age you had in mind, I collect."

She did not answer this directly. "You cannot have the breadth of experience I am seeking."

"You have me at a disadvantage," Restell said. He let Ferrin's letter dangle between his fingers rather than set it aside. It was a subtle signal that he would remain engaged only as long as she did. "I know nothing at all about what experience you require. Perhaps if you would begin with how you came to be here."

She hesitated, then asked, "You don't want to know my name?"

"Would it mean anything to me?"

"No."

"Then it's not important. You know mine. That seems to be the salient point."

"I learned about you from my physician."

Restell folded Ferrin's correspondence as he considered this information. He tapped one corner of the letter against his knee. "Might I know his name?"

"Bettany. Dr. William Bettany."

Restell did not reveal whether or not he was acquainted with the doctor. "And what did Dr. Bettany tell you about me?"

"Precious little." Making her decision, she backed into the chair behind her and sat down abruptly. The reticule remained clutched in her gloved hands. "That is, he was not speaking of you to me. I overheard some of what he told my . . . what he told someone else."

"Might I know *that* name?" Her pause let him know she suspected he might have some familiarity with that person. He let it pass and went to the heart of the matter. "What manner of things did you overhear?"

"The doctor seemed to think that you had certain peculiar talents that might be helpful to someone in my situation."

"Peculiar talents," Restell repeated. "It's an intriguing description. What do you suppose he meant by it?"

"He was speaking of protection. It's a service you offer, I believe."

"Are you quite sure that you comprehended the context. At the risk of offending you, you should know that when a gentleman places a woman under his protection it generally means—"

"He is setting up a mistress. Yes, I understand that. At the risk of offending you, that is not the sort of protection I am seeking from you. I do not believe I mistook the doctor's meaning. He was speaking of protection from harm. That is why I have come to you."

Restell folded his arms across his chest and regarded his visitor frankly. He did not try to penetrate her veil but took in the whole of her figure: the braced shoulders and narrow back, the quality and cut of her clothing, the stillness of her hands on the reticule. There was no glimpse of her hair and her feet were tucked modestly under the chair and hidden by her gown. She could be fair or dark or possess the olive complexion that suggested a Mediterranean heritage. She spoke in accents that were similar to his own and were influenced by years in London, attention to education, but nonetheless hinted at origins far north of the city. He could not deny that he was intrigued. He accepted that as fact. It did not necessarily follow that he was favorably disposed to taking up this matter of her protection.

"Is it shelter that you require?" he asked.

"No, not shelter. I have a home."

"Then you are not seeking to escape it." He saw her shoulders jerk and the brim of her bonnet lift as her chin came up. She was clearly shocked by the import of his words.

"No, of course not. I am content there."

Restell thought it a peculiar expression of sentiment, but he did not comment on it. "You will have to tell me more. It would be a good beginning to tell me why you need protection."

"I'm not sure that I do. That is a matter for you to determine. I thought I heard Dr. Bettany say that you make discreet inquiries. I am as interested in securing your services toward that end as I am in protection."

Was it too early for a drink? Restell wondered. He glanced past his visitor's shoulder to the drinks cabinet and actually considered removing the stopper from the decanter of whiskey and taking his fill. "Did you not just say you weren't certain you needed protection?"

"I'm not certain I need it for myself," she said. "I believe perhaps my cousin is the one who requires it."

"Your cousin. I don't suppose I might know her name."

"In time, I think. You can understand that I must be certain that engaging you is the right course of action."

One corner of Restell's mouth lifted slightly, hinting at both mockery and amusement. "I understand you think the decision is entirely yours."

"Isn't it?"

Restell did not respond immediately. Unfolding his arms, he picked up the letter opener on the tray at his side and lightly tapped the end of it against the palm of his other hand.

"No, in fact it ultimately rests with me," he said at last. It was just a fancy on his part, but he imagined that behind her veil she was frowning deeply. "I do not accept everyone who applies to me as my client. Conversely, I might choose to offer my services to someone who does not formally engage me. Once you announced your intention at the door to have this interview and stubbornly waited when I gave you sufficient time to think better of it, you surrendered your prerogative to decide the outcome. Whether you like it or not, I will determine how we go from here."

"But you don't even know who I am. If I do not hire you, you will never know it. You cannot offer your services to someone whose name you don't know."

"God's truth, you cannot be so foolish as to believe I will not discover it. If my peculiar talents do not extend so far as that, then why would you entertain any notion of engaging my services? It defies any sort of common sense. Have you so much in the way of cotton wool between your ears?"

Restell replaced the letter opener and stood. "Are you taking exception to my words? I hope so. If you are completely cowed, then there is no hope for it but that I will have to show you the door."

"I know where the door is," she said. "And sense enough about me still to get there on my own."

Restell permitted himself a small smile as he turned his back on her and skirted the desk. He dropped into the leather chair behind it and set his long legs before him at an angle. "How did you find me?" He did not miss the way she subtly shifted in her seat. The question surprised her.

"But I have already told you. Dr. Bettany."

"That is how you heard of me. I inquired as to how you found me."

"You are not the only one who can make discreet inquiries. I had it from a member of your family that you were temporarily using your brother's London residence."

"I sincerely doubt that someone in my own family characterized my stay here as temporary. All of them know I am quite satisfied with the arrangement; indeed, that I enjoy the distinct benefits of making this establishment my home. I will not be easily dislodged, even if Ferrin should raise some objection. The earl is my stepbrother, by the way, although we do not make too fine a point of it. I merely mention it so you will know that he possesses a generous nature that I frequently admire and regularly take advantage of but do not necessarily share."

"You are the poor relation, then."

The half smile that frequently lifted one corner of Restell's mouth now became a fulsome one, engaging his clear blue eyes and deepening the creases of twin dimples on either side of his lips. "Some would say so, yes."

"You do not seem to mind."

"I hadn't realized that I should." He shrugged, dismissing this line of inquiry. "So you had it from some member of my family that I could be found here. Dr. Bettany wouldn't necessarily know that, you see, which is what made me curious. I was yet living on Kingston Street when I made the acquaintance of the good doctor." Restell laced his fingers together and tapped his thumbs as he considered his visitor and all that she had not told him. "Are you yet prepared to share the whole of why you're here? I've had little enough sleep these three nights past and find I am weary of wondering. In truth, I am all for crawling back into my warm bed."

Restell had learned that silence was often the key to confession. When she did not respond immediately, he waited her out. He continued to study her as though he had long ago penetrated her veil and knew the nuances of her every expression, and when he had the urge to break the silence, he cautioned himself to wait that bit much longer.

In the end, he was rewarded for his patience.

She lifted the veil.

Restell had seen men leave the boxing ring after three rounds of rough sparring with fewer bruises than this woman had. The evidence of her beating had faded, to be sure, but there was color enough remaining to determine where the blows had landed. Beneath both eyes she sported deep violet shadows, proof that her nose had been broken if not completely smashed. Her complexion was suffused with the yellow hue associated with jaundice. In her case it was further confirmation of the fists she had endured. Her left cheek looked to be more tender than her right one; faint swelling was still visible across the arch. A thin cut on her lower lip had not healed, most likely because when she spoke it was laid open again. He could make out the faint line of bruising along one side of her neck. The high collar of her walking gown obscured what had been done to her throat, but Restell imagined mottled thumbprints at the hollow between her collarbones as testament that she had been choked, probably within a single breath of her life.

Restell took in the whole of her countenance in a single glance, then sought to see beneath it. The contusions obscured her features almost as well as the veil. Restell had to peel back every distended layer of bruising to find the true shape of her face.

She had a fine bone structure: a pared nose that had been set straight by a firm and skillful hand, a high arch to her cheeks that was made more prominent by the hollow beneath, a slender jaw held firmly—perhaps painfully—in place. Her eyes had a vaguely exotic slant to them that Restell supposed she could use to great effect if she lowered her lashes even a fraction. What she did, however, was hold his stare directly and give no quarter. The consequence of such forthrightness was that Restell only noted the color of her eyes upon his second appraisal.

"I had not imagined you would be so young," he said, echoing her earlier observation. "I am generally a better judge."

"Ah, yes, but you can see for yourself that I have recently garnered considerable life experience."

"Yes," he said, dipping his head in acknowledgment. "Yes, you have." Restell sat forward in his chair. "This was not done by someone you know?"

"No."

"Are you quite certain? Your father? Brother? Someone you do not want to reveal just yet. A lover, mayhap?"

"Why do you persist in thinking it is someone I know? I would tell you if that were the case, else why would I come?"

"Precisely. But many women do not tell it all, at least not at the outset. Fear, I suspect is the reason for it. Some are afraid of their tormentor; others are afraid to hope that anything can be done. Even when I explain that it is better that I know the whole of it at the first interview, the truth seems to reveal itself over time."

"A consequence of learning to trust you, I shouldn't wonder."

"You may well be right. Perhaps I expect too much." He shrugged and leaned back again, crossing his legs at the ankle. "Why hasn't anyone approached me on your behalf? You said you overheard Bettany discussing my talents with someone. Why hasn't that person followed where the good doctor pointed?"

"I can't be sure. I didn't ask."

"You must have wondered. What are your thoughts?"

She pressed her lips together, frowning slightly, then released her reticule long enough to press the back of her fingers against her mouth. She examined her glove for evidence of blood. Before she could find her handkerchief, Restell was standing before her, offering his own.

"Thank you." She dabbed her lower lip with the linen. "It will never heal if I persist on worrying it. I cannot seem to break myself of the habit." She withdrew the handkerchief, saw that she had stemmed the bleeding, and began folding the linen into a neat square.

"You may keep it," Restell said, returning to his chair. "I will not be put off my questioning and will give you cause to have need of it again. Now, tell me why you think no one save you has applied to me." He watched her take a steadying breath while he held his own and waited to see what she would do.

"I think it is because it's believed the danger is past, or rather that the danger existed only because I presented opportunity for it."

"You will have to explain the last."

"I mean that if I had not been just where I was no ill would have befallen me. I have thought a great deal about that."

"I see. So you are at fault for what happened."

"At fault?" Her eyebrows lifted in tandem. "No, I do not accept that. I am responsible for being where I was and that is all."

"So the thinking of your family is that this assault was random, one of opportunity rather than deliberate design."

"I have supposed that is their thinking. As I mentioned, I didn't ask."

"I do not recall reading an account of any assault such as you experienced in the *Gazette*. Did it happen here in London?"

"It began here. It ended in Walthamstow. Are you familiar?"

"I know where it is. Waltham Abbey is not far from there, I believe."

"Yes."

"Are you telling me you were abducted in London and taken to Walthamstow?"

"Walthamstow is where I was able to get away. I cannot say how long they meant to remain there."

"They?"

"There were two men, though sometimes it seems to me there was a third."

Restell kept his gaze steady, taking in this information as if it did not twist his gut. If she was willing to tell him, the very least he could do was honor her courage. "Your bruises look more than a week old. How long ago did this happen?"

"A bit less than three weeks. I am told I made my escape only days after I was assaulted behind Madame Chabrier's establishment. I cannot account for the time myself as it seemed to take no longer than the blink of an eye, yet was simultaneously only a few moments shy of forever. Because of the kindness of the village's innkeeper and his wife, I was able to send word to my family and was reunited soon after."

It was clearer to Restell why he'd heard no account of the abduction or her maltreatment. A family of some means and reputation would go to great lengths to keep such a matter quiet. Whether or not she bore any responsibility for events, whether or not she was sorely abused, it would be society's judgment that she was ruined. Restell thought that perhaps it was a judgment shared by her family.

"You were alone at the time of the abduction?" he asked.

She nodded. "I had not even my maid with me. It seems foolish now, but I cannot regret it as I think she might have been killed if she'd accompanied me."

Restell considered her attire again. "You are not in mourning."

She was silent for a moment, her expression grave. "Only as it applies to me," she said with quiet dignity. "I mourn the loss of self, of that part of me that enjoyed freedom of movement and freedom from fear. I might have been here days earlier if I could have left my home. I had opportunity but could not will myself to step outside. Twice I dressed and approached the door. Twice I retreated to my room. Today I took two spoonfuls of laudanum and depended upon their soporific consequences to help me find a balm for my terror. Do not suppose that I am muddleheaded because of my actions. The long wait in your drawing room did much to remove that effect."

"And are you fearful now?"

"Sick with it."

"Yet you sit so composed."

"I cannot move." She smiled slightly, sipping air as though through a straw. "I can barely breathe."

Her courage left him humbled. Some day he would tell her so, but not just now, not when a kind word might very well sabotage her resolve. "What do you suppose I can do for you?"

She did not answer this directly. That didn't entirely surprise him as she seemed more comfortable coming at a thing sideways.

"I am Emmalyn Hathaway," she said after a long moment. "Miss Emmalyn Hathaway."

As he'd suspected, her name meant nothing to him. "It is a very real honor to meet you, Miss Hathaway." She gave no indication that she reciprocated the sentiment or even that she believed him.

"My parents were Elliot and Teresa Hathaway, late of Peterborough."

Restell realized he hadn't been wrong about her accent. Peterborough was in Northhamptonshire.

"And later still," she continued, "of the fair ship *Emily Pepper* that was lost with all hands and passengers somewhere south of Ceylon."

"I know of the *Emily Pepper*," he said. In addition to apparently carrying Miss Hathaway's parents, the ship had been carrying a king's ransom worth of silks and teas. He had contemplated investing in the ship, but as he researched its prospects and, more importantly, its master, he had advised himself and others against it. The demise of the *Emily Pepper* and the loss of her crew, passengers, and cargo had spelled something of a reversal in his own fortunes.

People began to take him seriously.

Restell did not share this with Miss Hathaway. It would be difficult for anyone to reconcile the death of one's parents with the pivotal juncture it had been in his life, even more so because he was so ambivalent about the change it had wrought.

He realized the anniversary of the *Emily Pepper*'s sinking was almost upon them. "Three years next week," he said, and didn't realize he had spoken aloud until she stared at him. Her eyes were more green than blue, the color of water rushing toward the sea, not coming up from it, the color he had always imagined aquamarine should be and wasn't. "Three years," he said again, softly. "But then you know that."

She nodded. "Indeed."

"You are not alone, though. I believe you mentioned family. Brothers? Sisters?"

"Neither. I live with my uncle and cousin. Uncle Arthur is my mother's brother. My aunt died many years ago and he never remarried. Marisol is also their only child."

"She is of an age with you?"

"There are four years between us. She is eighteen."

Restell realized that Miss Hathaway was even younger than his second estimation of her age, and he was not successful in keeping this revelation to himself. The tiniest lift of his left eyebrow gave him away.

"You are surprised," she said. "When you remarked that I was so young, where did you place my age?"

Recovering his misstep, Restell said, "I do not think it would be politic to answer that."

Her slight smile communicated an appreciation for his response and that no offense had been taken. "You thought I was still older than you, I'd wager."

"You won't wheedle it out of me."

"It is a common enough error. I am judged by most people to be an ape-leader, a term generally assigned to a woman some seven to ten years my senior with no prospects for marriage. I mention it lest you think that it is my recent experience that has aged me. I assure you, that is not the case. I have always been accounted to be older than my years." She shrugged lightly. "A consequence of a serious temperament, I suppose, and an application of one's mind to study."

"No ape-leader, then, but a bluestocking."

"If I were a man, you would call me a scholar."

For all that her rebuke was softly spoken, Restell felt its sting sharply. "You are quite right. It was a fatuous comment and wholly undeserved. I beg your pardon."

"You needn't fall on your sword, Mr. Gardner. You have not scarred me."

Restell felt the tug of an appreciative smile and gave into it. "You are a singular piece of work, Miss Hathaway."

"Am I to take that as a compliment?"

"I certainly meant it as one; how you take it is entirely up to you." When she offered no rejoinder or gave an indication of the bent of her mind, Restell continued his questioning. "Your Uncle Arthur is well set up?"

"You are referring to his finances."

"Yes."

"He lives quite comfortably. Is it important? You are concerned about your fee, no doubt."

"We will discuss the matter of my fee if I decide to accept you as my client. It has no bearing on my question. I was wondering if your abductors could have had reasonable expectation of a ransom."

"A ransom? For me?"

"Your uncle would not have paid for your safe return?"

"Yes . . . yes, of course he would . . . it's just that . . ."

"Yes?"

"There is much I don't remember about what happened."

Restell watched her suck in her lower lip and worry it until she bit the tender spot. He almost winced on her behalf. She made a moue of apology and pressed his handkerchief against her lip. "Is there some question in your mind that there might have been a demand of ransom?" he asked.

"There's never been any hint of it, at least to me. Neither my uncle nor Marisol have indicated that they knew of such."

Restell marked the hesitation in her speech as signifying she was mulling over some aspect of her answer even as she gave it. "There is something more," he said, "something you are perhaps only now considering. Tell me what you're thinking."

Pulled abruptly to the present, she blinked widely as her chin came up. "It is just that I should have wondered about a demand for money myself. It fits with what *has* occupied my thinking of late, so I am disappointed that it didn't occur to me."

Sighing, Restell picked up the letter opener again and beat an absent tattoo against the edge of his desk. He felt rather like his childhood tutor who marked time with a ruler while he waited for a proper answer to his question. Glancing sideways at the letter opener, he wondered if it was as threatening as the ruler had been. He supposed that depended on whether Miss Hathaway thought he could be moved to rap it sharply across her knuckles.

"That is rather less information than I expect from a scholarly mind, Miss Hathaway. The whole of it, please."

"I am coming to that, Mr. Gardner, only you must stop banging the desk. The sound is like a timpani inside my head."

Restell hit it once more before stopping. He kept the letter opener in his hand, suggestive of a warning, then used it as a conductor might use a baton to encourage her to begin again. Her perfectly splendid eyes narrowed slightly, and Restell counted it as a good thing that she was not easily managed.

"I have had the suspicion for some time that the attack against me was not one of impulse and opportunity. I believe that Marisol may have been the intended victim."

"Your cousin?"

"Yes. Miss Marisol Vega."

"Your uncle is Arthur Vega? Pardon me, I believe he is now Sir Arthur."

"Yes. He is greatly honored by the crown's recognition. Have you met?"

"I have been privileged to view several of his paintings, but we are not acquainted. If I am not mistaken, my mother recently purchased one of his recent works." It reminded him that he must needs pay more attention to Lady Gardner when she rattled on about her views concerning art, fashion, and the theatre. It was too depressing for words.

"You're frowning," she said. "You don't find my uncle's work to your taste?"

"What I have seen I like well enough. I have not called upon Lady Gardner this past fortnight, so I cannot render an opinion about her latest acquisition. Although I generally take the time to form a well-reasoned position regarding matters of style, color, and brushstrokes, it is of no account to anyone but me. The sad fact of it is that I am a philistine, Miss Hathaway."

"You are kind to warn me."

Restell slid the letter opener aside. "Your uncle is comfortably set then."

"I believe I have already said so. His paintings command a goodly sum."

He waited to see if she would say that her uncle was also an inveterate gamer. Restell had had occasion to see his distinctive signature in the gaming books—and recently. One did not necessarily have to meet a man to know something about him, especially in the circle of the *ton* where gossip was the currency of exchange.

"Do you have any doubt that he would have met a ransom demand for his daughter?"

"Not one. Marisol is everything to him."

"Even if the demand was more than he could properly afford?"

"There is no such amount. He would have found the means to do so. She is beloved."

"Do you believe there would have been a demand for money if she had been taken?"

"It seems possible, though that supposes she was indeed marked for the abduction."

"It's your contention that she was," he reminded her. "Tell me why."

"I went to Madame Chabrier's in her place. I borrowed her bonnet and her favorite pelisse. Marisol and I are not so dissimilar in height or frame or coloring, and I have heard it said that there is a passing resemblance between us."

"You don't believe that?"

"I would be flattering myself too much to agree that an abiding likeness exists. Marisol is acknowledged to be a beauty. At a glance, however, especially if one did not know us well or had only a description to identify us, a mistake might be made."

"I see."

"And I was wearing her outerwear. I should not have, of course, but Marisol can be insistent and I saw nothing to be gained by arguing."

"Frequently nothing is, but in this instance one does wonder."

"It was all in aid of meeting Mr. Kincaid."

"I thought you were going to Madame Chabrier's. She's a milliner, is she not?" Restell watched her eyebrows climb. "I have four sisters, Miss Hathaway. I may be a philistine about the style of a woman's bonnet, but I know all too well who is judged to make the finest. Who is Mr. Kincaid and what purpose did he have at the milliner's?"

"You must promise that you will keep what I shall tell you in the strictest confidence."

"A tryst, then," he said in bored accents. "That is frequently the way of it. Why did she ask you to go in her place?"

"To end it, of course. Marisol is engaged, you see."

"And when was that done exactly? Before or after she agreed to an assignation with Mr. Kincaid?"

"Before."

"You will have to speak up, Miss Hathaway. Your reluctance to speak ill of your cousin is telling of your character but deuced annoying. Now, I believe you said *before*. Is that correct?"

"Yes. She was betrothed before she arranged to meet Mr. Kincaid."

"This was not the first time she agreed to it. You said she meant to break it off. From that I can infer that there were previous appointments with the man. She kept those, I presume."

"Yes."

"Your cousin's definition of what it means to be betrothed is rather different from what I understand is acceptable in society."

"She is very young."

"Is she not eighteen? Bloody hell, Miss Hathaway, if she doesn't understand the meaning of engagement, she's a foolish chit for agreeing to one. What sort of man is her fiancé? An ogre? Someone ready to turn up his toes? A widower with seven children of his own?"

"He is none of those things. Mr. Neven Charters is altogether an accomplished gentleman, and there are those who say he is handsome as well. He has had some business dealings with my uncle and has since become a patron. That is how he came to know us. Once he met Marisol . . . well, I think it is fair to say that he is besotted with her."

Restell was silent a moment, taking into account what he believed she *wasn't* saying. He didn't fail to notice that she was worrying her lip again. "And your cousin? Is she similarly addled?"

"Her behavior to the contrary, it appears to be a love match. I believe it is the prospect of marriage that frightens her—and what comes afterward."

Restell did not think his visitor's mottled complexion could make allowance for another hue, so it surprised him to see a hint of pink rise above the high collar at her throat and slip under her swollen jaw and bruised cheeks. The violet stains under her eyes deepened to indigo, and then the color took the path upward past her temples and spread across her forehead until it finally disappeared into her hairline and under her bonnet.

"Afterward?" Restell said, because he could not help himself. Goading females was the prerogative of someone with four sisters, at least he had always thought so.

"Children, Mr. Gardner. My aunt died in childbirth when Marisol was not yet five. She remembers it well enough."

Restell promised himself that he would not forget that when Miss Hathaway was pushed, she pushed back, almost always in unexpected ways. "Then you believe her flirtations are innocent?"

"Most assuredly. She is silly at times—some would say foolish—but she is not unintelligent. She realized what she was risking, thought better of it, and determined she must stop seeing Mr. Kincaid."

"Have there been other flirtations?"

"I don't know. I don't think so."

"Do you say that because you hope she's shown that much sense?"

"I say it because Marisol does not regularly confide in me."

"How did you learn about Kincaid? Did she tell you?"

"We attended a party at the Newbolts together. In January, I think it was. I observed the overtures made by Mr. Kincaid and saw that Marisol did not rebuff them."

"Others must have observed the same."

"They were rather more discreet than I have made them seem. Mr. Charters was not present, so Marisol was partnered in the sets by many different gentlemen."

Restell considered this for some time before he rose from his chair and crossed in front of the desk to the fireplace. He poked at the small fire that had been laid there. The morning had begun unusually chilly and the temperature had not improved greatly. In deference to his visitor's comfort, he added a small log and pushed it over the embers until it was captured by tongues of fire.

When he turned around it was to find Miss Hathaway

perched on the edge of her chair like some fledgling bird anxious to take flight. It occurred to him that if he had given her
more time, she would have seized the opportunity to escape.

"Have you changed your mind?" he asked.

"Pardon?"

"You look as though you wish yourself anywhere but here,
Miss Hathaway. I wondered if you've thought better of your
decision. Mayhap you'd like to leave."

"I'm not . . . no . . . that is . . ."

Restell required a coherent sentence to follow the bent of
her mind. Waiting for her to gather her thoughts, he absently
tapped the tip of the poker against the marble apron. Her response to the sound was nothing short of galvanic. Her head
jerked back as if struck and her hands finally released the reticule as she raised them defensively, protecting her face as
though from another blow. Restell dropped the poker. She
was already turning away from him by the time it clattered to
the floor. She burrowed into the armchair, drawing her legs
up under her skirt so her feet rested on the leather seat,
hunching her shoulders, and pulling in her elbows, all of it in
aid of making her as small a target as was possible.

Restell quelled his urge to cross the room and go to her. It
seemed self-serving to attempt to offer reassurance when his
very presence at her side was likely to provoke further agitation. He might derive some comfort from trying to assist her,
but she was unlikely to find any relief from it.

"Miss Hathaway?" He held his ground and kept his arms
loosely at his side, palms outward, showing her he had no
weapons, that even his hands were not to be feared. He maintained this posture even when she did not look in his direction, knowing that she would eventually risk a glance at him.
"I mean you no harm," he said calmly. "Was it the poker that
startled you? Were you struck with such a thing?"

Except for a shudder, she made no response.

"Will you not look at me, Miss Hathaway? Assure yourself
that I will not lift a hand against you."

He watched her lower her gloved hands a fraction, but she

did not turn her head toward him. "I admit to profound inadequacy in this situation," he said. "And I do not thank you for making me say so." He thought her hands lowered again, but it might have been a tremble in them that made it seem so. "I cannot decide what will give you the greatest ease. Should I offer refreshment? Perhaps you would like time alone to compose yourself and make your escape if that is your desire. Would cajolery work or should I remain silent?" For a long minute he did just that. He could observe that it made no appreciable change in the way she held herself. "I am going to step outside," he told her at last. "There is a matter I must attend to. You are free to remain or go as you will."

Restell reached the door by a route that maintained the most distance between himself and Miss Hathaway. He did not look back once he crossed the threshold but closed the paneled door quietly behind him.

Emma unfolded herself slowly, finding that she had become remarkably stiff during the time she'd spent curled so tightly in the chair. She touched one hand to her cheek where embarrassment had made her face go hot. She would have liked to indulge in a bout of tears but that release was denied her. There had been no tears since she'd escaped her abductors, nor many that she recalled while they held her. She'd been afraid to cry then and even more afraid since. She dreamed of drowning in tears or sometimes imagined being scarred by them, her face etched permanently as if by acid. Tears meant exposing that part of herself that she kept inviolate, that private, secret self where she still pretended that what had happened had in fact happened to someone else.

Uncle Arthur looked at her differently these days. She glimpsed disappointment in his sideways glance, even faint disapproval, as though because of her failure to protect herself she had failed him. Her inability to fend off her attackers reminded him that she was no stalwart son but a woman after all, with every one of a woman's vulnerabilities.

Marisol, in contrast, looked at her often. Her cousin was at once curious and repelled by what she saw and wholly unable to suppress that play of feeling in her features. In the first days of returning home, Emma had been helpless to keep Marisol from attending her. At first she believed it was guilt that brought Marisol so often to her side, but she now suspected that she had given her cousin credit for more tender sensibilities than she in truth possessed. The expression of relief on Marisol's fine features was perhaps a more accurate reflection of what she was thinking: relief that she had not been the victim here.

Emma could not find it in herself to blame her. Had their positions been reversed she might very well feel the same, and there had not yet come a moment when she wished their positions *had* been reversed. Emma could not imagine wishing what she had endured to be the experience of another person.

Hadn't she come here to avoid just that end?

Restell Gardner was not at all what she expected and the very least of it was his age. At first glance one could be forgiven for thinking they were in the presence of a god. His pale hair, so light that it might have been gilt with sunshine made Apollo come immediately to mind. Sitting or standing, he had a careless, casual way of holding himself that lent him an air of supreme indifference. That impression faded when one was held still by his eyes. If he willed it so, he could hold a glance for an interminable length and never blink. The intensity of feeling that was not expressed in his loose and lean frame was captured in eyes that could be as warm and clear a blue as a halcyon sky or as opaque and cold as frost on a pond in winter.

His patience, not his Viking warrior looks, made him a force to be reckoned with. Although she had been made to wait in his drawing room for what seemed an unbearably long time, she had not been able to use that opportunity to formulate any sense of what she meant to tell him. Snippets of thought simply tumbled through her mind so that no coherent whole was possible, yet he had been able to draw almost the sum of it all from her.

She never once felt pitied or pitiable, even when she raised her veil and showed him what had become of her face. He had regarded her openly, without revulsion, and made it impossible for her to duck her head or retreat behind the gauzy black curtain of lace. In that moment she became stronger because he expected her strength, as if he knew how to tap more deeply into the well of her resolve even as she would have sworn there never existed such a well.

So she had remained strong . . . up until the moment he began tapping the poker. If the banging of the letter opener against his desk had given rise to a timpani in her head, the sharp staccato of the poker against the marble apron was like a pair of cymbals crashing together on either side of her skull.

Her reaction—to curl hedgehog-like into the relative safety of the leather armchair—had been accomplished without any conscious thought. She'd just *done* it. There'd been no help for it and that terrified her. What if Mr. Gardner suspected she was a candidate for an asylum? Would he agree to help someone on so short a tether? He might very well suggest confining her to a madhouse, and how could she trust that her uncle would not approve of such a measure? There existed evidence that he could be convinced it was in her best interest, and if she failed to make herself useful, certainly he could be convinced that it was in his.

Emma stood abruptly. Her legs were steadier than she would have credited. Opening her reticule, she withdrew the cheque she had drawn on her quarterly allowance and savings and made out to Mr. Restell Gardner. She placed it on the blotter on his desk and laid the letter opener over it to serve as a paperweight, then she tugged on her veil and started toward the door.

Several sharp raps from the other side stopped Emma in her tracks. She opened her mouth to say something, to say anything, but discovered she had no voice to call out. The insistent knocking came again, harder this time, more urgent, as though someone thought she'd missed it the first time.

Emma couldn't say how long she stood there, only that she never saw the door opening. The darkness encroaching on the periphery of her vision had engulfed her by then.

Chapter 2

"Did I not say she is a female of the inconvenient variety?"
Restell studied Emmalyn's awkwardly positioned body as he
posed the question. He had had occasion to observe that some
women were able to manage a graceful faint. Miss Hathaway
was not one of them. Judging by the sound he heard just prior
to opening the doors, her impact with the floor had all the res-
onance of a two-hundred-year-old oak being felled. The
arrangement of her limbs suggested she had been overcome
quickly, with no opportunity to break her fall. He glanced
over at Hobbes who had wisely chosen not to answer what
was essentially a rhetorical poser. The man looked decidedly
uncomfortable. "Never say this is the first time you've been
confronted with a lady's swoon, Hobbes."

The valet cleared his throat. "Mary Stubbs used to fall on
her face when the gin was better than she was used to. Never
felt compelled to do more than turn her on her side, so she
could sleep it off without choking on her vomit."

"And you with no reputation for gallantry. There's a puzzler."
Restell hunkered down beside Emma and laid his hand near the
back of her neck. "Miss Hathaway?" When she did not respond, he glanced over his shoulder at Nelson who was hovering in the doorway. "Fetch whatever is at the ready to bring
her around. Consult Mrs. Peach if you must. She will know"

He broke off because he felt a slight stirring under his palm. "Wait. She is with us, I think." He carefully turned her over. The veil fell across her face, and he chose not to sweep it aside. "Hobbes, you will slip your hands under her legs. I will lift her shoulders. Then we shall place her on the chaise."

This transport was accomplished with rather more delicacy than Restell had imagined when he gave the order, but Hobbes was all for preserving Miss Hathaway's modesty and his own sensibilities. Clearly the sergeant made a social distinction between the gin-soaked Mary Stubbs and their deuced inconvenient guest.

"It occurs to me that you're a snob," Restell informed his valet as they eased Emmalyn onto the chaise. "Leaving poor Miss Stubbs to sleep off good gin in the gutter while demonstrating all manner of concern for a young lady you do not even know."

"I don't believe I mentioned a gutter, sir, and Mary, well, she would have accused me of trying to have my way with her if I'd done more."

"And you don't think this woman will do the same?"

This was a question Hobbes had not considered before. He could not step away from the chaise quickly enough.

"Make yourself easy, Hobbes. No accusation will be made here—even if there were cause for it. I think Miss Hathaway would sooner eat nails for breakfast than admit some terrible wrong had been done to her." Restell glanced back at the door. Nelson remained at his post awaiting further instruction. "Some tea, Nelson. A bit of whiskey would not be amiss, either." When the butler was gone, Restell addressed his valet. "You will want to absent yourself for the time being. I will make the introductions when I have determined she is all of a piece and prepared to depart. Have the carriage made ready. I will not permit her to walk and renting a hack is out of the question. You will ride with Whittier, won't you? Or has her faint given you pause?"

"I'll ride with him," Hobbes said. "He wouldn't know what to do if there's dustup."

"My thought also." Restell did not trust anyone so much as

the sergeant to act on what must be done should the occasion arise. "I should like to be confident that she will be returned to her home safely."

Hobbes bobbed his head once, acknowledging his employer's confidence was not misplaced, then left the room.

As soon as Restell heard the doors close behind him, he raised Emmalyn's veil. He was not surprised to find her staring back at him, although her mottled features made it challenging to determine the nature of her expression. It seemed that she was more out of patience than she was chagrined. When she started to rise, he placed a restraining hand on her shoulder.

"Allow yourself another moment's respite," Restell said. He saw her eyes dart to his hand and immediately lifted it. He straightened and took a step toward the foot of the chaise. "You took your fall on your face. I expect you will have another bruise to show for it."

Emma raised her gloved fingers and gingerly explored the length of her jaw, working it back and forth slowly as she did so. She winced when she happened upon the injury. "Am I bleeding?"

"No. It is merely a carpet burn."

She turned her head so she might see the Aubusson rug.

"Do not give it a thought," Restell said. "It appears none the worse for all that you attempted to plow it with your chin."

"It is good of you to evince so much concern for my person," she said wryly.

"Yes, well, the carpet is new."

"That explains it, then."

"And this is my brother's home."

"Of course."

"My mother had a hand in choosing it."

"I quite understand."

"You couldn't possibly, but it is good of you to evince so much concern for my person."

Emma was mildly astonished to hear herself laugh. The sound of it was not in the least robust, nor even particularly joyful, but as a first attempt she thought it was well done of her.

Restell watched Emma suck in her breath on a whimper of sound and what might have been an inkling of a smile was transformed into a wince. He inched closer to the chaise. "Are you certain you are recovered?"

Her response was to arch one eyebrow at him and raise herself on her elbows. "You will do me a great kindness by not encouraging me to laugh."

"Your lip is bleeding again."

Emma touched the small split in her lip with the tip of her tongue. She pushed herself upright, took out the handkerchief he had given her earlier, and pressed it to her mouth. After a moment she held it away long enough to tell him, "I blame you for it."

Restell inclined his head. "As you wish."

Emma regarded him suspiciously. His gracious capitulation was unexpected, and he seemed to be lending his words more gravity than circumstances warranted. There was also the merest suggestion of a smile playing about the edges of his mouth. She realized that he was agreeable to her blaming him but accepted no responsibility for the same. "So you make no admission of guilt."

"Hardly. I cannot be held accountable for what you find diverting. What if your sense of humor is tickled by the absurd, or worse, by farce? I cannot promise that I will never be caught in some improbable scheme, and if you knew my family better, you would not suppose for even a moment that I could resist it. If you fancy the ironic or the vaguely twisted, you might be less aggrieved in my company, but if you are amused by such observations as I make about circumstances of the moment, then there is no help for it but that you make a full recovery and come to embrace laughter as you would your dearest friend."

Emma removed the handkerchief from her mouth, but she was quite without words. She blinked widely instead.

"I know," Restell said sympathetically. "I have no argument for it myself." He indulged his urge to grin, offering it with an insouciant shrug of his shoulders. "Perhaps one will occur to me later." Nelson's light rapping at the door caused Restell to turn his attention in that direction. The careless air he'd affected vanished as he observed Emma's response to the sound. Out of the corner of his eye he was witness to her immediate wariness. She did not draw herself up like a hedgehog this time, but it seemed to him that she was fighting the urge to do so. Had it been his knocking at the door that provoked her faint?

Restell chose not to call attention to her reaction as she was struggling to do the same. He called for Nelson to enter. The pot of hot tea was exchanged for the cold one, and Restell dismissed the butler and poured a cup for his guest. "Will you take a dram of whiskey with it? It is mildly efficacious in calming the nerves."

"You know this for a fact?"

"Dr. Bettany assures me it is so."

Emma wondered if she could believe him. It seemed to her that Mr. Gardner was not above prevarication if it served his ends. As he obviously did not want an overwrought female on his hands—and truly, what gentleman did?—it was in his best interests to lie without compunction. She nodded and watched him add the whiskey to her cup. His notion of what constituted a dram was more liberal than her own, but she offered no comment. It was better to keep a sense of proportion about the whole, she thought, than focus too narrowly on the particular.

She accepted the tea, holding out both hands to balance the cup and saucer. She was gratified to see her fingers did not tremble. "Thank you."

"You're quite welcome. Will you have a biscuit?"

Emma shook her head. The thought of eating just now had the power to make her stomach turn over. "The tea is sufficient. More than that, really." She sipped from the cup and found the taste was not unpleasant. The tea settled warmly in her stomach.

Restell turned to his desk, hitching one hip on the edge, and observed the light pink color that flushed his guest's cheeks as she drank. The more subtle effect on her nerves would take longer to note, but Restell was confident that alcohol would serve her better than the laudanum had done.

Aware that his steady regard was not at all useful just now, Restell's glance fell on the bank draft lying on the blotter. He gave it a cursory look before turning it over.

"Is it not enough?" Emma asked when he made no comment.

"I have no idea. For what service did you mean to reimburse me? It is rather a lot for a cup of tea, even accounting for the whiskey."

"It is compensation for your time."

"I put no price on my time."

"That is very generous of you, but I think you are due—"

Restell held up one hand, palm out, effectively quelling her objection. "You misunderstand, Miss Hathaway, or perhaps it is that I was not clear. My time is priceless. You haven't sufficient funds to effect payment. No one does."

Emma's brow furrowed slightly as she considered what this meant. "Can you really think so much of yourself? Your time cannot be so precious as to be invaluable."

Restell simply shrugged.

"But what if I desire to engage your services?"

"I am not a hack driver, Miss Hathaway, waiting at the curb for someone to hire my cab." He waved aside her objection. "In any event, I do not deal in currency. I deal in favors."

"Favors?" The shadows beneath Emma's eyes deepened as she speared her host with a narrow glance. "What do you mean?"

Restell folded his arms across his chest. "Let us suppose there is a physician with a penchant for placing wagers on cockfights. Let us further suppose that he's had a run of bad luck so that his wagering far exceeds his ability to pay. He is profoundly motivated to change his habits, in part because the man he owes quite a bit of the ready to has threatened to break his hands, one finger at a time. To prove this is no idle threat, the man encourages the physician to make the acquaintance of a young gentleman who had a similar debt to pay."

Restell saw Emma's eyes drop to his hands. Not offended in the least, he held them up, splaying his fingers so she might view them clearly. "I am not that young gentleman." He wiggled his fingers for emphasis. "But you are right to suppose that I might have been. My brother made a timely financial investment in my future."

"So that you would have one."

"You have it exactly." Restell lowered his hands to the desk, curling his fingers around the edge. "For purposes of this illustration, our physician has no wealthy relative to see him clear of his debt, so let us imagine that he applies to me for assistance."

"You pay his debt?"

"Hardly. It's precisely that sort of interference that encourages more wagering. Ask Ferrin."

To suppress her laughter, Emma quickly took a sip of tea. She could not say whether it was the whiskey or Restell's discourse that was calming her nerves, but she knew herself to be more at her ease than at any time since her abduction.

Restell's grin underscored his lack of contrition. "Let us pretend that what I am able to do for this physician is to reverse his losses so that his debt is nullified. You might wonder how such a thing is possible without cheating, so I will tell you that it's not. Cheating was very much involved, though no more than was done to the physician. The fights are fixed, you see, and the physician is a mark from the outset, the object being to relieve him of his savings, of his livelihood, of his reputation, and most likely, in the end, of his life."

"But why?"

"For sport."

Emma's cup rattled in the saucer as she shuddered with the cruelty of it. "Can you mean it?" she asked softly.

"I mean it. Can you really doubt there exists such evil among us?"

She found herself oddly reluctant to answer him. Emma leaned forward and placed her cup and saucer on a nearby table. The small movement served to remind her of aches that had not yet healed and new ones that were surfacing. How had she forgotten that she'd been the victim of that sort of evil?

"For sport," she said on a thread of sound. "Yes, I understand." She shook her head slightly as if to clear it. "What of the favor, then? What do you ask of the physician whose debts you clear and hands you save?"

"I might ask anything of him," Restell said. "It is all hypothetical, you understand, but I might be moved to request that he attend a man who is gravely ill from a pistol ball lodged in, shall we say, an unmanageable location. Further, this physician would lend his expertise without raising a single question. He would be expected to offer his assistance at the precise moment he was asked, no matter the complication it presented to his own life. If all this is accomplished in a satisfactory manner, the favor is discharged."

"It is a rather ingenious approach."

"Hardly. It is barter. An eye for an eye, or at least something akin to that."

"Do the people you assist know what favor you will require of them?"

"No. They can't. I don't know myself."

"Does that ever give anyone pause?"

"I imagine it does—after their problem is resolved. No one hesitates to agree beforehand."

"What happens if someone is unable to meet the terms of the favor you ask?"

"I can't tell you." Restell could not miss Emma's look of dismay. He grinned. "I believe you've put the wrong construction on my answer, although I find myself unnaturally flattered that you think I could be so ruthless. The reason I can't tell you what happens is not because I cause harm to their person but because no one has ever failed to meet my terms."

"Astonishing."

He shook his head. "Do I strike you as unreasonable, Miss Hathaway?"

"No," she said cautiously, "but you will allow we have had a very short acquaintance."

"You are right, of course. You will perhaps appreciate that

those people I decide to help are often asked to agree to my terms on the strength of an introduction only—and my promise that I will resolve the situation that distresses them. They agree, I think, not because they know I am indeed a reasonable man, but because the circumstances of their life have become in every way intolerable. As it happens, though, I ask only what can be given. For instance, I would not demand that our hypothetical physician dishonor his oath to do no harm by asking him to mix a poison, nor would I require that he trod the boards at Drury Lane in the service of my amusement or the amusement of my friends. I have no notion whether or not he might agree to either or both of these things, but I am not inclined to place such disagreeable choices before him."

"Reasonable *and* honorable."

"Depressingly tiresome, but there you have it."

Emma managed a small smile without causing herself further injury. "It is kind of you to explain it to me."

"Not at all. You should know the whole of it before I accept you as my client."

A thin vertical crease appeared between her eyebrows. "I thought you understood I have changed my mind. I do not wish you to do anything on my behalf."

"On your behalf? Aren't you here on behalf of your cousin?"

"Yes, but—"

"Then whatever I might be able to do would be done for her, is that not right?"

"Yes, but—"

"So it is not on your behalf at all, is it? You would only have to agree to honor what favor I might ask of you. It is a small enough exchange for your cousin's safety and your own peace of mind."

"I suppose . . ." Emma worried the underside of her lip, trying to make sense of his argument. "It seems small enough, but—"

"Would you ignore the recommendation of Dr. Bettany?"

"No, but—"

"Sensible girl. Then I have your word on the matter."

"Yes, but—"

"Yes is all that is necessary."

"Yes."

"Good. It is settled. We have struck a bargain."

Had they? Emma knew herself to be breathless with no idea of how she came to be so. It must be how the fox felt after being run to ground. "You bullied me."

"That is a gross exaggeration and quite unfair of you. Do you wish to reconsider it?"

"My comment?"

"No. Our agreement. Did I recently remark that you were sensible? Perhaps the fall did more damage than is immediately evident to the eye."

Emma speared Restell Gardner with a significant glance and, lest he be oblivious to it, she added her most frosty accents to sharpen the point. "If there is damage to my thinking it is the whiskey that has provoked it."

"That seems unlikely given the fact that you managed to arrive here under the considerable influence of laudanum. What is a dram of whiskey compared to soporific effects of that opiate?" He did not permit her time enough to form a reply. Though he was credited to have considerable persuasive powers, Restell knew very well that he hadn't employed them with Miss Emmalyn Hathaway. He doubted that she would have been moved by his bullying in the past, but recent events made her vulnerable and he had shamelessly used that to his advantage. It wasn't fair, but it was necessary. "I want to introduce you to Sergeant Hobbes," he told her. "He will accompany my driver and provide additional escort so that you arrive home safely."

"That is not necessary. I came on my own."

"The less we refine upon that, the better."

Emma wished she might raise a more cogent defense against his high-handedness, but in truth, she was weary to the bone. He would have his way in the end; there was no benefit to her in making him labor for it. "I will be glad of the escort," she said. She was pleased that her tone communicated exactly the opposite.

"I hope you do not regularly mistake sarcasm for wit," Restell said.

Emma flushed. With effort, she managed to keep her chin up and made no apology. It was not worthy of her, she reflected, but she did not allow herself to care too deeply. She had not sought out Mr. Gardner to secure his good opinion.

"Hobbes is my valet," Restell told her, "though you should not make too much of that."

"Is he the man who assisted placing me on the chaise?"

"Yes."

"How did he lose his leg?"

Restell had wondered if she'd been alert enough to notice the valet's uneven gait. The peculiar sound of the peg's contact with the floor would have also alerted her. It may have even been that sound that brought her around to consciousness. "You will have to hear the particulars from him, but I can tell you that it happened in the final hours at Waterloo." He waited to see if she would offer some comment as people frequently felt compelled to do. She merely nodded and kept her own counsel, though he did not believe he imagined the wave of compassion that briefly crossed her features.

"Are you entertaining doubts?" he asked. "I assure you that he will provide superior protection."

"If you say it is so, then it is so, but I must remind you that it is Marisol who requires it."

"Yet you are the one with the bruises."

"I have explained that."

Not to my satisfaction. Restell let the thought turn over in his mind without giving it voice. He pushed away from the desk and rang for Hobbes. The valet appeared so quickly that Restell suspected he had been lingering in the entrance hall.

The former sergeant impressively filled the open doorway until Restell gestured to him to enter. Hobbes uneasily shifted his weight from his good leg to his wooden one while the introductions were made, then he stood at attention waiting for further instruction.

"At ease, man," Restell said. "Miss Hathaway is no threat to you."

"I am certain she is not," Hobbes said stiffly.

Restell shifted his glance back to Emmalyn. She had pulled her veil down the moment he rang for Hobbes. He did not upbraid her for wanting to obscure her face from Hobbes, though his man had certainly seen far worse on the battlefield and probably the equal in and around the pubs he frequented upon his return from the continent. "Hobbes will require your address, Miss Hathaway, and some directions as well."

"Number Twenty-three Covington. That is not far from Saint Mary's Church and the park."

"I know it, sir," Hobbes said to Restell.

"Good." Restell addressed Emmalyn again. "Who do you expect to be at home when you arrive?" He checked his pocket watch. "It is already after the noon hour."

"My cousin is likely to have returned from the modiste's. Uncle Arthur, though, departed earlier than I did in anticipation of sketching by the Thames near Greenwich. It is the sort of thing that will occupy him until the light is lost."

"What will your cousin make of your absence?"

"I don't know. Marisol is wholly unpredictable in that regard."

"You have some explanation at the ready?"

"She is familiar with my desire to be out of doors. It was my habit to be gone from the house most mornings, so I suspect she will want to believe that my actions are proof that I am ready to embrace my former routine."

"That is all to the good, then." He turned to Hobbes. "You will permit Miss Hathaway to exit the carriage at the park, then you will follow her at a safe distance. There is nothing to be gained by calling attention to your escort at this juncture."

"My thoughts exactly," said Hobbes.

"Afterward, I would like you to visit Madame Chabrier's shop on Bond Street. You will be glad to hear there's no need for you to go inside the establishment. I will do that with one or two of my sisters in tow. It is the mews behind the milliner's that is of interest. I will want all the particulars."

"Very good."

Restell approached Emmalyn. "I regret that I cannot accompany you myself, but I have an appointment I must keep."

"Of course." In fact, she was relieved. She was glad of the veil because she did not have to concentrate on schooling her features. She had no desire to have Mr. Gardner or his man living in her pockets. "You will not forget that it is Marisol in want of your attention."

"I could not possibly," he said. "You understand, don't you, that a complete accounting of events is in order."

"An accounting? But I have told you everything."

"You have told me what you know. At the risk of insulting you, that is hardly everything. It would be shortsighted of me to accept your perspective alone. It is but one aspect of the whole." He paused. "Do you agree?"

Emma found it difficult to dismiss the notion that he could see through her veil. His gaze was frank, expectant, and above all, piercing. "I am engaging you for your expertise in these matters, Mr. Gardner. It would be foolish of me to instruct you to act in opposition to what you believe must be done."

Restell was of a mind to tell her it would be foolish of her to instruct him in any matter, but in the interest of arriving at his appointment on time, he kept this to himself. "Very good. I will see you out."

Emma stood and waited for Restell to step aside before she retrieved her reticule. Clutching it in front of her, she thanked him for his invaluable time without any hint of sarcasm.

Restell stood just inside the entrance to the town house while Hobbes helped Emmalyn into the carriage. He noticed she did not cast a look in his direction once she was aboard. Her determination to act as if nothing extraordinary had taken place amused him, and for that reason alone he would have accepted her case with or without the promise of a favor to be returned.

Still, it was always better to have the favor.

* * *

"I trust you found something to divert you while you waited." Lady Gardner swept into the salon where Restell had been left to cool his heels in anticipation of her arrival.

Restell turned away from the painting he had been studying and regarded his stepmother with equal parts affection and wariness. "You are looking in fine health this afternoon. Solomon informed me you had gone to the park. I imagine you found your stroll agreeable."

"Let us say that I found it more enlightening than agreeable," she said, offering her right cheek, then her left, for his kiss. "But we will come to that."

Restell was all for coming to it now, but apparently Lady Gardner wanted to fit the noose snugly before she released the trapdoor. He had an urge to loosen the folds of his neckcloth.

"Have you been offered refreshment?" she asked.

"Yes." *The condemned's last meal.* "I declined."

Lady Gardner removed her pelisse and bonnet and held them out to the butler who had followed her into the room. "I will have tea, Solomon, and some of those iced cakes that Mrs. Trussle made this morning. Restell? Are you quite certain you will not join me?"

"Thank you, but I am not hungry."

"What has that to do with anything? I am attempting to foster civility." She threw up her hands as though she had quite given up on imparting good manners, then pivoted on her heel and addressed the butler. "Restell will have tea and cakes also, Solomon."

Restell was careful not to catch the butler's eye, fearful that one of them would be moved to sniggering, if not outright laughter. Lady Gardner would not appreciate either response if she believed it was at her expense. Restell doubted she could be persuaded to understand that he was the object of the jest.

As soon as Solomon vacated the salon, Lady Gardner gave her full attention once more to Restell. "Is that a new frock coat?" she asked, casting her gimlet eye on the cut of his garment. "It suits you."

"It is new," he said. "And thank you. I will extend your compliment to my tailor."

"It would be better if you would introduce your father to the man. I despair that Sir Geoffrey will never find a cut that flatters his figure."

"His figure is decidedly more round these days, Mother."

"Is it? I confess, he seems much the same to me as the day I met him." She paused, much struck by hearing herself say so. "Is that the nature of love, do you think?"

Restell smiled. "I suspect it is but one facet."

"Yes, well, it is good of you to venture an opinion when you have little enough experience with it."

"On the contrary, Mother, I find myself in love with irritating frequency."

"Oh, no." She shook her head with enough force to dislodge a lock of silver-threaded auburn hair. Sweeping it aside, she went on, "We will not have *that* argument. You cannot be in love with opera dancers and actresses."

"Not at the same time, certainly."

"That is not what I meant and you well know it."

"Someone should be in love with opera dancers and actresses. I have always found them so deserving."

"I wish you would not use that reasonable tone when you are being deliberately provoking. You know I find it confusing."

"I'm very sorry. I shall endeavor not to excite your nerves or your gray matter."

"You are all consideration." Her light blue eyes narrowed slightly as she regarded Restell askance. "You *are* all consideration, aren't you? I shouldn't like to discover that you are having me on."

"I shouldn't like you to discover that, either. It cannot possibly bode well for me."

Lady Gardner rolled her eyes. "You are a rascal, Restell. A dear one, to be sure, but a rascal nevertheless." She took his hand, drew him over to the upholstered bench set a few feet from the window, and urged him to sit when she did. He obediently sat. "You cannot conceive of whom I happened upon in the park this afternoon."

Restell remained silent, waiting, hoping that he looked appropriately interested. His neckcloth seemed extraordinarily tight again.

"Will you not at least venture a guess?" Lady Gardner asked.

"You said I could not conceive it."

"Well, certainly you cannot, especially if you do not make the attempt."

Restell chose not to educate his stepmother as to the accepted definitions of "cannot" and "conceive." He offered a guess instead. "Lady Armitage."

"No. Oh, heaven's no. Do you take no notice of what goes on around you, Restell? She has been dead these last three months."

"Then she is unlikely to enjoy a turn in the park."

Lady Gardner was saved the effort of a rejoinder by Solomon's arrival. She bade him place the service on the table in front of her and sent him out, then she poured tea for herself and Restell. Handing him his cup, she said, "It was Lady Rivendale. She is just arrived from the country."

"She is well?"

"Very well. She spent a fortnight with her godson and his wife at Granville Hall and another fortnight with Ferrin and Cybelline at Fairfield."

Restell realized he would have known of the latter visit if he'd had the opportunity to finish reading his brother's correspondence this morning. The missive was still lying on his desk beside the bank draft drawn up by Miss Hathaway. It occurred to him of a sudden that he should invest Miss Hathaway's money in some venture that would return a good profit to her. She might appreciate the means to be independent in her dealings with the world. Certainly it would not cause her distress to be less beholden to her uncle.

Lady Gardner snapped her fingers in front of Restell's nose. "You are not attending me, dear."

"I'm sorry. You were saying that Lady Rivendale spent a fortnight at Ferrin's estate."

"I have said a great deal more than that." She sighed. "The gist of it is that her ladyship has reminded me of her great success in bringing about perfectly acceptable matches. Your own sister benefited from Lady Rivendale taking an interest in her future."

The way Restell remembered it, Lady Rivendale's interest was confined to making a substantial wager on the likelihood that his sister would accept a proposal from Mr. Porter Wellsley. How that benefited Wynetta was outside Restell's understanding, but his stepmother remained persuaded it served as a catalyst to bring Wellsley up to snuff. The fact that Wynetta and Wellsley remained indecently happy after four years of marriage merely underscored her conviction. "I seem to recall that Ferrin was of considerable help in bringing the thing about."

"Does Ferrin say so?"

"No, he accepts no credit."

"Then you should not be giving him any. He is well out of it, and that is as it should be. The entire affair was havey-cavey; the less said about my son's part in it, the better."

Restell suspected Ferrin would agree. It was too much to hope that Lady Rivendale or his stepmother had their sights set on his younger sisters. Hannah was just turned sixteen and considered too immature to be the object of a serious match, even by Lady Gardner's standards. Portia was only twelve and showing unexpected signs of being bookish. It remained to be seen whether she could resist the tidal wave of entertainments that Lady Gardner would use to tempt her when she became of age. If it came to placing a wager, he would stake his living on his stepmother. One rarely was disappointed by depending upon Lady Gardner to achieve her goals.

For proof, he only had to recall how she had taken the twins in hand after her marriage to Sir Geoffrey. When they came of age, neither Ian nor Imogene had the inclination to resist her even if they'd had any weapons at the ready. They were turned out on the marriage mart virtually unprotected.

Imogene accepted a proposal her first season and was married at twenty. Ian did not last much longer.

Ferrin thwarted his mother's machinations for years, but that was largely because she was taken with his reputation as a rake. As she was of the opinion that one scoundrel in the family was all that could be properly managed, she did not indulge Restell's attempts to follow his stepbrother's lead. He had entertained some hope that when Ferrin married he might be allowed to embrace the role of family rogue. Sadly, Lady Gardner was proving resistant to this idea.

For his part, Restell was conscious of showing regrettable signs of respectability. It was quite possible his dear stepmama thought he had grown ripe for the plucking.

He sipped from the cup of tea he had not wanted, swallowed hard, and waited.

"A cake?" Lady Gardner asked, holding up the plate.

Restell shook his head, holding fast to the last bit of his resolve.

Lady Gardner helped herself and bit one corner of the cake delicately. She took no pains to hide her pleasure. "Mrs. Trussle is a treasure, though I suspect her iced cakes are at the root of your father becoming rounder. I shall have to have a word with her about that, I suppose." She plopped what remained of the cake into her mouth and finished it off with considerable relish.

"Now, where was I?"

Restell sidestepped the trap by remaining silent.

"Oh, yes, Lady Rivendale's splendid success on the marriage mart. She asked most specifically about you, Restell."

"Did she? That was very kind of her."

"I told her you were unattached and had no prospects."

Restell offered a wry glance. "It is to your credit that you did not puff the thing up."

Lady Gardner's lips flattened. "It gave me no pleasure, I can tell you that, but as she is in a position to offer assistance, what would have been the point?"

"Indeed. You did not enter into a contract, did you?"

"Do not be absurd."

"It is a perfectly reasonable question. I have no idea how these things are accomplished. Does she present you with a list of eligible females? And now that I think on it, what constitutes eligibility? Must they be females of a certain age? Say, between eighteen and death? Can they be widows or are you set on a virgin?"

"You are being outrageous."

Restell was unapologetic. "Is a substantial dowry a consideration? What of her face and figure? Can she have interests outside playing the pianoforte and embroidering pillows?"

"She will not be an opera dancer, of that I am certain. Really, Restell, you are intent on annoying me."

"No, that is not my intent, Mother, but it might well be a consequence of asking for the particulars. I do not even know if you and Lady Rivendale are prepared to make the proposal on my behalf or whether I am permitted to fumble through the thing myself. What opinion am I allowed to offer? I freely admit my thoughts have thus far been self-serving. I have not begun to consider the feelings of the female. She will have some thoughts on the matter."

"She will be pleased to have you, Restell. You cannot doubt it. What do you imagine will not appeal to her? You are possessed of an extraordinarily handsome countenance and a sharp wit. You have had benefit of a fine education, which you did not completely waste in spite of your best efforts to be sent down. You are an accomplished horseman, better than most of your set at cards, a superior partner in the waltz, and have much to recommend you as an excellent son and brother. You are discreet to a fault and your unfortunate predilection for actresses and their ilk aside, you have been known to demonstrate sound judgment. Do you lack so much confidence in yourself? I hadn't realized."

Her stout defense of him had the effect of taking the wind from his sails.

Satisfied that she had effectively silenced him for the nonce, Lady Gardner continued to present her position. "Can you not see why it is imperative that someone help us manage the match? You are already besieged by a veritable legion of marriage-minded females."

"Hardly a legion," Restell interjected.

"I beg to differ. I am speaking of the daughters who want you *and* their mothers who want you for them."

"Oh," he said quietly. "Then you might be right."

"There is no question but that I am right. You are six and twenty, Restell. That is an age where your father might reasonably expect you to marry."

Restell frowned. "Has he said as much?"

"No. You know he is absorbed in his political designs. He relies on me to manage the family."

"We all rely on you, Mother, because you are so very good at managing us. It hardly seems fair that you should take on so much responsibility. It must be wearing on your nerves."

Lady Gardner leaned toward Restell and divulged in confidential tones, "You cannot appreciate the extent of it."

"And the sacrifice."

"Yes, there is that."

"One wonders that you do not neglect yourself."

"It is a delicate balance, doing for others and taking care of oneself."

"I should think so," Restell said. "We take shameless advantage of your noble nature and profit from your good intentions. You would be well within your rights to throw up your hands and have done with the lot of us, unrepentant ingrates that we are. What a diversion it might be for you to step to one side and observe how we manage without your deft, guiding hand. Now, there would be a lesson for us and considerable comedy for you. Imagine the depth of our appreciation for you in such circumstances."

"You would all be humbled."

"Clearly that would be the way of it."

"I confess, it has a certain appeal."

"It would serve us right."

Lady Gardner chose another iced cake as she considered

the consequences of her inaction. "You are an original thinker, Restell."

"Your influence, Mother. It is the very nature of your arguments that compels me to think in novel ways."

She smiled. "That is a pretty compliment."

Restell was rather pleased himself, though he took pains not to show it. Deciding he had played his cards as skillfully as was possible at this juncture, he judged the better course of action was to change the subject. He set aside his tea and pointed to the painting he'd been studying when his stepmother entered the salon. "Is that your newest artistic acquisition?"

Lady Gardner swiveled on the bench to improve her line of sight. "The *Fishing Village*? Yes, that's new. I told you about it, do you not recall? Of course, you do not. It is as you said, I am taken completely for granted."

Restell rose to his feet, touching his stepmother's shoulder lightly as he did so. "Do not be so hard on yourself, Mother. You know that I do not recall much of what *anyone* says to me."

Lady Gardner snorted. "I am not fooled. You have a mind like a steel trap, Restell."

This was not the direction Restell wanted the conversation to take, so he did not attempt to argue the point. "So this is the Vega."

"That's right. Do you like it? It seemed as though you were admiring it earlier."

"I was, yes. It is a departure from his other work, I think. There is a sense of movement here, of activity. I do not seem to remember that Vega has ever rendered a scene with so much industry. The fishermen. Their wives. Children at play. Here is one woman who looks as if she means to abandon the fish she is cleaning and gut her husband. The humor is unexpected. The whole of it puts me in mind of Brueghel."

"That was my sense also. I wanted it very badly and your father appeased me."

"Vega still does portraits, does he not?"

"Yes. He has not abandoned his bread and butter. I understand Lady Greenaway has commissioned him to do a family portrait for her. Lord Greenaway is not enthusiastic about the engagement—I have that from your father—and how she will manage to make her five young children sit for it is beyond my comprehension, but she is set on the matter. Sir Arthur is commanding an indecent sum for his work, though I suspect that he will wish he had negotiated a much larger sum when he has met the children."

Restell chuckled. "When have you had occasion to meet Lady Greenaway's children?"

"The terrors interrupted the musicale I attended in her home last month."

"Bad form."

"They are undisciplined, but that is neither here nor there."

"On the contrary. Lady Greenaway might be grateful for such insight and advice as you can offer her. *We* have never interrupted one of your literary salons or evening entertainments."

"True, but you make no mention of the time the twins dangled you by your heels from the balcony."

"We didn't disturb anyone. You would not have known if Ferrin had not tattled."

She sighed. "That was really too bad of him. I did despair of that boy ever finding a sense of humor. Cybelline has been excellent for him."

Restell recognized dangerous waters. They were perilously close to discussing the benefits of marriage again. He nearly reeled at the prospect. "If you were to act as a mentor to Lady Greenaway, you could very well be invited to observe Sir Arthur as he creates the portrait. You should indulge your interest in painting, Mother. Think how such an intimate perspective might enhance your own happy talent."

"My, Restell, but you are clever today."

He shrugged modestly. "You inspire me."

"Your father says the same, but he is generally speaking of some political machination. It is difficult to know whether to be flattered." She finished her drink. "I think I will invite Lady Greenaway to tea soon. Obviously she is in need of some guidance regarding the continued employment of the children's nanny."

Restell winced. "Do not say you mean to tell her to release the poor woman from her household."

"It is sound advice and I intend to give it. I have no expectation that Lady Greenaway should take the children in hand herself. It is not done. Why, they are not even interesting at so young an age. The truth is that Lady Greenaway and her offspring are best served by a reliable, sober nanny. When the children are judged mannerly enough to be presented in public they may be sent to school. The boys will go to Eton or Harrow. The girls will have a governess to instruct them."

"It seems rather cold-blooded."

"Does it? I confess, it felt as if my heart was breaking to send Ferrin away, but that is the sacrifice a mother makes in the best interest of her child. You and Ian were already at school when I married your father, but watching you return there after holidays hurt my heart as well. It is only marginally easier with the girls, but they spend so much time with their governess, there are times when one wonders if they are even at home."

"I hadn't realized."

"Of course you did not. Do you imagine I could afford to show weakness? I would have been surrendering your futures. A mother does not do that." She paused and added softly, "A *stepmother* does not do that, not if she wishes to honor the woman who came before her."

Restell closed the distance to her side and bent to kiss her forehead. "You have done my mother proud, dearest. Never doubt that."

Lady Gardner's smile was a trifle watery as she patted Restell's cheek. "What plans have you for this evening? Will you join us for supper?"

"I should like that. Will you mind if I take my leave and then return? I promised Hannah and Portia that I would accompany them to Madame Chabrier's. They are in want of new bonnets, it seems."

"You spoil them, Restell."

"It is the privilege of being an older brother."

"Very well. They certainly enjoy time spent with you. You will not permit them to behave badly, will you? They have a tendency to gawk and dawdle. It is not the least attractive."

"No gawking. No dawdling. I understand. It does not even sound attractive."

She waved him off. "Go on. Supper is at seven. You will want to be on time. There will be smoked trout."

"Excellent."

Lady Gardner nodded and called after him. "And I remain hopeful that before the sweet is served you will offer a full account of this fresh intrigue that has engaged your interest."

Restell stopped in the doorway and slowly turned on his heel. He raised one eyebrow in a respectful salute to her perspicacity. "You are unnatural."

She smiled beatifically. "I'm a mother."

Chapter 3

"Your uncle wishes to see you."

Emma looked up from the book in her lap. The interruption was not unwelcome. She had been reading from the same page for some time and still had no comprehension of what had passed before her eyes. She closed the book and held up her hand, forestalling the maid who was already backing out of the room. "Wait, Miller, you have not told me where I can find him. Is he in his studio?"

"No, miss. In the library." She bobbed a curtsy and made a full retreat.

Emma raised one hand to her cheek, palming her jaw first, then gently exploring the bridge of her nose. There was no longer any swelling that she could detect, but Miller's hasty exit reminded her that the bruising had not entirely faded. This morning, when she had examined her face in the mirror, she had entertained the notion that she might take a turn in the park with Marisol and not be the object of stares, whispers, or worse, pity. The maid's discomfort in her presence served as a warning that this would not yet be the case.

Placing the book aside, Emma rose and smoothed the front of her white muslin day dress. Her pale green shawl had slipped to her waist, and she raised it to the level of her shoulders, knotting the fringed ends just below her bodice. Emma tried to make out her reflection in the window, but the late morning sun thwarted her efforts. Her attention was caught instead by the splintering of light at the corners of the beveled panes. She stepped closer and examined the rainbow that appeared in the glass. Following the angle of the light's entry, she looked down at herself and saw the ephemeral colors were spread across her bodice. She raised her hand so the light interlaced her fingers like a web of delicate silk threads.

"What are you doing, Emmalyn?"

The intrusion was so unexpected that Emma nearly lost her balance as she spun around. "Marisol. You startled me."

"That is obvious. You look as if you cannot quite catch your breath. What were you doing?" Marisol untied the ribbons of her bonnet as she stepped into the salon. She removed the straw bonnet with a flourish and gave her head a toss. Ebon curls fluttered first one way, then the other, and came to rest in a manner that made a perfect frame for her heart-shaped face. Her regard was not so much curious as it was demanding.

"I was studying the light," Emma said.

"Studying the—" Marisol waved one hand dismissively. "Oh, never mind. It cannot be important. Did I misunderstand? When I came in I thought I heard that Father desires to see you."

"He does. I just learned of it."

"You know he does not like to be kept waiting."

"No," Emmalyn said. "That is you who has no tolerance for waiting. In any event, I am going now."

Marisol stepped aside to permit Emmalyn to pass. "Do you know who he has with him?"

Emma wished she might have reacted less visibly to this intelligence. Was it not punishment enough that her stomach roiled and a weight settled on her chest? Why did she have to show her fear by faltering in her steps? "There is someone with him?"

"Are you all right?" Marisol asked, at once solicitous. "Why, you are ashen, Emmalyn. Except where you are still a bit jaundiced, of course."

Emma brushed aside the hand Marisol put out for her. "It's nothing."

"It does not appear that is the case."

"I'm fine," Emma said stoutly. "Really. It's nothing."

"You didn't know that Father has a guest."

"No, but that is neither here nor there."

"Shall I make some excuse for you?"

"No. I'll go. If Uncle is not embarrassed by my appearance, then I shan't be."

"You are very brave, Emmalyn." Marisol sighed. "I could not do it." She brightened suddenly. "I will allow you to use my rice powder," she said, seizing Emma's hand. "Come. Let me apply it to your face. You will be astonished at the result."

Emma shook her head and carefully disengaged herself from Marisol's hold. "You are kind to suggest it, but it is not necessary. I would not keep your father waiting so long as that. He is patient but not infinitely so."

"As you wish." She regarded Emmalyn critically. "I believe if you present a three-quarter profile Father's guest may not notice anything is amiss. It is only your left side that reveals the vestiges of your injuries."

"Stop," Emma said sharply. Marisol's head snapped back, but Emma could not regret her sting in her delivery. She did, however, draw a calming breath and offer in a less pointed tone, "Just stop. I'm certain that Uncle's visitor will not be so rude as to inquire about my disfigurement, therefore I am not in the least concerned that I will have to answer questions that might cause discomfort to any of us."

"That is a very good point," Marisol said. "I should have thought of it."

"You didn't think of it because *you* would ask the questions."

"I would not, and you are impolite to say so. And further, you are not disfigured, merely discolored. You cannot make me feel worse than I already do by making more of what was done to you than was actually done to you."

Emma blinked. Had there been a chair at the ready she

would have sat. "Do you think that's my intent? To make you feel guilty?"

"Guiltier," Marisol said. "I already feel guilty. Worse than that, really, except I do not know what word describes such a lowering emotion. I am heartily sorry for what happened to you, Emmalyn, and I will always regret that you went to Madame Chabrier's in my stead. But that is an example of your generous nature, is it not? I cannot accept all the responsibility. It would crush me. You know I am not as strong as you."

"That is what you say, Marisol, but I submit that it's never been put to a test."

Marisol's lambent blue eyes widened. Tears threatened at the corners. "I think you have grown wicked, Emmalyn, and that is the true, tragic consequence of the assault and abduction. There is no evidence of your fine sensibilities, nor any inkling that they ever existed. You say whatever comes to your mind with no regard for another's feelings. Have you not upbraided me for the very same? Now the shoe is on the other foot, and I must needs reproach you. I can only hope that gives you pause, for I assure you that I will be uncompromising in the application of the standard of conduct you used to set."

Emma closed her eyes briefly while she massaged her temple. The seeds of a headache had been firmly planted. "Marisol," she said softly, exasperation mingling with respect, "you quite take my breath away."

"Then it was an adequate setdown?"

"Better than adequate. I shall give consideration to all you've said, but just now—"

"Oh, yes. Father is waiting."

"Yes." Emma leaned forward and kissed her cousin lightly on the cheek. Her action surprised Marisol, but Emma turned and hurried from the room before she was delayed yet again.

Sir Arthur Vega's library was on the ground floor toward the back of the house. When he wasn't painting in his studio with its windows that opened onto a rooftop balcony, he favored the quiet that was only possible away from the street. Out of respect for his preference for peace, Emma tread lightly on the stairs and down the hallway. The butler was waiting at the door to usher her in. Her entry was accomplished so quietly that neither her uncle nor his guest immediately turned.

It was only when the door clicked into place behind her that her presence became known. Sir Arthur came about first, smiling warmly and waving her over.

"Ah, here you are. Come in, come in. You will like this news, I think." Arthur Vega was not a large man, but the arm he flung around Emmalyn's shoulders held surprising strength as he brought her closer. "Mr. Gardner, this is my niece, Miss Emmalyn Hathaway, of whom I have spoke with such affection. Emmalyn, you will be pleased to make the acquaintance of Mr. Gardner. It is his stepmother who recently purchased that piece I did of the fishing village."

Restell Gardner inclined his head politely. "Miss Hathaway. It is a pleasure."

"Mr. Gardner." Emma was only aware she had spoken after the fact. She further surprised herself by lifting her face to her uncle and announcing, "Mr. Gardner and I are already acquainted."

Sir Arthur's dark eyebrows lifted in tandem, the left one in a slightly higher arch than the right. "You are? That is unexpected." He cast a look at Restell. "Did you mention that? I don't recall you mentioning it."

"I did not," Restell said. He did not expound upon his answer.

"Do you know my daughter, then?" asked Sir Arthur. "I only raise the question because Emmalyn so rarely knows anyone I do not, while my daughter Marisol seems to be acquainted with the entire *ton*. I suppose some would consider that an accomplishment as she's only had one Season, but I have my reservations."

Restell smiled politely. "Fathers often do."

Emma noticed that Mr. Gardner had not answered the question, but it seemed her uncle was oblivious to this fact. Further, it did not appear Sir Arthur was going to inquire as to how she'd made their visitor's acquaintance. She had no idea how Mr. Gardner had presented himself to her uncle, but she was not going to be an accomplice to intrigue and subterfuge. Before she could offer any explanation, her uncle began to speak.

"Mr. Gardner has inquired about commissioning a painting similar to the one his mother purchased. I've explained to him that there is no other like it in the studio, but that there are the sketches and an early rendering in oil that I judged to lack the animation I was hoping to achieve. He is expressing an interest in seeing them."

"That presents no difficulty."

Sir Arthur gave Emma's shoulders another squeeze while he addressed Restell. "Did I not say that she was everything accommodating?"

"Yes," Restell said. "You did." He caught Emma's eyes. "Sir Arthur explained that you arrange many of his sittings and keep his schedule. He would have me believe that he no longer knows how he managed without your assistance."

"He is very kind," Emma said. "But for many years before I came to live here, he had an extremely competent secretary who did exactly what I do."

Sir Arthur cleared his throat. "Yes, well, Mr. Gardner does not wish to hear about Johnston, and neither do I. Will you show our guest to the studio, Emmalyn? Forgive me, Mr. Gardner, but as I told you, my knees are throbbing with distressing vigor today. It's the rheumatism."

"I understand. Do not give it another thought."

"It will not surprise me if there is a change in the weather, probably by nightfall."

"My grandmother made similar predictions. I do not recall that she was ever wrong."

Sir Arthur let his arm fall so that it rested lightly at the small of Emma's back. He gave her an encouraging nudge when she remained rooted to the floor. "Show Mr. Gardner every courtesy, Emmalyn. His mother is a singular woman, a force, I believe, to be reckoned with, and I am glad to have secured her patronage. Her presence at Lady Greenaway's sittings is enormously helpful. The children, remember? I told you about them."

"You did, but recall I did not arrange that commission." Still, she offered a commiserating smile because she had heard a great deal about Lady Greenaway's young heathens. What Sir Arthur had failed to mention was Lady Gardner's presence at any of the sittings. That would have raised her interest as tales of the children had not. "This way, Mr. Gardner. My uncle's studio is on the uppermost floor. Once you have made the climb you will appreciate his desire to remain behind."

Emma turned on him as soon as they were on the other side of the door. Through clenched teeth, she asked, "What are you doing here?"

Restell answered with considerably more warmth. "You receive full marks, Miss Hathaway, for waiting until we were in the hallway to put that question to me. I wasn't sure that you would. You did not make much effort to hold your tongue or wait to follow my lead."

"Can you not imagine that I was in shock? It has been some ten days since I saw you."

"Eleven."

"What?"

"It's been eleven days. When you visited my home you said it had been nineteen days since you were attacked. By my reckoning it's now been a month." He paused in his steps and held her up, taking her by the elbow so that he might examine her face critically. "The bruising has all but faded, except for that spot on your chin, and my recollection is that it is a remnant of a carpet burn." He released her immediately upon sensing her discomfort with both his touch and his study of her features. "The healing for the sake of appearances seems almost complete, but I wonder about the wounds that are not visible. How do you fare, Miss Hathaway?"

"I can't think why it concerns you, but I am well enough."

"Of course it concerns me. There is the matter of our agreement." He turned with her to mount the main staircase. It was wide enough for them to climb side by side. He noticed she did not merely run her hand along the length of the banister. Her fingers curled over the polished curve with a grip that was firm enough to suggest she was not as steady as she pretended. "You thought I reneged on our agreement, didn't you?"

"I believe I mentioned I have not seen you in ten, no, eleven days."

"You would have had to leave your home, Miss Hathaway. Take a turn in the park, for instance. Go shopping. Attend the theatre. Call upon a friend for tea. Join the revelers at Vauxhall Gardens. Dance at Almack's. Present yourself at a ball. In short, participating in any or all of the entertainments that have amused your cousin these last eleven days would have had us crossing paths. Miss Vega, by the way, is an inveterate flirt whether she is attended by her fiancé or not."

Emma was glad of the banister's support. She managed to go on without faltering. "You met Marisol?"

Restell shook his head. "No. Not formally. I think it is unlikely that she noticed me, surrounded as she was by her confidantes and admirers. That suited me, for my intent was only to observe her and make certain no harm befell her. That is what you requested of me, is it not?"

"Yes," she said quickly. "Yes, it is." She darted him a sideways glance as they reached the first landing. "You observed nothing untoward?"

"I observed a great deal that was untoward, but you will understand that I am in no position to cast stones. She is a lovely young woman, heady with the success of her connections and conquests, and she appears to be enjoying herself enormously. There is no finding fault there. Such comments as society is wont to make about her are generally favorable. I hasten to add that remarks of a critical nature must be interpreted cautiously, as they often seem to be taking root in jealous waters."

Emma frowned. "I do not like it that she is the subject of talk, no matter the nature."

"One cannot go about in society without occasioning talk. Many times it is simply a consequence of being seen. There are even those people who seek it out, if you can credit it."

"And my cousin is one of those people?"

Restell could not help but smile. She might have easily made a statement. That she offered it as a question indicated she retained some small hope that it was not so. "Miss Vega is yet an amateur, but yes, it is my sense that she would rather be the subject of conversation than a contributor to it. To the extent that her behavior remains above reproach, she will not be harmed by the wags and may even cultivate a circle of influence."

"Yet you said you observed things that were untoward." She led him around the landing, and they began climbing again. "What did you mean by that?"

"In spite of her following, she is able to escape the crush to find time alone with Mr. Charters."

"But he is her fiancé. It is my experience that society makes allowances in this regard. There is a certain amount of indulgence for engaged couples."

"There is, but she is not engaged to Mr. Glover. Nor Mr. Collier. Nor Mr. Truss."

Emma's shoulders sagged. "She was alone with those gentlemen?"

"To the extent that she did not know I was watching her, yes, she was alone with each one of them. They merely talked. I believe Mr. Collier was hopeful that he might take her hand, but she did not permit it."

"I don't understand. Was she encouraging them or not?"

"I cannot say. Mr. Charters happened upon your cousin and Mr. Truss and did not appear to take exception to what he observed."

"That does not surprise. He is ever charitable in his regard of Marisol."

"It begs the question of whether he knew about Miss Vega's assignation with Mr. Kincaid."

Emma's nod was reluctantly offered. "It occurred to me also, but I cannot make sense of what it might mean."

"It might simply mean that he is so intoxicated with her that he will forgive her everything."

"Intoxicated?" she asked. "That is a peculiar characterization. Do you not suppose that he is in love with her?"

"I imagine he thinks he is."

She stopped on the next landing and regarded him with interest. His features did not reveal the bent of his mind, making it difficult to know how serious he was about his remark. He had mastered an air of casual indifference that challenged her powers of observation. "You are not a romantic, then."

"Oh, but I am." He smiled down at her. "Very much so. It is why I can speak of intoxication with some authority. Do you know the feeling, Miss Hathaway?"

She was uncomfortable with the intrusive nature of the question, but she recognized that she was in some way responsible for it. "Only in passing," she said. She pivoted, giving him her back, and proceeded quickly to the end of the hall. "Through here," she said, opening a narrow door and stepping into an equally narrow stairwell. She started up after cautioning him to be mindful of his step.

"It seems an inconvenient location," Restell said. "You must encounter a certain amount of difficulty getting the paintings down."

"The larger ones, yes, but Sir Arthur designed the means to lower them to the street from the balcony. You will see. The complication is nothing compared to the advantages of the light."

Restell had been aware that the stairwell, while not lighted by any lamps, was nevertheless awash in light. Glancing up, he saw three skylights had been set into the roof. On a cloudless day such as London was enjoying, they funneled clear, golden sunbeams into Sir Arthur's studio. Canvases in a variety of dimensions were either covered or had their painted surfaces turned toward the walls to protect them from the direct and damaging effects of the sun. A window large enough to serve as a door opened onto a small balcony that overlooked the street side of the house.

Emma was not terribly surprised when Mr. Gardner did not wait for an invitation to explore the garret room that served as her uncle's retreat and began to go about on his own. She noticed that he touched nothing save with his eyes, lingering over the scarred pine table, which Sir Arthur used to mix his own oils, as if he could imagine the industry of the artist involved in grinding the ingredients, measuring the oil, and finally mixing the whole of it to create the exact color that had been in his mind's eye all along.

Restell stepped around half a dozen canvases stacked against the north wall without giving in to his urge to examine them. The studio had few amenities, most of them placed there, it seemed, for the relative comfort of those who came to sit for Sir Arthur. A loveseat was situated on a small platform under one of the skylights. The upholstered back of the piece gave up the original color, its golden damask covering having long since faded to a pale, nearly translucent, flaxen yellow. There was a winged chair turned toward the black iron stove and a footstool placed at comfortable distance from it, set there, perhaps, to raise the artist's legs and relieve the pain of his throbbing knees. A much higher stool—the artist's perch—rested in front of one of the covered easels; another of middling height rested in front of the balcony window. Used palettes were scattered on the tabletop; one lay on the floor by the easel.

The studio held the faint odors of linseed oil and turpentine, of musty fabrics and canvas. Open shelves were crowded with jars, bottles, and brushes. Muslin aprons, flecked and streaked with hundreds of stray brushstrokes in every conceivable hue from vermillion to violet, hung on a series of wooden pegs set into the shelves. A trunk and a narrow chest of drawers had been set side by side under the shelving.

Restell stepped toward the window and looked out past the balcony, past the rooftops of the houses across the street, and allowed his eyes to grasp the grand vista presented by even this small corner of London. "It is a view such as I have rarely seen," he said.

"Few people have unless they frequent the quarters usually given to the servants."

Restell glanced over his shoulder and regarded her quizzically.

Emma flushed. She spoke quickly to disabuse him of the construction he seemed to have put upon her words. "I didn't mean that you . . . that is, I never intended . . . I think you have mistaken my—" She cut off her inadequate explanation when she was finally able to divine that he was much amused by it. Irritation made her mouth flatten, which only seemed to amuse him more. Determined to ignore him by not making further comment, she took deliberate strides to the window where he stood and pushed it open, propping it in place with an iron rod made specifically for that purpose. Raising her hem a few modest inches, she stepped over the sill, ducked under the open glass, and came to stand on the balcony. "Would you care to view from here?" she asked.

Restell followed her example, though with less ease than she had shown. He also refrained from going to the edge of the wooden balustrade. "Does your uncle paint out here?"

"He has," she said, "but not in recent years. In fact, I do not believe I've ever seen him stand on the balcony."

"And you've lived with your uncle and cousin for three years, I think you told me."

"Yes, that's right."

Restell noted the stippling of paint on the balcony's floor, most of it concentrated in one particular area. He could make out the L-shaped corners where the easel legs had been resting. Paint dappled the balustrade, the colors still as rich and deep as they were on the floor. "Your cousin paints, Miss Hathaway?"

"Marisol?" she asked in incredulous accents.

"You have another cousin, mayhap?"

"Pardon? Oh, no. No, I don't." She tried to recover, realizing her reaction was hardly complimentary to Marisol. "I'm sorry.

It's just that I have never heard Marisol express the least interest in painting. It is difficult for me to imagine that she would find any pleasure in it. I've heard her remark that she finds it a messy, malodorous business. Her talents are the pianoforte and dramatic readings."

"Then you are the family's other artist."

"Me? Hardly. Why do you suggest it?"

He pointed to the balcony's floor and balustrade. "Someone has been painting out here recently. You say it hasn't been your uncle, and you've acquitted Miss Vega of the same. I think I can safely eliminate any of the servants, so I submit that it is you."

"You are not wrong with your facts, Mr. Gardner, but your conclusion is still incorrect."

A lock of pale, sun-gilt hair fell across his forehead as he leaned forward to regard her more intently. "Is it?"

Emma's own gaze did not falter. "It is. My uncle accepts students from time to time."

"So it is a student who paints out here."

"Yes. Is it important?"

"I doubt it, but you are gracious to indulge my curiosity."

"What is it precisely that you are curious about?"

"Why, you, of course." He retreated into the studio before she managed a reply, but not before he glimpsed her open-mouthed astonishment.

Emma followed Restell; this time exercising more caution as she crossed the sill. It was all in aid of giving her a moment to recover.

Restell considered offering his hand to assist her but thought better of it. She would not likely spurn his help; neither was she likely to be made comfortable by it. He waited beside the easel until she had crossed the sill and composed herself before he inquired about the painting he'd asked to see.

"I believe it's over here," Emma said. She moved to the loveseat where three canvases were leaning against the left side. She examined them quickly and found what she was looking for at the bottom. "This is it. I fear you will be disappointed. Uncle Arthur did point out to you that this is a first, and wholly unsatisfactory, early work."

Restell accepted the painting and studied it without comment for several minutes. It *was* an incomplete work. The canvas measured some eighteen by twenty-four inches, a little over half the size of the painting his mother had purchased. The right side of the painting was largely finished, though without the small details and richness of color and character that were so remarkable in the final work. The brushstrokes faded toward the middle of the painting and the left side was devoid of color. The rest of the scene was still visible because of the pencil drawing that remained.

"There are sketches also," Emma told him. "Would you like to see those?"

"Yes," he said. "Yes, I would."

Emma went to the chest and began rifling the contents of the bottom two drawers. She removed several sheets and carefully laid them on the table. "You will observe that none of them is like the finished work, yet elements from all of them are in the painting. When seen like this, end to end, one has the sense of the breadth of his vision."

To Restell's eye it seemed that Sir Arthur's initial vision had been far more ambitious than what he had finally put to his canvas. The sketches suggested a view of the village that allowed one's eye to travel a full three hundred sixty degrees, as if one were standing at the epicenter of all the activity. Nevertheless, these pencil drawings of the village were astonishing in their attention to detail and portrayed the villagers in such an intimate way that they seemed familiar. "The painting that hangs in my mother's salon," Restell said, "am I correct to assume it is but the first piece in a series?"

Emma stacked the sketches and made to return them to the chest. Restell reached across the table and lightly touched her forearm, halting her.

"You have not answered my question," Restell said. He straightened and allowed his hand to fall away.

"I have the intention to do so," she said. "You are not patient after all."

"And you are not the first to remark upon it."

It was not an admission, she realized, but did point to an awareness that others saw him in the same light. "Allow me to put these away."

"That is precisely what I meant to prevent. I am interested in purchasing the sketches."

"These? But they are—"

"Ambitious," he interjected. "And intriguing. It is why I wondered if there indeed would be a series of paintings. If these are of so little value to Sir Arthur that they are relegated to a drawer, then I should very much like to own them."

"I don't know what my uncle's intentions are regarding a second and third painting. You are correct that he considered a different project at the outset, but he was never quite satisfied with what could be accomplished and frankly could not wait to be rid of it. He was taken aback, I believe, when it aroused interest. Mr. Charters was helpful in that regard. He spoke most effusively about it to his acquaintances who value his opinion in matters of art and literature. He encouraged inquiries."

"I was not aware that my mother knew Mr. Charters."

"She may not. It may be only that she is familiar with his reputation. He has one of some consequence."

"The Brummel of artistic enlightenment," Restell said wryly. "I was right to avoid an introduction, then."

Emma's blue-green eyes flashed her disapproval. "He does not have the plague, you know."

"He was holding court at Lady Claremont's ball while his fiancé was slipping out to the gazebo with Mr. Glover. Miss Vega aside, his audience appeared to be enthralled with his discourse."

"Perhaps Marisol was desirous of his attention."

"That also occurred to me." He watched relief sweep through Emmalyn's expression. He could not fault her for wanting to see her cousin in the best light. She seemed to have a sound sense of Miss Vega's shortcomings of character and behavior, but she was perhaps too willing to view those foibles as a consequence of her cousin's age. Restell was reserving judgment in that regard. He accepted immaturity as a contributing factor, but was uncertain that it explained the whole of Miss Vega's precipitous disposition.

"Marisol is not quite all of a piece when she is not at the center of things," Emma said. "I have known her to embrace an uncharitable mood. She cannot seem to help herself."

"I'm sure she can't," Restell said neutrally. "I am given to understand Mr. Charters proposed some three months ago."

"Yes, in March. How did you learn that?"

He shrugged. "That sort of information is freely offered in the course of a general inquiry about Mr. Charters. Did Miss Vega immediately accept?"

"She gave him her answer after Mr. Charters spoke to Sir Arthur. I believe that was the following day."

"She did not seek your counsel?"

"No. She told me about the proposal, of course, but she did not ask me to offer an opinion as to the suitability of the match."

"What is your opinion? He is considerably older than she."

"My opinion is of no consequence. They are affianced. And he is eleven years her senior, not yet thirty himself, so it is hardly a chasm that separates them."

"Tell me about Johnston."

The abrupt shift in the tenor of his questions gave Emma a start. Her head came up a fraction and she frowned at him. "Johnston?"

"You mentioned him earlier in your uncle's presence. Do you recall?"

"I do, now that you have reminded me, but I fail to comprehend why he is a point of inquiry." She set down the sketches and held up one hand, forestalling his explanation. He would likely ask her to simply indulge him without offering any hint as to what provoked his curiosity. "Mr. Johnston was my uncle's secretary for almost a score of years.

Do not depend on my recollection regarding the length of his service. You would have to inquire of Sir Arthur."

"It seemed to me that your uncle desired not to speak of the man. He was quick to put a period to that conversation."

"You do not permit me to move you from your purpose so easily."

Her faintly accusing tone raised his smile. "That is because you approached me, Miss Hathaway, and asked for my help. It would not be in your best interest if I allowed you to dictate what questions are important enough to answer and what should be dismissed as mere fancy."

Emma could not find the flaw in his reasoning. Sighing almost inaudibly, she offered the information he sought. "Mr. Johnston was still in the employ of my uncle when I came to live here. It seemed to me that he worked tirelessly in the best interests of Sir Arthur, arranging viewings of my uncle's work, placating patrons, attending to all the pecuniary details, and occasionally accepting the brunt of my uncle's temper, regardless of what or who provoked it."

"A paragon, then."

"I would hesitate to name him as such, but he certainly impressed me as a capable and honorable gentleman. When I expressed interest in what he did for Sir Arthur, he made time for me and patiently answered my questions. I could not have assumed the responsibilities of his position if not for his tutelage."

"Did he realize he was preparing his successor?"

"It was not like that," Emma said. "There was no design that I would be appropriating his position."

"Yet he is no longer in the service of Sir Arthur and you are."

"My uncle believes that Mr. Johnston was stealing from him."

"What do you believe?"

"I am not as certain as Sir Arthur. There is compelling evidence to suggest that he is guilty of such a deed, and no other suspects, so one can comprehend my uncle's decision to release him, yet Mr. Johnston's protestations of innocence rang

Jo Goodman

true to me. That he should betray my uncle's trust after years of exemplary service did not make sense."

"Perhaps he was embezzling from the beginning and only became careless late in his tenure."

Emma shook her head. "No, that is not it. I went through the accounts with every attention to detail. Mr. Johnston kept meticulous records and had ledgers going back to the beginning of his employment. There is simply nothing to suggest that he was appropriating moneys for his own use."

"You cited compelling evidence."

"Oh, yes. There were discrepancies between commissions that were entered in the account book and the actual amounts that were paid for paintings. Mr. Charters is the one who stumbled upon the inconsistency."

Restell's clear blue eyes became vaguely distant in their focus as he considered this. He rubbed the underside of his chin with his knuckles. "How did that come about?"

"Mr. Charters overheard a friend remark that one must be prepared to pay a king's ransom for a portrait by an artist of some renown. I believe Mr. Charters pursued a line of inquiry until he learned the exact figure his friend was lamenting. In the course of conversation with my uncle, Mr. Charters realized that the commission Sir Arthur was expecting was much less than what the friend had agreed to pay. As Mr. Johnston acted as the agent for the sale, and as he had recorded the smaller figure in his ledger, it pointed to a clear incongruity. Mr. Charters's friend confirmed that he had indeed paid Mr. Johnston a larger commission than my uncle received. Mr. Johnston swore he was being wronged, but his protestations came to nothing. More evidence was uncovered in a similar vein, going back six months, I think. It was too much for my uncle to overlook. He dismissed Mr. Johnston without a character."

"That is when you assumed his responsibilities."

"Yes."

"You are compensated for your services?" Restell did not miss her surprise at this notion. Clearly she had not considered such an arrangement and apparently her uncle had not suggested it. "Mother says it is beyond vulgar when I broach the subject of money, so I beg your forgiveness if I have offended you, but clearly you are engaged in the same enterprise that put coin in Mr. Johnston's pocket. It cannot be outside all expectation that you might be reimbursed for your efforts."

"I should very much like to make the acquaintance of your mother, Mr. Gardner. She seems an infinitely sensible woman."

"She certainly takes pains to remind me."

Emma could not help but smile at his wry tone. She went on to explain, "I am not compensated for what assistance I lend my uncle. I do it gladly, and I am given food and shelter and an allowance sufficient for my needs. I am in no way neglected."

"You are the poor relation, then."

Unoffended by this characterization, Emma's slight smile deepened. Hadn't she said the same to him upon their initial meeting? She could hardly take exception. "Like you, Mr. Gardner. It is a position we share in our respective families."

Restell nodded slowly as he considered the import of her observation. He felt no obligation to correct her. "So it would appear, Miss Hathaway. Have you a need to marry for money?"

Emma's dark eyebrows rose almost to her hairline. "Do you never temper your tongue, Mr. Gardner?"

"To what purpose?"

"Civility."

What Restell did not try to do was temper his amusement. His grin was deep and hinted at the wickedness of his thoughts. In contrast, the dimples that appeared on either side of his mouth made him seem wholly innocent. His laughter was short and sharp, entirely robust and unrestrained.

"You have no use for observing proprieties?" Emma asked rather more sharply than she intended. "Or are you laughing at me?"

Restell reined himself in. "I have the greatest respect for you."

Emma supposed that answered her question. It was his regard for socially correct behavior that was suspect.

"You have not answered my question," he said. "I am noticing that you have a talent for turning me from the end I have in mind."

"It is a talent apparently in need of refinement. You are like a dog with a bone."

"You flatter me."

Emma sighed. He was perfectly intractable. "I have no need to marry at all, Mr. Gardner. My uncle is content to have me under his roof. I am given to understand that upon his death he will settle his fortune upon his daughter, but I expect to have a comfortable living."

"But not so much that you will become the target of fortune hunters."

"Goodness, no." She chuckled at the thought of it. "There is nothing about that prospect that is appealing."

"There is something to be said for being the poor relation," Restell told her. "At least I have always thought so."

"That view does seem to explain why you choose to accept favors for your services rather than expect remuneration."

Restell's small smile saluted her perspicacity. "Do you have occasion to see Mr. Johnston?"

Emma wondered what sort of partner Mr. Gardner would be in the waltz. She credited herself with being an accomplished dancer but in this particular milieu she was incapable of following his lead. More than once she felt as if she'd trod upon her own toes in an effort to keep up. "Mr. Johnston was able to secure a position as a clerk with the firm of Napier and Walpole. They underwrite business ventures, similar to Lloyd's."

"I am familiar. The firm is almost as revered as Lloyd's. It is somewhat surprising that Mr. Johnston was able to find employment there, given the fact that Sir Arthur supplied no character."

"My uncle is not vindictive, Mr. Gardner. He did not

oppose Mr. Johnston's efforts to seek another position. He expressed some concerns when he learned that Mr. Johnston would be working for the insurers, but he believed, rightly I think, that there would be such an examination of his work that there would be no opportunity for embezzlement."

"So no one, in fact, informed Napier and Walpole that they were employing a thief."

"No." She regarded him with sudden alarm. "You would not take it upon yourself to—"

Restell shook his head. "I would not. It is most assuredly not my place." He saw that her relief was palpable. "I imagine his current wages are not what they were in your uncle's employ."

"I don't know," Emma said. "It is likely you're right."

"Does he have a family?"

"His wife and his father."

"Can you conceive that he might be the sort of man to be moved to an act of vengeance?"

"Vengeance? Mr. Johnston? No, it is not possible." She considered why he was posing the question. "Are you suggesting that he might be responsible for abducting me?"

"I do not recall suggesting anything. Did it seem that way? I believe I asked if you could conceive of spiteful behavior in the man."

"Mr. Gardner, I can hardly conceive that he is guilty of theft. That he would act on a plan of revenge, or even entertain the notion, is quite outside my comprehension."

"That is all I wondered, Miss Hathaway. You might have simply said so."

Emma felt a measure of heat rise in her cheeks. She drew herself up, holding the sketches in front of her, and refused to look away from his implacable stare as if she'd committed a transgression. "Do you intend to pursue these same questions with my uncle and cousin?"

"With your uncle, your cousin, Mr. Charters, and most likely, with Mr. Johnston. I have many more questions for them. Didn't I say there would have to be a full accounting?"

Emma sat down abruptly on the stool behind her. "I never thought . . ." Her voice trailed off.

"It is frequently thus," Restell said sympathetically. "People rarely can comprehend the full consequences of applying for protection."

"Are you persuaded that what happened to me was not a random act?"

His voice was gentle. "I think you know it was not."

Emma's shoulders sagged. She expelled a puff of air between her lips that completed her deflation. "Was I the intended victim, Mr. Gardner? Or mistaken for Marisol?"

"I have not yet been able to determine that. There is still much to be answered, but it seems—" He stopped because he heard the creak of the door at the bottom of the stairwell. He had been careful to close it before he followed Emma to the studio, and now it was being opened.

"Emmalyn? Are you up there?"

Emma came to her feet. "It's Marisol," she told him. More loudly, she announced herself to her cousin. "I'm still here. I am discussing Sir Arthur's paintings with our guest." She heard Marisol's quiet tread on the steps before she'd finished speaking.

Restell turned in Marisol's direction just as she reached the top of the stairs. He made a slight bow and awaited the inevitable introduction. Marisol, he noted, appeared to be trying to recall where she might have encountered him. As he had not tried to avoid being seen at Lady Claremont's affair, he was not troubled that he had attracted her notice. In truth, he was more surprised that it might be so. It was his judgment that Marisol Vega saw little that was beyond the length of her own nose.

"Mr. Gardner, allow me to introduce my cousin, Miss Marisol Vega. Marisol, this is Mr. Gardner, your father's visitor. He has come to inquire about one of Sir Arthur's recent paintings."

Restell did not correct Emma's explanation of his purpose.

It was true enough, but did not encompass the whole. "A pleasure, Miss Vega."

"Mr. Gardner." She glanced at Emma. "Father sent me to find you."

Emma doubted that. It was much more likely that Sir Arthur had instructed a servant to do that task, and Marisol had offered her services instead. What her intention might be, Emma could not divine.

"I fear I have kept you overlong, Miss Hathaway. Are we settled on the sketches?"

"You truly want them?"

"I do."

Marisol walked over to the table and held out her hand to Emma. "Those sketches?" she asked. "Allow me to see."

Restell did not miss Emma's infinitesimal hesitation. He understood her reluctance as caution when he observed how Marisol held the drawings without regard for the placement of her fingertips. She seemed to have no awareness that she might smudge the sketches or curl the paper. He was tempted to take them from her hands himself but feared she would shred the paper with her nails, so tight was her grip.

"I do not understand, Mr. Gardner," Marisol said. She flicked her thumbnail across the upper corners of the papers to separate them. "These are singularly dull. Pencil renderings only. Do they not beg for the application of watercolor?"

Restell picked up the sketches the moment Marisol let them slip out of her fingers and drift to the tabletop. "I could not say whether watercolor would improve the look of them. I have no expertise in matters of art, so I purchase such pieces that interest me. These interest me, Miss Vega."

She sighed so deeply that a wayward strand of curling, ebony hair fluttered at her forehead. "As you wish, but I think it would benefit you to speak to my betrothed before you are seized by another impulse. Mr. Charters is completely agreeable to sharing his views on the essence of art. He is accounted to be an expert, you know."

"While your father merely creates it." He offered this with no trace of the irony it suggested.

"Well, of course there is that," Marisol said blithely. Her gaze swiveled sideways to Emma. "What is your opinion of the sketches?"

"I don't believe I've formed one."

"No, you would not, would you? You must needs sell everything my father has done, even when such a sale might cast a shadow on the whole of his work. Neven advises the exercise of prudence when putting new pieces before the public."

"Marisol," Emma said, her tone gently chiding. "Your father directed me to show Mr. Gardner these sketches as well as an early, and only partially complete, painting of the fishing village. It is possible that he is willing to part with them."

"He is the artist," Marisol said. "Not the expert. Did you not hear Mr. Gardner agree with me on that very point? Naturally Father wants his work to be seen, but you cannot always indulge him. It does not serve, Emmalyn."

Diverted, and in anticipation of blood sport, Restell's eyes darted between the combatants. Knowing he was of two minds, he wondered if he could trust his own judgment. While throttling Marisol Vega had a certain appeal, he believed it would ultimately be less satisfying than kissing her cousin.

Chapter 4

Sir Arthur did not rise to his feet when Marisol, Emmalyn, and Mr. Gardner returned to the library. He was comfortably ensconced in an oversized armchair—dwarfed by it, really—and had no desire to remove his aching legs from the hassock on which they rested.

"So you are come at last," he said by way of greeting them. "I hope, Mr. Gardner, that my niece did not insist you look at every piece in the studio. She is perhaps too ardent in her approval of my work."

Marisol went directly to her father and leaned over to kiss his cheek. "Emmalyn does indeed admire your talent, Father, but offers no more praise for it than is your due. Look, she has encouraged Mr. Gardner to consider the purchase of your fishing village pencil drawings."

Restell was much impressed by Marisol's tactics. She and Emmalyn had been unable to resolve their differences of opinion in the studio. The verbal sparring had simply ended when Emmalyn refused to engage her cousin by defending her own position. Once Marisol realized she'd had the last word, she turned on her heel and started down the stairs, supremely confident that she would be followed.

She was . . . eventually. Restell did not make to exit until he observed that Emmalyn had composed herself. That she was embarrassed by her cousin's behavior was evident in the

color in her cheeks and the hitch in her breathing as she tried
to calm it. He had considered telling Emmalyn that she was
not responsible for Marisol's impolitic attempts to discourage
the sale of the sketches, and hadn't she, in fact, tried earlier
to dissuade him of the same? He elected to keep his own
counsel. His experience with the women in his own family
suggested this was the wiser course. Females did not seem to
appreciate the interjection of logic and reason into their emo-
tional arguments. On the one occasion he pointed this out to
his mother and sisters, they turned on him.

A hint of a smile crossed his features as that memory came
back to him. He almost missed Sir Arthur's inquiry. "I am
quite taken with these sketches," Restell said, holding them
out to the artist. "Miss Hathaway was uncertain if you would
have need of them."

Sir Arthur accepted the drawings and studied each one for
several long moments before passing them back to Restell.
His fine, aristocratic features were set with a certain wistful-
ness as he explained, "I had entertained the notion of painting the village on a much larger canvas. It would have been
a self-indulgent exercise as there is no interest among my patrons for a painting of the dimensions I envisioned."

"Then it was not a series of paintings you meant to do,"
Restell said, glancing at the drawings. "But one."

Sir Arthur nodded. "It speaks to my dissatisfaction with the
finished work. Mayhap Emmalyn told you."

"She did."

Marisol moved to stand behind her father's chair and
placed her hands on his shoulders. "Neven's advice was
sound, Father. The painting would not have sold, and you
would have been heartsick that it was not well-received. How
you would have disliked seeing it sitting in the studio day
after day. I shouldn't wonder that you would eventually be
moved to pitch it from the balcony where it would fall on the
head of some hapless gentleman and strike him down. The
trial would be scandal, and although you would plead that a
fit of artistic temperament prompted your action, you would

nevertheless be transported to Van Diemen's Land. I would be inconsolable, and Emmalyn very nearly so. Neven might very well decide he cannot marry me. A gentleman does not, you know, often choose to marry the daughter of a murderer."

Sir Arthur's bright blue eyes, so like his daughter's, revealed his tempered amusement. "You quite make me believe it would happen thus." He reached up to his shoulder and patted one of Marisol's hands. "Certain tragedy has been averted. Would you not agree, Mr. Gardner?"

"I can find no fault with Miss Vega's exposition."

"I am accounted to be the artist in the family, but I daresay that it is Marisol who paints the more colorful and dramatic pictures."

Marisol gave her father's shoulders a squeeze. "You know I do not paint at all, so have off with your pretty compliments."

Restell observed Sir Arthur shared an indulgent, almost helpless, smile with Emma when Marisol failed to understand the import of his words. Clearly Marisol was the victim of her father's lowered expectations. The surge of pity Restell felt for her caught him unaware. He ruthlessly suppressed it but understood he would have to consider what it meant later. It was the sort of emotion, he'd found, that made him vulnerable.

"Am I to be permitted, then, to purchase these sketches?" Restell asked.

"Of course," Sir Arthur said. "I would make you a gift of them, but my niece will not allow it. Is that not correct, Emmalyn?"

"Someone must protect you against these moments of impulsive generosity," Emma said. "But before I arrange the sale, Uncle, I would be remiss if I did not tell you that Mr. Gardner's interest in your work is not all that brought him here today. You must listen to him first and then decide if you want him to have your drawings."

Sir Arthur raised an eyebrow. "Is that so, Mr. Gardner?" He brushed his daughter's hands aside as he sat up straighter. His feet remained supported by the hassock, but his bearing had

become more formal. "What is it that Emmalyn knows that I
do not?"

Restell placed the drawings on a walnut end table. "You
recall, do you not, that Miss Hathaway explained that she and
I are previously acquainted?"

"Yes, yes, what about it?"

Sir Arthur's query was made almost inaudible by Marisol's
exclamatory response. "Oh, there is to be a proposal! That is
it, isn't it? There has been an affair conducted entirely in
secret, and now there must be a proposal. Emmalyn, you are
a sly boots."

"Marisol!" It was Sir Arthur, not Emmalyn, who intoned
her name as a chastisement. After a moment, in more agreeable tones, he said, "Will you not ring for refreshment?
Unless I have misjudged the situation even more than you, I
suspect it would be welcome."

Behind her father's back, Marisol pressed her lips together.
The thin white line spoke eloquently of her annoyance, but
she honored his request.

Sir Arthur indicated the sofa opposite his chair. "Please,
Mr. Gardner. Emmalyn. Be seated. Marisol, you will bring a
chair from the window and place it beside me." His gaze
moved between Emmalyn and Restell, his expression merely
thoughtful, not judgmental. "What is there to tell me?" he
asked before Marisol joined them. "I think I should like to
hear from you first, Emmalyn."

Emma's hands were folded neatly in her lap, and they remained there while she spoke. It was only Restell who could
observe that beneath the cup of her hands, her thumbs wres-
tled nervously. "I fear you do not recall, Uncle, that Mr. Gardner's name was brought to your attention after I returned to
town from Walthamstow."

Just as if she had been visiting friends in the country,
Restell thought. *After I returned to town from Walthamstow.*
She might have been speaking of a journey she made regularly, so lightly did she offer this explanation. It did not entirely surprise him that she presented it in this fashion, but it

put a rather pretty bow on an ugly package. Even so, he saw Sir Arthur shift uncomfortably in his chair, while Marisol finished giving the butler her instructions about tea and hurried to take her seat beside her father.

"Did you mention his name to me, Emmalyn?" Sir Arthur asked. "If you did, then you are correct, I have no memory of it."

"It was Dr. Bettany. He was speaking to you outside my room. I was not eavesdropping, Uncle. I could not help but hear."

Sir Arthur's brow furrowed. He had a thick head of dark hair, and now he plowed it back with his fingertips as though he might be able to turn over the memory. "Can it be so important? You will have to speak plainly about the conversation because I cannot bring it to mind."

"Yes," Marisol said. "There is too much roundaboutation for my liking."

Emmalyn ignored her. "Mr. Gardner is the gentleman that Dr. Bettany recommended you seek out to assist in the apprehension of—"

"I've got it," Sir Arthur announced, his expression clearing. "The doctor suggested that we might wish to investigate. Discreetly, of course. If you overheard, then you know I thanked Bettany for his concern, but told him I would not be acting on his information. What he proposed was certain to be fraught with difficulties, not the least of which was assuring that strict confidences were kept. Discretion is much to be desired, often promised, and rarely realized."

"Emmalyn understands, Father," Marisol said. "She knows you were thinking of her reputation."

Out of the corner of his eye, Restell saw Emma's head droop slightly, as if it were suddenly too heavy for the slim stem of her neck. He knew, as she did, that Sir Arthur's refusal to act had been largely to protect himself from any hint of scandal. That Marisol should not be touched by it was also a consideration.

Sir Arthur shifted his attention to Restell. "Bettany is responsible for you being here? I hope that is not the case."

Emma did not allow Restell to answer. "I am responsible for Mr. Gardner's visit, Uncle. I have retained his services. It has been ten"—she glanced sideways at Restell and managed a small smile—"actually eleven days since he and I arrived at our agreement. During that time he has been engaged in acts of discovery and protection. At my insistence, he is attempting to learn the details of what happened in the mews behind Madame Chabrier's and whether I was mistaken for Marisol. As it will take some time before he can satisfactorily discharge this responsibility, he also has been acting as our protector."

For several long moments there was complete silence, then Marisol and her father began speaking at once.

"You cannot mean that you—"

"It is beyond everything sensible that—"

"That you should defy my express wishes, it is not to be—"

"You have ruined all. It is a complete betrayal, Emmalyn."

Restell decided it hardly mattered who said what. It was not as if either expected Emma to defend herself. Their objective was to make it clear that they now viewed themselves as the ones having been injured.

It was the outside of enough.

Restell stood. Although he made no threatening gesture, nor took a single step forward, the action of standing was sufficient to encourage silence. "That is quite all that should be said, I think." There was rather more charity in his tone than he was feeling. "I intend to speak forthrightly and not spare your sensibilities as Miss Hathaway is wont to do. Moreover, I will not seek your permission to do so, nor will I beg your pardon later. Miss Vega, if you believe you will be offended by such things as I mean to say, then you should excuse yourself."

Marisol had no opportunity to say whether she preferred to stay or go. Her father simply pointed to the door. The firmness of his expression did not invite protest. Marisol rose slowly to her feet and departed, looking over her shoulder only once before she slipped through the door. Emmalyn did not see the pleading expression cast in her direction, but Restell did not miss it.

Emmalyn wished she might call back her confession. By speaking out of turn she had forced Restell's hand. He never told her when he expected to receive the full accounting of events, but it looked as if the moment was upon them.

She noticed that Restell Gardner had secured Sir Arthur's full attention and a deeper measure of wariness as soon as he'd risen to his feet. He had a command of authority in his bearing that was bred in the bone, so intrinsic to his nature that he did not have to puff himself up to bring it about. He stood at his ease, just as he had when she'd met him, but it was as if the very air about him was charged with the force of his expectations. She had not observed this man before, the one who would brook no argument nor ask for favor. She no longer had any sense that he was but a few years older than she, so profound was his consequence. In the same vein, it was difficult to recall that she'd ever thought he was too easily amused. This man, the one who stood before her now, did not impress as one who smiled effortlessly or found humor in almost every aspect of the human condition.

Here was a man who gave no quarter.

"I will present you with the facts as I have come to learn them," Restell said, addressing Sir Arthur. "Whether you accept them as such is for you to decide. One month ago, your niece went to Madame Chabrier's as a kindness to your daughter. Miss Vega desired to end a flirtation with Mr. Jonathan Kincaid and asked Miss Hathaway to do the thing on her behalf."

Sir Arthur glanced at Emma, one eyebrow raised in question. She nodded faintly.

"Miss Hathaway wore a pelisse and bonnet belonging to Miss Vega. When Miss Hathaway arrived at Madame Chabrier's she was mistaken for Miss Vega at first glance by one of the shop girls. The reasons for this are twofold: the passing similarity of their features when Miss Hathaway is wearing garments associated with Miss Vega, and the relative infrequency of Miss Vega's visits to this particular milliner. I have this information from both the shop girl and Madame Chabrier. It was Madame who corrected her employee's mistake on the occasion of Miss Hathaway's visit."

Emma stared at her hands in her lap as she struggled to recall the events of that afternoon. She could not bring to mind any exchange of words with the shop girl and had not even a fleeting recollection of speaking to the milliner. The effort to bring these things to the forefront of her thoughts merely made her head throb. She was uncomfortably aware of a weight settling on her chest that was making it difficult to breathe. She forced herself to concentrate on what Restell was saying, though it was as if he were speaking to her from a great distance. She leaned forward slightly and strained to hear.

"Madame Chabrier remembered a gentleman coming into the shop while Miss Hathaway was there. Several young ladies visited moments later. She recalls this because Miss Hathaway was so gracious, even encouraging, in permitting her to inquire after the needs of her other patrons. She left Miss Hathaway to speak first to the gentleman, then the trio of young ladies. Assisting her latest arrivals took considerable time, and it was not until she finished the sale that she realized Miss Hathaway had absented herself from the shop. The gentleman was gone also, but this did not distress her as much as Miss Hathaway's departure. Madame Chabrier felt certain she had missed the opportunity for an important sale, such was the interest in her goods that Miss Hathaway expressed. The gentleman, she remembers thinking, was unlikely to have purchased anything. She acknowledged that occasionally a gentleman will wander into her shop for the express purpose of meeting young ladies. She identified this gentleman of that particular ilk."

"Was it Kincaid?" Sir Arthur asked.

"It seems possible, even likely, but to confirm it I need to have a detailed description of the man. Madame Chabrier offered information in the most general terms. Further inquiry on my part of so specific a nature would not have been prudent. You will understand that I did not want to entertain questions from the milliner."

"While there is much I have yet to comprehend," Sir Arthur said, "that particular point I can grasp. You must explain to me why you trifled with the milliner when you could have the whole of it from Kincaid."

"Madame Chabrier is easily found in her establishment, while Mr. Jonathan Kincaid does not seem to have established an address in all of London." Restell heard Emma's sharp intake of air, the exclamation point of her surprise. She was also in the line of sight of her uncle's disapproving glance. It occurred to Restell that permitting Marisol to leave had the consequence of bringing the full force of Sir Arthur's displeasure down on Emmalyn's head. She did not sink more deeply into her chair as he might have expected. This time she met her uncle's eyes full on and refused to accept responsibility for what she could not have known.

Restell brought Sir Arthur's attention back to him as he continued explaining. "There are nine adult men answering to the name Jonathan Kincaid that I was able to locate. Five of them could never be mistaken in any company as gentlemen, residing as they have for years in Holborn, St. Giles, and the Blackfriars. Of the remaining four, one is in his seventh decade, another so portly and ill with gout as to be confined to his bed. The third is a student at Cambridge and was not in town a month ago, and the last is the Negro manservant of Lord Honeywell.

"None of this means that Mr. Kincaid does not exist, but it casts suspicion on how he represented himself to Miss Vega. Indeed, for him to move with some freedom in the same circle as your daughter and Miss Hathaway, he has played false with many more of their society."

"There are rooming houses all over London," Sir Arthur said. He folded his hands, exposing his knobby, arthritic knuckles to some painful pressure as he squeezed his fingers together. "Gentlemen of modest means often reside in places of that sort when they are in from the country."

"They do indeed, yet none of my informants found a man answering to that name in any of the reputable houses. To the extent that he truly existed under the name of Jonathan Kincaid, he has disappeared. He might well be in London, but he is employing another alias, thus, the necessity of a respectable description of the man."

"You shall have better than a description," Sir Arthur said. "On the morrow you shall have a sketch of Kincaid. Marisol and Emmalyn will provide sufficient detail to render a drawing that you may use, within sensible limits, naturally. Is that satisfactory?"

"It is." Restell did not reveal his annoyance at the interruption caused by the arrival of tea. A maid set the tray beside Emma and disappeared without fussing over the service or inquiring if she might be of further assistance. At the brief entrance and exit of the maid Restell was able to see that Marisol was still hovering in the hallway. He had an unflattering picture of her pressing her ear to the door, hoping for some clear words that would indicate the depth of the trouble she was in with her father.

"There is another construction that might be placed upon Mr. Kincaid's disappearance," Restell said after he was seated again and served a cup of tea. "One must at least entertain the notion that he is dead, murdered perhaps during that assault on Miss Hathaway. It is not entirely satisfactory as an explanation, not if he was a gentleman. It does not account for the difficulty in locating his residence or the fact that no one save me appears to be looking for him. It does not account for the fact that precious little is known about him, even by those who engaged him in conversation or invited him to their homes."

Sir Arthur frowned deeply again. His tea sat beside him, untouched. "Emmalyn, did you or did you not meet this villain at the milliner's?"

The steadiness of her voice surprised her. She expected to open her mouth and reveal nothing but the echo of her thundering heart. "I cannot recall, Uncle. I think I remember looking at Madame Chabrier's hats, then the illustrations she put before me, but it may be because I have had other occasions to do those things. Sometimes I believe I spoke to Mr. Kincaid, but it has the flavor of a dream and I cannot give it the weight of fact. The scent of the alley, though, is in my memory, so I have to believe I used the back of the shop to make my exit. Do you see? I have to allow that I reconsidered meeting Mr. Kincaid and fled through the back door upon his arrival, or mayhap I fled before he arrived."

"Why can you not remember?" Sir Arthur asked. "You have no difficulty recalling all manner of inconsequential details. You manage my schedule with remarkable efficiency, keeping most of the appointments in your head, I have noticed. You can recall where I mislaid my brushes, what the cook charged at the greengrocer, and which slippers Marisol wore when she attended the Tidwell ball. It escapes me how you fail to recollect so many of the particulars about this . . . this . . . this *thing* that happened to you."

"I am given to understand that is often the way of it," Restell said. "This *thing,* as you call it, was an assault of the most vicious kind. You, who saw the full extent of her injuries, must know she is fortunate to have survived with any of her senses intact. That she cannot remember the details of a beating that nearly took her life, nor recall the moments leading up to it, seems more a gift of Providence than a curse. How much more might have been accomplished by this time if you had sought me out immediately is now only a matter for conjecture. In your eagerness to avoid attaching scandal to the family, you have allowed the full weight of shame to be carried by Miss Hathaway."

"You forget yourself, Mr. Gardner."

Restell was having none of it. "No, Sir Arthur, I do not. You would have Miss Hathaway remember details of her ordeal as it serves you, yet through your actions have demonstrated your desire that she never speak of it. In spite of that, she came to me, knowing it would displease you, but recognizing a greater risk. She is unconvinced, you see, that the assault was random, and further, that she was the intended mark." Restell set his cup and saucer aside, leaned forward in his chair, and made a steeple of his fingers. His regard was as frank as his speech. "When you feel compelled to upbraid Miss Hathaway for failing to recall all the particulars of her abduction, I hope you will not forget yourself, Sir Arthur, but keep in mind that it is your daughter who deserves the sharp edge of your tongue and perhaps the flat of your hand on her backside."

Sir Arthur actually flinched. Tea sloshed over the rim of Emma's cup as she did the same. Neither of them found their voice before Restell spoke again.

"I will want to interview Miss Vega, speak at length with Miss Hathaway, and discuss the course of further investigation with you. My arrangement, however, is with Miss Hathaway, and she is the only one whose opinion is of consequence. I will also want to speak with Mr. Charters and Mr. Johnston."

This last name caused Sir Arthur visible discomfort. "Johnston? Why? What can be the connection?"

"Did you not release him from your employ after years of service? You provided no character and replaced him with Miss Hathaway. Revenge is not a terribly complicated motive, but the manner in which it is carried out is often as involved as it is inventive. It is also an emotion in want of resolution. Miss Hathaway's escape suggests to me that someone is frustrated, not satisfied. Your daughter and your niece require protection such as you have no experience providing. You may require the same."

When Restell stood this time, he inclined his head a fraction. It was less a sign of civility than it was an indication that he was preparing to excuse himself. "Please tell me where I might speak to Miss Vega in private."

* * *

Emma tried to read again, but she was no more successful than she had been earlier. No book could hold her attention while her mind kept wandering to the drawing room where Marisol was being interviewed. The fact that it was difficult to imagine what sort of questions were being put to her cousin did not stop Emma from trying.

Sir Arthur said very little to her once Mr. Gardner left the room. She worried about his ashen complexion and hurried to get him a glass of port when he requested it. He asked her when she first had gone to visit Mr. Gardner and if there had been only one meeting. He did not chide her for not applying to him for advice or assistance before she went. Emma suspected her uncle knew now that he'd done nothing to make her think he would welcome her approach.

She'd watched Sir Arthur absently massage the swollen knuckles of his right hand as he contemplated what he'd learned. It seemed to her that he aged a full decade as he sat there, the chair growing bigger while he grew smaller. Creases that usually appeared about his eyes when he smiled were deeply and permanently etched when a smile was no longer in evidence. His eyes were flat and unfocused; she could not even say that he was seeing something in his mind's eye. He seemed to be seeing nothing at all.

"What is to be done about Marisol?" he'd asked. And because the question had been directed more to himself than her, Emma hadn't answered. She'd left quietly, suspecting long minutes would pass before Sir Arthur realized he was alone.

Emma set the book aside and went to the window where she stood with her forehead pressed against the glass. The iridescent spectrum that had been visible in the panes this morning was gone. Clouds in the distance had gray undersides and were spreading across the horizon. She smiled faintly, recalling her uncle's prediction of rain by nightfall. It made her wonder how painful he would find developing the sketch of Mr. Kincaid and how it would compare to her own pain in bringing the man to mind.

"You are tired," Restell said, observing Emma's posture from the doorway. "I have to return for the drawing of Kincaid that was promised me. Do you wish me to wait until then to speak to you?"

It was a measure of her weariness, Emma thought, that she had given a start upon hearing his voice. She turned and swept back a lock of hair that had fallen over her forehead. "I cannot imagine that you will keep me overlong, Mr. Gardner. What have we left to say to each other?"

"There is the matter of the three sketches."

"You still want them?"

"Yes. It will not surprise you, I think, that your uncle remains willing to sell them to me. You may ask him if you like. He and I have just completed our discussion."

So he had saved her until last. Emma hadn't realized so much time had passed. "No, that will not be necessary. I believe you." She named a price that should have given a poor relation pause. Restell Gardner, she noted, did not hesitate in his acceptance. "You are free with your brother's money," she said.

"He is as rich as Croesus and unlikely to be overset. If he objects, he may have the sketches. His wife will approve of them even if he does not."

Emma was reminded that he had an answer for everything. "Very well. You will bring your bank draft tomorrow, and we will conclude the transaction."

Restell nodded, satisfied. "As to the other?" he asked. "Do you wish to hear what Miss Vega told me?"

It was better to hear it first from him than to have Marisol shade her responses in the retelling. "I should like to know what she said."

"Good. Will you take a turn with me in the park? I have my carriage and we will not excite a great deal of comment if we are seen together. You have been confined to the house for too long." He paused, then suggested with dark humor, "Shall I fetch the laudanum or will you want whiskey in your tea?"

Emma's head came up sharply; she glared at him. He

merely tilted his head to one side and remained in calm expectation of her reply. "You are bullying me again," she said.

"A little, perhaps. Is it working?"

"A little. I cannot help but believe you will accept nothing less than my agreement."

"You read me very well, Miss Hathaway. I think you would be an excellent partner at whist, but I would not like to have you as my opponent. Will you want a pelisse or is your shawl sufficient?"

Emma looked beyond the window to the overcast skies. "We might well be caught in the rain."

"I did not arrive in an open carriage. Now, will you have your pelisse or your shawl?"

"My shawl will be adequate." It was only as she said it that she realized he had secured her agreement to go. Shaking her head at the ease with which she was manipulated, Emma led the way when he made a gallant gesture that she do so.

Restell watched her falter when they reached the front door. He allowed her to delay their departure another minute to tell her uncle where she was going—and with whom—and another minute while she sent one of the maids to fetch her bonnet and he collected his hat, then the moment was upon her when she had to step across the threshold. She held on to both sides of the doorway with a grip so tight that her fingertips were almost as white as the painted jambs. He waited behind her, not urging, not encouraging. He was hardly aware of holding his breath until he let it out as she put one foot on the stoop. Her fingers eased their grip on the doorjamb, then she brought her back foot up to meet the forward one. He followed quickly, almost standing on her heels so that she could not make an easy retreat.

Restell bent his head so his mouth was near her ear. "Breathe." He watched her shoulders rise as she sucked in a mouthful of air. "Go on. I will catch you if you start to crumple." He grinned as his words had the predictable and desired consequence of making her fairly fly from the stoop to his waiting carriage. Restell followed at a less hurried

pace, allowing Whittier to drop to the sidewalk from his
perch and assist Emma up the step and inside.

Restell informed his driver of their destination, then entered the carriage. Emma did not look entirely comfortable
sitting stiffly on the bench seat, but he counted it as a good
thing that she was not cowering in the corner. "Will you not
sit back?" he asked. "The leather cushions are as plump as pi-
geons and so easy at the back of one's head that you may wish
to sleep here."

Emma avoided his gaze as he sat on the opposite bench.
"That does not seem likely."

Restell turned so his back was in one corner and he could
angle his long legs in the space between the two seats. He was
careful not to disturb Emma's dress with the toe of his boots.
He removed his hat and placed it on the bench beside him.
Folding his arms in front of him, he made a critical study of
Emma's unnatural stillness. "Are you breathing?"

She nodded.

"That is something at least." The carriage began to roll forward. The movement put Emma back against the squabs
whether she wanted to be there or not. He was gratified to see
she did not fight it. "You are safe, you know."

"I understand," she said quietly. "It does not seem to matter
that I know it."

"You are very pale. Do you think you might faint?"

"It is discouraging that you sound hopeful."

Restell chuckled. "I assure you, I am not. You have yet to
look out the window. You have lovely hands, but I wonder that
they can be so interesting."

When she raised her eyes, they were not directed toward the
window. "Do you mean to nip at my heels for our entire journey?"

"It is only one turn in the park. Nipping will not tire me
overmuch."

She set her mouth in a tight, disapproving line, but it was
all in aid of tempering her smile. When he raised an eyebrow
at her, calling her to task, she simply shrugged. "I do not want
to encourage you."

"Now, there is a refrain I've heard before. One might reasonably expect that family and friends would support my excellent disposition, but they will not humor me."

There was nothing for it but to surrender. His wordplay set her lips twitching.

"There," he said, satisfied. "That is infinitely better. Your temperament is not so fussy as you would have me believe."

"Fussy?" That description gave her pause. "Do I seem so?"

"On occasion. It is a fraud, of course."

"A fraud? Are you certain?"

He nodded.

She said nothing, expecting that he would give her some evidence to explain himself. When he didn't, she was forced to express her interest or allow her curiosity to go begging. "I should like to hear more," she said. "I cannot decide if it is better to be fussy or a fraud."

"It is not a matter of being one or the other," he told her. "You are both or neither."

She held up a hand. "Pray, not another word. I shall grow dizzy."

Restell's chuckle rumbled at the back of his throat. His smile was easy as he regarded her. "It's your eyes," he said after a moment. "They betray you."

Emma immediately looked away. When she realized what she'd done, she met his gaze again.

"I was thinking that they reveal your amusement when your mouth does not," he said. "But I suppose it is true that they betray you in other ways as well. Your discomfort, for instance, a moment ago. Your annoyance that I knew you were discomfited just now." He laughed outright when she tried to shutter her expression. "And your determination that you will not expose another emotion to me."

"You are enormously vexing."

He underscored her observation by simply ignoring it. "Your eyes are a most unusual color, you know. More green than blue, yet unmistakably blue. At first I thought it was an effect of light touching them from without, but it occurs to me now that the light comes from within."

"You know that is nonsense."

"Perhaps. But it is a pretty notion, don't you think?"

Emma's mouth flattened.

"Your eyes are twinkling," Restell said.

"They aren't."

"Like stars."

Emma turned her head to look out the window. She thought she heard him call her a fraud under his breath, but she couldn't be sure. He might have said she was fussy.

Oak leaves turned their silver-green undersides upward as a rush of wind swept through the park. Slim birches shivered. Two young women walking side by side had to make an instant decision whether to save their bonnets or their collective modesty. They simultaneously put both hands on their heads and let their skirts snap and flutter so that silken ankles, calves, and even knees were revealed. Giggling, they spun about. The wind pressed their skirts against the back of their legs. The shawl on one of them began to loosen, and when she grasped it her bonnet was torn from her head. She gave chase, reaching for the ribbons as she might try to grasp the string of a wayward kite. The wind carried it like a spirit, then spun it in free fall until it was caught by a gallant rascal who used his ivory knobbed cane for something more than an affectation.

The surge of envy that Emma felt watching this scene threatened to overwhelm her. She thought she might faint, so dizzy was she made by the intensity of the feeling. Tears came unexpectedly to her eyes, and she turned her head a fraction more to swipe at them without being observed.

"It was good of you to suggest the park," she said.

"Was it?"

His question was put to her so quietly that she knew he had seen her tears. "Yes," she told him. "It was." She shifted on the bench to face him again as she considered how she might explain herself. "I am reminded that I must try to do more. I have not liked staying indoors, but it has been surprisingly simple to find reasons to do so. Today, I began to wonder how I will know when my face is healed if I always see disfigurement in my reflection." She smiled slightly, mocking herself. "You might not credit it, but Marisol is the one who opened my eyes. It was all convoluted and more than a bit self-serving, but sometimes she hits the nail squarely in spite of her talent for obfuscation."

It was fortunate, Restell decided, that she did not seem to expect him to comment.

Emma adjusted her shawl where it had slipped from her right shoulder. "It used to be my practice to come here of a morning. The sun was barely cresting the treetops by the time I made my second circuit. It did not interest me to be part of the fashionable promenade that began an hour or so later. I believe that those few people who spied me thought I was a maidservant or a governess enjoying a bit of freedom before being bound to my charges and my duties. It all was very pleasant."

"You make it sound so."

"I should like to know that freedom again," she said. "To be threatened by nothing so much as the gusting wind and decide only if I will secure my bonnet or hold my skirts in place. I have tried to tempt myself with it before I fall asleep, imagining that I am once again walking this path." Regret fashioned the shape of her mouth. "Then morning comes, the sun breaks the horizon, and I cannot watch it from anywhere but my window. It is completely disagreeable, and it is not long before I am the same."

"I understand."

The odd thing was, Emma thought, she believed he did. "It may be that tomorrow I will be ready, or perhaps it will be the day after that. I cannot allow myself to lose hope."

"No," he said. "You can't."

She nodded faintly. "You will suggest the park again, won't you? From time to time as it suits your convenience, of course, in the event I am feeling neither brave nor hopeful."

"You can depend upon it."

Emma felt as if he'd closed the distance between them, and

perhaps he had, if only with his eyes. It seemed that he held her as securely as if he'd folded his hands around hers or cradled her in the shelter of his shoulder. Had he done it in fact, she knew she could not have borne it, yet this was comfortable and comforting and made her think she might bear anything.

"I think you are a bit of a fraud," she said quietly.

"Am I? How so?"

"Well, you are very different here."

"Here?"

"In this carriage . . . with me . . . you are all consideration."

His eyebrows rose. "Do you mean to take me to task for it? I assure you, I have comments at the ready that will give offense if you desire to hear them."

Emma's shawl slipped again as she laughed. "On occasion you demonstrate some wit."

"Only on occasion? Apparently you also have comments that will offend at the ready."

Her smile deepened. "And I cannot help but think you are possessed of an extraordinarily even temperament."

"So where is the fraud?" he asked. "What have you observed to make you question the appearance of things?"

"Do you recall the manner in which you spoke to my uncle? How you stood to deliver your dressing down? It was far and away unexpected. I was prepared for you to make your point, but I would have anticipated moderation in your approach. Sir Arthur is, after all, a favorite of the king. He is also a gentleman to whom one generally accords respect. You looked as if you meant to take no prisoners and spoke in much the same way. I was not certain he would agree to see you after you spoke to Marisol."

"I offered him no choice. I could ill afford to retreat from my position."

"I understand."

"Did I seem insincere?"

"No. Did you mean everything you said?"

"Every word."

"And the way in which you said it?"

"I have no regrets." Restell sat up and leaned forward, resting his forearms on his knees and threading his fingers together. "Sir Arthur deserved to be planted a facer, but as you have already noted, I am possessed of an extraordinarily even temperament."

"He was discomposed that it might have been Marisol instead of me who was injured."

"He seemed so, yes, but you are under his protection also, Miss Hathaway. I thought he required a reminder. Mayhap he will reconsider his daughter's role in events before he reproaches you again." Restell sat up, though he did not return himself to his comfortable corner. "In any event, what you observed was no fraud. Not even a bit of one."

"You seemed ruthless."

"I am, when it serves. You would not want it otherwise."

Emma was less certain. "It was difficult to see my uncle so shaken. He is not by nature an unreasonable gentleman. I do not remember my aunt well, but everything I've been told is that Marisol is very much like her. I do not know how Sir Arthur would manage if my cousin was harmed. They are very close."

"You bear him no ill-will?"

She hesitated. "I am disappointed in him," she said, staring at her hands again. "And a bit embarrassed for him. If my defense of his behavior seems generous it is because I am not naive about my uncle's character. He is not as strong in his convictions as he would make himself, or others, believe."

"I will keep your concern in mind," Restell said. He was careful to refrain from promising that it would change anything. "We discussed the sketches. It was the last item of business between us. You are surprised?"

"It seems ill-timed."

"I did not raise the subject. He wanted to know if I still wanted them."

"Oh."

"Oh, indeed. It suggests a man who is in need of money." The space between Emma's dark eyebrows became deeply creased as she considered this possibility. "I do not think that can be right."

"He is a gamer, Miss Hathaway. Were you aware?"

"I know he has a club he favors. I imagine he makes the occasional wager as do other members."

"He visits the gaming hells. That is altogether different. I do not know if he's recently gone—there has been little time to pursue it—but I know he has visited in the past with some regularity."

"How could you possibly know that?"

"I've seen him."

Emma's features remained clouded. "You frequent gaming hells?"

"I find it rather odd that you seem to be more disturbed by the thought of me visiting such establishments than your uncle."

"I cannot explain it myself. Do you go to the hells often?"

"As I need to." Restell waited to see if she would ask for clarification. It looked as if another question hovered on the tip of her tongue, but she bit down gently and restrained herself. He realized she was afraid of what she might hear. "I cannot tell you very much about your uncle's gaming habits at this juncture, but you should prepare yourself for the possibility that he has lost more money than he can properly afford."

"I understand."

"You are taking this in stride."

"He will have to paint more," she said. "The problem is not without a solution. He will paint more, and I will negotiate better commissions for him."

"Then he will return to the hells with more money to lose."

"I cannot stop him from going. It seems to me it is the sort of thing that he must be prepared to curtail on his own. Am I wrong?"

Restell shook his head.

"Then I can only influence his schedule," Emma said. "Mayhap if I accept enough work for him, he will not have time for the hells."

"It has merit."

"You might want to consider it for yourself."

He chuckled. "You must not try to reform me, Miss Hathaway. My mother remains hopeful that she will yet win the day. I cannot conceive of her willingly giving over the task. She is also of the opinion that the problem is not without a solution."

"Oh? And what has she advanced as the answer?"

"Marriage."

"Really? That is an intriguing notion."

"I do not find it so."

"Of course you do not." She waved her hand dismissively. "It hardly matters."

"I think it matters."

His earnestness made her smile. "Not to Lady Gardner."

Restell's glance sharpened. "There is a gleam in your eye, Miss Hathaway. It is my experience with such gleams that they rarely bode well."

"You have nothing to fear, Mr. Gardner. As you pointed out, you are your mother's problem. Sir Arthur is mine. It occurs to me that Lady Gardner has hit upon an elegant solution. I must needs find my uncle a wife."

"I did not imagine that I would come to feel a surge of sympathy for Sir Arthur, but there you have it. The man is deserving of my pity."

"Confess. You are relieved that I have no designs upon your future."

"True. That is why Sir Arthur also has my gratitude. You may plot his likely marriage prospects to your heart's content. It will be a pleasant diversion for you, I think."

Emma laughed. "I believe you think I am in earnest."

"You aren't?" he asked cautiously.

"Of course not. Have I not made it clear that my uncle is deserving of respect? Unless Sir Arthur decides that he is in want of a wife, I will not be advancing marriage as a solution to any problem, not when it occurs that a paramour will do as well."

Restell still could not divine how serious she was, but he

remained hopeful regarding the paramour. "Perhaps you will speak to my mother. She is not the free thinker you are."

Emma merely smiled in response and encouraged him to make of it what he would. It was difficult to conceive of a place more fraught with danger than that bit of space existing between a mother and her son. Emma had sense enough not to wedge herself in it.

Lost in thought, she was unaware of the passage of time. It might have been seconds or as long as a minute or more. When she collected herself, she realized that there had been a shift in the bent of Restell's mind. He appeared infinitely more grave now than he had in her uncle's company.

"What is it, Mr. Gardner? There is something you wish to say?" She posed her question with considerable calm, but felt her heart begin to pound.

Restell did not answer immediately. "I am undecided," he said finally. "I believe it will cause you distress."

Emma's breath hitched once. She curled her fingernails into the heart of her palms and felt the dampness. In spite of this, she said, "I am no hothouse flower. You shouldn't treat me as one."

"You fainted in my library."

"I didn't break."

"Very well." He slipped one hand inside his frock coat.

"Pray, have done with it." Her eyes followed his hand and her voice was already sharper than she'd meant it to be. "You led me to believe you would tell me what Marisol said. Is that what you think will distress me?"

"It is actually something I mean to show you. I showed it to your cousin as well." Restell withdrew a handkerchief from his inside pocket. The green-and-white-striped Barcelona silk lay neatly folded in the palm of his hand. He saw immediately that it was unnecessary to ask if she recognized it.

Emma Hathaway was already clawing at her throat.

Chapter 5

Restell moved quickly to prevent Emmalyn from injuring herself. He put himself on the seat beside her and grasped her wrists. Her strength surprised him. She did not seem to be aware of his presence or of her own resistance. Her lips parted as she gulped air. Believing she meant to scream, Restell was not prepared when her head snapped forward and she sunk her teeth into the ball of his left hand. It was no delicate, pinching nibble. There was real menace to the bite, and it threatened to take a considerable portion of his flesh if he simply tried to pull away.

Restell pushed his hand *into* the bite. Releasing one of her wrists, he used the side of his free hand to apply firm, insistent pressure against the underside of her nose. This pushed Emma's head securely against the leather squabs and kept it there. She tried to avoid the discomfort of his touch. He rubbed the side of his hand back and forth until he felt her jaw begin to relax. Grimacing with pain, he nevertheless resisted the urge to yank his hand away until her mouth opened wider.

"Miss Hathaway," he said tightly between his own clenched teeth. She was unresponsive to his entreaty. "Emmalyn." He pressed harder and felt her jaw yield another fraction. "Emma. I'm not going to hurt you." He doubted she heard him, or if she did, that she believed him. He had reason to know that his hand against her nose, while not causing pain, was considerably uncomfortable. If he pushed even a little bit harder, he could force a break.

"Emma." He said her name more softly this time, closer to her ear, and he felt her teeth part that final, infinitesimal fraction he needed. He pulled his hand away quickly, wincing as he nursed it for a moment against his chest. He glanced down and saw blood beading on his skin. The Barcelona silk handkerchief was within reach, but Restell ignored it in favor of using his own handkerchief to bind the wound. He wrapped it quickly while Emma pushed herself more deeply into the corner of the carriage. She looked patently terrified, but she was no longer trying to claw at her own throat.

"Do you know where we are, Emma?"

She didn't respond immediately. Her eyes darted around the carriage, first to the opposite bench, then the window, and finally back to him. "In the park," she whispered. "This is your carriage, and we're in the park."

"That's right. Do you know my name?"

"Mr. Gardner."

"That will do," he said.

Emma glanced at the hand he was cradling to his chest. "Did I do that?"

He nodded. "There is some doubt in your mind?"

"I am still hoping I will wake up."

"You are awake, Emma."

She turned away and stared out the window. "You understand that I wish I weren't."

"I understand."

The sky was completely overcast now, and Emma thought how perfectly it complemented her mood. She shivered slightly as the tops of the trees bowed to the wind and the carriage swayed.

"You are cold?" Restell asked.

Emma shook her head. Her shawl had slipped down her arms and now lay mostly wrapped about her waist. She didn't try to raise it. "It occurs that I am becoming quite mad."

Restell had to strain to hear her. It was even more difficult to know if she was speaking primarily to herself or to him.

"You might well think I am a candidate for an asylum," she said. "It is done, you know, to put people such as I have become in places like that. I am no longer certain that I would make any argument against it."

"Now, there you are wrong," he said. "You would make the argument."

Emma discovered that she had not entirely abandoned her sense of humor. Glancing back at Restell, she let him see by her wry smile that his rejoinder had hit the mark.

"You are not mad," Restell told her. "Nor are you becoming so. Not in the least."

"It seems as if I am." Emma turned to face him again. She stared at his hand before raising her eyes to his. "I have never bitten anyone. That is the sort of thing lunatics do."

"Do they? I hadn't realized."

"Will you allow me to look at it?"

"It is nothing."

"Please." She extended her hand to take his.

Restell noted that while Emma appeared the very model of patience, she was not prepared to back down. Her hand remained outstretched, while her eyes practically dared him to decline. Refusing her began to feel rather childish.

"Thank you," she said, accepting his injured hand. She cupped it in her palm and began to unwrap the handkerchief. The bloodstains gave her pause, but she set her jaw and kept going until she could observe the wound and not merely the evidence of it. Her teeth marks were still imprinted in his flesh. A bit of blood welled to the surface as she unintentionally squeezed his hand. Instantly, she eased her hold and dabbed at the blood, apologizing for hurting him yet again.

"I took no notice," he said.

"You are kind to say so," Emma told him, "but I have seen that you take notice of everything." She ran her index finger lightly over the imprint of her teeth in his hand. "Have you a physician to examine this? Dr. Bettany, perhaps?"

Restell shook his head. "Hobbes will treat it. He was attached to Wellington's mounted regiments. He knows something about what must be done for bites."

"You are speaking of a horse bite. I shouldn't wonder that this is different."

"Primarily in the location of the bite, I expect. Hobbes informs me that horses tend to nip at the flank."

Emma flushed. For all that he expressed it delicately, she knew he was speaking of a man's arse. "This is easier to bandage, I imagine."

Restell chuckled softly. "I imagine."

She rewrapped his hand with considerably more care than he had shown and tied the handkerchief off neatly to keep it in place. "You should have used the Barcelona silk," she said, daring to glance at it lying on the opposite bench. Her throat tightened so that she finished in a more husky timbre. "It appears as if it's already stained."

Restell removed his hand from hers. "May I?" he asked, indicating the discarded handkerchief.

Emma signaled her permission with a short nod and at the same time placed more space between them. She watched him warily as he picked up the handkerchief and unfolded it to its full length. She saw the green-and-white-striped silk was flecked and streaked with something that was dark brown in some places and nearly black in others. "The stain," she said. "It's blood, isn't it?"

"Yes."

"Whose?"

"I don't know. Hobbes found this in the mews behind Madame Chabrier's. It was wedged under one of the steps leading from her establishment. I believe that accounts for its relatively clean condition and the fact no ragpicker stumbled upon it." He waited to see if she would offer anything. When she didn't, he went on. "Your cousin told me this handkerchief is like one she purchased to accent an older straw bonnet. You were wearing that bonnet when you went to the milliner's, weren't you?"

"Yes. That's right."

"And this adorned it?"

She nodded. "One like it, yes. It replaced a ribbon."

"I think we can dismiss the notion that this silk is merely like the one Miss Vega purchased and trust our intuition that it is the very same." Restell watched as Emma's right hand lifted slowly to her throat. In spite of the injury she had inflicted, he was prepared to intervene again. It proved to be unnecessary. Emma only cupped her throat and swallowed hard. "Did your assailant use this on you?" Restell asked. "Is that what you're remembering?"

"There is no memory."

"There is," he said gently. "Mayhap it is not one you can bring to your mind's eye, but I know you feel the power of it. It's there when you lift your hand to your throat. I think you feel this around your neck."

"No." Emma shook her head vehemently. "It is only that my throat is so tight of a sudden."

He ignored her denial. "And you want quite desperately to pull it away. You have already marked your skin with your fingernails."

"I couldn't breathe. It is difficult even now."

"It is difficult because you know the feeling of being strangled, of trying frantically to slip your fingers under this piece of silk so that you might draw another breath. That is the memory you cannot bear to put before you but which has its own stranglehold."

"You cannot know that," she said. Even to her own ears, the hoarseness of her voice seemed to play her false. She made her protest as a matter of form, not because she was convinced any longer that it was true. "No one can know that, not when I don't."

With a quickness that suggested a familiarity with sleight of hand, Restell balled up the handkerchief and tucked it out of sight. "Enough, Emma," he said quietly. "It is enough."

She nodded slowly and allowed her hand to fall back into her lap. She stared at it for a long moment before she spoke.

"You were right to bring me here. I should not like Marisol or my uncle to witness these petty dramas. I believe they . . ." She hesitated, then went on. "They would be frightened." Another moment of unease seized her. "As I am."

"I had but one motive for inviting you to take a turn in the park," Restell said, "and that was to see a measure of color in your cheeks. I wasn't certain that I would show you the handkerchief. There was no compelling reason to put it before you now. It might have easily waited until tomorrow. I must return for the drawing of Mr. Kincaid, remember?"

"Yes, of course. And for the village sketches . . . with your bank draft, naturally."

"Naturally."

Silence settled between them. Emma did not find it the least discomforting, nor was she disturbed by the roll and rumble of distant thunder. She was loath to raise the unpleasantness surrounding the Barcelona silk, but neither would the subject be dismissed from her mind.

"I understand you might have waited another day to show me the handkerchief," she said. "But I am less certain why you waited so long already. You said Hobbes found it. I recall that you sent him to Madame Chabrier's the very same day we met."

"True. He did not find it on that occasion. One of the shop girls spied him in the course of his investigation, and Madame Chabrier called upon the Charlies to run him off. As he tells it, he led them on a merry chase and escaped cleanly, but the incident forced him to bide his time until he could return. He only found the handkerchief two evenings ago. So, you see, I did not wait long to inquire about it."

"You said it was wedged under a step."

"Yes. Hobbes was fortunate to find it. That is his estimation, not mine. I believe it was diligence and thoroughness, not luck, that provided this outcome. Of course, had there been an immediate inquiry, it is likely that it would have been discovered. Hobbes was hampered by the fact he believed it was prudent to return to the milliner's only at night."

"Under a step seems an odd place to find it," she said. "Do you think it was put there of a purpose?"

"It occurred to me."

"Do you think I put it there?"

"It seems likely. When you are not biting me, I am reminded that you have great presence of mind. At some point your assailant stopped trying to strangle you and put the handkerchief aside. It is not unreasonable to assume you shoved it under the step to provide evidence of your abduction. Marisol knew where you had gone, so surely you would have believed that she would send someone to look for you."

"She did, didn't she?"

"Yes. She says she sent Mr. Charters."

"But—"

He held up his hand, indicating she should hear him out. "Do not imagine for a moment that she told him the true reason you had gone to the milliner's, and do not further imagine that she mentioned anything about sending you. She simply reported that you went to Madame Chabrier's and had not returned. It was after Charters came back without you that Marisol finally went to her father. Charters volunteered to supervise a discreet search. What experience he has in such matters is unknown to me. I do not think I would be wrong in suggesting it is very little as nothing came of his early inquiries."

"I did not realize so much had been done on my behalf. Marisol has never mentioned that Mr. Charters was involved."

"She explained to me that she wanted to be sensible of your feelings. She said you would be embarrassed in her fiancé's company and feel some obligation toward him. Is she right?"

"She is. Did I not tell you that occasionally she hits the nail squarely?" Emma did not ask him to explain the small sound he made at the back of his throat. It might have been agreement, but there was every chance that it was skepticism.

"Have you ever inquired about your uncle's response to your disappearance?"

"I think you already know it wasn't encouraged. He was

obviously relieved to have me back. In those first days I was not anxious to speak to anyone."

Restell had no doubt that Sir Arthur and Marisol had found any number of ways to discourage Emma from discussing the details of her abduction, even once she was prepared to talk. "You heard me tell your uncle that I must speak to Mr. Charters."

She nodded.

"Do you wish to be present when I make my visit?"

"You would permit it?"

"Yes. I do not mind if you bite him."

Emma glanced at his injured hand again. "You are taking it rather well, I think. Have you had a great deal of experience to draw upon?"

"Hannah was a biter," he said.

"Hannah?"

"My youngest sister. She captured my thumb regularly to teethe upon. Usually it did not hurt overmuch, but on occasion she sank those tiny pearls deep. I still have a scar on my calf. Her penchant for flesh made it necessary to acquire some way of dislodging her from my person. I discovered quickly enough that pulling away was not only considerably painful, but that it also allowed her to keep some portion of my anatomy between her teeth. I was moved to call her Shylock for the pound of flesh she was wont to extract."

"Shylock. Oh, but that was very bad of you."

"That is what Father said, but he was laughing behind his paper as he said it. Mother was less amused." He raised an eyebrow in inquiry. "Did I hurt you?"

"No, not at all. It was over very fast."

"You will understand that it seemed less so to me."

Emma tucked a stray tendril of hair behind her ear. It made her realize her bonnet was askew, a consequence, she was sure, of their tussle. She chided him for not telling her. "I am not vain, Mr. Gardner, but I do not like to appear foolish."

"I thought the tilt of it was charming."

She tugged on the ribbons and situated the bonnet on her

head at the proper angle. "When do you imagine you will see Mr. Charters?"

"On the morrow. He is in town, so there should be no impediment."

"You are assuming he will have no other engagements."

"I am depending upon Sir Arthur and Marisol to make sure he does not." The first fat droplets of rain splattered themselves against the carriage windows. "We are arrived safely, Emma." He pointed to his left as the carriage slowed to a stop in front of her home. "Give me one moment, and I will see you to your door." He swept up his hat and placed it on his head, then turned just as the driver appeared. The door was flung open and the step pulled out. Restell jumped down and held out his hand. He was heartened when she didn't hesitate to reach for him.

Oddly enough, it made the afternoon seem brighter. The fact that they were dodging raindrops was of no account.

The following morning, Emma carried her breakfast to the studio and set it outside on the balcony's wide rail. She chose the stool in front of the easel to take out as well and when all was arranged to her liking, she broke her fast in the day's first rays of sunshine. From this vantage point she could see the park, though the angle and the canopy of trees kept her from viewing those few early risers who were taking a turn. Below her, there was already activity on Covington Street. There was not a house on the block where the servants had not been up for an hour or more. Deliveries were being made to the trade entrances of some homes, while trusted helpers slipped out of others on a mission to buy the freshest produce and meats from the vendors setting up at market.

Chewing on a triangle of toast, Emma leaned over the rail to watch the comings and goings of Covington Street's lesser known denizens. She saw the Harveys' kitchen maid slow her steps as she neared the Fords' home in order to affect a meeting with one of the young footmen coming from that house.

Cocking her head, Emma could hear snippets of a heated
conversation between the Allens' cook and the tinker who al-
legedly sold her inferior goods. The milk wagon rumbled
along the cobblestones, late again this morning because of a
mare that could not be coaxed to good humor by her driver.
Two lads from Sir Harold Wembley's home waited impatiently at street side to take delivery of the milk. Emma imagined that inside the home, Sir Harold's twins were showing
signs of impatience as well.

Fascinated by the patterns of purpose and industry below
her, Emma was unaware of Marisol joining her until her
cousin helped herself to a piece of toast. Startled, Emma sat
back on the stool with force enough to tip it alarmingly.

"Goodness," Marisol said mildly, observing Emma's grace-
less surprise. "I had no idea you did not hear me coming.
What were you doing leaning so far over the balustrade? You
might have fallen, you know. Do you never consider the consequences of acting so precipitously?"

Emma recognized that Marisol was mocking her. She had
captured, with remarkable accuracy it seemed, Emma's own
intonation and accent. "Do I really sound so insufferable
when I deliver a scold?"

Marisol nodded. "I have always thought so."

It was clear to Emma that Marisol's mood was mercurial
this morning. "Then I beg your forgiveness and promise I will
be more tolerant in the future." She pointed to the orange
slices on her plate. "Will you have some? They're very sweet."

"No, I mean to take breakfast in my room." Grinning slyly,
she plopped what was left of the piece of toast she'd filched
in her mouth and chewed with obvious enjoyment. "But it is
good of you to offer."

Emma seized the last piece of toast on her plate and her
cup of hot cocoa before Marisol could do the same. "Why are
you here? It cannot be so late. You are usually still abed at this
hour."

"I was curious about the sketch of Mr. Kincaid. You and

Father were still discussing it when I retired. I wondered how it turned out."

"It's on the table. Didn't you see it?"

"I didn't notice." She glanced behind her and saw several sheets of paper lying on the table. Pencils and brushes were scattered across the top of them. "Did you work late?"

"It was gone midnight when I was able to convince Uncle Arthur that he should be for his own bed."

"I am glad for your consideration, Emma. He is most out of sorts when he's not had enough rest, and yesterday was trying in the extreme."

"Will you not look at the likeness of Mr. Kincaid?" asked Emma. "I should appreciate your opinion. After all, you spent more time in his company than I did."

"True, but I do not think I paid him the least attention. Did you notice that Father was put out with me when I could not describe the man to his satisfaction?"

"It is not enough to say the man has a pleasant countenance," Emma said dryly. "That is precious little information for an artist to begin a portrait. Your father required more in the way of detail."

Marisol sighed. "I'm certain he thought it was little enough to ask, and I felt badly for not being able to accommodate him. Do you think it is because I am so extraordinarily self-centered that I did not attend closely to Mr. Kincaid's features?" Her satin robe rippled as she rose on tiptoes and twirled sharply, giving Emma her back. "Don't feel compelled to answer that question," she said, returning to the studio. "If you are truthful, it will surely be lowering, and if you lie, well, you will not lie so it will surely be lowering."

Shaking her head, Emma carried her plate and cup inside and set them down on the table. "There are four drawings," she said. "You saw two of them before you went to bed."

"They were adequate, I remember thinking." Marisol swept the pencils and brushes aside and studied the two drawings that were closest to her. "Are these the ones? It seems as if they might be."

"I believe so, yes," Emma said. "Here, look at the others."
She pushed them across the table to Marisol and watched her
cousin's face as she studied them. Marisol's concentration
was absolute. All the telling indicators were there: the crease
between her brows, the pressed mouth, the faintly narrowed
gaze. With so much effort applied to her study, Marisol was
in no danger of giving her thoughts away. Emma was forced
to ask for her opinion.

"What?" Distracted, Marisol looked up, her glance rather
vague. "Oh, you are wondering what I think." Straightening,
she pointed to the drawing on her left. "You know I haven't
my father's eye for such things, but I believe this one is the
best of the lot. Do you see how Mr. Kincaid is smiling here?
It is somewhat sly, isn't it? Or perhaps it is only secretive. I
confess, it is what drew me to him from the first. Do you
know who I think has a smile like this?"

Emma's eyes darted to the drawing then back to Marisol.
"No. Who?"

"Your Mr. Gardner."

"What an absurd thing to say. He is not *my* Mr. Gardner."
Emma raised her cup of cocoa and sipped. "In any event, his
smile is nothing at all like Mr. Kincaid's. Cunning is not at all
the same as clever. Mr. Kincaid has proved himself to be cunning. Mr. Gardner is clever."

"I think he is both," Marisol said, indifferent to Emma's
opinion. "Mr. Gardner, I mean." She returned to her study of
Mr. Kincaid's features. "His eyes are rather more brown than
the hazel color this suggests, and I do not think they are
spaced quite right."

"Really? Should they be closer?"

"Farther apart."

Emma frowned. "I do not remember him that way." She
picked up the first drawing that Sir Arthur had done. In it
Jonathan Kincaid's eyes were widely spaced but with the
left eye being a fraction closer to his nose than the right.
"Like this?"

"Yes. It is the feature that I think we captured exactly at the beginning."

"All right," Emma said. "I hadn't realized. Is there anything else?"

"His ears are not so prominent. They look rather comical here. Did you find them so?"

"They are hardly rendered prominent."

"They look like jug handles. Do you think I would arrange an assignation with a gentleman with jug handles where his ears should be?" Her brow creased anew as she considered what she'd said. "You will not mention the assignation with Mr. Kincaid to Neven, will you? I could not secure that same promise from Mr. Gardner, and frankly, I am concerned he will upset all manner of things when he speaks to Neven. I was much relieved when I realized you had been invited to join him. I wish only that I might go as well, though I don't suppose Mr. Gardner will be amenable to that suggestion."

Emma could not fail to notice that Marisol said this last rather more as an entreaty than a statement of fact. "I don't pretend to know what Mr. Gardner would think of you accompanying us. You could ask him, you know."

"I did. Yesterday. When I thought he was going alone, I asked if I might join him and make the introduction myself. He does expect me to make certain Neven accommodates his visit, so it did not seem an unreasonable request."

"He said no?"

Marisol nodded. "I thought it was small of him to do so, but he was unapologetic and intractable."

"That is very much like him."

"Then it is good that he has a charming smile, otherwise I am sure I would not forgive him." She paused only a beat. "Will you not ask him? I do not think he will refuse you, not if you say that my company will give you ease."

Emma did not commit herself. "Perhaps." If she decided to make the request, she would have to propose some reason other than her cousin's company giving her ease. To be believed, she had found, one could not stray so far from the truth. "Will you choose one of the drawings? Even better, arrange them in order of preferred likeness, with the best on top."

"Very well." Marisol offered no enthusiasm for the task. "Do I at least have your word you will not speak of the true reason you went to Madame Chabrier's? I did not tell Neven the whole of it. He is everything loyal to me, but I have no wish to test the strength of his tether by having him learn I had arranged to meet Mr. Kincaid."

"He is not a lapdog, Marisol. You would do well to reconsider your metaphors."

"One does not put a lapdog on a leash. What a silly idea."

Emma felt helpless to do naught but shake her head. "I will do my best to talk around the thing," she said. "And before you ask, I will also strive to steer Mr. Gardner along a similar path. It cannot hurt anything to maintain, as you did, that I went to the milliner's of my own accord."

"To what purpose?"

"To purchase a hat, of course."

Marisol drummed her fingers on the single pile of drawings she had collected. "You are not very good at this, are you? You cannot tell him that you were there to purchase a hat. He knows you depend upon me for your sense of fashion and would not go without me. Really, Emmalyn, you must think these things through to their end. Further, there is no hope that he will not learn about Mr. Kincaid, else why have we applied so much effort to these drawings? You must put in the notion that you were secretly meeting Jonathan. It explains why you went out alone, why you went to a milliner that I do not regularly frequent, and why I was so often in Jonathan's company."

"Excuse me, but I do not seem to know the answer to this last. How does it explain your time in Mr. Kincaid's company?"

"Why, I was the excellent go-between, naturally."

"Naturally."

Marisol waved one hand airily. "Smoothing the waters for the course of true love."

"Promise me you will rethink your metaphors." Emma again directed Marisol's attention to the drawings. "The preferred order, please." When Marisol had sorted the lot, Emma scooped them up quickly lest they be rearranged. "Do you think Mr. Charters will believe that Mr. Kincaid and I formed an attachment?"

"Why not? I did."

"That is not what I meant. I do not think I danced even once with Mr. Kincaid. If I did, it was completely forgettable. Where is the evidence that he and I shared a mutual interest?"

"Now you are overthinking the thing. Neven will not have noticed how often Jonathan was your partner in a set or even if you exchanged above three words with him, not when Neven only had eyes for me."

Emma was thoughtful. "There is truth enough in that, I suppose. He does attend you."

"When he is not engaged in discourse with his pretentious friends."

"Pretentious? I did not realize you found them so."

"Insufferable know-it-alls. They are quite tiresome with all their talk of art and drama and the like. I am inclined to forgive Neven, but he does have a tendency to countenance their company and conversation." Marisol raised her hand to indicate the whole of her father's studio. "He forgets—they all do—that I have had my fill of paint and turpentine. I suppose it seems romantic to them that I have grown up in a home where great works of art are lowered from a garret balcony to the street like so much manna from heaven, but I am heartily weary of making it seem so. It is truer that I can no longer tolerate the odors peculiar to this place, nor appreciate that my father confines himself here for hours—sometimes days—on end. You cannot grasp what it is like to share neither your father's passion nor talent. You were fortunate that your father was a merchant. No one asks if you have a head for figures and investments. They do not expect it. I, on the contrary, am asked with irritating regularity if I paint."

"It is a common enough question," Emma said gently.

"People are curious about a young woman's accomplishments." She added quickly, "But I comprehend your dislike for it. I imagine you are often confronted with their unreasonably high expectations."

"That is it precisely," Marisol said. She shook her head as though to clear it and shrugged her shoulders helplessly. "How did we come to such a disagreeable conversation? And at so early an hour. The sun has barely topped the trees." She pointed to the drawings that Emma held. "I hope that Mr. Gardner will find them helpful. Do you know, Emma, I do not think I have thanked you properly for engaging his services. I realize how poorly I received the news when it was first put before me, but you know the reason for that. I have had time enough to think, and I realize you have done right by all of us."

Marisol skirted the table and threw her arms around Emma. She hugged her hard.

"The drawings," Emma said. They were in danger of being crushed. "You'll ruin—"

"Oh! Sorry." Marisol kissed her cousin on the cheek before she drew back. "Are they damaged? I most sincerely hope not."

Emma examined them, smoothing them on the tabletop as Marisol retreated to the top of the stairwell. "They are only wrinkled. It is nothing that cannot be pressed out."

"Good. You will not forget to ask Mr. Gardner if I—" She stopped because Emma's look made it clear she had not forgotten. "I'll be in my room if you have need of me."

Emma nodded, waving Marisol off while she studied the drawings as they had been arranged for her. She picked up a pencil and lightly numbered each sheet on the back to indicate Marisol's preference. She did not recall that Mr. Kincaid's hair was quite so dark as the favored drawing indicated, nor that his hairline peaked in the manner shown in the second. The more she studied, the less any of the sketches seemed to capture the man Marisol had sent her to meet. She wondered now if she would have recognized him at all or would again if their paths crossed. Still, in spite of her uncertainty, or perhaps because of it, Emma set her pencil to paper once more.

Restell arrived just as the entrance hall clock was striking two. He was shown to the drawing room and left there to amuse himself while he waited for Emma. He anticipated that Marisol would steal a march on her cousin and announce herself first, then proceed to enumerate all the reasons she should accompany him to her fiancé's home. When that was unsuccessful, she would simply plead with him. She could not know that he had considerable practice in ignoring such entreaties as females were wont to put before him and was only occasionally vulnerable.

He did not expect that Emma would appeal to him on Marisol's behalf, but that is what she did when she joined him. He found he was more than a little reluctant to turn her down. She was looking remarkably pretty, for one thing, and Restell knew his Achilles' heel was a pretty woman, not a beautiful one. Although he could not precisely define the difference, he knew very well that one existed. Often a woman who was pretty at the outset became beautiful in his eyes, but the reverse had never happened. Pretty denoted a liveliness of affect that he had never found in strictly beautiful women. He appreciated the turn of the head that was prompted by curiosity, not vanity. The smile might be a shade too wide and was almost always a bit crooked in its presentation, but Restell was inevitably beguiled by its inherent honesty.

It was such a smile that Emma gave him in greeting, and he had not yet recovered his footing.

"You can understand that she is concerned we will give her up," Emma was saying. "In her position I might think exactly the same."

With some effort, Restell pulled his eyes away from her mouth. "You would not be in her position."

"All of us do foolish things," she said quietly. "I have never found it wise to cast stones."

"That is because you are sensible."

Emma supposed it was a compliment, though it made her feel inordinately dull. "Will you allow her to attend us, Mr. Gardner?"

Agreement was on the edge of his mind when something in Emma's eyes stayed the thought. Instead of saying yes, he asked, "Do you want her to?"

It was the question Emma had hoped to avoid. Here was her opportunity to tell him that Marisol's company would give her ease or at least offer some other reason that might be believed. She turned over several in her mind and decided in the end that only the truth would serve. "It is always easier when Marisol has her way."

Restell threw back his head and laughed. "I can well imagine that's the case, so I regret informing you that you will have to endure her disagreeable mood at some point in the day, for she is not going with us." That it was the correct decision was immediately apparent to Restell. Emma was not quite able to shutter her expression before he glimpsed her relief. "Do you have the likeness of Kincaid?" he asked.

"I do."

"Good. I will look at it on our way. What about the sketches of the fishing village?"

"Did you bring payment?"

Restell smiled. "You do indeed look out for Sir Arthur's interests." He patted the area of his frock coat above the inside pocket. "I have the draft here."

She bobbed her head once. "I'll get the sketches. I have placed them in a box to protect them. You will want to consider how best to store them if you desire that they should last."

"At the price you extracted from me, can you doubt it?" Restell caught her beginning to chuckle before she made her retreat. It made her eyes crinkle at the corners. Pretty, he thought, and was not entirely displeased for noticing it yet again. It was not as if he'd been unaware of it. For all that it had been difficult to see past her bruised and swollen features at the time of their introduction, it had not been impossible. Her lower lip had cracked as often because she could not quite tamp her smile as because she was worrying it. What he remembered about that smile was that he'd nearly been undone by it, and he was not helped by the fact that she regarded him from the vantage point of her most excellent blue-green eyes.

Restell exited the drawing room in favor of waiting in the entrance hall. Emma appeared in very little time carrying the box containing Sir Arthur's sketches. The exchange was made with no fanfare, and she excused herself only long enough to put his bank draft safely away. When she returned a maid appeared with her pelisse and bonnet. Restell accepted his hat and walking stick from a footman.

"Shall we?" he asked, inviting her to lead the way. The front door was already being opened for them. The only encouragement he offered was the expectation inherent in his single raised eyebrow. He watched her steel herself to leave the house, then march ahead with all the dignity of condemned royalty on their way to a beheading. Once she crossed the threshold, she seemed to embrace the idea of certain death because her feet barely touched the ground between the stoop and the carriage. When he joined her, she was flushed and a little breathless.

"Are you all of a piece?" he asked. He rapped lightly on the roof with the crystal knob of his cane to alert Whittier that they were ready to go.

"I wish you would not do that," Emma snapped.

Bewildered by her waspish tone, Restell frowned. "Do what? Inquire after the state of your nerves?"

"Do not be ridiculous. My nerves are in a fine state for you have jangled all of them." She reached across the gap separating them and wrested the walking stick from his hand. She slapped the knob sharply against the flat of her palm. "That," she said firmly, beating out a series of staccato sounds. "Do. Not. Do. That."

Although each note was a dull thwap, he immediately

understood her reference to the tattoo he'd made against the roof. "What is it about that sound that sets your teeth on edge?"

If only that were all it did, Emma thought. Every hair on her body came to attention, and a rush of fear ran through her as quickly as the blood in her veins. She was left with a pounding heart and a thick head and little understanding of why it was so. "I cannot explain it," she said. It was with some reluctance that she returned the walking stick to him. "I imagine it is much the same for the fox upon hearing the call to hounds. That creature, though, has his earth. I have nowhere to go. I know you did not do it of a purpose, but that has no bearing on how it makes me feel."

"And how is that?"

"Dreadful. It fills me with dread."

He nodded, thinking it over. "Has the sound always caused you such distress?"

"No."

"Then it is related to the assault and abduction. Does it seem that way to you?"

"Yes."

"You were not bothered by the thunder yesterday. I noticed that."

"I have never been afraid of storms."

"But the sound, that doesn't distress you?"

"Not in the least. Why should it?"

"It seems infinitely more threatening to me than the drumming of this stick against the carriage roof."

"Then I'll offer you protection in a thunderstorm," she said, "but I promise I will clobber you with that stick if you pound the pavement with it."

Restell's eyes narrowed, while Emma's did just the opposite. Her hand flew to her mouth, covering it before any more ridiculous utterances escaped it.

"I think you mean it," Restell said.

She lifted her hand a fraction but did not let it fall away. "I did when I said it."

Restell lay the walking stick along the bench beside him so it was partially wedged in the seam between the leather seat and back. "As a precaution," he told her. "In the event I forget myself and you are compelled to act as you promised."

"Oh, but I wouldn't."

"I think you would. You might believe you have no choice." He raised his right hand and pointed to the angry bruise left by her teeth marks of only the previous afternoon. "I did not want to call attention to it, but it is perhaps better that I do. For my own well-being, I will accept you at your word." He watched a series of hard to read emotions flit across her face. "What is it? Have I embarrassed you?"

She offered him a faintly guilty smile. "Oddly enough, no. I am not embarrassed in the least, or rather I was, but I am no longer. The idea that you believe I can threaten you, even carry out that threat, well, it makes me feel strangely powerful . . . and a bit unsettled." She regarded Restell squarely, looking to him for perspective. "What do you think of that?"

"It seems to me that good will come of it. You will not put it about, will you, that I have uncovered the fierce, ruthless heart of an Amazon? I fear the collapse of society, or at least the society of men, when women come to embrace the power they have."

"Now you are having me on."

"Not as much as you think. Have you not read Wollstonecraft? Her *Vindication of the Rights of Women* is only marginally less frightening than her daughter's *Frankenstein*."

It was the perfect gravity of his expression and the dryness of his delivery that made Emma smile. He made it difficult to know when he was amusing himself and when he was in earnest. "I have read neither," she told him. "But I am sufficiently intrigued to begin both."

"I hope you will share your opinion. Now, what of the drawing of Kincaid? May I see it?"

Emma pointed to the box on the seat beside him. "I placed them with the sketches."

"Them?"

"There are four," she said as he lifted the lid. "Marisol and I could not agree on the details. Uncle Arthur did his best to manage the debate, but we strained his patience. You can appreciate that he was not in the best humor at the outset. I'm certain he was relieved when Marisol finally retired for the night."

Restell nodded faintly as he sifted through the drawings. "The differences between them are subtle, at least I find them so, yet it is as if I am seeing four distinct individuals. I am left with the impression that one of them might be Jonathan Kincaid, while the other three are his brothers."

"I understand. I thought much the same."

His fingertips caught one of the corners so that it curled forward. It was then that he saw the small pencil mark on the back. "What is this? It looks like an E."

"You are looking at it upside down. It's a three."

"What does it signify?"

"I asked Marisol to place the drawings in the order she preferred. The first is the one she considers most like Mr. Kincaid. The one on the bottom least resembles him."

"There is another mark on this first one," he said, tilting his head to examine it more closely. "It is a D; I am certain of it."

"I placed them in the order that I preferred. I used the alphabet so there would be no confusion."

Checking the back of each, Restell reordered the drawings according to Emma's preference. "You have almost the opposite opinion."

She sighed. "I know. I was discouraged to realize it. Marisol admitted that she did not think the first two drawings that were done before she went to bed did full justice to Mr. Kincaid, but those are the ones she chose this morning as the best likenesses."

"I suppose it is understandable. She had no say in the other two." He studied the drawing that Emma liked the best. "He has a less pleasant countenance in your recollection than your cousin's. Perhaps that's what she objected to."

"Perhaps. She did remark that his ears looked like jug handles."

Restell chuckled. "There is that."

"May I look, please?" Emma asked. She took the drawing and examined it with a critical eye. "They are conspicuous, aren't they? I could not see it when Marisol pointed out the same."

"I have observed that females sometimes enjoy disagreement for its own sake."

"That is absurd."

"My thought exactly."

"You are deliberately misunderstanding. It is your observation that is absurd."

He shrugged and accepted the drawing when she passed it to him. "I do not think it would hurt to ask Mr. Charters for his opinion."

"You do not think he will find it odd?"

"Why would he?"

"I imagine because he would expect you to trust my judgment. I am the one who formed an attachment to Mr. Kincaid, after all."

"So that is the story you wish to tell him."

"I promised Marisol."

"I did not."

"But you'll do it, won't you? Support me in this, I mean. There is nothing to be gained by sharing all of the truth with Mr. Charters. Marisol had already had it in her mind to end her flirtation with Mr. Kincaid. Where can be the harm in pretending there never was any affection between them?"

"I don't like it," Restell said. "It rarely serves to advance a lie when one expects the truth in return."

"Please," she said quietly. "If I am willing to pretend an attachment where none existed, it cannot be so terribly hard for you to say nothing to contradict me."

"If you knew me better you would not say that."

"I am serious."

"So am I. You are asking me to disregard my experience and my judgment."

Having it put before her so plainly gave Emma pause. "I will not renege on my promise to Marisol," she said finally. "But you must do as you think best. It seems to me that is the nature of the agreement I have with you."

"I'm relieved you realize it." Restell returned the drawings to the box and covered it. "Allow me to see how the interview unfolds, then I will know better what can be left unsaid. That is not my pledge to say nothing, only that I will consider it."

"Thank you."

Restell shifted his gaze to the window and away from her splendid blue-green eyes. He could have told her that his judgment was already impaired and that it had been thus since she raised her veil. She wouldn't have believed him, so he might have said it without fear of being taken at his word, but he did the difficult thing and said nothing at all.

Chapter 6

Neven Charters impressed Restell as a gentleman who thoroughly enjoyed life's finer offerings and made no apologies for it. It seemed quite purposeful, Restell thought, that he and Emma were shown to the gallery. The room had pretensions of being a museum, boasting works of art from all over the continent and from civilizations that no longer even had a living language. The walls were crowded with portraits, pastoral scenes, and medieval Madonnas. Egyptian artifacts shared space on the mantel with Greek urns and beautifully detailed Chinese vases. The tables—and there were four of them, all influenced by Roman design and realized by master craftsmen—were crowded with figurines of jade, porcelain, and gold. The rugs were Persian and Oriental. Rich, jewel-toned fabrics covered the appointments. Silk. Velvet. Damask. One wall was concealed almost entirely by a tapestry that told the whole of Chaucer's *Canterbury Tales* in its threads.

Restell caught Emma's eye and pointed upward. She glanced at the vaulted ceiling and was unsuccessful in reining in her reaction. She gasped inelegantly.

Restell bent his head toward her. "The twelve plagues visited upon Egypt," he whispered. "As the subject for a mural, it is thankfully rather rare. I find the locusts particularly frightening." He waved a hand in front of him, batting ineffectually at the air. "No, I beg your pardon. It was naught but a fly."

"You must stop," she said under her breath. "Mr. Charters could walk in at any moment."

"And we will be caught with our mouths open as wide as fledglings. I tell you, he will be flattered."

"Flattered?"

"That we are properly awed, of course. It will not occur to him that you and I are appalled."

"You cannot possibly know that."

"Would you like to engage in a wager?"

"Do not be foolish."

"Do not be fussy. I can see you are intrigued. You are wondering what we might wager."

"I am not," she said primly. Her eyes darted toward the door. "What would we wager?"

Restell managed not to grin, but it was a narrow thing. His light shrug suggested that the thing won or lost was of little interest to him. "I have nothing in mind. A marker would suffice."

"But what would the marker be worth?"

"You are mercenary," he said. "I hadn't realized. I was thinking of something you might do for me."

"Another favor? But then I would owe you two."

"Only if you lose. If you are so certain that will be the outcome, then you shouldn't make the wager." The regard of his clear blue eyes was faintly challenging. "On the other hand, if you think there is a chance you will win . . ." Quite purposely, he did not finish his sentence. She would complete it for him, he knew, if only in her mind. Watching her contemplate that he might be the one owing the favor caused Restell to wonder if losing would not be the better result for him. If he did not mistake the mischief in her eyes, she looked to be contemplating something at least moderately wicked. He could not help but support that.

"Very well," Emma said. "I will have your marker."

"You haven't won yet. But the opportunity is upon us. Look up."

The door opened just as Restell and Emma returned their attention to the vaulted ceiling. Their mouths fell open of their own accord. The plagues were as shocking upon this second inspection as they had been upon the first. For Restell it was the subject matter that seemed grossly inappropriate for a painted ceiling. For her part, Emma could forgive the content but not the execution. The composition was poorly realized, and the choice of pigments could only be described as garish. The subjects, however, were rendered with enormous attention to detail. This had the unfortunate effect of lending the whole of it the irrational realism of a nightmare.

"Perfectly dreadful, is it not?" Neven Charters strode into the room. "I have considered having it painted over, but I cannot bring myself to do it. I fear I should miss the thing, and it does amuse me to watch visitors struggle to find appropriate adjectives to describe it."

Out of the corner of his eye, Restell saw that Emma was finding it difficult to keep her own amusement in check. Although he had considered that there were worse things than losing the wager to her, he was hard pressed to enumerate them now. She was enjoying herself a bit too much at his expense. His mood was not improved when Neven Charters took both of Emma's hands in his and regarded her warmly while he welcomed her.

"It is a pleasure to have you here at last," Neven said. "But the greatest pleasure is seeing that you are faring so well. Marisol spoke to me regularly of your progress, yet I find that seeing it for myself is infinitely more satisfying."

Emma carefully drew her hands from his. "You are good to inquire after me, and I hope you have not been inconvenienced by our visit. It is a poor manner of thanking you for your many kindnesses to me and my family. Please, allow me to make the introductions."

"Of course."

Emma performed the function calmly enough, though she was aware of a shift in the very air about her. Both men seemed perfectly at their ease, even politely interested in each other, but she did not trust that it was sincerely felt. She did not think that either man had moved a fraction, yet Restell

Gardner once again had the look of a Viking warrior, and Neven Charters seemed to be preparing to wave a cutlass and repel all boarders. Although Restell was as fair as Neven was dark, they were of a similar height and build. They held themselves confidently as men who were comfortable in their own skin were wont to do. She suspected they shared an interest in athletics, and she would not have been astonished if they had grappled with each other instead of exchanging courteous nods. To avoid just such an end, Emma quickly sought neutral ground and found it overhead.

"Who is the artist?" she asked, indicating the ceiling.

"My grandfather."

"Oh."

Neven's green eyes settled warmly on Emma as he chuckled. "I did not mean to put you at such an awkward disadvantage. So few people inquire that I forget there is no politic response when I tell them the truth. Grandfather was an enthusiastic painter but not an accomplished one." He looked at Restell. "You have formed an opinion, Mr. Gardner?"

"Indeed, I have," Restell said. "The politic response, I believe, is not to share it."

"Right you are." Neven gestured to one of the velvet-covered sofas. "Won't you be seated? I have already arranged for lemonade and sandwiches. I recall that you enjoy lemonade, Miss Hathaway."

"I do. Thank you. It seems absurd that you remember that."

"I cannot easily account for it myself. My interest is often caught by what others would find to be the most inconsequential of details."

"It must serve you well," Restell said. "In the course of collecting your artwork. I am given to understand that an unsuspecting public or an overeager patron is particularly susceptible to fraud."

Neven nodded. "Most people cannot imagine the breadth of the problem. Victims are often unwilling to step forward because they do not wish it to be known they were duped."

Restell sat beside Emma on the sofa. He watched Neven

choose a Queen Anne chair and place it within the perimeter of the Oriental rug but closer to Emma's end of the sofa. He wondered if Mr. Charters would be interested in knowing that he also was often intrigued by what others would find to be the most inconsequential of details.

"More and more I am asked to judge the authenticity of a particular work," Neven said. "Some people have been generous in their compliments, and that has led to more opportunities to judge other works. I hope I do not flatter myself when I say my services seemed to have discouraged false claims."

"I recommended you to Mrs. Stuart," Emma said. "It is a Tintoretto, I believe, that she wishes to learn about. She brought it back from Italy. Did she seek you out? It was some time ago."

"She did. Only last week. She failed to mention how I came to her attention. In truth, I thought it was Marisol. The piece is not a Tintoretto, though I think you suspected that." He leaned forward a fraction and offered in more confidential, knowing tones, "Mrs. Stuart is a lively, vastly entertaining woman, but a bit of a Philistine, don't you think? Did you know she purchased the painting because she thought it complemented the wall color in her morning room?"

Emma was not in the least dismayed. "I am delighted to hear it," she said. "The piece gives her pleasure. She will see it every day when she looks up from her sewing or her reading, and she will smile, quite satisfied that she had the good sense to find such a remarkable work. She will be reminded of her tour of Italy, perhaps of an evening in Tuscany where she shared the balcony view with her husband, and the whole of it will make her happy. Such a memory can only improve her mood. She will be kind to her children, her servants, and even kinder to her husband. Mr. Stuart, as it happens, sits on the high court, so it is of some consequence to a great many people when he is treated kindly." Emma concluded her justification of Mrs. Stuart's artistic choice with a beatific smile. "Such is the power of art."

Restell did not think that Neven Charters was often at a loss for words. Emma was to be congratulated for bringing the thing about. Charters looked as if he'd been pushed back in his chair by the force of Emma's peculiar defense. Restell suspected that while the man might be used to this sort of recounting from Marisol, he was unprepared for the same from her cousin.

"You have convinced me," Restell told Emma. "I am cheerfully content to be a Philistine."

"You do not wish to improve yourself?" Neven asked.

"I confess, it has never held much interest. I count myself fortunate to know a great many people who regularly apply themselves to improving me."

Emma placed her fingers against her lips and politely cleared her throat, all of it in aid of keeping her laughter in check. She could not help but notice that Neven was not amused. He smiled, but there was no appreciation in it. It seemed he was not prepared to give Restell Gardner the least forebearance.

Emma decided it would be prudent to discuss the purpose for the visit. For reasons she had no wish to refine upon, her companions were nipping at each other's heels. It occurred to her that Marisol had not been wrong to adopt the canine metaphor. Restell Gardner reminded her of a playful retriever, while Neven Charters had much in common with a bull terrier. In any event, she was prepared to fit them both for leashes.

"You know why we are come?" she asked Neven.

"Sir Arthur explained it in the note he sent round this morning. He was somewhat cryptic in his correspondence, but I believe I understand the gist of it. You wish to discuss the events of one month ago."

"In truth," Emma said, "I would prefer to discuss anything else, but it is necessary that we do so. I have engaged Mr. Gardner's assistance in the matter. He will explain the whole of it to you."

Restell was prevented from beginning because of the ar-

rival of the refreshment. He observed Mr. Charters control-
ling the interview by taking his time in instructing his housekeeper to set the service and offer the lemonade and
sandwiches. The tactic was infinitely more interesting than it
was irritating, and Restell simply waited out his host.

"We will not keep you overlong," Restell said when they
were alone again.

Neven's response was directed at Emma. "Whatever you
need, Miss Hathaway, for as long as you need it."

Restell's lips twitched. He pressed the glass of lemonade
to his mouth to hide his reaction and sipped. "We would like
to hear what you can recall from the day Miss Hathaway was
abducted. Sir Arthur and Miss Vega have given us to understand that you volunteered to begin an investigation."

Neven turned slightly in his chair and took several long
moments to appraise Restell. "What exactly is the nature of
the assistance you are providing Sir Arthur and his family?"

"Miss Hathaway, not Sir Arthur Vega, is my client. She has
applied to me for protection for herself and her cousin."

Neven's dark brows drew together as he glanced at Emmalyn. "Is this true?" When she nodded, he asked, "Why did you
not come to me? And for Marisol also? She has said nothing."

Emma offered the explanation before Restell could speak.
When she finished, she saw that Neven was only marginally
mollified. She could appreciate that as her cousin's fiancé he
believed it was his responsibility to act on Marisol's behalf.
That he appeared to think he had some obligation where she
was concerned was unexpected. "Marisol only learned yesterday that she may have been the intended target of the
attack," Emma reminded him. "I should not have borrowed
her pelisse or her bonnet. There would be no suspicion otherwise." It was not entirely true, but she had managed to keep
her promise to Marisol thus far and hoped to continue.

"Why did you borrow them?" Neven asked. "That seems
unlike you."

"Convenience, I'm afraid. They were at hand."

"Marisol did not tell me this at the time."

"Are you certain?" Restell asked.

Ice edged Neven's tone. "I would remember."

Restell did not argue the point. It was probably true. "When you went to Madame Chabrier's, did you speak to the milliner?"

"The shop was closed when I arrived. It was already late in the day. I went back the following morning and spoke to one of the shop girls. She was less than helpful."

"You never spoke to Madame Chabrier?"

"I returned again on the pretext of making a purchase and observed the woman was a gossip of the worst sort. Sir Arthur was clear that he did not want to arouse the wags. I elected to look around and found nothing to support Marisol's claim that Miss Hathaway had gone to the milliner's."

"The shop girl did not remember her?"

Neven shook his head. "No. At least not the girl I spoke to. I recall that she was young and mayhap dull-witted, but she was earnest and wanted to please. There was no reason to doubt her account."

"The fact that she was earnest and wanted to please is the very reason one must be suspicious. Perhaps she was speaking the truth as she knew it, but it is also possible that she suspected you did not want confirmation of Miss Hathaway's presence, and so she answered you accordingly."

"Ridiculous. Why wouldn't I want to know if she had been there?"

"Because you knew she had gone to meet Mr. Kincaid."

Neven's attention swiveled to Emma. "This is true?"

Emma could not fathom what had prompted Restell to make his assertion. While it was certainly true that she had visited the shop to meet Mr. Kincaid, she didn't understand why Restell was so sure Neven knew it. It required a moment longer for her to realize that Marisol must have lied to her fiancé from the beginning. She sighed, more out of patience with herself than her cousin. Marisol, at least, had been acting predictably. Emma found her own gullibility troubling.

"Didn't Marisol explain all to you when she asked you to find me?"

"She did," Neven said. "Of course she did. Perhaps I should not admit it, but I found the whole of her story suspect."

Restell's position as Emma's protector dictated that he remain properly skeptical. It was not difficult. "What did she reveal to you?"

Neven set his glass of lemonade on the serving tray. He crossed his long legs as he leaned back in his chair. "I trust that you will not speak of what I am going to say to Miss Vega. I must have your word on that." He looked to both of his guests for their promise. When they nodded, he went on. "While my affection for Marisol knows no bounds, I find that she is given to prevarication when the truth would serve her as easily. I'm afraid I assumed a lie when she revealed that Miss Hathaway went to the milliner's to meet Kincaid."

"What did you imagine the truth to be?"

His eyes shifted momentarily to Emma, but he returned his attention to Restell when he answered. "I don't know that I gave it a great deal of thought."

"Truly?"

"Truly," Neven said flatly. "It seemed to me that the pressing matter was the task at hand. Regardless of the reasons Miss Hathaway had for leaving her home, the salient point was that she had not returned. When my visits to Madame Chabrier did not reveal anything of import, I prepared to make other inquiries. As it happened, Miss Hathaway revealed her whereabouts before I took that action."

"You saw her soon after her return?" Restell watched Neven and Emma exchange a glance that he did not immediately understand. As soon as he realized Emma was preparing to respond he hit upon the answer, interrupting her before she'd uttered a single word. "It was Mr. Charters who came for you, is that it?"

Emma nodded. "When I sent word to my uncle that I was safe, he asked Mr. Charters to do him the great favor of traveling to Walthamstow to attend me on the journey back to London. Sir Arthur also sent my maid."

"Marisol did not go?"

"No," Neven said. "She wanted to accompany me, but I refused her request. Rightly so, I believe. She would not have been comfortable at the pace I set."

"I assume Sir Arthur's health prevented him from making the journey."

Neven nodded, rubbing his chin. "The rheumatism. Traveling would have been difficult. He was anxious to have Miss Hathaway returned with all due speed. That necessitated that he remain behind."

"He holds you in great esteem," Restell said.

"I was honored to be asked to assist him and happy to oblige. Naturally, I wish the circumstances had been different."

"Yes," Restell said. "There is that."

Neven Charters made no reply. His jaw was so firmly set a muscle jumped in his cheek.

Restell politely excused himself as he stood. He went to the table just inside the doorway and retrieved the box he'd set there upon entering. "I wonder if you would be so good as to look at some drawings?"

Neven glanced at Emma. "Drawings? To what purpose?"

"They are sketches of Mr. Kincaid," Emma said. "You might be able to settle the question of which one is most like the man. Marisol and I were ever at odds choosing among them."

Restell removed the drawings of Kincaid from the box and carried them to Neven. "To my way of thinking, your ability to authenticate one of these will be your most important contribution in matters of art."

Neven held out his hand without comment. He looked at all four sketches briefly before he studied them in earnest. "This one," he said. "You must allow that I spent little enough time in Kincaid's company. He seemed wholly unexceptional, and I cannot recall that he ever entered into a discussion of the sort that interested me, but this one may have captured the look of him. It is the brow, I think, that sets it apart. You can see that it is high and wide, though perhaps not so pronounced as this drawing suggests. However, I recall thinking he had deeply set eyes. That would explain the attention to the forehead."

Restell accepted the drawings and returned to his seat. He turned over the corner of the one Neven had selected and saw that it was Marisol's second choice and Emma's third. "Thank you. That is helpful."

"I fail to comprehend the purpose for this. If you want an accurate sketch of Mr. Kincaid, shouldn't you apply to the man himself?"

Restell explained all the reasons it was not possible. "Is there anything you can tell us that would aid our search?"

Neven Charters shook his head slowly. His expression was no longer shuttered, but a revealing mix of surprise and concern. "I'm afraid there is nothing. I do not know if you can appreciate how I wish it were otherwise."

"I think I can," Restell said quietly.

Emma's clasp on her glass of lemonade tightened. She was not prepared for Restell to let it go so easily. "What about his friends? Are you aware of any?"

One of Neven's dark brows kicked up. "How is it you are not?" he asked. "Clearly, you had some affection for the man, else you would not have agreed to meet him. Can you have made the arrangement knowing so little about him that you cannot name a single intimate?"

Emma flushed deeply at the rebuke. Knowing it was well-deserved did not make it easier to receive. It was Marisol who needed to hear it, and Emma felt a passing urge to give her cousin up. She did not act on it, however, suspecting that Neven would not deliver the same admonition to his fiancée. In a moment of clarity, Emma understood that Neven's expectations of Marisol were significantly different than the expectations he had of her.

"I comprehend that you think it is out of character for me," Emma said, forcing herself to meet his critical study. "But I cannot be the only person who acts precipitously when she imagines herself in love."

"In love?" he asked. "That is what it was to you?"

Restell thought Emma looked as if she'd been thrown into the Thames with weights tied around her ankles. He did not think she'd come up again for air. His sigh was inaudible as he prepared to extend a figurative hand and pull her out of the drink. "Love regularly makes a fool of me," Restell said, bringing Neven's attention around.

"One imagines it is not that difficult," Neven said.

Restell's smile was good-natured. "Yes, well, I retain wit enough about me not to judge others when my own imperfections are so apparent."

Neven set his jaw again and his nostrils flared slightly. He did not attempt to speak for several long moments. When he did address Restell, it was in answer to Emma's earlier question. "I am unfamiliar with Mr. Kincaid's friends. If you like, I can ask the Newbolts. Kincaid was a guest in their home on several occasions."

"It will not be necessary," Restell said. "I have spoken to them and several others besides. They cannot agree on how they came to invite him."

Neven frowned. "How can that be?"

"Gentlemen like Kincaid have any number of ruses they use to insinuate themselves into a particular social circle. In my experience it is generally for purposes of developing a plan to rob their hosts. That does not appear to be the motive here, but then we do not yet entirely understand the motive."

"I thought there was a robbery." Neven slanted a look at Emma. "Did you not tell me your reticule was taken?"

"Yes, that's true. I did not have coin for the innkeeper."

Restell shook his head, not in negation of what Emma said, but to prevent a misunderstanding. "Any street thief would have cut the strings of her purse and run off. The idea is to be quick. Snick. Snack. Done. Unless the victim puts up a fight or gives chase there is often little harm. Emma's injuries were far too extensive to have been sustained in a single struggle. Her reticule was taken, but it was an afterthought, not the purpose."

Emma stared at Restell. She had never mentioned the loss of her reticule, yet he understood it so well that he might have witnessed the very thing she could not remember. "I wish I could be more helpful. I cannot recall when I was relieved of it."

"It is no matter," Restell said under his breath. The look he darted in Emma's direction cautioned her from speaking further. When she didn't, he wasn't certain if she was respecting his warning or if it was simply that she had no more to say. He suspected it was the latter. Emmalyn Hathaway was not the most tractable of females.

Restell rolled the sketches into a cylinder and lightly tapped his knee. "If you think of anything that might be helpful," he said to Neven, "I hope you will seek me out."

"I certainly will make Sir Arthur privy to my information."

Restell chose not to take issue with Neven's slight. He simply nodded as if his host's response was entirely satisfactory and prepared to take his leave. He was prevented from doing so when Emma unexpectedly seized his wrist. Her fingernails dug into his skin. Surprised, and not a little discomfited by her grip, Restell looked to her for an explanation. As soon as he saw her tight-lipped smile and the set of her jaw, he understood. Without realizing it, he had been beating a tattoo against his knee with the cylinder he'd made of the sketches. He was fortunate, he supposed, that he'd left his walking stick in the carriage. The half-moon impressions that her nails scored in his skin were quite enough consequence.

"Why don't you take the sketches?" Restell said. He felt Emma's grip ease immediately. He thought she showed admirable restraint when she did not snatch the drawings from his hand. The presence of Neven Charters was no doubt responsible in some measure for the care she took. The pains taken to produce the drawings accounted for the rest.

Emma smoothed the sketches across her lap. She was aware of Neven's consternation. The small drama that he'd witnessed could not have possibly made sense to him, but she had no intention of explaining it to him. "Mr. Gardner and I have imposed upon you long enough," she said. Both men stood in unison when she rose to her feet. "I hope you will come to dinner soon. We so enjoy your company at our table."

"I should like that."

"I will speak to Marisol. She has been remiss in not extending an invitation."

"I believe that was in deference to your own health."

Emma nodded. "I thought it might be the reason. Thank you for your help, Mr. Charters. I am most grateful for all you have done."

Neven inclined his head, accepting her thanks, then stepped aside so she could lead the way from the gallery. He escorted his guests to the entrance hall and stood looking out the window until the carriage began to move. Turning away, he addressed his butler. "I want a note delivered to Miss Vega," he said. "Allow me but a few minutes to compose it, then come to the library."

As soon as they were in the carriage, Restell placed the box on his lap and lifted the lid. He indicated that Emma should put the drawings inside. "I apologize for playing percussion upon my knee," he said. "I was completely unaware of doing so. Do you want to take the box?"

"I want to box your ears." Emma no longer found it odd that she was perfectly comfortable threatening him. "Did you see how Mr. Charters regarded me? He is yet another person who will be moved to question the state of my nerves."

"Hardly. You only took a small liberty. I imagine he thought your grip was more in the way of an affectionate squeeze."

"Affectionate? I'm sure he didn't place that significance upon it."

Restell shrugged. "You were smiling when you did it."

"I was gritting my teeth."

"It looked like a smile. In fact, I am emboldened to say that your hand on my wrist was remarkably similar to one of those small intimacies that I have observed between engaged and married couples." He chuckled when Emma's lips parted as if she meant to offer an objection, then simply pressed them closed as no argument occurred to her. "You comprehend, don't you, that Charters was disposed to see us in that light?"

Emma frowned. "Disposed to see us as a couple? Why would he think that?"

"Because we so obviously were enjoying each other's company when he came upon us."

"We were arguing over the points of a wager—which I won, by the way. We were not exchanging tender words."

"It hardly matters what words were exchanged," Restell said. "It is all in the manner in which it is done. Confess, Miss Hathaway, you find some modest pleasure in sparring with me."

"If I do, I am not likely to admit it, and it suggests a certain arrogance on your part to think that I would."

Restell laughed. "Have a care. You will turn my head with your pretty compliments."

What Emma did was turn her own to prevent him from seeing her smile.

"It's no good," Restell said. "I know you are amused."

"It is exasperation." Facing him again, she set her mouth primly. "You understand there is a difference, I collect."

"Have you ever considered that you might do well as a governess?"

She was aware that Restell's gaze had dropped to her mouth. For a moment her thoughts tangled and she couldn't think what she wanted to say. It made no sense that his cool blue eyes were responsible for the warmth she was feeling in her cheeks. "I suppose you mean to explain that remark."

"No. Not if you don't wish it."

Emma's fingers tightened around the box in her lap. It was all she could do not to raise it like a shield. It required a few moments, but gradually her wary expression became thoughtful. "I am come to the opinion that you are a skilled angler, Mr. Gardner."

"Not skilled enough, it seems. You will not take the bait, will you?"

"Not this time," she said. "But I doubt that will discourage you from trying again."

His grin flashed his parenthetical dimples. "No, indeed. I have never shied from a challenge." He reached across the distance that separated them and gently removed the box from her hands. "Before you crush it," he explained. He set it on the seat beside her. When he leaned back against the leather cushion, his manner was changed. His eyes were more remote in their regard, his expression grave. "What did you make of Mr. Charters's recounting of events?"

"I'm not certain what you mean. It seemed straightforward to me."

"Why didn't you mention that it was Charters that Sir Arthur sent to Walthamstow?"

"I suppose it didn't occur to me. Is it important?"

"That you omitted it? I have not decided. That your uncle asked Charters for a favor of such import? Yes, that's important. I did not understand until learning of it just how respected Charters is. It makes me think that Sir Arthur sets great store by his opinion in matters other than art."

"I trust that is so. Isn't it to be desired? Mr. Charters is going to be his son-in-law. The fact that there is mutual respect and admiration must all be to the good."

"Perhaps."

Restell's noncommittal reply disturbed Emma. "What provokes you to reserve judgment?"

"Cynicism. Experience. The knowledge that things are not always what they seem to be. An inclination to distrust gentlemen who are bent on impressing others."

"That is how you view Mr. Charters?"

"We were shown to his gallery, and that was by his design. If the purpose was not to impress us with his collection of paintings and antiquities and gauge our reaction to that horrible painting on the ceiling, then why not have us wait in a drawing room?"

"You make it sound as though he were watching us."

"It would not astonish, no. A gallery such as he has could easily accommodate a peephole. Several of them."

"You know you are being absurd." Emma said it with a shade more vigor than she truly felt. "You disliked him at the outset. What I could not determine was if he disliked you first."

"You noticed that, did you?"

"It would have been difficult to miss. You were both barely civil. I do not believe Wellington and Napoleon paid as much attention to their positioning on the field at Waterloo as the pair of you did in that room. It struck me as rather silly."

Restell offered up a sheepish, faintly crooked, smile. "That is unfortunate, then."

"Unfortunate?"

"Well, yes, as all that posturing . . . that is, the positioning, was in aid of securing your favor."

Emma's eyes widened a fraction. "Securing my favor," she whispered. "You do not mean that."

"Very well. I do not mean it."

"It suggests that Mr. Charters had a similar intent."

"I believe that's precisely what it suggests."

"It is Marisol he favors, else why would he propose marriage?"

"Why, indeed," Restell said. He saw Emma's features remained troubled as she considered what he was telling her. Still, it did not surprise him that she remained cautious in her interpretation.

"You are implying Mr. Charters desires my good opinion because he will be marrying my cousin."

"No, but you are welcome to think it if the alternative is so discomfiting."

"I am not discomfited by the truth." She was taken back by the sharpness of her protest. It was perhaps too forceful to be believed. "That is, I am not usually unsettled by it. You may say whatever you like, but please say it plainly."

"As you wish. Mr. Charters has feelings for you." Restell

saw almost at once that she was wholly resistant to the idea he was trying to put before her. He tried again, this time holding nothing in reserve. "Your cousin's fiancé may very well be in love with you."

Emma simply had nothing to say. She glanced away, caught herself, then met Restell's considering gaze directly. That he may be right was more than discomforting. It was disturbing in the extreme.

"Was there no part of you that suspected?" Restell asked gently. "Even a little?"

"Some things are not worthy of examination."

"But you are not saying that I must be mistaken."

"It would do no good."

"True, but is that really the reason you haven't objected?"

Emma stared down at her lap. "I don't suppose it is," she said softly. "It is the sense that you might be right." She glanced up at him. "What made you suspect?"

"In part it was his reaction to me, which you observed— but mostly it was his reaction to you, which you chose to deliberately ignore."

"It was not a conscious decision."

Restell wondered if that were true, but he didn't challenge her. "Perhaps not," he allowed. "But Charters gauged your every response. The lift of your chin. Your smile. When you were appreciating his rejoinders—and when you were not. He was always aware of your presence, not casually, but intensely. He watched you without seeming to, in the way a gentleman does when he cannot be openly admiring."

"I am sure you have mistaken the matter."

Restell shrugged. "I am almost moved to feel sympathy for Charters. It is a piece of good luck, then, that I am occupied licking my own wounds."

"Pray, in what manner are you wounded?"

"You tempt me to check myself again," he told her. "God's truth, but you draw blood with the scratches you inflict."

Emma's feathered eyebrows came together until only a

small, vertical crease separated them. "You are not speaking of your wrist, are you?"

"No. I am most definitely not."

She sat back suddenly, comprehension upon her. "Oh."

"Oh," he said, mocking her.

"You are saying that you also hold me in some affection."

"That seems to be the way of it. As I mentioned, it is some-what lowering that you did not suspect."

"But I did suspect," she said. "It simply did not occur to me to trust the feeling. You admitted to me almost at the beginning of our acquaintance that you are a romantic. If it is love that you imagine, it will be infinitely more practical if you allow the feeling to pass. That way neither of us is undone by it."

Restell considered her suggestion. "Allow the feeling to pass," he said, turning it over in his mind. "As if it did not set well in the stomach, like a bit of curdled milk or a bite of spoiled meat pie. Is that what you mean?"

"I had not thought of it in quite that way, but I suppose it might be similar."

"That is where your inexperience is revealed. There is nothing at all disagreeable about the feeling."

"Perhaps not, but it seems to me to be of an ephemeral nature, at least in the manner in which you are acquainted with it. Whatever it is that you imagine you feel, it is not an enduring condition of the heart."

Restell realized he was enjoying himself immensely. "You have done it again." He pointed to the back of his hand. "Just here. Another prick to my skin."

"You are making yourself ridiculous."

"No, see for yourself." He held out his hand to her. "There, below the bite."

"There is nothing there."

"Look closer."

Sighing, Emma took his hand in hers. It was in every way against her better judgment to support his foolish claim by looking for an injury, yet here she was, doing precisely as he

bid her. As she knew would be the case, there was no
evidence of a new wound.

She looked up, prepared to chide him, and discovered that
his head was now bent close to hers. Their foreheads almost
touched, and she'd missed his nose by the narrowest of mar-
gins. She was caught, not because he held her, but merely because she'd lost the will to look away. His eyes, so clear a blue
they seemed translucent, did not waver once from her gaze.
Their centers widened, darkened, and grew warmer all at
once. Watching them, her breath hitched, then she felt as if
she stopped breathing altogether.

He did not ask permission but gave her time all the same.
She'd understood his intent from the moment she lifted her
head. Honesty compelled her to admit she was relieved he
didn't speak. She didn't know how she would have answered
his question. This way there was no need. It would happen—
this kiss would happen—because she wanted it and would not
have to say so aloud.

"Breathe," he urged softly.

Her lips parted.

"Yes," he said, then his mouth was on hers.

She had not noticed him smiling but it seemed to her that
his smile was what he pressed against her lips. It was no
broad grin, to be sure, but a more subtle shape that was at
once encouraging and pleased. It was only for a moment that
she had the sense of it. When it was gone, what she knew was
that a peculiar heat was slipping under her skin and that his
mouth was its source.

If she had had to guess at the taste of his kiss—if she had
even thought it might have a taste—she would not have supposed it might be lemonade. This kiss hinted at the sweet-tart
tang of lemons and sugar and would be indelibly fixed in her
mind.

His lips lay lightly across hers, not terribly presumptuous,
but insistent nevertheless. The pressure was gentle, but there
was no mistaking that it was there. Of her own design she
inched forward. She was hardly aware that she still clasped

his hand or that her fingers were tightening around it, yet there was some part of her that understood she was grasping a lifeline. Nothing could have persuaded her to let go.

His mouth moved over hers, catching her upper lip, tasting the delicate underside with the tip of his tongue. The humid warmth of his breath did nothing to prevent her shiver. She felt the contraction, first as a ripple across her skin, then as something wholly unfamiliar deep inside her. She had always imagined that her heart would be the organ most affected by a kiss, but what she experienced now was the contraction of her womb.

At first she did not recognize the sound she made as coming from the back of her throat. Neither protest nor sur- render, this small whimper was all naked need. She did not mind overmuch that he'd heard it. What she regretted was that it gave him pause.

Restell gingerly removed his hand from hers as he raised his head. He sat back in his own seat in the same fluid motion. Emma's bonnet was slightly askew, and he was re- minded that she did not want to appear foolish. He touched a finger to his own head, made a tipping motion, and smiled a bit ruefully as she tugged on the ribbons to set it right.

"If you like," he said, "I'll make an apology."

Emma found she wanted to lift her hand to her mouth. She already missed the pressure of his lips on hers. It was too re- vealing of a gesture to make in front of him, but she suspected she would do it later when she was alone, perhaps when she was lying in bed. At the great age of two and twenty she would finally have the opportunity to savor her first kiss.

"If you apologize," she said, "I shall be hurt beyond measure."

"You understand, don't you, that you may demand satisfac- tion? There are females who would be moved to slap me."

"Truly? And it hasn't deterred you in the least. That is worth noting, Mr. Gardner. I'll slap you if you like, of course, but I'm accounted to be a credible shot and would prefer pistols at twenty paces. I will aim to wound. As you have noted, I am accomplished at it."

Restell laughed. "Why do I think for a moment that you will behave in the manner of every other woman of my acquaintance? I hope you will forgive me for my impoverished expectations. You are in every way a singular individual."

"Not so singular," she said, shaking her head. "If I had not permitted you to kiss me, well, *that* would have been singular. I doubt there has ever been a woman who refused you." She could not help but smile watching his brow crease as he tried to think of the exception to the rule. "Please, you must not strain your cognitive powers. An admission that I am right will suffice."

"You are right."

She tilted her head to one side as if giving full consideration to his response. "Yes, it suffices. It is unexpectedly disappointing, though, to realize that no member of my sex has been able to resist you."

"I have not approached them all," he said. "That should hearten you."

A bubble of laughter tickled Emma's lips. It was reminiscent of his tongue against the soft underside of her mouth. She felt a bit like she was all liquid of a sudden. "It is little wonder that you oppose your mother's wish for you to marry. There is yet so much for you to do."

He was tempted to kiss her saucy mouth again. The vulnerability he glimpsed in her eyes kept him from doing so. She was not quite as cavalier as she would have him believe. He respected her need to hold her own, more than that, he applauded it. "I hope you will explain my position to Lady Gardner. She appears unable to grasp it when I set the thing before her."

"I am making no promise," she said. "But I will consider it if I judge you are marching to the altar against your will."

"You are all kindness."

Emma smiled, returning to her more comfortable position in the corner of the carriage. She was remarkably at her ease, no longer as boneless as she'd felt moments before, no longer as deliberately distancing. "What is next, Mr. Gardner?"

"Next?"

"For us." Her eyes brightened with amusement when she observed his frown. "Do not be alarmed that I mean to march you to the altar myself. I am speaking of the reason I came to you. You have met my uncle, my cousin, and Mr. Charters. You have the drawing of Mr. Kincaid, and you have spoken to Madame Chabrier and her shop girls. You've watched over my family for almost a fortnight and put questions to any number of people who might have crossed paths with Mr. Kincaid. Therefore, I am wondering: what's next?"

"Walthamstow."

"You are going there? When?"

"On the morrow. I leave at first light. You look surprised, but my trip has been planned for some time. It is the reason I insisted upon visiting Charters today. I did not want to wait until I returned to speak to him."

"What do you imagine you will find there?"

"It is not so much what, but who. You were helped by an innkeeper and his wife in Walthamstow. I desire to talk to them. It is clear that Charters did not question them."

"Not in my hearing," Emma admitted. "He was very anxious to get me away from there."

"Understandable."

"It is what I wanted," she said.

"Also understandable."

She frowned. "I cannot help thinking you do not mean it."

"I mean it," he said. "It is all perfectly understandable. It is also indulgent. What either of you wanted is of little account when compared to what you needed. Admit it, Emma, you were in no physical condition to make so hasty a return to London."

She would not admit it. Childishly, her mouth snapped shut.

Restell merely smiled, his point made. "I will be gone a sennight, perhaps a few days longer. There is no cause for you to be concerned for your safety or that of Miss Vega's. All is arranged, and I have every confidence you will be well looked after."

"I am certain to be," she said, "as I will be with you."

"Pardon?" He honestly believed he could not have heard her correctly. The clatter of the carriage wheels effected a waver in her voice. "Did you say you would be with me?"

"Yes."

Restell thrust one hand through his hair. "Well," he said, much struck by her assertion. "That is wholly unexpected."

"For me, also."

"You cannot go, of course."

His answer was predictable, but Emma was not going to let it stand unchallenged. "Why?"

"I won't permit it." He raised a hand, interrupting her argument. "I am not Neven Charters, and I won't indulge you. It is reckless to entertain the notion of doing so. There is the matter of a chaperone, your comfort, the speed at which I plan to make the journey, your uncle's permission, your inevitable confrontation of places and memories that can only cause you pain, and finally there is the fact that it takes great effort of will for you to step outside your own home. How do you imagine you will make it so far as Walthamstow?"

"I cannot imagine it," she said. "That is why I am claiming the marker I won. I must make the journey, and you owe me a favor."

Chapter 7

"Come away from the balustrade, Emmalyn. You look as if you mean to throw yourself off the balcony. Consider what that would do to my health if you cannot appreciate what it would do to yours." Sir Arthur stepped back from his painting and regarded it critically. "Come here. I have need of your eye and your honesty. No, no. Leave the doors open. The air is fine today, and it gives me pleasure to pretend I am painting out of doors."

Emma stood at her uncle's side and studied the painting much as he was doing. She had the back of one hand under her chin as though to support it, while the other hand rested on her hip. "You have captured the color of the kite's tail quite brilliantly but not the sense of movement. It appears to just hang in the air as if there is no current to support it. Mayhap if you were to go to the park and watch the children at play . . ." She did not finish her sentence as he began making noises of protest. "Then observe how a fish swims. Think of the water as air current and the undulating of the fish as the kite's tail. If you like, I'm certain we can arrange for a few fish and tub of water to be brought here."

Sir Arthur considered this as he began to paint out the unsatisfactory kite. "Such suggestions are precisely why I have need of you."

Emma was relieved to hear it. "I truly was not considering

throwing myself off the balcony. I was watching the lads from the Wembley house trailing after the Fords' maid. They appear to be taken with her."

Sir Arthur nodded absently and continued to apply his brush to the canvas. "Are you coming with us to Lady Rivendale's this evening? It would give me comfort to know you are ready to rejoin society. I'd hoped that might be the way of it when you accompanied Mr. Gardner to the park, then to Mr. Charters's home. Do not misunderstand, I was relieved when you did not go with him to Walthamstow. I regretted giving my permission as soon as I'd done it."

Emma sat on the stool her uncle had recently vacated and rested an elbow on the table as she watched him work. It seemed prudent not to comment. The humiliation of her failed attempt to accompany Mr. Gardner still stung.

She'd argued her case to Restell with convincing logic. There had been a moment's triumph when he had agreed at last to take her. Then came the conditions. He demanded that she secure a traveling companion—someone other than her cousin—and obtain Sir Arthur's permission. He consented to slowing his journey to accommodate a carriage if she was able to acquire the use of one, but would make no other allowance for her comfort. Every arrangement would be her responsibility.

She'd accepted each term as he put it before her without the slightest hesitation. It was only when he came to the final condition that she wondered at her ability to see it through. He expected her to come to him.

The short journey from her home to his should have been the simplest part of what he demanded. She'd accomplished it before—with no companion—and with no idea what to expect when she arrived. Still, after winning her uncle's approval, securing her maid's assent, and making arrangements for the carriage, she woke up the following morning knowing she would be unable to leave the house. A dram of laudanum or a few fingers of whiskey might have proved efficacious in calming her nerves and urging her to rise from her bed, but

Restell had strictly forbidden that she use either of those sub-
stances or anything like them. He was most insistent that she
arrive without benefit of a clouded mind, in large part so his
own conscience would be clear.

Emma had had no choice but to send her maid around with
a note that she would not be joining him after all. There had
been no reply. Bettis could not report if he was disappointed
or relieved as she had only passed the note to his butler. It had
been six days since he'd left and there'd been no word that
anything had come of his trip. She did not expect to hear from
him, but that did not keep her from waiting for the post each
afternoon. The imminent arrival of letters was the reason she
had been leaning over the balustrade, though she did not
desire to share that with her uncle.

"I have not decided if I will go," she said. "I have never met
Lady Rivendale, nor do I imagine I will know any of her
guests."

"You will know Marisol and me. Mr. Charters will also be
there."

"Then you will be in very good hands."

"I already accepted on your behalf."

Emma did not attempt to hide her dismay. "I wish you had
not done that, Uncle. I never said I would go, only that I
would consider it."

"Yes, well, it's less an aggravation to our hostess if I must
make some excuse for your absence than to bring you along
without the favor of a reply. She can manage fewer guests at
the table more simply than accommodate additional ones. In
any event, you would not go if I had not already accepted for
you. You were hoping for just such a reason to stay behind."
He waggled his brush at her. "Tell me I am not right."

She sighed. "I cannot."

Sir Arthur nodded, satisfied. He used his brush to mix a
patch of white and marine blue on his palette and began to
paint again. "Mr. Charters thinks that Lady Rivendale could
be an important patron. He was quite pleased to receive his
invitation."

Jo Goodman

"Is he the reason we have been invited?"

"I imagine so. He speaks highly of my work and people seem to take notice of his opinion."

"They do, don't they? He has a great deal of knowledge at his fingertips."

"Years of study, I expect." Sir Arthur placed one hand at the small of his back and stretched. "Do you find it odd that he and Marisol are so well-suited?"

"I cannot explain it, but it appears to please both of them."

"So it does," Sir Arthur said.

Emma observed the grimace about his mouth and divined the cause. "Won't you sit, Uncle? You have been at the easel for the better part of the morning and afternoon. A rest would not be amiss." The fact that he didn't argue told Emma how much he ached. She accepted the brush and palette when he handed it to her and stepped aside to clear his path to the sofa.

Sir Arthur arranged a pillow behind him and placed his heels on the footstool. "Much better," he said. He rested his head against the curved back and closed his eyes. "Lady Rivendale is the godmother of the Viscount Sheridan. At least that is what Charters tells me."

Emma dabbed the paintbrush into the color Sir Arthur had already mixed. "It's the sort of thing he would know," she said. "Also from years of study."

Sir Arthur chuckled. "Quite right. I am also given to understand that Sheridan's sister is married to the Earl of Ferrin. I suppose that makes the pair well-known to Lady Rivendale."

Emma looked around the easel at her uncle. "The Earl of Ferrin? Did I hear correctly?"

"Hmm. You did."

If the stool had been directly at her back, Emma would have put herself upon it. She felt a bit unsteady on her feet, but perhaps, she thought, it was because there was so little room to stand as the world had become considerably smaller.

* * *

Marisol Vega, looking resplendent in pink and white silk, sidled close to her cousin and hissed in her ear. "Stop fidgeting, Emmalyn. It is grossly unbecoming." She smiled while she imparted the admonishment in spite of the fact that no one could see her mouth behind her ivory fan. She was, however, a believer that a smile was perfectly visible in the eyes, and both of hers were in plain view above the fan's delicately scalloped edge. "You do not want to call attention to yourself, yet it is precisely what you are doing." Having said her piece, Marisol slipped away and joined her fiancé beneath an elaborately framed seascape by the seventeenth-century English painter Anthony Eden.

Emmalyn stared after her. Marisol's intrusive entry into her thoughts had had the desired effect. Emma ceased to fidget.

Trying to be inconspicuous was more difficult than she supposed. Glancing about the large music salon in search of a conversational group that she might join, Emma dismissed following Marisol to Neven Charters's side. She could well imagine what he was saying about the Eden painting to those in his circle, and she had no desire to hear his opinion when she had yet to formulate her own. Her uncle had disappeared into the card room so she could expect no rescue there, and Lady Rivendale, their gracious and genial hostess, seemed to have gone in search of him. Emma was intrigued by that notion, but she hadn't the nerve to confirm her suspicions as it would have meant crossing the salon on the diagonal and attracting notice as she did so.

A man introduced to her as Porter Wellsley was in earnest conversation with Ian Gardner. Ian's twin, Imogene, and her husband, Edward Branson, were in an animated debate with two other couples that, judging by the few words that Emma could occasionally overhear, seemed to be of a political nature. Staying clear of that was much to be desired. There were several clutches where the latest *on dit* was being exchanged. Emma saw Wynetta Gardner Wellsley flit from one group to another with the lightness of a hummingbird, catching her husband's eye each time she did so. Lady Gardner hovered beside the harp at the opposite side of the salon. Each time she seemed determined to leave her post, Emma noticed she was set upon for advice, gossip, or opinion. This was all to Emma's liking, though she called herself a coward for it. How often had she told Restell that she desired to meet his mother? Now the moment was upon her—or would be eventually—and she quailed at the thought of it.

It was all because of his kiss, that infinitely compelling and vaguely wicked kiss. She had come to attach more importance to it than it deserved, and as often as she reproached herself for it, she was unable to make herself believe it was wrong.

Emma snapped her wrist so the fan she carried opened. Warm of a sudden, she waved it close to her face and bare throat, grateful that a fashionable woman's accessory was more practical than a man's. While gold and crystal tipped walking sticks were collected in the entrance hall with hats and gloves, almost all the female guests dangled silk or ivory fans from their wrists.

"It's a bit of a squeeze, isn't it?"

Emma gave a start. The voice was so unexpected that for a moment she was in danger of losing her balance. A hand at her elbow steadied her.

"Forgive me," Sir Geoffrey Gardner said. "I did not realize you were so unaware of my presence. I find it is always satisfactory to be alone with one's thoughts in a crowded room, though how it is possible remains a mystery to me." He smiled warmly, then inquired after her health.

"I am well, thank you," Emma said. "It was but a momentary start. I confess, I thought you were your son. Mr. Restell Gardner, I mean."

Restell's father chuckled, revealing twin dimples and a faintly crooked smile. "I knew who you meant. It is the voice, I expect. I am told that we sound a great deal alike."

"It is more than that," she said. "Indeed, he must look at you and glimpse a sense of his future countenance."

"Oh, I sincerely hope not. I am a good deal rounder these

last few years, a consequence of a whole and happy life, of course, and an earnest affection for sweets. Lady Gardner has determined recently that I must deny myself pastries." He sighed. "It is a sacrifice I will make, not for the sake of my figure, mind you, but for the sake of my marriage."

Emma smiled appreciatively. Sir Geoffrey's engaging manner drew her in now just as easily as it had at their first meeting. She'd been standing off to one side of a gathering on that occasion also. There had been an introduction soon after she arrived at Lord and Lady Greenaway's musicale, but when he approached her after the soprano had entertained them, she had had difficulty recalling his name. He had come to the entertainment without his wife, she remembered, and she'd been initially wary of his interest. Her guarded manner had been without cause, for Sir Geoffrey's warmth and curiosity had been genuine and appealing. He had spoken at length about his family—none of whom were in attendance—and shared the most delightful story of how they had conspired to abandon him so that he must needs attend the musicale alone. "They cannot abide sopranos," he'd told her. "I do not understand it myself, but I appreciate the effort they made to remain behind so that I might not be embarrassed by their complete boredom. They would yawn, you know, even my lovely wife."

Recalling that comment now, Emma stole a glance in Lady Gardner's direction. Sir Geoffrey had not exaggerated his wife's charms. The spirited exchange she was having with her intimates emphasized her energy and animation. She used her hands extensively when she spoke, making broad, expansive gestures. Although she was slimly built and did not rise much above her husband's chin, she was neither dainty nor fragile. She looked as if she wielded power as easily as she wielded her fan. It was little wonder that Restell considered her intention to see him married as a real threat to his freedom.

"I understand Lady Gardner is well-pleased with her painting," Emma said. "You could not have made her a better gift, I think."

"I spoil her," he said, unapologetic. "I cannot help myself. She spoke of the painting so often that I had to have it for her. I am given to understand that Restell admires it also."

"He has told me the same. He recently purchased the original sketches."

"Did he? I didn't know."

"It was only a week ago. I don't suppose he had occasion to tell you."

"No, we see little enough of him these days. He is always engaged in some intrigue, though the details are never forthcoming. I cannot fathom it, but he has no interest in politics, and it is filled with intrigues and schemes." He lifted his chin in the direction of his other son. "Ian will be the one to follow my course. Gambling hells—if you will pardon me for speaking plainly—hold no allure for him, while Restell finds them endlessly fascinating. He announces regularly that he aspires to be a rake though Lady Gardner will have none of it, I am happy to say."

"A rake?" Emma asked weakly.

"Hmm. He is amusing himself with us, you understand. One cannot precisely accept Restell at his word. It is Ferrin's influence."

"The earl?"

Sir Geoffrey nodded. "It is odd, but once Ferrin married Restell no longer found him as worthy of emulation."

"I confess, I wondered if Lord and Lady Ferrin would be here this evening."

"Heaven's no. They rarely come to town. Lady Rivendale visited them not long ago and could not persuade them to accompany her when she returned. Likewise, her godson and his wife. I remark on this because the absence of those she holds most dear leaves her at sixes and sevens. She and my dear wife have been exceptionally cozy these last weeks and experience tells me that a strategy is being planned. At first I thought Restell might be the recipient of their well-intentioned entanglements, but I've recalled that my wife was present at Lady Greenaway's while Sir Arthur was making her portrait, and now I've noticed your uncle has been Lady Rivendale's partner at whist for several hands. You will want to consider what I've said and determine whether he might be in need of rescuing."

"Is he playing for money?"

"Oh, no. No, my dear. I did not intend to give you that impression." He inclined his head and spoke in confidential tones. "I suspect Sir Arthur is playing for his life."

Emma blinked. This bit of intelligence was wholly unexpected. "His life?" she asked when she'd recovered her wits. "You do not mean that literally, I hope."

"Literally? Certainly not." He chuckled at the thought. "Lady Rivendale takes her cards seriously, but even she is not likely to murder her partner for bad play. No, I meant that it's likely your uncle is being fitted for a leg shackle. I felt compelled to bring it to your attention. Mayhap I have been wrong to do so, but I had the sense that he depends on you to protect his interests."

"In matters of business," she said. "Not marriage."

"Why, you are an innocent yourself, Miss Hathaway. Marriage *is* business." Sir Geoffrey's attention was caught by his wife who looked in need of rescuing herself. "Pardon me. It seems Lady Gardner is in want of my company." He made a slight bow and took his leave.

Emma stared after him, much struck by the extraordinary conversation. When the invitation to Lady Rivendale's dinner party arrived, Emma had no reason to suspect that it was anything but what it appeared to be: a desire by the countess to effect an introduction to Sir Arthur and perhaps secure his agreement to paint her portrait. This afternoon, when she'd learned that Lady Rivendale was connected to the Gardner family through marriage, it occurred to Emma that if she attended on Sir Arthur's arm, she would be placed squarely in front of the Gardners for their inspection. Once that moment of panic had passed, she was able to reason that her fear was nonsensical. It was unlikely that Restell had shared any part of the arrangement she had with him with his family. He had impressed her as a gentleman who meant to keep her confidences.

It was the kiss again that had addled her mind. The guilty pleasure of it made her want to confess all to someone. It was perhaps fortunate that she had no one immediately to turn to. Marisol was unsuited to the role of confessor, and Emma knew her uncle would not want to thank her for unburdening herself. She could hardly say anything to Neven Charters. It struck her that she led an insular life well before her abduction, and it was not a happy epiphany.

Emma closed her fan and skirted a large potted palm so she could slip along the perimeter of the salon without attracting attention. It helped that Wynetta Wellsley was encouraged by her friends to play the pianoforte. While strains of Haydn's *La Roxelane* were coaxed from the instrument, Emma eyed her destination. The entrance to the card room seemed as great a distance away as Walthamstow. There were moments when she did not think she could go so far, and it was frustrating in the extreme. What she told herself rationally had no impact on her fear. She arrived at the card room by sheer force of will and was nearly sick with the effort.

Standing just inside the doorway, Emma was forced to raise her fan to hide the fact that she was winded. She sipped air until her breathing calmed, then she wandered as casually as she could toward her uncle's table. Her purpose in coming to the room was quite different than she imagined Sir Geoffrey supposed. She did not truly believe her uncle required protection as much as he required encouragement. Still, Emma could not entirely abandon him. She decided that if Sir Arthur was being fitted for leg shackles, the very least she could do was make certain the marriage irons didn't chafe.

"I am no longer inclined to favor the name Arthur," Lady Rivendale was saying as Emma approached. "I had a dear friend by the same name, and as I am out of sorts with him, you will understand why the name gives me pause."

Fascinated by this rather novel conversational tack, Emma veered away from the table and chose a seat near the open

French doors. The evening was warm but not uncomfortably so, and the light breeze carried the fragrance of Lady Rivendale's spacious garden into the room. Emma pretended interest in the fountain that she could glimpse just beyond the portico. Tilting her head to one side, she listened to the exchange between Lady Rivendale and her uncle.

It was incidental that two other players shared the table with them. Except for occasionally gathering a trick or making a bid, the pair had nothing to contribute. Emma suspected they had already learned that their silence was much appreciated.

"My given name is Arturo," Sir Arthur said.

"Arturo." She tested it on her tongue. Lady Rivendale was still a handsome woman in her fifty-seventh year. A complete beauty in her youth, she had lines about her eyes and mouth that she liked to think reflected a life being lived to the fullest. She had known heartache but also great joy. She expected good fortune but was prepared on those occasions when it proved elusive. "Is it Italian?" she asked. "I have always liked the Italians."

"Spanish," he said. "You have kind regards for Spaniards, I hope, even those of us who trace our origins on these shores to the Armada."

"We were all from somewhere else first," she said. "The Gardners are of Viking descent. I, myself, am Norman. Barbarians and invaders, the lot of us, though I find it oddly comforting to know we are come from such fierce stock." She snapped trump on the trick on the table and drew it to her side. "Do you often have opportunity for cards?" she asked as she made her next play.

"Occasionally at the club."

"You are a credible partner."

He smiled. "You are carrying me with your exceptional play. I know I have made errors."

Emma quickly raised her fan to hide her own smile. She had been mistaken to suppose her uncle would require encouragement. While he always conversed easily with others, she had not known him to engage so comfortably in conversations of no particular importance. Except with Marisol, she amended, coming to her feet. Marisol could draw her father into a lengthy discussion about hair ribbons, he was that indulgent. On the heels of that thought, Emma was reminded that Marisol was reputed to be very much like her mother in that regard, and she could not help but think her uncle's light flirtation with Lady Rivendale boded well for the future.

Emma went to stand in the open doorway leading to the garden. With her back to the card room she could no longer catch snippets of conversation, but she was pleased to hear Lady Rivendale's robust laughter rise above all other voices in response to something Sir Arthur said.

She looked longingly at the garden. Although the hour was late, it was not yet dark. Summer's long days were upon them, and the torches that marked the perimeter of the portico would not be lighted until dinner had been served. As hungry as Emma was, she still dreaded the meal. She had it from Marisol that she was seated at the table between Sir Geoffrey and Porter Wellsley, a placement that would not have caused distress if it were not for the fact that Lady Gardner would be across the table from her. She would be saved from conversing directly with her ladyship, but she fully anticipated that she would be observed. It was in Lady Gardner's nature to take account of everything . . . and everyone.

Emma raised her cashmere shawl so that it covered her bare shoulders. The bodice of her pale yellow bombazine gown was rather more low cut than was her usual fashion, but Marisol insisted that it should not be worn with a betsy. Deferring to her cousin in matters of style was something Emma did as a matter of course. Upon arriving at Lady Rivendale's and observing the manner in which other young women were dressed, Emma was grateful for Marisol's unsolicited advice. She would have appeared more matronly than the matrons if she had slipped a modest betsy under the mint green rosettes that trimmed her bodice.

"You look as if you cannot decide whether to stay or go."

Emma lost her grip on the tails of her shawl as her suddenly nerveless fingers tangled. She had not seen or heard Neven Charters's approach. "I did not realize you left the music room," she said. "Have you made your final judgment on the Eden painting, then?"

"I have." His eyes shifted momentarily to Lady Rivendale's table. "Why don't we step outside? You seemed to have been contemplating doing just that when I came upon you."

Emma tilted her head so that she could look past his shoulder. "Where is Marisol?"

"I couldn't say. She found my conversation tiresome, I expect, and went in search of some pleasant gossip." He cupped Emma's elbow and gently urged her to turn in the direction of the garden. "Shall we?"

Short of making a scene, Emma did not think she could easily remove herself from Neven's side. Accepting his escort would have been uncomfortable in any circumstance, but Restell's comments gave her another reason to pause. Still, she *had* been wondering how she might step outside and enjoy the garden, so perhaps the more considered approach was to take advantage of his escort. Surely she could do that without encouraging him.

"I should like that," she said. "It is a pleasant evening." Emma was aware of her faltering first steps, but if Neven felt them he was too polite to comment. "Have you had opportunity to view Lady Rivendale's collection?"

"She invited me to go where I desired. The Eden painting aside, many of the best works are in the music room."

"I promised myself I would form my own opinion about the Eden work before I heard you pronounce judgment, but you have intrigued me. What did you find objectionable about the painting?"

Neven Charters came to a halt as they reached the marble balustrade. "You will understand why I thought it best to remove ourselves from the card room when I tell you that the Eden is a most excellent fake."

Emma's features betrayed her disbelief. "You are quite certain?"

"I have not gone so far as to remove it from the wall, you understand."

"Oh, no. Of course not. It's just that—"

"I am teasing," he said gently. "I am certain because I purchased the original from the Battenburn estate. I suppose you did not see it in my gallery as your attention was caught by the ceiling. Set yourself at ease, Miss Hathaway, I am of no mind to apprise Lady Rivendale of the truth. She did not ask for an appraisal so I am not honor bound to give her one. You convinced me with your impassioned speech that it is not the authenticity of a painting that gives the masses pleasure. Collectors care, naturally, but we are not great in our numbers."

"Only in their influence," Emma said with a certain wryness in her tone.

"I did not mean to suggest—" He stopped. "Ah, you are teasing me, I think."

"I am."

"Shall we walk to the fountain? It is just the sort of garish garden monument that I find so fascinating. Cherubim should not be made to spout water from their mouths. That is best left to fish."

"Mermaids?" she asked, allowing herself to be led down the steps.

"Well, there you have me."

Emma's soft chuckle was lost in the crunch of gravel underfoot. She was glad for their companionable silence as they walked to the fountain. Neither of them exchanged a word as they circled it slowly. The chubby marble cherubs were a heavenly symphony of sorts, each one of them playing an instrument. There were two with flutes, a trio of violinists, one with a drum, and another pair with cymbals in their hands.

When they'd made a second complete turn, Neven asked in mildly appalled accents, "What do you suppose they're playing?"

"Handel's *Water Music,* I should think."

Neven's laughter was cut off so abruptly that Emma turned her head to look at him. She felt him sag against her before she had any sense of what was happening. The dead weight of his body shoved her hard against the fountain. Stumbling, she threw out a hand to keep from tipping over and opened her mouth to call for help. Her effort came to nothing. Her fingers could not find purchase against the wet marble, and her cry could not be heard as her head was pushed under the water in the fountain's basin. Neven's body lay heavily on top of her, pinning her in place. She got her hands under her and pushed hard against the basin, trying to raise her face and shoulders above the waterline and dislodge Neven. She came up only a few inches before the effort failed and her arms collapsed. Lungs burning, she tried again. The desire to draw a breath made her light-headed, and darkness clouded her vision. She wanted air, *demanded* it, and when she finally surrendered to that most basic need, her nose and mouth filled with water.

Her last thought was not of her life as it had been thus far, or even of loved ones. As consciousness faded, her last thought was both prosaic and absurd. Emmalyn Hathaway realized that she was going to die in a most ignominious fashion: face down and bottom up in a marble fountain with her cousin's fiancé lying sprawled on top of her while fat cherubs played their instruments and spouted nonsense.

"I grabbed Charters by the scruff of the neck," Sergeant Hobbes said, making a fist of his hand to demonstrate the action, "and yanked him out like a sack of sand. He was about as heavy as one, too. Collapsed on the ground, he did, though I paid him no mind as all my attention was for Miss Hathaway. I was more gentle with the lady, you understand. I pulled her from the fountain more like she was a half-drowned kitten—which she was. Someone from the dinner party saw us and gave a cry, so there was no hope for it but that we should attract attention."

Restell still had mud on his boots, dust on his riding breeches, and a riding crop in his hand. He sat mostly sprawled in a wing chair in his bedchamber while his bath was being drawn. Servants marched in and out of the dressing room pretending not to listen to Hobbes's account of the Rivendale party but hanging on every word all the same.

For Restell's part he could not have suffered the tale if he had not already learned the ending. Hobbes wisely began his report by announcing that no one was dead. It begged for any number of questions, but Restell allowed Hobbes to tell the story in his own fashion. The questions could wait until the end.

"Go on, man," Restell said. He tapped the quirt against the toe of his boot as Hobbes turned to set out towels. "Cease with your fussing."

Hobbes paid no attention to the characterization that he was fussing and placed the towels neatly on a warming pan. "Well, I wasn't certain what to do with Miss Hathaway once I had her. Her head hung backward over my arm, and I couldn't tell if she was breathing. That's when I remembered Mary Stubbs."

"Gin-soaked Mary Stubbs," Restell said. "It's good you have the experience of regularly saving that woman's life, Hobbes, else you would have little to recommend you as a gentleman of great sensitivity."

"It breaks my heart to know you're right, sir." The valet shooed the last of the malingering housemaids out of the room and closed the door. "There was nothing for it but that I place Miss Hathaway on the ground and turn her on her side. I delivered half a dozen brisk slaps between her shoulder blades."

"What made you think to do that?" asked Restell.

"Burping babies, I expect." In response to Restell's raised eyebrows, he explained, "I did a little of that moving among the camp followers. There were always babies about, and it was a pleasure to hold them. That doesn't reflect favorably on my sensitivity because mostly I held them after I had carnal knowledge of their mothers or killed some Frenchies."

"It is good you clarified it. I was prepared to revise my opinion."

Hobbes nodded. "It looked as if you were." He picked up Restell's mud-flecked Carrick coat and began brushing the capes. "Miss Hathaway coughed up water, choked and gagged a bit, though I recall thinking she did it altogether like a lady."

"She will be glad to hear it," Restell said wryly. "Proceed."

"After she drew a full breath I helped her sit up. Guests were crowding around by then and a few of them were assisting Mr. Charters. I heard someone remark he had a lump at the back of his head the size of a hen's egg. Seems there was a bit of blood also."

"He was attacked?" Restell sat up, alarmed. "I thought you said he merely collapsed."

"I said that's what I supposed happened. I'm far and away into explaining that I was wrong to assume it. Charters and Miss Hathaway were on the far side of the fountain from where I was standing. I didn't see anyone approach them, but I don't think I could have, not from my vantage point. It seemed little longer than a blink of an eye that I had no view of them. They'd made two tours of the fountain, and I thought they meant to make another. When they didn't appear immediately I imagined they stopped to inspect it more closely. It's the kind of piece that lends itself to study. Fat, naked babies with drums and fiddles. I've never seen the—"

Restell slapped his quirt with considerable force against the side of his boot. It had the desired effect: Hobbes picked up the important thread of his story.

"It was the disruption of the water flow that caught my ear. The pitch of all those spitting cherubs changed. I hobbled closer and saw splashing. By the time I rounded the fountain the villain was gone, not that I could have given chase, not with Miss Hathaway drowning under Mr. Charters's weight."

"What evening did you say this occurred?" Restell pushed

himself to the edge of his chair and made to rise. "And where is Miss Hathaway now?"

Hobbes positioned himself squarely in front of Restell to prevent a precipitous exit. "Three nights ago," he said. "Thursday evening. Lady Rivendale is a managing woman— if I may be so bold to offer that observation—and she took charge in the aftermath. There was nothing I could do to prevent it. It is perhaps fortunate that liveried servants look so much alike to their masters and mistresses because your parents took no notice of me, and they were early to the scene."

Restell closed his eyes and rubbed them with his thumb and forefinger. "Bloody hell, Hobbes, but this is a mess."

"I know, sir, and I'm sorry for it. I'm prepared to take my leave at once if you like. I don't expect a character."

"Take your leave? Don't speak nonsense. I haven't the patience for it. Again, where is Miss Hathaway?"

"Didn't I say? No, I suppose I didn't. She's still at her ladyship's."

"My mother's?"

"No. Lady Rivendale's."

Restell realized he was more weary than he had been wont to admit. He could barely follow where Hobbes led him. "I imagine the countess felt some obligation as the attack happened in her home." He frowned, struck by an unhappy thought. "Charters? Did she allow him to stay there as well?"

"No. I understand that she offered, but he insisted on seeking the treatment of his own physician and would not hear of troubling hers. As he had but the lump on his head and Miss Hathaway was the one in acute need of the physician's care, he had his way. Miss Vega accompanied him home and Sir Arthur stayed with Miss Hathaway." Hobbes motioned to Restell to lift his left foot and bent to remove the boot. "These details such as I am able to report came to me by others. I was not privy to the conversations, but Lady Rivendale's personal maid was forthcoming."

Restell leaned back in his chair as Hobbes attended him. He closed his eyes and almost groaned with relief as the left boot was removed. "I hope you are not so forthcoming when I am the subject of inquiry."

"I expect I shall be perfectly mute, but as no one has ever put an inquiry to me, it is all supposition."

"Just as well," Restell said. "How does Miss Hathaway fare?"

"Very well, I believe. Jamie McCleod watches the house during the day and nothing untoward has occurred. Lewis and Shaw continue to observe the activities of Miss Vega and her father."

"Ferrin will not approve of the use I've made of his footmen, but those three are infinitely better suited to intrigue than service."

"Perhaps that is because you hired them."

Restell roused himself enough to open one eye and give Hobbes benefit of his wry glance. "True, but my brother is paying their wages."

"An excellent arrangement," Hobbes said.

"I have always thought so."

Chuckling, Hobbes released Restell's right foot and let it fall to the floor. He noticed that not a drop of brandy was lost, that in fact, Restell barely stirred. "Do you wish to postpone your bath?"

He did, but the thought of falling asleep with the stink of the road upon him was equally unappealing. "No." He finished his brandy and held out the snifter for Hobbes to take. "God's truth, but I can still feel the horse under me."

Hobbes stood back as Restell got to his feet. "Did you come straightaway from Walthamstow?"

Restell nodded. "I thought I would stay one night at an inn, but . . ." He didn't finish. How to explain the sense of urgency he'd felt to return to London when he didn't understand it himself? "The weather held," he said after a moment. "It seemed a piece of good luck so I rode on."

Hobbes did not comment. He opened the door to the dressing room and waited for Restell to follow, then he assisted Restell with the removal of his frock coat, waistcoat, and linen. While Restell stripped off the remainder of his clothes, Hobbes retrieved the warm towels. By the time he returned to the dressing room, Restell was up to his neck in water and looked as if he intended to sleep in his bath. "More hot water?"

"A little." Restell didn't move while Hobbes tipped the kettle and a stream of hot water was added to the copper tub. "Who was the doctor that attended Miss Hathaway? Bettany?"

"Harris, his name was."

Restell supposed it was too much to have hoped that Lady Rivendale and Sir Arthur shared the same physician. "What do you make of the incident that landed Miss Hathaway in the drink?"

"It's a puzzler. I watched her the whole of the evening and didn't think she would ever leave the music salon. That was all to the better, I thought. She was safe enough there. Now, Miss Vega, by way of contrast, flitted about like the veriest butterfly. That young lady doesn't know a stranger."

"What prompted Miss Hathaway to go outside?"

"I couldn't say," Hobbes said, "not being privy to her mind, but she went to the card room after your father spoke to her, then Charters approached her and it was no time at all before she was outside."

"Did he force her?"

"No. Leastwise not as I could tell. It seemed to me that she was happy for his company."

Restell grunted softly.

"I do not know how their assailant moved so quickly," Hobbes said. "I know this old peg slows me a bit, but I can still give a good chase. This villain was like a wraith. Come and gone on the back of the wind. It was not yet dark so it seemed to me that I should have seen *something*."

"I believe you said the fountain blocked your view."

"Yes. But it strikes me as a good piece of luck for the attacker to have made his approach so squarely behind the fountain. It made me wonder if he knew I was observing."

Restell had wondered the same thing. "What was Charters's account of the events?"

"You will want to inquire of him. I was only able to learn that he was struck down."

"The weapon? Was it found?"

"A crystal-knobbed walking stick. A gentleman claimed it as his own but denied that he'd used it in such a fashion. There were witnesses that he was in the music salon when the attack occurred. His name is Gibson. I had no opportunity to examine the stick."

Restell began lathering his arms and chest. "Did guests speculate about the attack?"

"I heard none of those conversations."

"What do you believe, Hobbes? Was Charters attacked because he stood in the way of getting to Miss Hathaway, or did Miss Hathaway come to injury because she happened to be standing beside Charters?"

Hobbes was long in answering. Finally, he shook his head and shrugged a bit helplessly. "I don't know."

Restell nodded. It was an honest answer, but nothing about it settled well with him.

Emma sat on the piano bench with her back to the keys and studied the painting on the far wall. It was the seascape by Sir Anthony Eden that held her attention. The fine brushstrokes, the liberal use of blue-green pigments, the careful observance of the manner in which light glanced off the waves, all of it was the hallmark of Eden. Emma knew it was not at all unusual for someone studying art to try their hand at imitating those artists whose work was admired. Learning the nuances of color and light and brushwork required instruction and application, and application meant practicing the techniques used by others. Often, the most effective way to do this was by copying a painting.

Emma had observed the students her uncle mentored imitating his style as they began to experiment and develop their own. She wondered if that's what she was seeing here. If it was indeed the work of a student, it was well-done and most likely sanctioned by the artist. Sir Arthur did not permit his students to remove the works they copied from his studio. He required them to paint over the work. As a consequence, a single canvas might have two or even three complete paintings beneath the one visible to the eye.

"Miss Hathaway?"

Lost in thought, Emma was slow to recognize that she was being summoned. She swiveled on the bench and saw Lady Rivendale's housekeeper standing in the doorway. "Yes, Mrs. Posey?"

"You have a visitor, Miss Hathaway. Mr. Gardner wishes to speak to you. Will you receive him?"

Emma's fingers curled around the edge of the bench. She did it so that she might keep her seat. "Has Lady Rivendale been informed?"

"She is gone from home."

Emma could not imagine that Lady Rivendale would object to a visitor, but she did not want to overstep. "Please tell Mr. Gardner he should return when Lady Rivendale is here."

"If you like," Restell said from behind the housekeeper. "But I'll see you now as well. Please, step aside, Posey."

The housekeeper looked in such a misery of indecision that Emma took pity on her. "It's all right, Mrs. Posey. I will see Mr. Gardner now."

Restell slipped past the housekeeper before she had completely given way and closed the pocket doors firmly behind him. He made a quick appraisal of Emma first, and upon assurance that she was all of a piece, his eyes followed the same head-to-toe path again, this time as a study.

Emma suffered the inspection, her mouth flattened in a disapproving line to emphasize that she had no patience for his scrutiny.

Restell was having none of it. "I might do the same, you know. Your mouth is all priggish displeasure and your eyes are . . . well, let us say they are betraying a like interest in my person."

If anything, her expression became more severe. "Can you not see that I am mocking you?"

"You are?" His head tilted to one side as he entertained the possibility. "No, I don't think that's so. You were regarding me with the same careful attention you give to the examination of a painting. I am choosing to be flattered."

Emma threw up her hands. "It is not possible to offend you."

"I had not considered it, but you may well be right."

Not wanting to be at a disadvantage as Restell approached, Emma shot to her feet. She was unhappily aware that his slow, deliberate advance pulled every one of her nerves taut. Had she ever been so anxious in his presence? Emma did not think so, not like this, not when anticipation was part of what she felt. This was not the dread she experienced when stepping past the threshold of her own home, but that hopeful, pins-and-needles state she knew when she was in expectation of something good coming her way.

Of something very good.

The moment he inclined his head, Emma rose on tiptoes. Her arms went around his neck with enough force to bring her body flush to his. His hands at the small of her back held her there. She lifted her face and the distance that separated their mouths ceased to exist. When he whispered her name, it was as if she could taste the sound of it on her lips.

She was delighted to learn her name tasted like warm brandy.

Restell edged Emma backward against the pianoforte, and her hip brushed the keys. Neither of them noticed the oddly discordant accompaniment to their kiss, nor would they have done anything differently if they had.

This kiss would suffer no trivial interruption.

There was little that was gentle in the press of their mouths. Need did not make much allowance for tenderness. There was heat here, and passion. Nothing about the movement of his lips across hers was hurried. He drank slowly, tempered by the knowledge that he had been thirsting for just this end for a very long time and desiring that the end should not come too quickly. Emma's desire matched his own.

Her fingertips brushed the damp, curling ends of his hair

just above his collar. The color and texture of it was so light she might have been threading sunshine. She felt him shiver, then knew a like response in herself and realized it was not a shiver at all, but a nerve plucked so sharply that the pleasure of it veered perilously close to pain. She needed him for support, for heat, for air, and as a balm for her wounded heart. Her breasts swelled, and they ached with an unfamiliar heaviness. She welcomed the cup of his hands there and the pass his thumbs made across her turgid, sensitive nipples. It never occurred to Emma to deny herself the relief his hands offered. If it was a liberty that he took, then she wished he might always make himself so free.

His tongue swept across the ridge of her teeth. She opened her mouth wider and her own tongue tangled with his. The intimacy of it made her want to weep. She held nothing back, not the tremor that he roused in her, not the harsh breath that she drew when he lifted his head.

"Emma?" He held her face in his palms, and his thumbs supported her chin. The slightest pressure raised her face. "Look at me."

She opened her eyes and found herself staring into his. He was still so close that she imagined it was her reflection she saw in the wide, dark mirrors that his eyes had become. "You will not tell me you are sorry," she whispered.

He shook his head. "No. I couldn't."

"I am not sorry, either."

Restell's faintly wry smile revealed a single dimple. Emma sounded a bit defiant. "Do you mean to convince yourself that's true?"

"It *is* true."

"Very well." His voice was gentle. "Until the kiss, your greeting was not at all warm."

"I thought you said I was studying you as closely as I would a painting."

"Yes, but not one you particularly liked."

"And yet you chose to be flattered. I think you enjoy being perverse."

"I'm sure you are right."

Emma could only shake her head. For reasons she could not comprehend, her response seemed to invite his kiss. The surprise of it was a large part of its charm since it was neither as thorough nor as heated as the last time he'd put his lips to hers. She was left with sense enough to ask, "What was that in aid of?"

Restell was not given opportunity to reply. Lady Rivendale chose that moment to make her presence known. Her raised eyebrow and artful smile was proof to even the meanest intelligence that she had observed the better part of the exchange.

"La! but I hope it was in aid of a proposal. Of marriage, I mean. That is the only sort of romantic entanglement I can support in my own home. You understand, don't you? It is not that I am against an offer of protection, but it must not be made here."

Restell turned slightly to face the countess. "I mean to propose both to Miss Hathaway," he said. "Marriage and protection."

Chapter 8

Lady Rivendale did not remain in the salon long. After assuring herself of Restell's honorable intentions and hinting that she rather admired his unconventional approach, she ordered refreshment brought to the room and excused herself in light of other pressing matters requiring her attention.

"No doubt she wants to write a note to my mother," Restell said once she quit the salon. "And send it by messenger at once." He turned back to Emma and saw that his wry amusement was not shared. "Come, are you so out of sorts with me that you cannot raise a smile? Lady Rivendale means no harm. She is an enthusiastic meddler and enjoys supposing she holds considerable sway over affairs that are almost entirely beyond her control. She likely believes she is responsible for just this end, though how that is remotely possible is incomprehensible to me."

Emma gave him the sharp edge of her tongue. "Perhaps she thinks the fact that I almost drowned in her fountain is what brought you up to snuff."

"My, but you are put out with me."

"With you and your proposal." Emma desired to give him her back, but she was already pressed against the pianoforte. There was no easy escape unless he allowed it. "Pray, what do you imagine my answer is?"

"As I haven't yet put the question to you, I hope you have

not set your mind on a reply. I stated my intentions to Lady Rivendale, but I have not acted upon them."

"Are you going to?"

"I imagine that depends on whether you mean to sheathe your claws or tear another strip off me."

At her sides, Emma's fingers curled into her palms so the nails made half-moon impressions in her skin. She drew a deep breath and released it slowly. Both were only marginally helpful in calming her. "It would be better, I think, if you were to remove yourself to that chair across the way. I cannot leap so far as that."

Restell appreciated the warning. He was not at all certain he should turn his back on her while he made his way to the chair, but he chose to do so because if she spied his grin he *would* claw at him. By the time he was seated, Emma was once again on the piano bench. Her hands lay in her lap, though neither of them was open. She kept them curled in fists, rhythmically squeezing them so the knuckles turned pink and white by turns.

Before Restell could put any question to her, Emma asked, "When did you return to London?"

"This morning."

"This morning? But it is not yet eleven. Did you ride all night?"

"I did."

It was not a trick of the light, she saw, that placed pale shadows beneath his eyes, but the unenviable stamp of weariness. "I did not realize," she said quietly. "I should have seen it at once."

"You were not meant to see it at all. It is unimportant."

"I don't think so." It was his eyes that she'd noticed when he came upon her. His eyes studying her. She'd been so caught by the intensity of his gaze, the heat of it, that she failed to notice what lay beneath. "Why?" she asked. "You might have stopped along the way."

Shrugging, Restell offered a partial truth. "I already had

spent more time in Walthamstow than was my wont. Perhaps you can appreciate my desire to return."

"How did you find me here?"

"Hobbes told me."

"Did he tell you that he saved my life?"

"That is not quite how he regards it. He thinks his inattention is the reason you almost drowned."

Emma shook her head most vehemently. "That isn't so. No blame can be attached to him."

"I didn't say I blamed him. Only that he blamed himself."

"What happened to me was an accident. Didn't he explain that it was Mr. Charters who was attacked?"

"He explained that Charters was hit in the head. Did you see the attacker?"

"No. And I didn't hear him, either. I was looking at the fountain. It all happened very quickly. One moment Mr. Charters was laughing, then he was falling. I tried to assist him, but he was too heavy for me. There was no opportunity for me to move out of the way. When he fell on top of me, I couldn't lift him. It was Sergeant Hobbes who managed it, else I would have drowned."

"Emma, has it occurred to you that you might have been the intended victim?"

"Of course it occurred to me, but I dismissed it. Mr. Charters was struck, not I."

"You should consider that was the accident," Restell said. "The assailant aimed badly, or more likely, struck Charters first to remove the threat he presented. When he fell against you, and you could not remove yourself, the attacker was able to flee without striking a second blow. He believed you would drown."

"No." Emma's response was immediate and firm. "No, it couldn't be thus."

"Why do you persist in believing that you are not the one threatened?"

Agitated, Emma's fingers splayed across her lap. Her

palms were damp. "Can you not understand what a terrible thing it is to contemplate?"

"You are the common thread in both attacks. Is it less terrible to believe that your cousin or Mr. Charters is the intended target?"

"No. No, of course not. There is nothing about this that settles easily on my mind. Who could hate any one of us so much that he would be moved to murder?"

"I doubt that hate is the motive."

"No? Then what? Not money. If you are right and I was left to drown, then the point of the attack was that I should die, not be taken and held for ransom."

"That is not entirely clear, not when Hobbes was on the scene so quickly. There is the possibility that his presence chased your would-be abductor away."

"It is all speculation."

Restell gauged she had heard as much as she could and did not press further. "It cannot be anything else without facts."

Emma smoothed her muslin gown across her lap. It served to dry her damp palms. "You have not told me what you found in Walthamstow."

"That will have to be left to a later time. I have sketches for you to consider. It was what required that I spend so much time there. I hired a local man with a modest talent for drawing and watercolor to make a number of drawings for me."

"Of what?"

"Of what I saw," he said, watching her closely. "Of what I hope you will remember."

"I'd like to see them."

"I didn't bring them. I believe they will be best viewed away from here. I would prefer that we review them where there is no chance for interruption."

Emma understood very well what he was not saying. If there was something in them that would upset her, he was granting her the opportunity to experience it away from her family. "I told Lady Rivendale last night that I mean to leave today. She has been very kind, but there is no reason for me to stay any longer. There are no lasting ill effects. I did not breathe in so much as a thimbleful of water, though I admit it seemed like a great deal more. My uncle is sending a carriage for me this afternoon."

"No, he's not."

Emma's eyebrows lifted. There was no point in asking the question when she knew the answer. "You've spoken with him already."

Restell nodded. "I thought I should."

It was the manner in which he said it, vaguely apologetic, perhaps even a bit uncertain, that made Emma think they were no longer talking about precisely the same thing. "I meant that you told him not to send the carriage for me."

"Yes, I know what you meant."

She was certain now that he was being deliberately ambiguous. "What else did you discuss with my uncle?"

"His health. My trip. The painting he is working on. He told me that prior to the moment you and Mr. Charters were attacked, he had been enjoying Lady Rivendale's companionship at cards. I thought I detected your fine hand in that piece of work. Was I right?"

Emma dismissed all of what he'd said with a wave of her hand and asked the question that was foremost in her mind. "Did you tell him you intended to make me an offer of marriage?"

Restell sighed. "So we are returned to that. It seemed that you did not want to discuss it earlier."

"Please, Mr. Gardner, if you will be so kind as to answer my question."

"Then, yes, I told Sir Arthur that I wished to marry you."

"Without a hint to me that you meant to do so?"

"Would you have been receptive to a hint? Frankly, I did not think so. It seemed you liked the kissing well enough but not necessarily what might come of it."

"Your ability to put me out of patience is unnatural. What do suppose would come of a marriage between us?"

"Children, I suspect." He glanced at her lap and saw her

hands were bunched into fists again. It seemed prudent to elaborate. "We would have mutual respect and admiration, tolerance of each other's foibles and vanities, and a partner for the waltz and whist. We would share a home, the newspaper, a box at the theatre, perhaps a piece of fruit from time to time—I am fond of oranges—and naturally enough, a bed."

"Naturally enough," she said faintly. "So it would not be a marriage of convenience."

Restell snorted. "I should like to know the origin of that bit of nonsense. Marriage and convenience in the same breath? It is oxymoronic. Oh, I understand the premise well enough, but marriage, even when it is arranged for pragmatic reasons and not because of shared affection, is hardly a convenience. And further, such unions do not exclude marital relations."

Emma wished he did not have such a knack for amusing her. "Clearly," she said dryly, "you have formed an opinion on the subject."

Restell realized he had been perhaps too adamant in his response, although he was encouraged that the edges of her mouth were curling upward. "Yes, well, there it is. Have you known anyone to have entered into a marriage of convenience?"

"No, not of my acquaintance. I do not think it is generally announced as such, but the royals have engaged in the practice for centuries."

One of Restell's eyebrows kicked up. "You have made my argument for me, you know."

"Oh, very well. We are agreed there will be mutual affection and no conveniences."

"Then you are accepting my proposal?"

"You haven't actually asked." She held up one hand. "Don't."

He leaned back in his chair and stretched his legs before him. He made a steeple of his fingers and regarded Emma over the tips. It had required considerable effort to remove himself from his bath only a few short hours ago, then put on his best appearance for Sir Arthur. He had arrived at Lady

Rivendale's bone weary, yet strangely restive. In Emma's presence, though, as much as she tried and challenged him, she still gave him ease—often at the same time. He did not imagine that he would ever be able to explain it.

It was oxymoronic.

"There is something you wish to say?" he asked.

"Several things."

"That hardly surprises. Go on."

"What about love?"

He tapped his fingertips together as he considered his answer. "You gave me most excellent advice on that subject. Do you recall? You suggested I should allow the feeling to pass, and oddly enough, it has. I find I am considerably more clearheaded than I was on that occasion."

"Really?"

He smiled wryly. Clearly, she was skeptical. "As you have noted, it was a long ride from Walthamstow. If I do not seem of sound mind, I expect that accounts for it."

"It is as good an explanation as any." Emma ran a finger across several of the pianoforte's keys. She did not touch any of them hard enough to create a sound. "We have affection, then, not love. A good beginning, some would say. Will you want a mistress?"

Restell took his time answering, hoping she believed that the question deserved serious contemplation. What he was, however, was dumbstruck. "I don't think I will, no."

"You don't think you will?" she said, softly echoing his words. "That is not precisely an endorsement of fidelity."

"I take your point, and as I don't want to offend your sensibilities, I am agreeable to forgoing a mistress."

"Oh, good for you. I am taking note of your sacrifice."

Since she had neither paper nor pen, Restell supposed she made the tick in some mental ledger where it would never be lost or forgotten.

"How shall we live?" asked Emma.

Restell realized he should have anticipated the question. With the nonsense about mistresses out of the way, this was the most logical tack for her to take. "Why, I hope we shall live quite happily."

Emma's eyes narrowed, and she gave him the sharp edge of her frostiest stare. "I am in expectation of a better answer than that."

"Yes, well, you are referring to our finances, then."

She nodded. "We are both poor relations, Mr. Gardner. You must not hope that my uncle will settle any great amount on me. He did not lead you to believe that would be the case, did he?"

"No, not at all. He expressed concern that you should still be able to attend him, but he did not ask how I would provide for you."

"He imagines that you are well set in your own right. I have never explained to him that you engage in business for favors."

"I am not without means."

"The Earl of Ferrin. Do you intend we should live in your brother's home? Draw an allowance from him?"

"I take it you are not as satisfied with that arrangement as I am."

"You suggested to me that I should be paid for the services I do for my uncle," Emma said. "Perhaps you might find something you could do for your brother."

"Ferrin as my employer? Perish the thought. He is generous to those in his service, but I prefer his largesse. You know he has a perfectly vulgar living, don't you? He has amassed a fortune that no one man can spend in three lifetimes. Even he says as much. If he finds pleasure in supporting his family, it would be churlish of me to deny him."

Emma sighed. "I believe we are at an impasse. It is not that I object to charity, indeed, I have been the fortunate recipient of it, but I also think we must make ourselves industrious."

"I shall be industrious, or is protecting you of so little consequence?"

"Let us speak of that, shall we?"

"As you wish." Were all proposals so damnably difficult? he wondered. He was regretting he had not made some inquiries.

Ferrin or Wellsley, even Ian, might have had experiences that would have better prepared him. "What would you like to say on the subject?"

Emma did not hesitate. "I cannot help but believe your proposal is wholly predicated on this matter of my protection. Do you think you failed to protect me?"

"Not entirely. Hobbes pulled you from the fountain, but it was a narrow thing."

"Hobbes was there because you told him to be. In every way you were successful in securing my safety."

"I should prefer a different arrangement."

"You would have me live in your pockets."

"I admit, it has a certain appeal."

"It is a ridiculous notion. Have you considered how you will feel later, once you have discovered who is threatening me and put a period to it? And, truly, you do not yet know that I am the one threatened. Mr. Charters is Marisol's fiancé. It is still possible that I was mistaken for her because I was with him at the fountain."

"Yes, you were. Why is that?"

"You will not move me from my point, Mr. Gardner."

Apparently not. Restell was wise enough not to say so aloud. He glanced at the door and wondered what had happened to the promise of tea. An interruption at this juncture would serve him well. Unless he missed his guess, Emma was about to suggest that he should perhaps propose marriage to her cousin.

"If I follow your argument to its logical end," Emma said, "then you should consider making your proposal to Marisol."

Restell was saved from revealing his rather smug smile by the housekeeper's timely entrance. He rose to meet her before she had taken but a few steps into the room. He knew a spy when he saw one, and Mrs. Posey had the watchful eyes of someone who regularly apprised her mistress of events within the home. He did not want Lady Rivendale to know that his proposal had not yet been accepted.

Restell took the tray, thanked the housekeeper, and dismissed her. When she was gone, he carried the tray to the pianoforte and set it on the lid. "Nosey Posey," he said. "Lady Rivendale's spy mistress."

Emma nodded, amused. "You observed that also. I imagine she is in want of more information." She stood and poured tea for both of them. "These biscuits are quite good. Will you have one?"

"No." He sipped his tea. "I am not going to propose to your cousin, Emma, so you should not entertain hope on that score."

"I only suggested it to point out the failure of your reasoning, not because I hoped you would act on it. If we were to marry, you could expect to hear regular reports on your failures of reason. That should give you pause."

"That depends. Would you apprise me of them at breakfast or dinner?"

"Breakfast, I suspect."

"Then it presents no problem. I will be reading my paper and am likely to ignore you."

It was the teacup she was holding that prevented Emma from throwing up her hands. "You are determined to do this, aren't you?"

"I am, yes."

"After avoiding just this end for years? It makes no sense. I thought you were bent on defying your mother."

"Defying her? I would not characterize it as anything so bold. I was bent on making my own decision in my own time. I have done so. That it happens to coincide with her own plans is a happy accident. She will think she has persevered, and who is to say that she hasn't?"

"You don't know that she will accept me."

"Have you ever trod the boards at Drury Lane or harbor aspirations of doing so?"

Emma blinked. "No!"

"Then you will be entirely acceptable. Mother has very few standards, but she holds them as absolute."

Emma was not proof against Restell's sharply angled grin

or the deep dimple that caressed it. Still, she was also not prepared to give in just yet. "What if you come to regret it?"

"My proposal, you mean?"

"No. The marriage."

He shook his head, his eyes suddenly grave. "I won't."

"You can't know that. Please, humor me. What if it happens that you cannot bear to share even the newspaper with me?"

Restell said nothing for a moment. He set his teacup aside, then hers, and took her right hand in his. He hunkered down in front of her so that he was looking up. "I don't know, but believe me when I tell you I cannot conceive of it happening."

She did believe him. She was the one with doubts. "You must promise you will divorce me."

"Aren't you putting the cart before the horse?"

Emma went on as if he'd said nothing. "If I observe that you are unhappy in the marriage, if I suspect you have come to regret your noble gesture, then I will ask you to divorce me. I want your promise that you will do so."

"That is your condition to accept my proposal?"

"When you make it, yes."

Restell didn't have to consider it, and he suspected she would misinterpret any argument he made as hesitation on his part or signaling a lack of sincerity. "Then I agree," he said. "It will be as you wish."

Emma nodded once.

"Your hand is cold," he said. "Here, let me have the other." He folded her hands together, then surrounded them with his own. "Are you so frightened, then?"

"Terrified."

His smile was gentle, encouraging. "Then let us have it done quickly." He dropped to one knee. "Is this what you imagined?"

She flushed a little. "Sometimes."

"I understand from my sisters that young women often entertain such notions. If you have a preference for the manner in which it should be done, I would certainly like to hear it. I do not think I am at my best on one knee."

Emma was unprepared for the tears that suddenly gathered in her eyes. She managed a watery smile. "I doubt there is ever a time when you are not at your best."

"It is promising that you think so." Restell gave her hands a light squeeze. "Miss Hathaway . . . Emma . . . it is my belief that we are well-suited in temperament and inclination, and I suspect that a longer acquaintance would not diminish that belief, but strengthen it. It occurs to me you may share the same belief, and that has emboldened me to set the question before you: Will you do me the very great honor of becoming my wife?"

"I will." Her answer was so light of sound that she was compelled to nod to confirm it. The movement caused a tear to slip free of the rim of her lashes and mark a trail down her cheek. She gratefully accepted Restell's handkerchief. "It was a lovely proposal."

Restell found that a lump had settled in his own throat. He coughed politely, clearing it. Still, his voice was husky. "Thank you."

Emma dabbed at her eyes. "Did you rehearse it?"

"No. It was extemporaneous."

She nodded. "I wondered at the word 'emboldened.'"

"Did I say that? You will have noticed that I was not standing at the time. I begin to comprehend why gentlemen are wont to kneel and hold the lady's hand."

"Then it is not a romantic gesture," Emma said. "I have always had that question."

"You will not share this epiphany, will you? Ladies should be allowed to keep their romantic fancies, and gentlemen should not be made more nervous than they already are."

Recovering a bit of her poise, Emma smiled and shook her head. "I will tell no one. Are you able to rise, or must I assist you?"

"I think I can manage the thing." He stood, and because he still held one of Emma's hands, he drew her to her feet as well. "See? Steady."

Emma placed her free hand on Restell's shoulder and lifted

herself just enough to brush her mouth against his. When he
didn't engage, she kissed him again, this time nibbling lightly
on his upper lip as he had done to her. He was not entirely resistant to that effort. She felt his mouth begin to move over
hers, slowly at first, and lightly. As she returned it in kind, he
pressed with more ardor until she was quite without breath.
When they drew apart, the question of steadiness did not arise.

Emma dropped to her heels and stuffed Restell's handkerchief back into his frock coat pocket. "So I will know where
it is," she said, "in the event I have need of it later."

He chuckled. "I should have thought of it myself." He
glanced at the door. "Do you suppose we should inform Lady
Rivendale of your answer now or wait for Nosey Posey to deliver the particulars?"

"I think we should tell her. It cannot have been easy for her
to wait us out."

"As you like. It is quite possibly the last time we will announce it to anyone."

"What do you mean?"

"Lady Rivendale circulates more widely than the *Gazette*."

Before Emma agreed to marry Restell she thought she had
touched on every concern of import. A point she failed to
clarify was the speed at which the thing was likely to occur.
She had imagined there would be time enough to visit a
modiste and have a gown made for her. She thought there
would be fittings. She wanted to speak to the priest who
would marry them, and she had particular thoughts about the
flowers she would carry. She had depended upon the banns
being read.

She presented all of this to Restell the same evening they
became engaged. He listened to her quite closely, tilting his
head just so as she rattled on about gowns and flowers and
vows. He listened to her argue in favor of tradition without
offering an opinion of his own. He listened to her discuss
the guest list at great length, not inquiring once how she had

come suddenly to have so many friends. And when she fell silent, finally satisfied with the persuasiveness of her discourse, he presented her with the special license he had procured a few hours after securing her promise.

"We'll exchange vows in the morning," he'd said.

It had been the end of the subject as far as he was concerned. Emma was of a different opinion, but he was intractable. Pig-headed was the term she'd used to describe him. For some reason he found that vastly entertaining and kissed her so thoroughly that she forgot she was out of patience with him. She remembered afterward, but it didn't seem as important as it once had. Indeed, she began to look forward to the kiss they would share following the exchange of their vows. If that had been his intent, she decided that he was diabolical and that she would do well to remember it.

She found herself recalling it as Ian Gardner made a toast to their good health and happiness at their wedding breakfast. It had not occurred to her last night that Restell's family or her own would attend such a hasty wedding, nor did it occur that there was but one reason that explained their lack of protests and all of their cooperation.

They thought she was carrying his child.

Emma's fingers tightened around the stem of her wineglass. It suddenly felt extraordinarily heavy in her hand. As though she were watching from a distance, she saw herself raise the glass and touch it to her husband's. She also saw that she was smiling. The fact that she was baring all her teeth did not appear to alarm him in the least.

The carriage was waiting for them when they descended the steps outside his parents' home. The family—hers and his—crowded at the windows to see them off. Emma leaned forward and waved through the open door before the footman closed it. Marisol, she observed, was standing arm in arm with Mr. Charters, both of them looking oddly abandoned. Her uncle seemed happy enough, but it may have been that Lady Rivendale had secured herself a place at his side. The Gardners were largely smiling. Hannah and Portia stood on either side of their father and bounced in place with their energetic waving. Sir Geoffrey looked particularly handsome in his morning clothes and waved only marginally less enthusiastically than his daughters. Ian Gardner and his wife stood paired at another window, sharing some private amusement that made them laugh. Imogene and her husband shared a small upper balcony with Wynetta and Porter Wellsley. Wynetta and Imogene were tossing flower petals from a basket that the men held between them.

"You will not expect me to do that, I hope," Restell said when a shower of pink and white blossoms swirled around the carriage as it moved forward.

"Hold the basket or throw the petals?"

"Either." He sat back and regarded her steadily. "What is it, Emma? You have been biding your time, but I think the time has come."

"How did you come by the special license?"

The question surprised him. "A favor. One I was owed. It was the only way even I could get one with so little notice. It is all quite legal. Everything was put in order so you should have no concerns on that count."

"We were married with indecent haste, you know."

"I suspect there will be those who think so."

"Is your family among them?"

"I'm not certain I follow," Restell said carefully.

"Does your family think I am carrying your child?"

Restell frowned. "Did one of them intimate as much?"

"No. I want to know if you intimated as much to them."

"I did not. Even if you *could* be carrying my child, it is too early to know. We have not been acquainted above two months." He saw immediately that he had not done well to put that fact before her again. She looked very young of a sudden. It was odd, that. He had always thought of her as older than her years, more determined and practical. She was fragile. He knew that, too, but what had made her fragile had also made her strong. It was a paradox that he did not yet fully comprehend, although he observed the truth of it on every occasion they were together. "What raised this gremlin thought?"

"Your family was everything solicitous. All the preparations were made at a moment's notice. Their eagerness to move forward without raising a single objection seemed unusually co-operative, and I could not imagine any other explanation for their haste. I feared they must believe that I permitted you to compromise me."

"My family *is* everything solicitous," he said. "It is our nature to rally to a challenge, not turn our backs on it. The preparations were hardly elaborate, and quite frankly, Lady Gardner has been planning something like them for me since she married my father. Their eagerness, I believe, was predicated on a fear that I would change my mind." Restell touched Emma's slightly wobbly chin with a gloved fingertip. "I have told no one in my family what you were made to endure at Madame Chabrier's or later in the country outside Walthamstow. If they learn of it, it will be because you choose to tell them. I won't. It must be your decision."

Her nod was almost imperceptible. Restell felt the movement against his fingertip and removed his hand. She was the one who reached for it and folded her own hands around it.

"Last night, as I was readying for bed, Marisol came to my room. She was curious about my decision to marry you. Perhaps she is the one who put the idea of compromise in my mind. She never revealed her thinking to me, but as I reflect on our conversation, I believe it's what she meant."

"She did not anticipate that you would steal a march on her."

"I thought of that also."

"She is jealous of you."

"It is not a simple matter for me to understand, but I am coming to accept that it's true."

"I would have your mind at ease, Emmalyn."

"Emma," she said softly. "I prefer it to Emmalyn."

"Very well. Emma. I prefer it also. I have noticed that Sir

Arthur and Miss Vega call you Emmalyn, but I am put in mind of a reprimand when I hear it from them."

"That is my sense also." She smiled a shade wistfully. "It was the manner in which my parents used it. Emmalyn was for those occasions when my behavior disappointed them. Emma never was in trouble."

He chuckled. "You were fortunate to have such clear lines drawn for you. I had but the one name for my parents to use. I had to depend upon the tone to know if I was about to be praised or pilloried. Sometimes I missed the mark. That was never a good thing." He glanced sideways at Emma and saw that her smile was still in place. "Do you mind that we are not taking a wedding trip?"

"It did not occur that we might. I am not eager to leave London just yet, even in your company. It is a kindness to me for us to remain here."

"Good. I hoped you would not be disappointed."

"I have few expectations regarding how we shall go on."

"I see."

She stole a look at him. He was facing forward, his features set in such a way as to be impenetrable. "I am still catching my breath," she said. "The expectations, I think, will come in time."

Restell nodded but offered no comment.

Emma suddenly felt desperate to fill the uncomfortable silence. "There is another reason I am happy to remain in London: my uncle has need of me. You will not be surprised that he required more assurances last night that I did not mean to abandon him. I hope I was not wrong to provide them."

"I suppose that depends on the promises you made. If you told him that nothing would be changed, that you would continue to help him in the manner you always have, then I believe you overstepped."

"I said that he could depend upon me to visit him regularly, that I would discuss the arrangements for those visits with you, and that you would be reasonable. Was I wrong to make those assurances?"

"I wish you had not said I would be reasonable."

"Did you not tell me once that you are exactly that?"

"If I did, I could not have been speaking of your safety."

His answer, rather tersely given, still warmed Emma. "We were speaking of the favors you request. You assured me you were not an unreasonable man."

"And you took me at my word."

She smiled, squeezing his hand lightly and urging him to look at her. "I believe I was right to do so. Was I?"

Restell sighed. "I only wish you were not so confident of it in this case. You and I may yet disagree about what is reasonable."

"We will find a solution that satisfies both of us. Have you noticed that we do that?"

"I have." He raised his hand to her cheek and tucked a tendril of dark cocoa-colored hair under her bonnet. The carriage began to slow. His smile held an edge of regret. "We are arrived."

"Are we?" Emma felt no compunction to look away from him. She'd thought she already knew every nuance of his expression and the angle of every one of his features. But she was not familiar with the way he was looking at her now, nor had she known that his smile could tilt at so perfect an incline as to pierce her heart.

"We are." Restell dropped a quick kiss on her slightly parted lips and pointed over his shoulder as the carriage came to a halt. He watched Emma's face as her eyes darted to the window. Her puzzlement was not unexpected. "It's my home," he said, answering the question before she asked. "I did not think we should spend our first night together in my brother's house. You argued quite effectively in favor of financial independence, so I thought I would begin as I mean to go on."

Emma stared at the town house as if she'd never seen the like before. In truth, it was very much on the order of every other house along the row in size and design, with only its black door and shutters and stately iron fence setting it apart. Alarmed of a sudden, she sat back and gave Restell the same incredulous regard that she'd given his house. "How is it possible? Please say you have not indebted yourself because of some ill-conceived suggestion I made?"

"I have not indebted myself," he said calmly. "Come. Let us go inside, and you will tell me if all is to your liking. I am depending upon your honesty. I cannot assure you that everything has been made ready, though the staff has been working with considerable diligence since you gave me your answer."

Emma could barely make sense of what he was saying. "You did not secure this home only yesterday, did you?"

Restell chuckled. "No, Emma. I could not have anticipated I would be in immediate need of a dwelling."

"I cannot fathom why not. You are frighteningly well-prepared for all manner of things."

"My, how you flatter me." The door to the carriage opened. Restell made a nimble descent, then held out his hand for Emma. It seemed to him that her feet barely touched the ground, she was that light on his arm.

The household staff was assembled in the entrance hall. They stood at something resembling regimental attention as Restell escorted Emma inside. The butler took Restell's hat, gloves, and stick and Emma's bonnet. She declined to give him her shawl. Her fingers were wound too tightly around the knotted tails.

Restell kept one hand on her elbow as he introduced her. Mr. Crowley served as butler, Mrs. Underwood as the housekeeper. The misses Payne and Hanley were the upstairs' maids; Mrs. Wright and Miss Miller performed the downstairs' functions. Mrs. Wescott held the important position of cook. Her two young helpers were Becky Morrison and Eliza Shepard. Hobbes stood to the rear of the line, closely attended by the footmen McCleod, Lewis, and Shaw.

Out of the corner of his eye, Restell observed Emma nod and smile and find something pleasant to say to each servant as the introduction was completed. She comported herself with the effortless confidence of one who was practiced in managing a household. If any of his staff noticed that she had only been able to loose one hand from her shawl and that the one that rested at her side curled frequently in the folds of her white bombazine gown, not one among them gave any indication of it. Even Hobbes and the footmen, all of whom had better than a passing familiarity with her, seemed quite taken with her manner.

"Grace under pressure," Restell told her when they were alone.

"Hmm?" Emma stopped running her index finger along the spine of the book she was holding and returned it to the tabletop where she'd found it. It seemed doubtful that she'd have occasion to read *Nightmare Abbey* this evening. She looked up. Restell was sitting in a wing chair that he'd angled away from the window. A light breeze caused the drapes to billow behind him. He watched her with his eyelids at half-mast, and she was struck by how extraordinarily tired he must be. She approached his chair and sat on the upholstered footstool he seemed to have no use for.

"You were the embodiment of grace under pressure," he said. "That's what I was thinking when you met the staff. You demonstrated a great deal of poise."

"Did you mean to test my nerve?"

"No. Is that how it seemed?"

"No, it was merely startling," she said. "I cannot say if I would have done better or worse to have been forewarned." She lifted her hands to indicate all of the sitting room they were in, then broadened the gesture to indicate all of the house. "You can collect, I think, that it is rather a lot to absorb."

"But you find it satisfactory?"

She was struck again by Restell's concern that she approve of her new home. It was perhaps the most appealing aspect of his character that he placed some value on her opinion. "It is all to my liking."

Restell had presented her with a large set of keys that made her feel every inch the chatelaine, then escorted her on a tour of the home himself, taking her even to the bowels of the house and showing her the kitchen, the wine cellar, and the meat safe. She observed that the pantry was well-stocked, that the cutlery was sharpened, and that there were coals enough in the scuttle to sustain fires in every room when they would have need of such. He urged her to open cupboards and closets and see for herself that there were linens, china, and silver. He allowed her to wander about the drawing room and the library, picking up and examining such items that caught her eye. She was struck by his exquisite taste in the appointments and artwork, and when he had urged her to consider how she might change any of the rooms to please her, she had been unable to imagine what could be more pleasing.

As she walked from room to room and took in the arrangements of each, she could not help but recall Neven Charters's home. He seemed to have amassed all of his most impressive treasures in one room. The purpose—and she had come to conclude it was purposeful—was to inspire awe in his visitors. In contrast, Restell's treasures appeared everywhere. There was the delicate Ming vase filled with hothouse flowers in the entrance hall, the sumptuous, damask-covered window seat in the library, the medieval tapestry in the sitting room. Every piece of furniture was elegantly curved so that the eye slipped easily from one appointment to the next. No single piece stood apart from the rest, yet they were not designed or crafted by the same artisans. An ornate gilt birdcage hung in one of the bedchambers. The bird, a nightingale, perched on the highest point of the equally ornate gilt mirror above the mantel and seemed to be quite full of himself now that he had the whole of the room for his home. Neither she nor Restell had been able to coax it down, although only Emma's soft urgings could truly be interpreted as coaxing. Restell simply demanded that it remove itself. The bird showed his disdain for this approach by leaving a bit of guano on the gilt scrollwork, and Restell had been sufficiently motivated by Emma's laughter to stand on a Chippendale chair and snatch the felon.

"I find all of it to my liking," she repeated. "Even the nightingale."

Restell grunted softly. "If he had more meat on his bones, we would have him for dinner."

"I am certain Mrs. Wescott has a recipe for it. She seems frightfully competent."

"She is. She is also given to tantrums and opinions not shared by my mother, the latter being the reason I was able to lure her away. I promised her I would have no opinions of my own, and we have gotten on famously."

"But I have opinions."

"Yes, and you are as skilled as the entire diplomatic corps in negotiating terms. I fail to see that Wescott will present you with the least challenge."

"My, how you flatter me." She saw his lips twitch as she echoed his earlier comment to her. "Why did you choose to live in Ferrin's home when you might have lived here?"

"For the advantages, of course." He saw this did not placate her in the least. Before she could begin her interrogation, he explained, "Chief among them being that mamas with eligible daughters were not quite certain that I would come up to snuff. I had no visible means of support except for Ferrin, and he regularly made noises—very public noises—that he would not settle so much as a farthing on me while I avoided responsibility."

"I can understand what might move him to tell you privately, but it is not the sort of thing families are usually wont to make public."

"You are quite right, but I asked Ferrin to put it about. It was as good a ruse as any to keep certain females from making me the target of their pursuits."

"Your mother must have been extremely put out with you."

"An understatement, but she has never known the whole of it. She does not, for instance, know about this house."

"Mr. Gardner! Oh, but that is very bad of you."

Restell's eyebrows approached his hairline. "If you are going to admonish me, and I suspect you will find many reasons to do so, I insist that you use my Christian name."

Emma's mouth flattened momentarily. "Well, I have already said my piece so there is no reason to belabor the point." She ignored his chuckle. "Is your father also uninformed?"

"No, but he can never admit that he's known. His life would not be worth living."

"To have such secrets from your mother." She shook her head. "Will she forgive you?"

"Eventually," he said, turning the full force of his smile on her.

"You think you are charming," she said primly, "but your mother will not be so easily persuaded."

"*You* will not be so easily persuaded," he said, reaching for her. "For all her noises to the contrary, Mother does not entirely mind that I am a rascal." He caught Emma's fingers, then clasped her hand and pulled her off the stool. Before she could straighten fully, Restell tugged harder so that she simply fell into his lap. She made to scramble free, but he caught her by the waist and quieted her. He watched her face closely. A pale pink wash of color highlighted her cheeks. She was not quite meeting his eyes but looking just past him. "Are you uncomfortable?"

"I am discomfited," she said. "I am not certain it is at all the same."

"Probably not." He was aware of the slight tremor that slipped beneath her skin. His hands spanned her narrow waist, and just beneath her rib cage, he could feel the thud of her heart. "Did you sleep well last night?"

"No. Did you?"

"I do not think I slept at all."

She nodded faintly. "It was the same for me." Quite without knowing that she meant to do it, Emma lifted her hand and cupped the side of his face. Her thumb lay lightly against his skin, then made a pass across the high arch of his cheek. "Does it seem curious to you that we have come to just this end?"

"Curiously inevitable, perhaps." He turned his head and kissed the underside of her wrist. "And exactly right."

It was the warmth of his mouth against her skin that made her feel weak of a moment. If he had asked her to remove herself from his lap, she wouldn't have been able to stand. She passed her fingertips across his temple and made a small furrow in his sun-gilt hair. When he simply closed his eyes, she did it again. And again. His small sigh of contentment was as warming to her as his lips had been on her wrist.

Without opening his eyes, he said, "You will have noticed that our bed is large."

Her fingers stilled, then resumed their gentle threading. She glanced toward the entrance of the adjoining room where the curtained four-poster occupied considerable space. "I did in fact notice that."

One corner of his mouth edged up at her effort to remain composed. "So large, I believe, that we might lie comfortably together."

Emma's eyes darted to the open window behind Restell. "There are many hours yet before nightfall."

"I am thinking we might have a nap, Emma."

"A nap. Oh, but that is a splendid idea."

Restell's slight grin deepened, and he offered in dry accents, "I am choosing not to be insulted by your enthusiasm for it."

Her sweetly warm kiss did a great deal to assure that was so.

Chapter 9

Restell opened one eye, saw it was dusk, and promptly shut out even this meager light by burying his face in his pillow. He stretched but only so he could find a more comfortable depression in the mattress. He was vaguely aware of a conversation taking place in the dressing room and that both participants were female. The hushed tones did not permit him to hear the particulars of the exchange, but he recognized Emma's carefully modulated accents. The other voice was unfamiliar to him, which he counted in his favor: It meant Emma's personal maid and all of her trunks had arrived from Sir Arthur's.

Restell fell in and out of sleep. Sometimes he awakened and heard the flutter of activity in the dressing room and sometimes he heard nothing at all. Once he glimpsed Emma folding a blanket at the foot of the bed, then she was gone.

It was the fragrance of warm bread and a savory roast that nudged all of his senses to wakefulness. His empty stomach was a powerful motivator. Pushing himself up so he could rest on his elbows, he watched Emma uncover the dishes that had been set on the small, round table in front of the fireplace. It was a pleasure to watch her at this task as she breathed deeply of the aromas that were revealed and gave evidence of her satisfaction in a smile that was at once expectant and replete.

"Your appetite appears to match my own," he said.

Caught unaware, Emma nearly dropped the cover she was holding. It bobbled in her hands before she secured it against her chest. She saw Restell's gaze drop to her covered breasts and did not mistake the mischief going on behind his eyes. Flushing, she turned her back on him and replaced the domed lid over the roast. She heard Restell leaving the bed, then his soft tread as he approached her from behind. He placed his hands on the curve of her shoulders and brushed the crown of her head lightly with his cheek.

"I imagine that I will learn to temper my teasing," he said.

Emma twisted her head just enough to glance at him. "Oh, I hope you will not do so on my account."

He saw that she was perfectly earnest. "Then you were not offended?"

"No." She hesitated. "I was . . ." She halted again, searching for the right words. "That is, your teasing . . . well, it made me . . . *warm*."

"Warm." He pressed his smile into her hair. It was like silken threads beneath his lips. "Warm. That is a good beginning, I think." He gave her a quick kiss on the temple, then nudged her gently toward one of the chairs. "May I seat you?" At Emma's nod, he pulled out a chair and waited for her to sit. When she was comfortable, he took the seat opposing her.

When they had taken to their bed earlier, Emma had removed all but her modest shift and stockings, while Restell had stripped down to his linen, trousers, and hose. He could not fail to notice that she'd taken some pains to dress for dinner and looked quite lovely for the effort. In contrast, he was aware that he looked rather disreputable. His shirt was open at the throat and only slightly more wrinkled than his trousers. He'd left the bed without stepping into his shoes and hadn't given a thought to applying a brush to his hair. Conscious of his appearance, he quickly ran a hand through his hair and fumbled with the chitterling on his shirt. When he glanced over at Emma and saw she was watching him, he realized his efforts did little to improve his appearance.

"I should dress," he said, starting to rise.

Emma reached across the small table and placed her hand on his forearm. "No. Do not. It is of no import to me, and your food will grow cold."

"If this is a dream, I pray I will not wake from it. My mother would never permit my father to sit at supper in this wise."

"And I submit, sir, that you do not know what manner of dress is accepted in your parents' bedchamber. That is surely a private place."

Restell almost blanched. "Your point is taken," he said quickly, "and we will say no more on the matter."

Emma chuckled. "It is disconcerting, is it not, to think of one's parents as intimate."

"I beg you, stop."

Still chuckling, Emma removed all the covers and began serving herself from the platters. The thinly sliced roast was rare and lay in its own dark juices. Small buttered potatoes were surrounded by carrot medallions and pearl onions. At Emma's insistence there was half a loaf of warm, crusty bread, pear and cheese wedges, and a bottle of red wine. She accepted the half glass of wine that Restell poured for her and raised her glass when he did the same.

"This is right, Emma," he said quietly, touching his glass to hers. "For both of us." Although she nodded, Restell could not divine whether she believed or merely that she wanted to believe. After they both drank, there was silence. Restell applied himself to filling his own plate. Emma spread a serviette across her lap and waited politely for him to finish before she picked up her fork.

They ate in silence for some time before Emma was moved to note it. "It is still a bit awkward, isn't it?" she said, spearing one of the carrots. "The two of us, I mean."

"I must say, you go at a thing head-on. Have you never injured yourself?"

"On occasion. You will have noticed that I persist."

"I have noticed," he said. "From the outset, in fact."

She looked down at her plate, thoughtful now as she cut

into her roast. "Why do you suppose I cannot persist in other ways? Do you realize I still can go nowhere unattended?"

"Nor should you."

"That is not the point. A woman in society is granted little enough independence. A solitary walk in the park is not outside the pale if the hour is not too late. I want that back, Mr. Gard—" Seeing the dramatic arch of his eyebrow, Emma stopped. "Restell," she said. "I want that back, Restell."

"And so you shall have it."

"You cannot know that."

He shrugged lightly, lifting a potato to his mouth.

"It is no good if you will not argue," Emma said.

Restell chewed and swallowed. "At this juncture, I can think of no argument that will persuade you. Given that, I prefer silence."

Emma's sigh was sufficiently dramatic to cause the candle flame to flicker. Seeing it, she had the grace to offer a smile rife with self-mockery. "As a rule, I am not given to sulking."

"I know, and I'm appreciative."

"Do you sulk?"

"I brood. It is the masculine form of the expression."

"I did not realize." She speared a small stack of carrots. "What of fussing? Do men fuss?"

"They stew."

"Yes, I can see how they might. It even sounds masculine. Very meaty."

Restell was having difficulty maintaining a tone as dry as hers. "Men are not harried either. We are plagued."

"I see. It must be a great trial to you, being a man. I am sure I would not have the stamina for it."

Restell was forced to wash down a bit of meat with some wine before he choked. "Enough. You will kill me."

Emma's smile was all innocence as she regarded him closely. "You will not like to know this, Mr. Gardner, but you are looking a bit harried."

"And you are a plaguey wife." Restell struck with the speed of a cobra on a mongoose. He had Emma out of her chair and hoisted in his arms even before she understood his intent. The fork she still held in her hand was poised to puncture his neck. It did not give him pause until she went perfectly rigid. Only then did he recognize that what he meant as an impulsive, playful gesture was neither of those things to her. "Emma?"

He risked glancing away from her slightly glazed eyes to look at the fork. It was all too easy to imagine those tines sinking deep into his flesh, and the wound she could inflict might well be fatal. "Emma. It is Restell. Look at me. Look at *me*." As he spoke, he carefully lowered his arm that supported her under her knees until she unfolded and her feet touched the ground. Holding her securely against him with one hand, he used the other to quickly wrest the fork from her. There was no battle for it. Her nerveless fingers simply surrendered it.

Emma was already trembling with the sure knowledge of what she had been prepared to do. "I'm sorry," she whispered. "I'm so sorry. I didn't—"

Restell tossed the fork away. He held her loosely, supporting her more with the frame of his body than his hands at her back. "Hush. Nothing happened, and if it had, it would be no more than I deserved."

She raised her face. Her eyes pleaded with him, though she had no sense of what she wanted to say.

"Emma," he said gently. "I provoked you to it. Come, lie down. You are yet unsteady." He was grateful that she did not resist him or his suggestion. More meekly than he would have thought possible, she accompanied him to the bed and sat. "Will you allow me to play the lady's maid?"

"Yes. Yes, please. I do not want Bettis to see me thus."

That made him smile, albeit only faintly. He stooped, raised her right leg, and removed her leather slipper. He made equally quick work of the other. Earlier in the day she had disappeared into the dressing room to remove her gown. Now she made no protest as he loosened the ribbons that defined the bodice and helped her pull it over her head. Sitting beside her, he tugged on the laces of her corselet so that she might remove it. She gave it to him without a word.

He was on the point of carrying her garments to the dressing room when she indicated that he should remove her stockings also. He placed what he was holding on the bed and dropped to one knee in front of her. She rested her foot on his thigh and raised the hem of her batiste chemise to the midpoint of her calf. Restell reached under the chemise, found the ribbons that held her silk stockings in place and tugged. His palms lightly grazed her legs as he rolled the stockings to the tips of her toes.

"Bettis is not as efficient as you," she said, watching him.

"She probably does not enjoy her work as much."

"Nor is she so well-practiced. You have done this before, I think."

Restell stood and gathered her clothes a second time. "That is not something you truly want to know."

But I do. Emma was not sure if she had spoken aloud or if he was merely pretending not to hear her. When he turned away without comment she had further cause to wonder if she had even spoken aloud. It was this last possibility, she supposed, that seemed to indicate that he was right.

When Restell returned from the dressing room, Emma was still sitting precisely as he'd left her. "Won't you lie down?"

She nodded but made no move to do so.

"Very well," he said. He began to gather the remnants of their meal, replacing the covers on the platters and putting the whole of it on the tray.

Emma was openly curious. "What are you doing?"

"I am removing this to our sitting room, then I am ringing for someone to take it all away. I did not think you wanted any intrusion here." He managed the task with brisk efficiency, and this time when he reappeared in their bedchamber, Emma was sitting at the head of the bed. It was an improvement of sorts, he decided, that her legs were no longer dangling over the side.

He closed the door to the sitting room so there would be no

interruption when the maids took the tray. Only the wine bottle and two glasses remained on the table as proof that they'd shared some part of a meal here. Restell carried all three to the bedside where he poured a second half glass for her and only a little more than that for himself.

Emma gratefully accepted her glass. While the urge was upon her to drink it greedily, she did not allow herself to give in to it.

Restell set the bottle on the bedside table. He started to back away, his intention to retrieve a chair, but Emma stopped him.

"Please," she said. "Sit here." She laid her hand at the side of the bed closest to her.

He regarded her uncertainly. "I don't know if that's a good idea, Emma."

"It is."

Her flat assertion made Restell's lips twitch. It seemed to him that she meant to brook no argument, a sure sign that she was well into recovering herself. He sat at her side and hooked his heels on the bed rail. "You are feeling more the thing, I collect."

Nodding, she took another sip of wine. It was considerably darker outside, but the candles inside the bedchamber cast warm, golden light across the coverlet bunched about her knees. Emma alternately plucked at the spread, then smoothed it over. She did this several times before she was able to pose the question uppermost in her mind. "Have I given you cause to fear me?"

Choosing his words carefully, Restell's answer was not immediate. "I am not afraid of you, Emma. It is more accurate to say that I am afraid *for* you."

Her eyes wandered from his face back to her wineglass. She rolled the stem in her fingertips. "The difference is of some import," she said quietly.

"I think so, yes."

"Then you would not entirely be opposed to consummating our marriage tonight."

Restell cupped her chin with the side of his index finger and gently nudged her face upward. "I would not be opposed," he said, surprising himself with the neutral tone he affected. "What I would wonder is whether you are prepared for such an end."

Her eyes darted to the right and left before they settled on him again. "Perhaps if we remove what might be used as weapons."

It was the perfect gravity of her response that raised his smile. "I do not think we must go to those lengths, Emma. My point is that I do not want to give you cause to reach for any."

"It is only that you startled me earlier. I did not expect you to lunge at me."

"I may startle you again. That can happen in the natural course of things."

"You are infinitely more experienced than I am," she said. "Can you not explain your intentions as you go?"

"Explain my intentions," he repeated with considerable deliberateness. "I'm afraid you will have to explain yours."

Emma finished her glass of wine and set it on the table, then she took Restell's glass from him and placed it beside hers. "I like the kissing well enough," she said. Pushing the coverlet aside, she rose on her knees and edged closer to him. "I am going to kiss you. On the mouth, if you like, or on the cheek if you prefer. It is only by way of demonstration."

"On the mouth will be satisfactory."

Emma nodded. She leaned into him and placed her lips against his. She lingered there a moment, sipping at his mouth much as she had the wine, resisting the urge to surrender to greediness. When she felt the first inkling of a response from him, she sat back. "Do you see?" she asked. "I didn't startle you. You knew precisely what I was going to do as I announced myself."

Restell was more than startled. She had rendered him speechless.

Emma regarded him anxiously. "Restell?"

"A moment more," he said. "I am in want of my wits." He

held up one hand, forestalling her comment. "That is not
entirely bad, you understand."

"I do. It is the same for me."

Restell's smile mocked them both. "God's truth, but we
are well-suited. As witless a pair as ever embarked upon a
marriage."

"Imagine how much worse it would be if we were in love."

Wishing he had fought to retain his glass of wine so that he
might finish it off now, Restell still was able to consider the
consequences of her assertion. "Infinitely worse," he said.
"We might make ourselves ridiculous."

She nodded. "The wags would have it all. Gossip to Gospel
in a nine days' wonder."

Restell's eyes dropped to her mouth. It was hardly necessary for him to announce his intentions. Still, he did so as a
courtesy. "I'm going to kiss you now. Just there, at the corner
of your mouth. You have the sweetest curve . . ." His voice
trailed off as he bent his head.

His lips touched hers at the edge of her tremulous smile.
He kissed her there, then moved slowly across her mouth
until he had engaged it all in the kiss. "And here," he whispered, touching his lips to her jaw. "Here also, at this hollow
just beneath your ear."

His breath, warm and humid against her skin, raised a *fris-
son* even before he touched her. She tilted her head to one
side, surrendering the spot. The tip of his tongue made a
damp line in the curve.

"I'm going to put my hand at the back of your neck."

She nodded once. His fingers slid under her hair and lifted
it just slightly. His mouth moved to her ear.

"A bite," he said softly. "Just a small one."

Her breath hitched as his teeth caught her earlobe and
tugged. The pleasure that tripped down the length of her spine
didn't end there. It went all the way to her toes. She wrig-
gled them.

Restell felt the movement under his hip. He was leaning
at an awkward angle around her bent knees. She could not

stretch and neither could he. "Will you lie down now?" he asked, raising his head a fraction. "It would be a comfort to me."

She gave him a slightly bemused smile. "Yes, of course."

He sat up to make room for her to unfold. "Shall I extinguish the candles?"

"No!" Her vehemence surprised them both. More softly, she said, "No. I am . . . that is, you will think me a child, but I am afraid in the dark."

"Always?" he asked.

She shook her head. "Only recently."

Restell was careful not to reveal a shred of pity for her. "Then the candles will remain as they are. If you like, I will light others."

"No, it isn't necessary."

"Shall I draw the curtains around the bed?"

"A little, if you like."

"What I like is that I shall be able to see my wife's flushed cheeks." Just as he knew she would, Emma obliged him by blushing. "You are in some ways predictable."

Except to show her distaste for it, she did not favor that with a reply.

"I mean to kiss you again, you know." He shifted his position on the bed so he was not lying across her, then he placed one finger to her lips. "Right here on your sulky mouth."

"It is not sulky," she said. "It is brooding."

"Not even by half." He leaned down and kissed her, thoroughly and warmly. He traced the seam of her lips with his tongue until she opened for him. When he had her mouth, he deepened the kiss, pressing his advantage more insistently, tangling his tongue with hers. He teased her senses with short raids and long explorations, and both made her slightly breathless.

"Your throat." He said the words huskily against her skin. It was less a warning than a statement of fact. His fingers slid deeper into her thick hair. One of her ivory combs slipped from its moorings, and when he withdrew his fingers her dark hair spilled over the back of his hand, then the pillow. He raised his head to look at her, to admire the way her hair framed her face and the candlelight softened her features. The centers of her eyes had widened so that he could only glimpse the blue-green iris, but she regarded him as intently as he regarded her, mirroring the search of his face as he searched hers.

"What do you see, Emma?"

"You." Her voice was but a thread of sound. Even more softly, she added, "My husband."

He nodded, encouraged. His eyes dropped to the curve of her neck and shoulder. He thought he could make out the faint pulse of her heart. He placed a kiss there, sipping her skin lightly. She would bear a mark later, a faint bruise that would bring to mind this intimacy. He hoped she would think of it more fondly than all the other bruises she had suffered at a man's hands.

He made a trail of kisses across her bare shoulder, then lower still as he followed the neckline of her soft chemise. Her hands had come to rest lightly at his own shoulders. Her fingers fluttered as if she was hesitant to rest them there, then they fell still when his mouth grazed her breast through the batiste. He realized she had not expected that.

Emma cut short his apology. "No," she said quickly. "It was surprising in a different way, that's all. I quite liked it." She saw his faint frown. "Should I not have said so? Perhaps it is not done."

In response, Restell rolled away from her and lay on his back. He stared at the ceiling where the flicker of candlelight against the curtains created waves of shadows. "I cannot do this, Emma."

She sat up. "I have ruined it, haven't I? I should have said nothing."

"You may say whatever you like. It is not something that should be suffered in silence."

"But I was not suffering." She stared at him, comprehending. "You were, weren't you? I didn't realize. I thought—"

"I was not suffering," he said firmly. "At least not in any

way you can yet conceive." He shifted his attention from the ceiling to her. "You understand, don't you, that there may be some pain? I have never lain with a virgin so I cannot say if it is always thus or whether something might be done to make it less disagreeable."

"I think the pain must be tolerable, else women would not submit."

"I would have it that there is no pain."

"Then you may as well place me upon the mantel where the maids can dust me from time to time. Even better, I will share a cage with the nightingale and be even less of a bother than that bird." She brushed his hair gently with her fingertips. "I am not afraid of you, Restell. I have never been afraid of what you will do to me. Here, in this bed, I have never mistaken you for one of my attackers. Dr. Bettany says I was not touched in such a way."

"I know."

"Perhaps you wish I had been. I would not be a virgin."

"Bloody hell, Emma."

"I'm sorry." She sighed. "Are we at an impasse?"

Restell placed his forearm over his eyes. "I don't know. Mayhap we are."

That was when she startled him. Her softly expelled breath, the faint fragrance of red wine, the warmth of her skin close to his, all of it alerted him—and all of it came to him at once. He only had a moment's warning before her lips touched his.

Restell was not proof against her advance. He *had* been suffering, and what she promised him now was relief. Groaning softly, he gave himself up to what she was offering.

Emma stretched out beside him, fitting herself against him in the way she had when they were standing. The familiarity of his body was pleasing to her. The scent of his skin, the flavor of his mouth, the curve of his sheltering arm, the whole of it imparted to her a sense of sanctuary.

She eased her fingertips under the opening of his shirt, tracing the edge first, then laying her hand flat against his chest. His heart beat steadily beneath her palm. She moved aside the linen and pressed a kiss to his skin. "Will you not remove it?" she asked.

Restell tugged on the tails and pulled it free of his trousers. Holding up his hands, he allowed Emma to remove it for him. He watched it out of the corner of his eyes as it sailed over the side of the bed. "I showed a great deal more care with your clothes."

"True, but you were playing the lady's maid. I am your curious and anxious wife, not your valet." To satisfy her curiosity and ease her anxiety, Emma began a tender exploration, first with her hands and eyes, then with her mouth. She traced his collarbone, drawing on his skin much as he had done to her. Her tongue teased a response from him as she kissed his shoulder, then the curve of his elbow, and finally the back of his hand, raising it up to her mouth, then holding it against her cheek.

She walked her fingers down his chest, gauging the ease of his breathing as she came closer to the button fly of his trousers. His abdomen retracted. Her hand slipped under the fabric of his drawers, and it was difficult for her to know which one of them was more shocked by her temerity. She would have withdrawn immediately if not for Restell taking her by the wrist and holding her exactly as she was.

"Do you have the least notion what you are about?" he asked.

She freely admitted she did not. "But I am depending upon you to tell me when I am about it wrong."

He grunted softly and closed his eyes, somewhere between pleasure and purgatory. He released her wrist. "You have not erred thus far." He glanced at her again. "Go on. Unbutton them."

Emma removed her hand first, then allowed it to slide over the taut fabric of his fly. She could feel the heat of him through the material. His blood pulsed heavily here. She imagined that his heart was no longer as steady as it had been before. "I have studied anatomy, you know."

"I didn't, but you are good to mention it."

"This is a bit different."

"For me, also."

"Illustrations are flat and sculpture is cold. You are neither."

"Did you also study torture?" It was the end of enough. Restell sat up and quickly shucked himself of his trousers, drawers, and stockings while Emma slid under the coverlet and sheet to remove her shift. He was certain he heard her soft laughter, but when he turned, she was only smiling.

It really was the most splendid smile.

Restell joined her under the covers when she raised them. The invitation was clear. He had had mistresses who never tempted him so well. He raised himself on one elbow and used his knee to gently urge hers apart. "You will tell me if I hurt you."

She nodded.

Restell did not believe her, but he could do no more than extract her promise. He laid his hand on her shoulder, passing his thumb across her collarbone. His hand drifted lower slowly, carrying the coverlet and sheet with it until her naked breast was visible through his splayed fingers. Her nipple, puckered and pink, arose at the center of an aureole that was the precise color of the blush he had observed in her cheeks.

He caressed her breast, first the slope, then the underside. He felt her swell slightly beneath his attentive hand. "I mean to kiss you here." But he didn't, not yet. He knew something about preparing his way and meant to do it.

The scent of her filled his nostrils. There was lavender and musk, one light, the other heady, and yet they arose from her skin in a harmony of fragrance. His palm made a pass across her rib cage and the inward curve of her waist. He stroked her hip, her thigh, then with infinite care, between her legs.

She stirred under his hand, restless now and unable to contain it. He watched her face and listened for the sounds that she could not help but make at the back of her throat.

She sucked in a breath as his palm passed over the flat of her abdomen. When he cupped her breast again he bent to kiss it. The suck of his mouth was hot. She arched beside him, wanting and not wanting, but giving him the right to choose for her. He chose not to neglect the other breast.

Restell slipped an arm under her back and fit himself closer, cautious of not lying heavily on her. She accommodated the change by shifting on her side so she faced him. He cupped her bottom. Her hips tilted forward until she was cradling his heavy, swollen sex against her belly and thighs.

He raised the knee he'd insinuated between hers, parting her thighs a fraction wider and slipping his hand into the space he'd made. His light caress rose higher each time he made a pass. He eased his fingers into the soft, springy nest of dark curls between her legs, then slid deeper, searching, finding, stroking until he had wrested a keening little cry from her.

He kissed her then, swallowing that cry, claiming the need and passion that he had coaxed from her as his own. She held his face in her hands and gave all to him willingly. Heat curled inside her, flushing color into her skin that he found so perfectly suited to her cheeks. She was like a pale pink rose, and where he caressed her most intimately her flesh had much in common with the velvet petals of that flower.

"It must be now," he whispered against her mouth.

"All right."

The simplicity of her response nearly undid him. Restell hitched her upper leg over his thigh, then guided himself into her. He watched her closely, anticipating resistance, even fear. She showed neither. Except to catch her lower lip between her teeth, she gave no sign of discomfort. When he judged she was ready, he turned her so she was finally under him and seated himself fully between her open thighs.

Her eyes, already so wide at the center as to be nearly colorless, widened further, this time starting with the lift of her eyebrows and lashes. Her nostrils flared slightly as she caught and held her breath. She shifted, lifting her hips for a moment, then raising her knees. Her heels found purchase in the mattress and bedsheets. Her palms slid from his shoulders, to his chest, then on either side of his ribs until they rested at his

hips. It was all done in an effort to accommodate his entry, and
none of it was the least bit conscious on her part.

"I seem to know what to do," she whispered, imparting this
as the profound revelation it was to her. It was then that
Restell moved the narrowest fraction and her body contracted
around him. Her mouth formed a perfect O of surprise.

Restell's eyes closed momentarily, his self-control mastered with great effort. "You do." His voice, then his kiss, was
rough, and she answered in kind. When he broke away, his
breathing was harsh. "You certainly do."

"The illustrations I studied did not show me this."

"That's because you didn't go to school at Hambrick."

Emma was uncertain what that meant. It flitted through her
mind to ask him, but he began to move and the thought she
had became as nothing. His hips lifted then thrust, rocking
her, and she became a counterpoint to that rhythm, rising and
falling with each beat of his body.

Her fingers tightened; the nails made half-moon indenta-
tions in his flesh. She closed her eyes, all feeling now. Her
skin seemed stretched too tautly to contain her much longer.
Heat flickered, but there was no flame. It rolled through her
in waves, every crest rising like a crescendo, leaving pleasure
behind when one broke. She welcomed each tug on her
senses, the spark that was part excited nerve and the rest that
was nervous excitement.

Emma could not say when she stopped riding the wave and
began climbing, only that something had changed and where
she thought there might be a peak was naught but a plateau.
Her hands dropped from Restell's hips to the bed. She clutched
the sheets in her fists and held on.

Restell plunged deeply. Once. Twice. He watched her face,
wanting more for her. He wanted . . . Cursing softly, he felt
the rhythm of his thrusts change, becoming quick and shallow and beyond what little control he had left. His climax approaching, he surrendered to it because no other course was
possible.

He spilled his seed, remembering at the last moment not to

rest himself heavily upon her. He collapsed to one side of Emma's still body and withdrew more quickly than was his desire. Out of the corner of his eye he saw her inching the sheet upward to cover herself. He lifted his hip, then his leg to make it easier for her to take back what covers he had stolen in the tangle of their limbs.

Restell felt his heartbeat slow and his faintly ragged breathing quiet. Emma had the sheet bunched in both fists just above her breasts, and she was regarding him with a certain wariness.

"That is not the expression I'd hoped to inspire," he said.

Emma said nothing, though she continued to stare at him.

"Have I given you fear of me after all?"

She shook her head.

"You will have to tell me what you're thinking, Emma. I cannot divine your thoughts."

Still, she hesitated. Her eyes narrowed a bit as she searched his face. "I am wondering if you are all of a piece," she said finally. "You shouted, you know. And it seemed as if you might have been in pain. I thought perhaps it was I who hurt you."

Restell might have howled with laughter if she had not been so grave in her concern. Turning on his side, he slipped one arm under his pillow, raising his head slightly while he reached for her with the other. He laid his hand over her clenched fists. "I don't know that pleasure such as you gave me has ever been pretty, but I am certain it is rarely quiet."

"Then you enjoyed it?"

"Yes," he said honestly. "Except for knowing that you did not. I am sorry for that, Emma. I wanted it to be different."

"It was not so painful as you were wont to believe. You made it quite tolerable."

He grinned crookedly. "Now you damn me with very faint praise."

"Oh, but I did not mean—"

Restell put a finger to her lips to stop her explanation. "I think it is for me to explain, better yet, to demonstrate." He pried her fingers carefully from the sheet so that he might slip his hand under it. His fingertips glided between her breasts to her navel, then lower still. He cupped her mons. It was damp with the musk-scented dew of her previous excitement. The velvet folds were still as soft as they had been, but now they were wet. His fingers spread these lips in search of the hooded bud between them. He only had to graze the surface to elicit a response from her.

"See?" he said gently. "It is not possible to be quiet, not if the thing is done well." He leaned toward her and whispered in her ear. "Shall I make you scream, Emma?"

He could not do that, she told herself. And if he thought he could, it was because he had so little experience with women of her resolve and too much experience with opera dancers.

Restell observed the firm set of her jaw. "I think you mean to challenge me," he said. "Good for you. It will only make what is inevitable that much sweeter." The look she flashed him let him know she had misunderstood. She was too naive to comprehend that he was talking about her satisfaction, not his own.

His hand continued its gentle manipulation while he gauged the nuances of her every response. He listened for the subtle changes in her breathing and watched the fractional parting of her lips. She had taken up the sheet again, and her fists alternately loosened and tightened their grip. Sometimes she worried her lower lip; other times she dampened the upper one with the tip of her tongue. He judged it was better for her when she showed the ridge of her teeth. He applied just that much more pressure to see it again.

Emma's hips jerked. The movement was not in avoidance of his caress but in wanting more of it. She was vaguely aware that half-formed thoughts became unintelligible phrases whenever she spoke aloud. Although she had little understanding for what she said, Restell was fluent in the language.

What Emma did recognize was the slow, sweet climb that led to her eventual return to the plateau. The difference was that when she reached that plain there was no moment to collect herself. This time she did not simply linger there. This time she was urged to climb higher.

Emma felt every muscle grow taut, all of them drawn in such a fashion by Restell's insistent, intimate caress. She threw back her head as much as she was able and pushed her heels deep into the bedding. She released the sheet and made to reach for him, though her intent was not clear even to herself. The effort came to nothing. Her hands fell to her sides and the fingers splayed wide. Her lips parted wider than before and the breath she had captured in her lungs was released.

The short burst of sound she emitted had a pitch that might very well have made it a scream.

"Well?" Restell waited to pose the question until Emma's breathing had calmed. He determined that the fact that she was still flushed a deep rose was no deterrent to speech.

Emma looked at him askance. "You are a trifle too superior for my tastes. It is not becoming."

"You tempered your outburst beautifully," he said. "A carefully modulated trill."

She continued to regard him suspiciously. "Did you say a carefully modulated *thrill*?"

"That also, I suspect."

Emma was sufficiently moved to poke him in the ribs with her elbow.

Restell had not thought it possible to manage a wince and a chuckle at the same time, but he did both. "Why did you do that?"

"Because I don't have a fork."

He pulled her close and kissed her saucy mouth, then lingered there because the taste of her was so fine. When he raised his head, he saw she was smiling rather smugly. It occurred that she had wanted to provoke him to just this end. There was naught he could do but surrender to her. "I am convinced you are in every way my better. There is no need to be smug about it."

"Women are not smug," she said. "We are haughty."

Restell sat up and took her by the hand. "This way, your haughtiness. There are matters that must be attended." He allowed Emma to take the sheet with her as he pulled her out of bed, but when wrapping it around her became a task she could barely manage, he found her chemise and presented it to her. While she slipped it over her head, he located his shirt draping over one of the chairs and put it on. He led her into the dressing room where he poured water into a basin and tossed in a sponge.

"For your ablutions," he said. "The screen is behind you in the event you are still in a modest frame of mind. If you are not, I will be happy to do the—" He stopped because she had already fled behind the screen. Restell crossed his arms and leaned against the washstand, content to watch the slim silhouette she made on the screen's silk fabric. She set one foot on a stool, then raised the hem of her chemise to the level of her thigh. Water dripped in the basin as she squeezed water from the sponge. She touched it to her inner thigh, drawing it up her leg, then for no reason that he could discern, she stopped.

Emma could not say what suddenly caused her skin to prickle, but she knew to pay attention to that discomfort. She was aware of her surroundings in a way she had not been before. The candlelight behind her, her shadow on the screen, the provocative picture that she made poised as she was to begin her ablutions.

"You are watching me, aren't you?"

Restell knew immediately that he had made a grave error in judgment. "I'm leaving," he said. He exited the room quickly, closing the door behind him.

Emma looked around the screen to make certain he was gone before she applied the damp sponge to her nether parts. That this was a private, personal act did not entirely explain her reaction. She felt violated and more than a little ill. When she wrung out the sponge a second time, she realized her hands were trembling.

It was difficult for Emma not to rush her ministrations. She was horribly aware of being alone though not of any specific danger. It seemed to her that she could no longer draw a full breath, and her chest ached with the pressure building inside it. Her field of vision was limited by darkness at the periphery.

"Emma?"

She jerked at the sound of her name. Restell was inquiring after her. Had she been in here so long, then? How had time fled when she was unable to account for it? She glanced down at herself and saw she was no longer holding the sponge nor even standing behind the screen. She was sitting on a stool, her knees drawn close to her chest. The sponge was in the basin that was now on the floor beside her, and what was in her hand was a towel. She stared at it, unable to grasp the import of what she was seeing. Almost against her will, she felt the length of it and realized it was damp. She had already dried herself.

"Emma?" Restell called again. He hesitated to knock because he had seen the consequences of raising that sound to her consciousness. He held the handle, debating whether he should turn it and enter without her permission.

"I require but another moment," she said.

Another moment? "Forgive me," Restell said. "You were gone such a time that I feared all was not well."

Emma stood and found her brush in the case where her maid had left it. She picked it up and quickly ran it through her hair. Her robe, she recalled, was in the large armoire. She took it out, slipped into it, and belted it on her way to open the door. Restell stood directly in her path on the other side when she opened it. It required considerable effort not to push him out of the way.

Instead, she forced a smile. "You may wish you had arranged for me to have my own dressing room. I shall endeavor to be more mindful of my time in the future."

Restell was tempted to seize her by the shoulders while he studied her face. He had to be satisfied with a cursory inspection before she slipped past him and headed directly for the bed. He did not think he was mistaken in his assessment: her eyes and her smile were both a shade too bright.

Emma kept her back to Restell as she straightened the bed-clothes. After a few moments of this activity with no word passing between them, she heard him close the door to the dressing room. She risked a glance over her shoulder and saw that he had disappeared. It was then that she felt free to sag against the bed and put her head in her hands. Not knowing when Restell would return, weeping was a luxury she could ill afford.

She tried to think of what she could tell him that would explain what had happened in the dressing room, but no explanation occurred to her. Even the truth did not suffice, not when it pointed to the very real possibility that she was going quite mad. Restell would want to do something. It was in his nature to make things right, to return balance where it had been lost. But what if he failed? What if the assurances he offered were merely platitudes and there was nothing he could do? Things could not always be made better. He might be able to find her attackers, but it did not mean that he could save her.

Emma was not yet prepared to tell him that or why it was so. The risk was too great—for both of them.

Restell thought that Emma would be abed when he returned to their room, but she was sitting up in the wing chair he had occupied earlier that morning. She had a book in her lap, and he recognized it as one his sister Wynetta had recommended: *Nightmare Abbey*. He'd had it for several years without opening it. Emma, he noticed, had not opened it either.

"Gothic novels are not to your taste?" He saw her brow pucker. It cleared only when he gestured to her lap. She could have given him no better indication of her mind being somewhere other than in this room.

"Oh, this," she said, lifting the book. "I cannot decide if it is worth the effort. Can you recommend it?"

Restell shook his head. "Wynetta gave it to me. I had forgotten that I brought it here."

"Perhaps you should return it."

"She thinks she gave it to Imogene. I am out of it."

Emma managed a small smile. "You are good at giving the appearance of avoiding responsibility."

"Thank you. It requires more in the way of skill than one would think." Restell padded barefoot to the bed and sat down. "Did I tell you how lovely you looked this morning?"

"You may mention it now if you like."

"Lovely," he said. "My father remarked on it. I overheard him tell Mother."

"Your father is very kind."

Restell hooked his heels on the bed frame and rested his forearms on his knees. "I think you have a previous acquaintance with my father. Am I wrong?"

"You're not wrong, but what makes you say so?"

"You informed me when we met that it was some member of my family who told you how to find me. I watched you with all of them today, and the only person with whom you struck an easy conversation was my father."

"Oh, I hope I was not so stiff with the others that it was evident to all."

"You were cordial and gracious, and no slight could ever be made regarding your manner. It is only that with my father you seemed at rest, and he did not speak of politics once. There is something worth noting in that."

"I met your father at the Greenaways. It was an afternoon musicale and a soprano entertained us. Sir Geoffrey and I struck up a conversation. Perhaps it will not surprise that he spoke at length about all of you, and he demonstrated a perfectly delightful sense of humor in telling his stories. I did not know then that I would have need to recall any of the details of his discourse, but when Dr. Bettany mentioned your name, I knew where you could be found. Your father seemed to find the idea that you lived under Ferrin's roof rather amusing, though I did not understand why that might be so until today."

"Remarkable. I would not have suspected he was the source of your information. I wonder if Mother knows he converses with young ladies about peculiarities in the family."

"I don't know," Emma said. "But I should be put out with you if you tell her. He purchased my uncle's painting for her. Did you know that?"

"Did he? She never said. She told me she wanted it and that he indulged her, but I didn't realize that he'd made the purchase himself. Isn't he a deep one? Secretive about his own business and a veritable wag when it comes to the rest of the family."

Emma was certain she did not want to entertain any conversation that dealt with keeping secrets. "Do you regret that Ferrin and his wife could not attend our wedding?"

"It is not precisely regret. I would not act differently tomorrow than I have today so regret seems like an indulgence. What I wish is that he was more often in town and that of necessity I did not have to exclude him."

"Will he understand?"

"He will understand perfectly."

Emma waited. It seemed he was on the verge of saying more, then he caught himself and the moment passed. Emma glanced toward the mantel where an ormolu clock ticked off the time. It was gone ten, late enough for them to retire if they had not already slept the better part of the day away. She at least had gotten up to greet Bettis and sort through her clothes when her trunks arrived; Restell had slept like the dead, making up for every hour lost on the road between London and Walthamstow.

Restell was not privy to the leapfrogging of Emma's thoughts, so he was not prepared for her to ask about the drawings he'd carried back from Walthamstow.

"May I see them?" she asked. "You said you would show them to me when we were in your home." She raised her hands to indicate the room. "Here we are."

"It is late, Emma."

"I am not tired."

"Another time."

She was not entirely sorry that he denied her the opportunity. "Well, then, do you suppose that we might find something to eat? I am astonishingly hungry. I do not think we ate more than a third of what was on our plates. "

Restell stood and approached her chair. He removed the book from her lap and held out his hands for her to take. "That is because we satisfied a different hunger. Come. Mrs. Wescott will have left us something in the kitchen."

Chapter 10

Emma wondered how her marriage might have been different if she had been honest with Restell. If she had been more resistant to his proposal, would he have pressed for the truths she concealed? It was not that she had lied to him but that she had omitted so much—and continued to go on in that manner.

He did not press, a fact that she found curious in its own right. Did he truly imagine he knew her so well, or was it that he was waiting for her to come forward? The morning after their wedding night, she'd awakened with the return of such dread that throwing off the covers required an act of supreme will. Restell had seemed oblivious to her distress, and she was both relieved and angered by it.

She hardly knew what to do with herself. He'd presented her with a house that was already well run by a staff that was almost slavishly loyal to him. They anticipated his needs in a way that she doubted she ever would, even if she was of a particular mind to do so. She found herself often going to the house where she was needed. Her uncle's home provided some small respite for her. Passing part of each day in Sir Arthur's studio was preferable to wandering about Restell's home at sixes and sevens.

She was prickly and out of sorts and could not seem to help herself. Again and again, her thoughts flitted back to the time she could not account for on their wedding night. She saw herself standing behind the dressing screen, then sitting on the other side of it with no memory of what she'd done in between. Daydreaming did not account for it. There was a sickness upon her, and she could not hope to keep it hidden forever.

Restell did not remain oblivious. Emma watched him grow bewildered by her uncertain moods. He approached her directly, then with kid gloves. He invited her to tell him what manner of things troubled her. He played to what remained of her humor with his own. He escorted her to the theatre, but she found the crowd uncomfortable in spite of Restell's constant presence. He kept his promise to return with her to the park, and they took the phaeton there on warm evenings. He never begged off if she suggested they play a game of chess or cards. When she finally discovered how he earned his considerable income investing and recommending investments to his family and others, he allowed her to sit with him poring over newspapers and journals and daily reports from the insurance houses and banks. It was the one interest she'd never imagined they would share.

She had married a kind and generous man, intense and intensely curious. She'd known that at the outset and wished she might complement him in that regard. Emma witnessed the arrival of strangers to their door, men and women like her who came to him for help, sent there by a friend or acquaintance or another stranger who had once benefited from Restell's intervention. She knew he did not agree to act on every situation that was presented to him. No such commitment was possible. For all that he seemed to have an informant or foot soldier in every part of London, he was still but one man. She had never considered how it might settle on his conscience to turn people away. In contrast, her own concerns seemed trifling and selfish.

She was careful not to place demands upon him. There was often one or two nights each week that he had to leave the house. She always knew when he'd been to a gaming hell but not where he went on other occasions. She admired him for maintaining the confidences of the people he helped, but she was also kept distant by it.

Several different times she asked about the drawings he'd had made at Walthamstow. He always found some reason not to show them to her. They avoided speaking about her abduction, though Emma did not have the sense that it was for the same reasons that her uncle and Marisol never spoke of it. She did not believe that Restell was willing her to forget what had happened, but rather that he was willing her to remember.

It frightened her in ways she could not describe, and the shame of what she felt kept her silent.

For his part, Restell was ever mindful of the tactics that Emma used to set herself from him. Sometimes it was a word exchanged; sometimes it was a word left unsaid. He knew the moment she'd stepped out of the dressing room on their wedding night that something had been profoundly altered. He apologized for his blunder, and she graciously accepted it— even made light of it—but Restell came to understand over the course of the next days and weeks that what had been changed was Emma's thinking about herself and their marriage and no apology, no matter how sincerely made, could turn her thoughts to make all right again.

Restell was not accustomed to feeling helpless. It did not rest easily on his shoulders. He would have rather borne the weight of her fears than be forced to watch her shoulder them alone. She was maddening. She was afraid. Mostly, Restell thought, she was inconsolable.

He was never so far from her as when he held her in his arms. She did not deny him. He thought it probably did not occur to her that she could. In their bed she turned to him easily, yet held herself from him at the same time. It seemed to Restell that Emma became less a participant in making love and more an observer of it. She remained curious but not connected, eager but not engaged. She might have been any whore and that had no appeal to him.

There were glimpses of the woman he'd married from time

to time. When her guard was lowered, usually late in the evening, he could surprise a genuine smile from her or coax her to laughter. One night he awakened from a pleasantly erotic dream to discover that her hand was nestled between his thighs. He'd placed one hand on her wrist, though whether his intent had been to keep her there or remove her was never fully answered. Her fingers curled around his rigid cock and his last coherent thought dissolved.

It had been Emma who'd given him pleasure on that occasion, though he couldn't say how conscious she was of it. She seemed to linger in that drowsy state between sleep and wakefulness. She spoke in hushed tones, most often with her eyes closed, and when her eyes were open they were openly wanting. But they wanted *him*. He did not mistake that, and it gave him hope.

The following morning he realized he had been naive. Within minutes of waking, he observed that the breach between them had not been narrowed. Indeed, it was wider than ever.

Restell came to understand then that he was a man very much in need of a bridge.

The offices of Napier and Walpole were a hive of activity. Located only a few short streets from the Thames, they were ideally situated to receive news of arriving ships. They had a sophisticated system of communication involving runners and beacons that went all the way to the sea, and now that the war on the continent was ended, they received reliable reports from Marseilles, Genoa, and Athens. Even the Russian ports on the Baltic were not beyond their reach.

Restell's appointment with Mr. Martin Johnston was for the one o'clock hour, but Restell purposely arrived early to make his observations. Johnston was one of more than a dozen clerks who worked hunched over small desks making their calculations. Every desk faced the same direction: the spacious and finely furnished room that had once been the office shared by Mr. Napier and Mr. Walpole. Their heirs now held claim to the investment and insurance house and after so many generations, the surnames were no longer those of the founders. Still, there was respect for tradition because the brass plates on the great mahogany desks—the only desks to face each other—still read Mr. Napier and Mr. Walpole.

Restell was a frequent visitor to the firm and well-known to the managing partners. He was shown every courtesy upon his arrival and entertained polite inquiries about his health, his newly married state, and with some effort at delicacy, when they might expect him to make another investment. He had inquiries of his own, but his manner of asking questions was so far and away more subtle than what had been put to him that the partners were unaware of the interrogation.

The unusual feature in the office of Napier and Walpole was a large window set into the interior wall that allowed one or both partners to observe the clerks simply by standing at their desks. Restell had the same view each time he made an excuse to rise. He never caught Johnston out. The man remained stooped over his work, his pen moving steadily across the page as he made his entries. If Johnston was concerned about the interview, he gave no indication of it.

Promptly at one, Mr. Johnston left his desk and appeared at the partners' door. Introductions were formally made, then Restell and Johnston were allowed the use of a private room where business affairs of a sensitive, often secret nature were conducted.

"It is good of you to meet with me on so little notice," Restell said, indicating that Johnston could seat himself anywhere at the long table. When the clerk made his choice, Restell took the chair directly opposite him.

"I was encouraged to do so," Johnston told him. "Your patronage is much valued by Napier and Walpole. How may I serve you?"

"I have not come on a matter of my usual business, although I am prepared to make a substantial investment in the *Numidia* to compensate you and the firm for your time. I will recommend that ten shares are placed in your name."

"That is extremely generous of you."

Restell was impressed with Martin Johnston's composure. He carried himself quite correctly, with none of the obsequious demeanor that Restell had had occasion to observe in some of Johnston's colleagues. He was obviously a proud gentleman, and Restell had cause to wonder if that was his nature or a consequence of being released from Sir Arthur's employment. The latter would have broken some men, but there were also those who would refuse to be damaged by it, especially if they knew themselves to be innocent.

Johnston presented the solemn countenance of a man who did not smile easily. The evidence that he was in or nearing his fiftieth year was in his graying temples and the lines engraved about his eyes and downturned mouth. He was slimly built, altogether average in height and weight, and wearing his black frock coat and unimaginatively tied stock, he appeared little different than every other employee of Napier and Walpole.

"Perhaps you are aware, Mr. Johnston, that I recently had the good fortune to marry."

"I was not aware, sir, but may I wish you happy?"

"You may. It has been some six weeks. I confess, I had every intention of visiting you before now, but my wife discouraged me."

Johnston's brow knit in a perfect puzzlement. "I'm afraid I don't understand, sir."

"You are acquainted with my wife, Mr. Johnston. She is Emmalyn Hathaway . . . Emmalyn Gardner now."

"Miss Hathaway." Johnston's dour countenance was dramatically altered by his broad, satisfied smile. "Oh, but this is good news indeed. She has always been a favorite. It has been some time since I have had occasion to see her. The wedding preparations, I suppose, account for her absence." His smile faded as a troubling thought occurred to him. "Or perhaps it is that I gave her offense. She never mentioned her engagement. You say she discouraged your visit?"

"She did, though not for any reason you might conceive. I have come on a matter that concerns her uncle." Restell did not miss the immediate shuttering of Johnston's features. That carefully set expression did not change even after Restell revealed that his visit also concerned his wife. "I cannot discuss the details, Mr. Johnston, but I believe such information as you were privy to as Sir Arthur's man of affairs could be helpful."

"I will not discuss Sir Arthur Vega. I understand why Miss Hathaway attempted to dissuade you. Whatever you wish to know, you will have to apply to your wife for answers."

Restell was not deterred. "She believes you are innocent of the accusations Sir Arthur leveled against you."

"I *am* innocent, so it is of no consequence what Miss Hathaway . . . forgive me . . . what Mrs. Gardner believes."

"I think it is of consequence to you. You value her good opinion—as do I. She told me that when the accusations were first made you assigned some fault to her. After all, she did usurp your position as Sir Arthur's most trusted agent, and you taught her every skill she needed to do so. In your place I would think the very same."

"It was a moment's anger that made me speak so incautiously. She is as innocent as I am."

"How can you be so certain?"

Johnston said nothing.

"It is most damning, I think, that she benefited from your release."

Johnston started to rise. "I do not wish to hear what you think, Mr. Gardner. I have made my peace with your wife. Indeed, I have made my peace with the whole of what happened."

Restell pointed to the chair that Johnston was bent on vacating. "Please sit, Mr. Johnston. I will determine when the interview is concluded."

The clerk sat and stared stonily across the table.

Restell continued as if there had been no interruption. "I have wondered if you could be sufficiently moved by your reversal of fortune to exact some payment from my wife."

"Payment? What manner of payment?"

"Money is the usual request."

"Are you suggesting that I have engaged in blackmail?"

"Perhaps a favor," Restell said. "On occasion a favor may be granted. Have you asked my wife for such a favor?"

"You insult both of us."

"Revenge is also payment in kind. What of revenge, Mr. Johnston?"

"No shares are worth this affront. I beg you keep them and permit me to return to my work. It is infinitely more satisfying sharing a room with fourteen of my fellow clerks than remaining in your company."

Restell hardened himself to finish. "Tell me why you are so certain that my wife is blameless."

"Do you doubt her character?" Johnston rubbed his forehead as his brow furrowed. "I believe she's made a grave error in judgment in accepting your offer of marriage."

"Something more than my wife's character is at stake here," Restell said.

Johnston simply set his jaw.

Restell knew then that he would not be able to pry it open.

Emma recognized Restell's voice as he greeted Marisol in the hallway outside the entrance to the studio. In anticipation of his visit, she draped a cloth over the easel and turned to clean brushes at the table. Restell did not linger long with Marisol. He was halfway up the stairs before she finished sorting the brushes.

"I am becoming fond of the fragrance of turpentine," he said, brushing her proffered cheek with his lips. It was a cool, perfunctory kiss of the kind they shared more and more frequently. "Where is Sir Arthur?"

Emma pointed to the sofa where her uncle was sleeping.

"He began painting early today and lay down only a short time ago."

Restell examined the posture that sleep had visited upon the artist. "He will suffer a stiff neck if he remains there for long."

"Perhaps I will wake him before I go. You are here earlier than I expected. Have you concluded your business so soon, then?"

Restell set himself upon the stool at the table. "It did not require as long as I thought it would. Mr. Johnston sends his regards."

Emma nearly upended the jar of turpentine. She managed to catch it before it tipped and placed it firmly at the center of the table until she had need of it again. "That is where you were this afternoon? You never said a word."

"You did not inquire." Breakfast had been a quiet affair this morning. The distance between them was far greater than the length of the table.

"You know I wish you hadn't gone," she said. "But I'd hoped that if you felt you must, you would have asked me to accompany you."

"You would not have tolerated my ill manners."

Emma's shoulders sagged a bit as she set the brushes to soak. She did not look at Restell. "You behaved badly?"

He did not apologize for it. "It was necessary. You will not be astonished that he acquitted himself. He defended you most ardently."

Emma's voice conveyed all of her disappointment in her husband. "Oh, Restell. What did you say to him?"

"I asked him if he suspected you of having played a part in his dismissal, and when he said he did not, I pointed out the reasons that he should. He refused to name you."

"Of course he refused," she said quietly. "I had nothing to do with it, and he is not a man who lies to save himself. Was it so important that you must needs attack him?"

"He has a powerful motive to hurt you, Emma. I cannot dismiss that."

"He would never hurt me." She reached behind her and

tugged on her apron strings, then impatiently removed the apron. "He would not hurt anyone."

"I believe you."

"Now," Emma said. "You believe me now." She hung her apron on one of the wall pegs before she turned on Restell. "Because you have judged it for yourself. Why could you not accept my sense of the matter and spared him?"

"Because I no longer trust your sense on this matter or any other."

She stared at him.

"Bloody hell, Emma." Dispirited, Restell closed his eyes and rubbed them with his thumb and middle finger. He could not say he didn't mean what he said, only that he hadn't meant to say it. He let his hand fall away and held her wounded gaze because he owed her that. She did not pretend that he had not hurt her. "I do not know what I should say," he told her.

"Then let silence carry the day. We will both be served better by that." She picked up her paisley shawl and wrapped it around her shoulders, then she stepped past Restell, deliberately not touching him, and started down the stairs.

Restell did not follow immediately. He sat where he was, feet propped on one of the rungs of the stool, and stared off into space.

"You've made rather a mess of things, haven't you?" Sir Arthur Vega pushed himself into a sitting position on the sofa and stuffed a worn, faded pillow behind the small of his back. "And there is no apology that will suffice at this juncture. You will have to do something extraordinary to put yourself in Emmalyn's good graces again."

That was not encouraging. "I don't know what I did to fall out of her good graces."

"We never do."

Restell rested one elbow on the tabletop. "Did you hear the whole of it?"

"Enough." Sir Arthur regarded Restell from beneath his hooded glance. "I understood you to say that you'd met with

Johnston. Frankly, I'm surprised you hadn't done so already. I cannot believe it of the man, but I suppose he should be eliminated as a suspect."

"I allowed Emma to persuade me that he couldn't possibly be a suspect."

"She liked Johnston immensely. It was a blow to her when she learned of his perfidy. To both of us, really."

Restell nodded faintly. "She still visits him. Not recently, of course. Not since her abduction. But before then, she met with him."

"Met with him? Are you sure?"

"He told me. I'm certain he didn't realize that I had no knowledge of it."

"What would have been her purpose?"

"I don't know that she had one beyond visiting a gentleman she considers to be a friend and mentor."

Sir Arthur released a sigh with enough force to vibrate his lips. "I cannot comprehend it myself. She never breathed a word."

"Perhaps she knew you would disapprove."

"The man stole from me. Naturally I would disapprove."

"The evidence is damning," Restell agreed. "You have the statements of your patrons. I imagine they provided you with the bills of sale that point to the discrepancies between what they paid and what Johnston recorded in your books."

"Oh, yes. Neven presented it all to me and explained his suspicions. No charge was leveled until then."

"I thought that must be the way of it." Restell offered no other comment. His gaze wandered to the easel. "Emma said you've been painting all day."

"Indeed. I must take advantage of the fine weather as it makes the rheumatism tolerable."

"May I see? Emma says so little about your work." At Sir Arthur's frown, he added, "Pray, do not take offense. She says little on any subject these days."

"It is a touch of the melancholia, I think. One must remain

hopeful that it will pass. She puts me in mind of how she was after her parents died."

Restell nodded slowly, thoughtfully. *I mourn for the loss of self,* she'd told him once. And later in the park, watching a pair of young ladies laugh with abandon as they playfully pressed themselves into the wind, she'd said, *I want to know that freedom again.*

"You can view the painting, if you like," Sir Arthur said.

Lost in reflection, Restell was several moments in responding. He ran one hand through his hair, leaving it only slightly more furrowed than his brow. "Pardon?"

"The painting. You asked to see it."

"So I did." Restell dropped his feet to the floor and pushed the stool under the table as he stood. "Has someone commissioned it?"

"No. It is for my pleasure alone, although it will also be my pleasure to see it sold."

Restell carefully raised the drop cloth that covered the painting and threw it over the back of the easel. For the longest time, he could only stare as he was transported to the very place he had been thinking about only moments earlier.

Every aspect of the scene before him was familiar. He recognized the beginnings of an overcast sky on the horizon and sensed the movement of air in the swaying boughs of the oaks and pines and chestnuts. There were carriages on the gravel path, one in the distance moving away, the other approaching. A shadow fell across the carefully manicured lawn at the heart of the park, and there, just at edge of the painting were two lovely young ladies facing down the wind. One of them still managed to retain her bonnet, but the other had been captured on canvas in the act of trying to catch hers. She was portrayed almost as though she were airborne, her slim figure so light and delicate that she barely touched the ground. Her fingertips were fully extended in the pursuit of her bonnet's long, curling ribbons. Most telling was her face, for her features portrayed no hint of frustration with the effort she was making. Her impulsive pursuit was all delight.

Restell knew that just beyond the painting's aspect was a gentleman rogue with an ivory-knobbed cane who would rescue the bonnet and the lady. What would happen after that he couldn't say, but he suspected the gentleman, the lady, and the lady's good friend would find shelter from the storm and find enjoyment in the vagaries of nature that brought them together.

Sir Arthur cocked his head to one side, studying Restell's reaction. "You will have to say something, Mr. Gardner. For myself, I am yet uncertain of this new direction in my work. It is more in the nature of an experiment. As I said, for my pleasure. Perhaps it is not to your taste."

Restell stepped back, regarding the painting from a slightly different angle. "It is exactly to my taste," he said quietly. He heard the reverence in his voice and was not embarrassed by it. What he observed in the painting, the naked expression of a moment's abandon and joy, filled him with awe.

He finally turned to Sir Arthur. "You will have no difficulty finding a buyer for this piece."

"Do you think so? Frankly, I have wondered, though I often entertain these doubts until the moment the painting is sold."

"What does Emma think?"

"She is guarded in her assessment."

"Truly? This work is of a piece with the painting my mother purchased."

"The *Fishing Village*." Sir Arthur moved from the sofa to stand beside Restell and study the painting from the same vantage point. "You are correct, of course, but I should like to hear what leads you to that conclusion."

"I am no expert."

"And that is of no consequence."

"Well, it is primarily the emotion of the piece. I am not familiar with the entire body of your work, but it seems the choice of paints here is a departure for you. The colors are particularly vibrant. They are not quite as they appear in nature, are they? Yet they are not unnatural. I am put in mind of a dream." Restell shrugged. "Perhaps it is accounted for because this is not a portrait."

Sir Arthur considered this last observation for a moment before he answered. "No, I do not think that accounts for it. Tell me about the emotion you observe."

Restell could have told him that it was not observed emotion that set the painting apart, but felt emotion. He held that comment, appreciating for the first time that it would not necessarily be comprehended by this artist. "There is humor in the *Fishing Village*, or at least I found it there. Here it is joy of the moment."

"You do not find it disturbing?"

"Disturbing? No, not at all."

"I wondered if perhaps it is not a trifle vulgar. Does it strike you as such?"

"It is not a word that comes to mind."

"These young women here . . ." Sir Arthur pointed vaguely at the canvas. "You do not think they appear to be lacking a certain moral firmness?"

"May I speak plainly?"

"Please."

"Are you asking me if these women look like tarts?"

Ruddy color suffused Sir Arthur's thin face. "I suppose I am."

"Then, no. I do not see them at all in that light." Restell's eyes darted between the painting and Sir Arthur, and he observed that Sir Arthur's study was as intent on the canvas as his own had been. "Who else has seen this?" asked Restell.

"Mr. Charters has had occasion to visit."

"While Emma was here?"

"He may have. I cannot say."

"Your daughter? Has she seen it?"

"Marisol rarely ventures up here."

It was not precisely an answer to his question, but Restell let it pass. "Servants?"

"No. Emmalyn takes care of this room for me. I don't trust anyone else to leave things as I like."

Restell's lips thinned a little, but he bit back the comment that came to the tip of his tongue and asked instead, "What of Lady Rivendale? I understand you have been together of late."

Sir Arthur chuckled. "So Emmalyn is not entirely silent."

"I had it from my mother."

"Oh. Well, she is quite right. The countess is altogether fascinating, I must say. She has been here on several occasions, but I cannot recall if she viewed this particular work."

Restell had heard enough. "I apologize for disturbing your rest, but I am glad of your permission to view this latest piece. I'm afraid, though, that I must take my leave."

Waving the apology aside, Sir Arthur said, "I wish you success of this evening."

"Success?"

"With Emmalyn . . . returning to her good graces."

Restell considered this a moment before he answered. "What I need to do, Sir Arthur, cannot be accomplished in a single evening, but you have made me hopeful that it *can* be accomplished."

Emma was waiting for Restell in the entrance hall. When he appeared at the top of the stairs she nodded to the butler and the door was opened for her. She stepped outside unassisted and went to the waiting carriage. She was already situated inside by the time Restell reached the doorway.

Restell observed Emma's progress with interest. Anger had its place, he supposed. It certainly had a liberating effect on his wife.

Following at a deliberately slow pace, Restell could see Emma's profile through the window. She stared straight ahead, purposely not looking in his direction, he thought. Just above an hour ago, her behavior would have irritated him. Now it merely made him smile.

He schooled that smile before he boarded the carriage. There was nothing to be gained by allowing his sudden good humor to nettle her.

"You spent rather more time in the studio than I would have

credited," Emma said. Although she made an attempt to communicate a neutral tone, there was still a clipped cadence that let her know she fell far short of the mark. Fearful she would simply begin to weep, she could not bear to look in Restell's direction.

"It was not my intention to linger. Sir Arthur awakened."

"He awakened?"

"He did not comment on our disagreement," Restell said, lying without compunction. "I think he did not hear us."

"Or perhaps he considered it the wiser course to remain well out of it."

"Naturally that is a possibility." Restell leaned into one corner of the bench and tipped the brim of his hat forward so that it shaded his eyes. He folded his arms across his chest. "I think your uncle is quite taken with Lady Rivendale. He speaks kindly of her."

"So that is what detained you," she said.

"You sound relieved."

"Do I?"

"Was there another topic perhaps that you feared was under discussion?"

Emma put forth a remarkably even voice when she replied. "You entertain peculiar notions."

He shrugged.

Emma's jaw tightened at what she considered to be a lack of response. "Will you not tell me what he said to you about the countess?"

"Of course. He said that she has visited his studio on more than one occasion."

"Truly?"

"You didn't know?"

"No. I knew she visited, but I was unaware that she'd made the climb to the studio."

"It suggests there is mutual interest."

"They share a passion for painting," said Emma.

One of Restell's eyebrows kicked up. "When I spoke of mutual interest, I did not mean painting. I believe they share passion."

Emma felt heat rising in her cheeks. She glanced at Restell and saw that he was not looking at her. His eyes in fact were closed. "Did he say anything else?"

"I believe he called her fascinating."

"Fascinating."

"Indeed. Has he never said as much to you?"

"He has only mentioned that he enjoys her company. Marisol has more to say but very little of it is fit to repeat."

"Is that why you've never spoken about your uncle and Lady Rivendale?"

Emma frowned. "You have someone watching my uncle every time he leaves his home. What can I tell you that you don't already know?"

Restell tipped his hat back and regarded Emma frankly. "No one is watching your uncle any longer, at least when he is gone from home. It isn't necessary. Not since we were wed."

"I don't understand."

"Sir Arthur is not at risk for harm, Emma. Not his physical person. He could be immeasurably harmed by you or Marisol being hurt, but he does not require someone looking to his safety."

"You are quite certain?"

"Yes."

Emma nodded slowly. "Well, that is good, then," she said quietly. "You have less with which to concern yourself. You are still watching Marisol, aren't you?"

"Yes."

"And I am living in your pockets, so all is well."

"Is it? It does not seem that you live in my pockets of late."

Emma glanced out the window as the carriage slowed. The timing of their arrival could not have been more fortuitous as far as she was concerned. When the door opened she quickly took the exit offered her and hurried up the walk. It was a temporary reprieve at best. She could sense that Restell would have his reckoning.

It was not as if she could hide from him, Emma thought

as she was relieved of her bonnet and shawl. He did not precisely dog her steps, but he was already at the foot of the stairs by the time she reached the top. She rang for her maid as soon as she arrived at the suite of rooms she shared with Restell. Her pounding heart masked the sound of Restell's tread, but she knew that he had to be close. Emma fled into the dressing room and shut the door.

She was a thorough coward, and a glimpse of herself in the cheval glass confirmed it. Beads of perspiration gave her flushed skin a sheen. Tendrils of hair fell raggedly about her face because she had all but torn the bonnet from her head when she'd reached the house. There was a wildness to her eyes that spoke to being hunted and a stillness in her frame that spoke to being found.

The scratching at the door almost caused her knees to buckle. Instead of sinking to the floor, she leaned against the armoire for support.

"Mrs. Gardner?"

Tears of relief welled in Emma's eyes. It was Bettis, not Restell, at the door. "A moment, Bettis." Emma poured water into the basin on the washstand, then splashed her face. She remained bent over the stand for several long moments as she collected herself. The weight of dread that made her shoulders stoop and her chest ache gradually lightened so that she was able to stand and draw a full breath. When she was sufficiently calmed, she told Bettis to enter.

Restell dismissed the maid with a pointed look and waited for her to vacate the suite before he opened the door. By then, Emma had called for her a second time. "You will have to be satisfied with my services," he said. "I recall one occasion that you welcomed them."

"I want Bettis." Emma looked past Restell's shoulder. "What have you done with her?"

"Done with her?" Restell shook his head. "Are you able to hear yourself, Emma?"

She could hear herself. She could hear every mean-spirited

thing she thought before she said it and still could not stop. "I don't wish to speak to you."

"Then you don't have to. I will do the speaking. Unless you wish to clap your hands over your ears, you will do the listening."

It was not encouraging that he knew the bent of her mind so well. "I wish to bathe. I smell of turpentine and paint."

"I will not be put off, Emma. If you wish to bathe, then it will be in my presence. You will have to hear me out while you do it."

She squared her shoulders and lifted her chin. "Then I give you joy of the stink of me."

Restell stepped out of the way as she marched determinedly for their bedroom. She looked ill-tempered enough to desire to push him out of the way. "Here?" he asked. "Or our sitting room?"

In way of an answer, she made for the door to the sitting room. She turned on Restell once they were both inside. "Well?"

Restell sighed. "You are purposely making this difficult, more so for yourself than for me. It's precisely what I have come to expect since our wedding night. You need to comprehend, however, that my patience is not infinite."

"And what will you do when you have reached its end?"

"I will tell you what I will *not* do. I will not strike you, Emma. No matter the provocation, I will not raise my hand against you."

"You make it sound as if that's what I want you to do."

"Do I? I suppose that's because I've suspected as much of late. I think you would willingly suffer the blow so that I might suffer in the aftermath. If I can no longer trust myself to deal better with you, you would have your divorce. It makes no sense to try to protect you from others if I cannot protect you from myself."

Emma shook her head, but there was no vehemence behind it. She took a small step backward as though a physical blow had been delivered. Restell reached for her, but she avoided his hand by pivoting suddenly and presenting him with her back.

"Tell me what I've done, Emma. Tell me what I can do. I want to make this right between us."

Emma's fists clenched at her sides. "You cannot make everything right."

Restell took a steadying breath. Already he knew he had begun the thing badly, starting out where he'd meant to end it. "Won't you sit? Please, Emma, allow me to explain."

She hesitated, her head turning sideways as she surveyed her options. Finally, she nodded and went to the upholstered window bench. She plucked a heavily embroidered pillow from the seat and held it in front of her as she sat. Her fingertips ran along the short, fringed ends that bordered all four sides.

Once Restell saw that Emma was settled, he went to the drinks cabinet and poured them each a glass of sherry. He handed her the drink, then stepped back to the sofa where he sat. He sipped his drink, regarding her thoughtfully over the rim of his glass.

"Where is it you go, Emma?"

"I don't know what you mean."

"No, I suppose you don't. I hardly do myself. I watch you slip away, yet I could easily take your hand. You are closer to me when you are gone from home than when we are dining together. What is happening to you no longer happens *only* to you. It is happening to *us,* Emma, and it is happening so quickly that I cannot make any sense of it. We are not grown distant by separate interests and years of disaffection and indifference. Our marriage can only be measured in weeks, not months, and already there is a rift so wide that when we speak there is an echo."

Restell thought she might say something. Her lips parted as though it was her intention, but she stayed the thought and continued to sift the pillow's fringe with her fingertips. He was put in mind of an old Indian gentleman he knew who did the very same with worry beads. Her glass of sherry, he noted, was still untouched. He took another sip from his own glass.

"I have kept things from you," he said. "It has been done of a purpose, but it has failed to make a difference. It seems to me that you should know all."

Emma's fingers stilled. The hand that held the glass of sherry was lifted to her lips. She took a large swallow, then said, "You are speaking of the drawings you brought back from Walthamstow."

"In part, yes. Would you like to see them now?"

"I would have liked to have seen them every other time I asked."

"No. It is no good pretending that it's so. You asked several times, true enough, but you were not prepared any better to view them then than you are now." He held up his hand. "Before you disagree, consider that you have not answered my question in a straightforward manner and allow me to pose it again: Would you like to see them now?"

Emma's hand tightened on the stem of her glass. She worried her bottom lip as she considered the consequences of her answer. She finally nodded.

"I need to hear you say it, Emma."

"Yes," she said. Her lips moved around the word, though it was largely inaudible.

Restell set down his glass and stood. "The drawings are in the library. It will take me but a few moments to retrieve them." He left then, and was as good as his word, returning with the drawings in time to see Emma finish the last of her sherry. He took the glass from her hand, placed it on a nearby table, and sat beside her. The drawings had been rolled into a cylinder and secured by a string. He untied the string, pushed it into his pocket, then unrolled the drawings. They did not remain flattened. As soon as he let go of one end, they snapped into a curl.

"Perhaps if you give them to me one at a time," Emma said. "How many are there?"

"A dozen."

"So many. I hadn't realized."

"They are different perspectives of the countryside around Walthamstow. After speaking to the innkeeper and his wife I was able to narrow the direction from which you approached the inn. Mr. and Mrs. Broadstreet were most eager to assist me. Mr. Broadstreet served as a guide as I tramped around looking for evidence of your passing. He is also the one who suggested Mr. Matlack when I inquired about an artist."

Hoping he had not badly misjudged the timing of his presentation, Restell offered the first sketch for her examination. It was of a wood just beyond Walthamstow. It might have been any stand of trees along almost any route from London, except for the posting at the fork in the road that marked direction and distance to the village.

"Do you recall seeing this?" Restell asked.

"No."

"All right." He gave her another, then another. They reached the fifth one before she reacted to what she saw. Restell removed the watercolor from her hands before she crumpled it. "This cottage?" he asked. "Or another like it? There are many similar in the area."

"No. The exact one you showed me. The little brook that ran next to it, did you notice?"

"Yes."

"That's what I followed when I escaped."

"So you remember that."

"I do now." Emma turned to Restell and regarded him with some astonishment. "How is that possible?"

"I have no idea." He handed her another drawing. "Look at this one. Perhaps it will nudge another memory loose."

Emma shook her head at the pastoral scene he showed her. The gently rolling hills and winding stone fence were unfamiliar to her. "This looks to be a view from an upper window. Is that right?"

"Very good. That is precisely the artist's perspective." He took back the sketch on her lap and gave her yet another. "What of this one?"

The drawing was also from a window view, but this time the artist was almost in the boughs of the trees he drew. The winding brook was just visible beyond one corner of a thickly thatched roof. "I left the cottage by this route," she said slowly. "Your artist is looking out on the same view I had." She poked her finger at the thatching as if she could test the strength. "I did not know if it would support me. It did not look as thick as this when I slid out the window. The kitchen is below, I think. Is that right?"

Restell nodded. "Did you leap to the ground or go to the trees?"

"The trees."

"I thought you might have. I found bits of fabric in the bark that suggested someone had been there. It seemed possible that it might have been you." They had only a few more drawings for her to study. Restell looked from them to Emma and began to shake his head. Her complexion was almost as pale as salt and her breathing was both shallow and rapid. "It is enough," he said.

"I will see all of it." Emma took a deep, calming breath, held it, then released it slowly. As evenly as was possible given her racing heart, she said, "You cannot decide for me, Restell. Not at this juncture."

"Very well." He passed her another. She glanced at it and pushed it back at him. "That is the room where I was held."

He nodded. "And this one?"

It was another view of the wood but from deeper inside it. The cottage could be seen at a distance through a break in the trees. Emma looked at it for a long time. "Who was the artist?" she asked.

"Mr. Matlack."

"Was Mr. Matlack standing in a small clearing here?"

"Yes."

"The cottage is rather more distant than this drawing suggests."

"Mr. Matlack does not have your uncle's skills."

"He did well enough. I recognize this spot. I rested here until daybreak. When the sun rose I could see in which direction the village lay. I made my way there by staying clear of the road."

Restell passed her the last picture. "And what of this place?"

Emma regarded it, but she shook her head from the first. It showed a steep descent to the brook, most of it a rocky incline with occasional tufts of grass sprouting between the stones. "I don't know it. If this is the same brook I followed, then this embankment is beyond where I left the path. What is its significance?"

"It's where Jonathan Kincaid's body was discovered."

Emma was silent for several long seconds absorbing this fact. "His body." She stared at the steep incline rendered in the artist's drawing. "He fell?"

"A logical assumption, and perhaps the one that was intended for others to make, but if it was a fall that broke his neck, it didn't happen here."

"I don't understand."

"Mr. Broadstreet and several villagers told me there was evidence in Kincaid's home to suggest he might have been injured there. Overturned chairs, a cracked wall in the stairwell."

"You saw this?"

"No, everything had been put to rights or repaired by the time I visited. His body was discovered within days of your return to London."

She frowned. "Then he was in Walthamstow when I was?"

Restell nodded. "Yes. Sir Arthur's sketches established that. Several villagers could place him there. No one I showed the sketches to had any difficulty identifying Kincaid. He grew up there and until recently resided in the home his parents left him. It is the home where you were held, Emma."

Emma was sick with the knowledge that it was so. She forced herself to listen to the whole of what Restell had to say.

"Trips to London took him away these last few years. Frequently, from what I gathered. The people who knew him better than others—and no one would admit to knowing him well—said he was putting on airs. He apparently boasted of an arrangement he'd made in London that would see him heavy in his pockets before the end of spring. You may be interested to know that the two sketches of Kincaid that you favored were the ones considered most like him."

"It does not seem so important now."

"No, perhaps not. His true name was William Peele. In

Walthamstow he was known as Billy Peele. There are two cousins he counted as confidants and cronies. They have not been seen since before Billy Peele was found dead. Neither came to his grave site for the service. They are Elliot and William Peele, the latter going by Will to avoid the inevitable confusion."

"The names mean nothing. I do not think I ever heard my attackers address each other by name, but mayhap it is only that I do not remember." Emma laid one hand against the right side of her face and gently massaged her temple.

"Is it a headache?"

"A small one only."

"Would you like to lie down?"

"No."

"Perhaps more sherry."

She smiled a bit unevenly. "In a little while, I think."

Restell rolled the drawings back into a single cylinder and slipped the string around it. He tapped it lightly against his knee until Emma took it from his hands. "Bloody hell," he said, running one hand through his hair. "I didn't realize what I was doing."

"I know." Emma laid the sketches on the floor. "I acquit you of being intentionally cruel."

"Do you understand yet why the tapping bothers you so?"

She shook her head. "I have racked my brain to think of it, but nothing comes to me. I suppose it is not a memory I can force, like the cottage, or the room, or even certain aspects of my escape. I could not bring those things to mind in their entirety until you provided these sketches. It was an inspired idea. I wish you had showed them to me before now."

"I don't think we can assume your reaction would have been the same. You were attacked at Lady Rivendale's only days before I returned to London. That did not suggest itself as a good time to put these in front of you. Then we were married and—"

Emma laid her hand over his. "I understand. The time was never right after our wedding."

"Why is that, Emma? Why did that happen?"

She squeezed his fingers. "I cannot tell you."

"Do you mean you don't know?"

"No, I mean I cannot tell you."

"Emmalyn."

She smiled a shade ruefully at his use of her full name. "So I am in trouble, is that it? Because I choose to keep my own counsel? That is not fair, Restell, not when you have withheld so much from me. You are still not telling me all that you know. You are as afraid of what will happen to my mind as I am." Too late, she realized she had said more than was her intention, and her sharp intake of breath merely served as an exclamation point to her confession.

Restell's head snapped around, and he pinned her back with his implacable blue eyes. "You still fear you are going mad." It was more an accusation than it was a statement of fact. "That's it, isn't it? Something happened on our wedding night that confirmed it in your mind."

Caught out, Emma merely stared back at him.

"What was it, Emma?"

She refused to answer.

Restell did not allow that to deter him. He recounted the events as he remembered them. "I followed you into the dressing room. You went behind the screen. I made the colossal error in judgment to suppose that you would be flattered by my attention to your silhouette, and you railed at me. I left you alone, then, and you . . ." His voice trailed off because he was not privy to her thoughts. "And you were . . . embarrassed? . . . angry? . . . frightened?" He realized she was holding his hand so tightly her nails were digging into his skin. He didn't care. "It has to be said aloud, Emma, and you have to be the one to say it. What happened after I stepped out of the room?"

Emma took a steadying breath. "That is when I stepped out of my body."

Chapter 11

Restell desired to discover more about Emma's confession, but she began to weep softly, and he didn't press. It made him smile when she reached for the handkerchief he carried rather than one of her own. In spite of her attempts to set herself from him, there were still small intimacies that made him feel that she was very much his wife.

"Excuse me," Emma said, rising to her feet.

Restell let her go without asking for an explanation. He watched her disappear into their bedroom, then heard faint sounds of movement coming from the dressing room. He stood and went to the bedroom. She had not closed the door behind her, and he saw her standing at the washstand holding a damp cloth to her eyes. Satisfied that she was all of a piece, Restell turned away before she saw him. He sat on the arm of a wing chair, waiting for her to come out. A few minutes later, she did. Her eyelids were slightly swollen, but her eyes were clear. The small smile she gave him was regretful, not watery.

Restell glanced at the damp cloth she carried. "Shall I ring for Bettis?"

"No. I would like something to eat, though. I have had nothing since this morning."

She had eaten little enough then, Restell remembered. He didn't say as much. His cause would not be served by any admission that he watched rather more closely than even she might suspect. "I'll take care of it," he said. "Will you lie down?"

She nodded. "Yes, I think I will."

Restell returned to the sitting room before he rang for Hobbes. He asked for their supper to be brought up and informed his valet that his plans for this evening were yet uncertain. Once Hobbes was gone, Restell picked up the bottle of sherry from the drinks cabinet and carried it and the glasses back to the bedroom. Emma had removed her gown and was sitting up in bed wearing her chemise. The combs that had secured her hair were lying on the table beside her. Her hair fell in thick waves on either side of her shoulders. She'd drawn her knees forward to her chest and was holding the compress against her forehead.

"Sherry?"

Emma stole a glance at him. "A little."

He set the glasses on the table and poured some for each of them. He took his glass but left hers where it rested. "When you're ready for it," he said, returning to his perch on the curved arm of the wing chair. "And when you're of a piece that you can explain yourself, I should like to hear that also."

"There is not a great deal I can tell you."

"Something more, I hope, than you stepped out of your body."

Holding the compress in her hands, Emma raised her head. Her regard was frank. "It sounded every bit as absurd as I thought it would, and to call it absurd is to consider it in the most gentle light. Admit that what I said to you is quite mad."

"I will admit nothing of the sort. I do not yet comprehend what you mean by it."

"And I comprehend it no better than you."

"Then let us see if we can make sense of it together. What did you fear, Emma? That I would suggest an asylum?" When her face drained of color, he realized he'd hit the mark. "You did, didn't you? Do you trust me so little?"

"I *know* you so little."

He could not argue her point. He sipped his sherry and waited her out.

"My grandmother lived the last ten years of her life in such a place," she said finally. "There is madness in my family, Restell."

"There is madness in mine as well," he said, "but we prefer to call it eccentricity and adapt accordingly." He intercepted her pained look. "I am not making light of you. What I'm saying is quite true. My mother—not Lady Gardner, but the woman who bore me—had a great aunt who regularly tried to poison her husband. There are those who say he deserved it for fathering nearly a dozen bastards and leaving her childless, but who is to know the truth of it all? No one thought to put her in an asylum, though. On the other hand, I am familiar with a gentleman who had his wife put in such a place for simply disobeying him. My point is that whether one is relegated to a lunatic asylum is often a matter of what others are willing to tolerate."

"I have always thought you were tolerant."

"Then you should say it as if you believe it. I cannot help but think you are merely hopeful."

"Perhaps I am hopeful that you believe it."

He smiled. "I *am* tolerant, Emma. Like madness, tolerance also runs deep in my family."

Emma slowly released a breath as she considered this. "Then let me explain as well as I am able." She set down the cloth and picked up her glass of sherry. "My discomfort began before you left the dressing room. I was almost immediately ill when I realized you were watching me. You left, but the feeling did not pass. In fact, it became worse. I saw I was shaking, and I could barely draw a breath. Both those things have happened before, many times actually since I was attacked, so while the experience is frightening, it is also familiar. I have even learned to expect that darkness will sometimes appear at the corners of my vision, but what I could not anticipate was the calm."

"Calm?" asked Restell, as Emma sipped her drink. "Is that not to be desired?"

"Not when it caused me to become removed from myself." She sighed. "It's clear you do not understand, and I can say it no better than that. I cannot account for my time in the dressing room. I remember washing behind the screen and then . . ." She shrugged helplessly. "And then nothing. I went through the motions of washing and drying, even walking from behind the screen, yet it was as if all of those things were done by someone other than me. I was sitting on a stool when you called to me. It was then that I came into myself again. I became *aware*. What happened in between, that is what I cannot explain."

Restell had no explanation for it either. Emma's description of events was clear enough, however. "Have you ever known the like before?"

"I think it's why I cannot recall what happened when I was attacked."

"Then perhaps it is not a terrible thing, Emma. It is protection of a sort."

"It does not feel like protection, not when it happens in my own dressing room. There was no threat there."

"No, but I think you felt threatened. It is not so dissimilar from what happens when you hear the steady, deliberate tapping. You act to physically protect yourself. Why can it not be that your mind does the same?"

Emma said nothing. She pressed the rim of her wineglass against her lower lip as she considered what he'd said. Finally, she tipped the glass and drank, then set it aside. "You did not ask me if it's happened since our wedding night."

"Then I have been remiss. Has it?"

She nodded. "Twice. Once when I was in my uncle's studio and just two days ago when I was in his library."

"You felt threatened in both those places?"

"I thought I was being watched."

"There is always someone around, Emma."

"No, it is different when it is Hobbes or Lewis or one of the other footmen. I expect them to be there. I *know* they will be there. In the dressing room . . . when you were watching me . . . it was unexpected. I had the same sense in the studio and again in Sir Arthur's library."

"Was anyone there?"

"I don't know. I cannot account for my time in either place. I was on the studio balcony when I became aware again; in the library I was on the upper rung of a ladder reaching for a book. I almost took a tumble."

"From the ladder or the balcony?" Restell was able to pose the question with considerably more composure than he felt.

"The ladder."

"I suppose that is the lesser of two evils."

"Only because I had not yet reached the balcony rail."

Restell finished his drink in a single swallow. She was getting a little of her own back, so he didn't mind if she saw she'd unsettled him. She should know that she was not the only one who could be unnerved.

Their supper arrived and Restell held back his questions. He ate at the table in the bedroom while Emma had her meal in bed. She would have objected to being treated as an invalid, but he made that argument moot by treating her like a queen. When their trays were cleared and Emma looked as if she could get her feet under her again, he invited her to sit in the chair he had occupied. He spun his own chair away from the table and straddled it, resting his forearms across the back rail.

"Is it often that you're alone in the studio?" Restell asked the question as if there'd been no interruption. "I was under the impression that your uncle was always there."

"Not always, but it is mostly the case. Sometimes when his knees are bothering him, he paints in his library. I am charged with getting him what he needs from the studio as he does not have confidence in the servants."

"Should I ask McCleod or one of the others to escort you everywhere you go?"

"I will place myself in an asylum if you do that."

Restell counted her dark humor as a sign that she was recovering herself. "Very well, then what will help you ease your mind?"

"I don't know."

"You're not going mad, Emma."

She smiled tentatively. "It is good to hear you say so."

Restell watched Emma raise her bare feet onto the chair and tuck the hem of her chemise around them. "Tell me about your grandmother's madness," he said. "Did she try to poison anyone?"

"No." Emma gave him a sharp glance. "Have you fathered a score of bastards?"

He grinned. "Nary a one. I swear it."

"Then you are safe. My grandmother was visited by long bouts of melancholia and seized by unpredictable humors. At least that is how it was explained to me. She did not want to eat or change her clothes. She refused to allow the servants to help her bathe, and I understand there were days she could not climb from her bed."

"Did you know her?"

"No. She died when I was yet an infant."

"This is your father's mother?"

"No. My mother's. Sir Arthur's as well, of course."

"And your grandfather on that side? Where is he?"

"Dead before my grandmother. It's why I went to live with my uncle when my parents were lost at sea. There was no one except my father's sister, and she has lived in India with her husband and children for a decade. I did not want to go there."

"Understandable." A small crease appeared between Restell's eyebrows as he attempted to follow the sequence of certain events. "So it was your grandfather who gave permission for his wife to be cared for in the asylum."

"No. I suppose I wasn't clear. My grandfather had already died before my grandmother was sent to Bellefaire. Uncle Arthur made the arrangements for her to go."

"Your uncle." Restell spoke the words under his breath, more to himself than to Emma. Had even two hours passed since

Sir Arthur had spoken to him about Emma? *It is a touch of the melancholia, I think. One must remain hopeful that it will pass.* "Bloody hell." He shook his head, wondering what else he had failed to comprehend about his wife, her family, and her fears. It was not as if she leaped at shadows. Her fears were grounded, and he was the one that had not fully realized their import. "Bloody, bloody hell."

"What is it?" she asked.

Restell knew she would not stand for him to say it was nothing, not when the opposite was so clearly true. He asked a question instead, as if it were the thing that had been on his mind. "Your mother had nothing to say about her own mother's care?"

"My mother did not have any legal standing to gainsay him. She and Uncle Arthur were estranged for years because of his decision. I do not know the whole of it. Children never do."

"There was money involved," Restell said flatly.

"Why do you think so?"

"Experience suggests it. The husband that I mentioned earlier? The one who had his disobedient wife locked away?"

"Yes."

"There was a fortune at stake. Her fortune. It was money he could not touch in any other way, established for her in trusts that their marriage contract did not alter."

A slim smile edged the corners of Emma's mouth upward. "Does she owe you a favor now?"

"Indeed she does."

"Good. I'm glad you helped her." Her smile faded. "You're correct that money was a factor here also. The best I understand it, my grandmother had a steward who managed her estate and all aspects of her finances. My mother and father reviewed the accounts from time to time to be certain that everything was in order. When she went to Bellefaire everything came under my uncle's control."

"He is not that rich, Emma."

"I know. He lost a great deal of money making bad investments."

"And gaming."

"Yes, I suspect from what you've told me that it's so. One hopes that time spent in Lady Rivendale's company will diminish his urge for that pursuit."

"Do you manage all of his finances or only keep records of income and expenses related to commissions?"

"It is the latter. I have some awareness of the rest, but no responsibility for it."

"Who does?"

"Mr. Johnston used to, but when he was released the responsibility was given to solicitors. Meriwether and Stockwell."

"I am not familiar with them."

She shrugged. "You cannot know everyone." Emma smoothed her chemise over her knees. "May I inquire about the sketches you showed me?"

"Of course."

"I want to know how you came upon that particular cottage, and what suggested to you that I was held there. By your own admission there are many in the countryside like it."

"It was surprisingly simple. It is where Kincaid—Billy Peele, that is—lived. I learned that he was dead as soon as I showed Mr. Broadstreet the sketches. He was happy to take me to the site of Peele's demise as well as open the cottage for me. I believe we can depend on his discretion, Emma. Mr. Matlack's also."

She waved that aside. "That does not concern me as I will never visit Walthamstow again. I still cannot divine why you suspected so strongly that I was held there."

"I believe I mentioned I found bits of fabric in the bark of a nearby tree."

"I imagine you found those after your suspicions were so clearly aroused. Am I wrong?"

"No. Predators often take their prey back to their cave. It struck me that humans are not likely to do it differently, especially if their plan is not well-conceived. It seemed to me that Peele was deviating from a plan. It made him careless."

"What do you mean?"

"I think the abduction occurred because Peele began to think for himself." Restell held Emma's curious eyes steadily. "The plan, or rather the directive he was given, was to kill you."

Emma blanched. "Or Marisol," she whispered.

"Or Marisol."

"But why?"

"When we know that, we shall know everything."

"Could not Mr. Kincaid—" She stopped, collecting herself. "Billy Peele, I mean, could he not have planned the thing in its entirety? He was clever, after all. He was able to make himself welcome in a society to which he did not belong. That is no small feat. He encouraged Marisol's attentions and arranged the assignation at Madame Chabrier's. For all that Marisol is foolish at times, she is still no one's fool. If anyone could have seen through his pretensions, it would be Marisol. I think we must consider that, Restell."

Emma set her bare feet on the floor and scooted to the edge of the cushion. She clasped her hands together to keep from flinging them far and wide as she pressed her argument. "I realize that Mr. Peele did not act on his own. The men I heard from time to time on the journey to Walthamstow, neither of them was Kincaid. I know I'm right about that."

"Perhaps you are, but I submit that you cannot know it for a fact. There are too many things you don't remember yet."

Emma offered her agreement, but only reluctantly. "It is entirely possible that his cousins assisted him."

"I agree. I have men looking for them for precisely that reason. I should like to find them before they come to as bad an end as Billy."

"One of them might be the murderer," she said. "You must have thought of that. Why, it might not have been murder at all. You mentioned that it appeared there was a fight in the cottage. What if they fought after I left them? Blamed each another for my escape. It could be that Mr. Peele's death was an accident. The cousins panicked and moved his body where they hoped it would not be found. They fled, then. They may well be on the continent by now."

Restell nodded slowly, his head angled to one side as he considered the points she made. "It is not that what you say is impossible," he said after a moment, "only that it is unlikely. I admit to contemplating something much like it during my return to London."

"Yet you discredited your own thinking."

"Upon my arrival, I learned that you almost drowned in Lady Rivendale's fountain. That was certainly enough to give me pause. Who do you suspect of that bit of business if the cousins are on the continent and Billy Peele is already dead?"

Emma blinked. "Oh."

"Indeed."

She recovered her wits quickly. "We do not know with certainty that I was the intended victim at the fountain. I still may have been mistaken for Marisol, and do not forget that Mr. Charters was the one clobbered with the walking stick."

Now it was Restell who offered reluctant agreement. "I do not understand the whole of it yet." He rose from the chair. "There is one more thing I must show you."

Emma called after him as he disappeared into the sitting room, but he didn't respond. She got up and ran to the doorway just in time to see him go into the hallway. She did not follow further. Puzzled, she slowly retraced her steps to the wing chair and sat, this time drawing her legs toward her chest and resting her chin on her knees.

Restell was not gone long. What he had in his hands, he held behind his back. "I do not want to make more of this than it is."

"Then I suggest you simply show it to me."

"Do you recall what happened when I showed you the Barcelona silk handkerchief?"

She nodded. "Is it like that?"

"Yes," he said. "And more besides." It was as much preparation as he could give her. He watched her steel herself: her arms embraced her curled legs even more tightly. He took a few more steps toward her before he revealed what he held.

Emma stared at the satin straw bonnet. It was an exact match for Marisol's bonnet. Even the green-and-white-striped Barcelona handkerchief was the same.

"I found it in the cottage," Restell said. "Not in the room you identified as the place you were held, but in the room you didn't know." He did not think Emma's complexion could become paler than it already was, but she was very nearly as colorless as her chemise. "Emma? Are you all right?"

She nodded slowly. "That is not something I expected to see again."

"I understand." He set it aside. "It's the bonnet you wore, isn't it?"

"Yes." She frowned. "The handkerchief, though, that is your doing. You tacked it on."

"I'm afraid not. I found the bonnet exactly as it is." He reached inside his frock coat and removed a striped silk handkerchief from his pocket. Shaking it out, he showed her that it had never been cleaned. "This is the one that Hobbes found behind Madame Chabrier's."

Emma's brow creased. It was difficult not to gulp air. Had the weight of dread not kept her in the chair, she would have fled the room. "Two of them? It makes no sense."

"It does if your attackers needed some means of identifying you or Marisol easily. That suggests that Billy Peele was not present, but left it to others to take you. The handkerchief served as a marker, if you will, that the person wearing it was indeed their target."

"Marisol purchased that handkerchief to make the bonnet fashionable again."

"Perhaps Peele was with her when she bought it," Restell said. "You mentioned there were other assignations."

Emma remained unconvinced. "I suppose that's possible."

"Or it may be that he simply told her he found the bonnet particularly fetching and asked her to wear it. Would she find such a suggestion flattering?"

"Certainly. I recall proposing that she should wear the black leghorn, but it was raining and she said it would be ruined. I was the one who thought of the satin straw."

Restell shrugged. "That hardly matters. She might very well have suggested it if you had not. You simply didn't give her time. You did mention to me that she insisted you wear her pelisse."

"That was in aid of fooling Mr. Kincaid until the last possible moment. She wanted me to gauge his response."

"It would seem he had another plan in mind."

Emma pulled all of her hair over her left shoulder and absently began to plait it. "It might all be over, Restell. I know that you think what happened to Mr. Charters at Lady Rivendale's is related to all of this, but what if it is not?"

"What if I am wrong, you mean."

"It's possible, isn't it? You are not omniscient."

"This is the first I've heard of it."

Emma cocked an eyebrow at him. "I'm perfectly serious."

Restell saw that she was. "Very well. Yes, I might be wrong. It does not mean that I'm willing to act as though I'm wrong. If Billy Peele is solely responsible for the attack and abduction, then I will have the truth of it from his cousins before I'll allow you to go about unprotected."

"You may never find them."

Restell scowled at her.

"I do not mean to be discouraging," she said, "but merely practical. You agreed they may be on the continent. And you must consider that nothing has happened to me, Marisol, or even Mr. Charters that is the least untoward for weeks now." She tossed her plait behind her and regarded him earnestly. "In truth, Restell, the point I am making is probably moot since I cannot go anywhere without someone to attend me. I simply do not want to be afraid any longer. Can you appreciate that? I do not want to be afraid."

Restell hesitated, then walked to her side. He sat on the arm of the chair, turned slightly toward her and laid one hand on her shoulder. She did not try to evade his touch. "Are you ever not afraid, Emma?"

She did not lift her head to look at him, but she nodded.

"Tell me about those times," he said gently. "I think we need to have more of them."

Emma was quiet for a long time. Without conscious thought, she leaned into Restell's hand when he lifted it to brush her cheek. "I am not afraid now," she said, risking a glance at him. "I am never afraid when you're with me."

"Never? I haven't been certain that's been true of late."

She nodded faintly. "I understand, but it's different if what I fear is myself."

He waited, thinking she would tell him more. When she didn't, he chose not to press. "Are there no other times, Emma?"

"None come to mind."

"What about when you are in your uncle's studio?" He watched her closely, gauging her reaction to the question. He suspected that in this case it was second nature not to give herself away.

"It is comfortable there, but I am not without fear."

"Then if you are most easy when you're with me, it seems we must endeavor to spend more time together."

"You will not like that, Restell. I do not want you to resent my presence in every aspect of your life. Besides, it is not that I am entirely comfortable with you, only that I am not afraid. It is better, I think, that we go on as we have. You are free to go your own way of an evening as you are wont to do. It is no hardship for me to remain here."

He chuckled. "It sounds as if it might be a hardship. Have you never wondered where I go?"

"I know where you go most of the time. I have it from your own mother. You go to the gaming hells."

"My mother cannot know the whole truth of it, Emma. You should apply to me for the particulars." When Restell observed that she would not ask the question even when he invited her to do so, he understood that she feared hearing the answer. His hand dropped away from her cheek. "Do you think I've been unfaithful?"

"No, but I think you are tempted. I smell perfume on your clothing. The tobacco and liquor. You return to our home with it on your person."

Restell did not attempt to defend himself. "Would you like to accompany me to a gaming hell?"

Emma's head snapped up. "Accompany you? You would permit it?"

"I would welcome it. It is immensely boring work. I suspect that it would be considerably more interesting if you were there."

"But it is not done."

"You cannot visit one as my wife, you understand. That is what is not done. Women of a certain reputation, though, are free to come and go. Should you like to be a woman of a certain reputation?" When she didn't reply, he prompted, "Well?"

"I am attempting not to appear too eager."

Restell took Emma by the wrist and stood, drawing her to her feet at the same time. "So it intrigues you," he said. He cupped her face in his hands. "I confess, it intrigues me as well." Smiling a trifle wickedly, he kissed her.

Emma welcomed the touch of his mouth. She closed her eyes and simply allowed herself to feel. His lips were warm and damp, and she had wanted to know the taste of his mouth again. She engaged his tongue, sucking it gently as she deepened the kiss. Flinging her arms about his neck, she stood on the tips of his toes and kept him rooted to the floor.

"I'm not going anywhere," he whispered against her lips when they both drew back for air. "Never doubt it."

She nodded, pressing her lips to the corner of his mouth, his jaw, then against his neck just above the line of his stiff collar.

"Never doubt it," he said again.

Emma felt the vibration of his voice in his throat, then against her lips. She raised her face and found his mouth again. The kiss was more urgent this time, needier now than it had been only moments before. She was flush to him and wanted to be closer still. If she could fit herself inside his skin, it may not yet be close enough.

Emma knew she wanted to be inside his heart.

The sound that was torn from her throat was somewhere between a sob and a gasp. Her slender frame shuddered with the effort she made to restrain herself, and still the sound was wrenched from her. She held on tightly as Restell lifted her, and when he made to lower her to the bed, she held on then as well.

He tumbled and rolled with her. She ended up under him, slightly breathless and pinned to the bed by his weight, but when he began to move away, she shook her head. "No. It's all right. I want to know this."

"I will crush you."

She smiled. "The weight of my own fears is far heavier than you are. I can still breathe." To prove the truth of it she sucked in a mouthful of air. Her cheeks were drawn inward while her mouth formed a perfect bow that gave her a rather fishlike countenance.

Grinning, Restell kissed her.

"I suppose you would also kiss a trout," she said.

"I would if I'd been angling for it long enough."

"Has it been so long, then?"

Restell didn't answer, or rather his answer was to kiss her thoroughly and allow her to draw her own conclusion. Her mouth was sweet, tasting faintly of sherry, and like the wine, the effect was intoxicating. Each kiss was satisfying and still not enough. He wanted more.

He slid down her body, making a damp trail with his mouth as he went. He kissed the underside of her jaw, the hollow at her throat, then lower until he reached the scooped neckline of her chemise. He paused for a moment, allowing himself to absorb the warmth and fragrance of her. Tugging lightly on the chemise, he placed a kiss on the skin he revealed.

He continued on a path that took him over the soft, delicate batiste, not under it. His mouth made a damp circle around her aureole, teasing the nipple to pebble-like hardness. He rolled it lightly between his lips until he heard her small whimper. Raising his head, he allowed her a moment's reprieve before he turned his attention to her other breast.

Emma felt as if he'd found the cord that kept the whole of her together. When he sucked on her breast, she felt contractions in her womb. Her fingers curled into fists. Her toes simply curled. The small of her back lifted off the bed as her heels dug in. Sensation washed over her, prickling her skin and infusing her with warmth. She discovered it was possible to be hot and cold at the same time, to feel as if she were coming apart at his touch yet being made whole by it.

Her fingers threaded in Restell's pale gold hair, and she held him loosely to her breast, stroking his head, lightly caressing the nape of his neck.

Emma knew the crisis was upon her. Pleasure pulled every one of her muscles taut. Her hands dropped to his shoulders; her fingers tightened. She schooled her breathing, hearing herself sip the air, the rhythm of each breath matching the suck of his mouth on her breast.

In the end, she closed her eyes and softly cried out his name. Her body quivered for a long moment, then was still. Warmth crept upward from her breasts to her face as her skin was flushed with color.

Restell raised his head and regarded Emma's pink cheeks. "You blossom like a perfect rose." When she opened one eye and added the arch of an eyebrow in her regard of him, he amended his description. "A perfectly thorny rose."

Emma's slight smile came and went, and she closed her eyes again, replete. The weight that was upon her now was her own heavy lethargy. She thought she might never move, nor ever want to.

"That has never happened before," she whispered. "You didn't . . . that is you only . . ."

Chuckling, Restell rolled onto his back. "Your breasts are extraordinarily sensitive." He sat up and removed his frock coat, then threw his legs over the side of the bed and loosened his stock. Glancing at Emma over his shoulder, he said, "Do not fall asleep. There is a matter of quid pro quo."

"That is not terribly gallant."

"Oh? Have I ever represented myself as a gentleman?"

"No." Emma plucked at her chemise where it clung damply to her breasts. "Your father thinks you aspire to be a rake."

Restell paused in the removal of his boots. "He told you that?"

"The conversation took place before we were married. Shall I tell him that you've abandoned the dream?"

"I do not intend to pursue it," Restell said. "But I'm certain that I shall never abandon it." He let his boot thud to the floor to punctuate his intent. "You would not like it if I did." He removed his stockings before he stood and shrugged out of his linen. Turning slightly as he began to lower his trousers and drawers, he caught Emma watching him. She did not try to hide her interest. "You are rather more openly curious than is strictly flattering."

"Am I? I do not mean to be." Still, she did not look away. "You have a pucker."

"A pucker?" He followed the line of Emma's sight and attempted to look at his backside. "This?" He pointed to the vaguely star-shaped scar just above the curve of his left buttock.

She nodded. "The cicatrix. How did you come by that?" Before he could answer, she was sufficiently intrigued to roll toward him and come up on her elbows for a closer examination. "It looks as if it might be a puncture wound." Her eyebrows lifted in tandem as she stared up at him. "Were you shot, Restell?"

"Move over." He dropped his trousers, pulled the string on his drawers, and stepped out of both, kicking them out of the way. When he turned around, Emma had already made room for him again and was obligingly holding up the bedcovers. "You do not want to know the particulars."

"But I do."

Restell slipped between the sheets, then between her parted

thighs. He lay hot and heavy in the cradle she made for him. His hips ground once against hers.

Emma's breath hitched. "Perhaps the particulars can wait," she said after a moment. She raised her knees, then her pelvis, and felt him move into her with a slow, deliberate thrust. "Perhaps I will hear them . . . but . . . just . . . not . . . now."

Seated deeply inside her, Restell held himself still until Emma's dark lashes fluttered open. "You have the most splendid eyes," he whispered. Bending his head, he brushed his lips against hers. "Do you ever watch us?"

Emma stared at him. "You wish to talk?"

His slight grin dissolved as she contracted around him. He required a moment to catch his breath and master himself. "I wondered if you ever watch us."

"I watch you." Restell's beautifully sculpted features were taut just now, every aspect stamped with desire denied. The jaw was set firmly enough to cause a muscle to jump in his cheek. His clear blue eyes, so frosty on occasion, burned brilliant and hot. She lifted one hand and brushed back a lock of his pale hair that had fallen over his forehead. His skin was warm. She cupped the side of his face and passed her thumb across the arch of his cheek. "I always watch you."

He kissed her again and whispered against her lips, "It is a good beginning. Now watch us." He threw back the covers so only candlelight and shadow bathed their bodies. Lifting his hips, he drew her eyes in the direction of their joining. He thrust again.

Emma stared and saw the rise of her own hips as she met him. She had hardly been aware of the effort. How easily she responded to him. How simply he made it happen.

When she finally closed her eyes and gave over to all the feeling, the vision that she had in her mind's eye was clearer than ever before. This time she watched them as if from a distance, seeing him, but herself as well, and this remarkable moment of stepping out of her body was not the least bit frightening. She observed all of it. The slope of his back. His tautly curved buttocks. Her fingers tightening against the flesh

of his upper arms. The arch in her own throat. The long line of
his legs. The swell of her breasts.

They rocked in unison, hard at first, then with less urgency.
The cadence of his breathing changed, while she could not
hear herself at all. His pale hair was burnished gold by the
candlelight. Dark copper strands highlighted her own. She
could make out the corded muscles in his arms and the tension across his back. Her own body seemed sleek and smooth
by comparison. They fit in unexpected ways. His mouth at the
curve of her neck; the hollow at the back of her knee against
his thigh. His palm on her hip; hers cupping the nape of his
neck.

She climaxed quickly with barely a whimper. Restell threw
back his head and surrendered to pleasure with a deep, husky
groan.

They lay side by side, and except for the rise and fall of
their chests, they were still. Neither of them spoke. An occasional breeze stirred the curtains at the window, but it was a
warm evening, and they were not troubled by the threat of
rain to rise from the bed and close the sash.

Emma was the first to move. Still lying on her back, she
walked her fingers across the small space separating her from
Restell and found his hand. She laced her fingers with his and
was satisfied with the gentle squeeze he gave in return. Moments later, she was sleeping.

Restell felt her hand relax in his. He carefully pulled away
and turned on his side, gauging the depth of her slumber
before he rose from the bed. He gathered up his clothes, then
went to the dressing room where he washed and put on his
nightshirt and robe. He did not ring for Hobbes until he removed himself to the sitting room and closed the door.

Hobbes frowned slightly when he entered and saw that
Restell was already dressed for bed, but that mild disapproval
vanished when he saw the door to the bedroom was closed. It
seemed that Bettis would not be required to attend the mistress either.

"There is something you need, sir?" Hobbes asked.

"Who is watching Miss Vega this evening?"

"That would be Lewis. He pulled the short straw. It is to be the theatre, I believe. A drama. He has no fondness for dramatic works."

"Indeed," Restell said dryly. "It will be a hardship. Do you know if she will attend with her uncle or Mr. Charters?"

"I understand it will be Mr. Charters."

Restell nodded, not surprised. Sir Arthur had not indicated any plans for this evening. "I think there is no help for it but that I must go out tonight. I also have need of some specific items, not for this evening, however. You will have perhaps a sennight to collect them. I trust that will be sufficient." He sat down at the small writing desk and quickly penned the list. "I will depend on your discretion, Hobbes, as always."

Hobbes regarded the paper in his hand for several long moments before looking to Restell. "All of them, sir?"

"Is there a problem?"

"It is . . . *unusual*."

"None of it is for me, Hobbes."

"Oh. Well, you might have said so from the first. It did give me a bit of a start, wondering what queer turn your mind had taken." He glanced at the list again. "So it is for a young lady, then."

Restell could see that Hobbes wanted to say more. Clearly the man had the wrong idea about what he was being asked to do. "I haven't taken a mistress. You would do well to look to your own mind for queer turns of thought."

Suitably chastened, Hobbes said, "Well, then, if I might know the approximate size of the—"

Restell interrupted. "It is all for my wife."

Now the valet's sandy eyebrows jumped in the direction of his hairline. "Miss Hathaway?"

"Yes, but we're calling her Mrs. Gardner now, remember?"

Hobbes did not respond to Restell's wry rejoinder. He simply stared.

Restell stood. Rather than wait for Hobbes to recover his wits, he opened the door to the hallway and ushered him out.

"Send Mr. Crowley to me, if you will. I will be making some changes that will affect his staff." That announcement, he thought, would be sufficient to stir everyone from the kitchen helpers to the housekeeper.

The butler arrived only a few minutes later. Restell noted that the man appeared somewhat ill at ease owing to the fact that he was out of breath. It was not difficult to imagine that Hobbes's own bemused state had something to do with the butler's haste in answering the summons.

"How many servants have quarters in the garret?" asked Restell.

"Four," Crowley said. "Mrs. Wescott's two young helpers share a room. The upstairs maids, Payne and Hanley, have another."

"There are two rooms empty, then."

"Yes. At the front of the house. Do you wish to hire more servants?"

"No. Is the house not adequately staffed?"

"I believe it is, sir. I thought you might have need of someone else like Lewis or McCleod."

"No, I have them in sufficient numbers at present. They must be a sore trial to you, Crowley. They are barely adequate as footmen."

"I make do, sir."

"They were excellent footpads."

Crowley did not raise an eyebrow. "One hopes they are reformed."

"I don't think we have to worry about the silver," Restell said as he returned to the writing desk. He gestured to the butler to join him. He smoothed out a sheet of paper and applied his pen to it, scratching out a rough floor plan of the uppermost story. "This is fairly accurate?"

"I believe so," Crowley said. "What do you have in mind?"

"I want to remove this inside wall and add windows here and here. There should be a small balcony as well with doors wide enough to accommodate an easy entry and exit. The furniture should be kept simple. A table. Stools. A chaise longue,

I think, and a few comfortable chairs. Shelves along both these walls."

"You wish a library, sir?"

"I wish a sanctuary," Restell said. "Can you arrange this?"

"If you like. It will necessitate hiring craftsmen and laborers."

"I will leave all of those details to you." Restell scrawled an amount that he was willing to pay for the renovations. "There is your allowance. If all can be accomplished in one month, then you and your staff shall share in a bonus equal to five percent of this total."

"A month. That is very little in the way of time."

"I am fully aware," Restell said. "There is one more thing. You must keep this from Mrs. Gardner."

"Sir?"

"She is not to know. She spends the better part of most days with her uncle. I will make certain that if she is not there, she is gone from the house. I am hopeful that my mother or one of my sisters will arrange an adequate diversion if I cannot. What you make of the time she is gone is up to you and the men you hire. Five percent hangs in the balance."

"You mean to keep your sanctuary a secret from her?"

Restell thought Crowley was going to say more on the subject, but the butler visibly reined himself in. His disapproval had already been made clear. Restell realized that while he and Emma may have been estranged these last six weeks, the same could not be said of Emma's association with the staff. Whatever they had observed, their sympathies apparently lay with his wife.

"I mean to build a bridge," Restell said after a moment.

"A bridge." Crowley looked doubtfully at the plan lying on the desk. "Mayhap you should consider applying to the earl for help. I understand he knows something about building bridges."

"Ferrin knows something about everything." Restell's tone held no rancor. "But I do not require him for this." He sat back, folded his arms across his chest, and looked up at his butler. "Well, Crowley? Are you the man to see this through, or shall I put the challenge to another?"

The butler picked up the drawing. "Everything will be as you wish."

Restell had never doubted it. He permitted himself a small smile as Crowley departed. Emma's sanctuary. His bridge. Yes, it was in all ways the right thing to do.

He got up and poured himself a small drink that he then carried into the bedroom. Emma was stirring but not awake. He found *Nightmare Abbey* still unopened on the bedside table and picked it up. After nudging the wing chair closer to the candlelight, he sat down, made himself comfortable, and began to read.

"Is it good?" asked Emma.

Jerking at the sound of her voice, Restell almost spilled his drink. *Nightmare Abbey* tumbled off his lap and onto the floor. "I cannot say whether it is good, but it is diverting." He picked it up and put it to one side. "You slept well?"

Emma was lying on her side, her head propped on a pillow, which rested on her arm. She nodded. The cotton was smooth against her cheek. "Have you been awake long?"

"I never slept. I have to go out, Emma."

"You do?"

"It is regarding a matter that was brought to my attention before our introduction."

"Is it dangerous?"

"No. It is sensitive." He saw by Emma's expression that his explanation was in no way adequate. "The French ambassador's son is involved. The poor fellow's fallen in with a pair of young bucks who are regularly taking advantage of him. Being French, he assumes he is not so naive as to permit himself to be misled. His superiority makes him a most perfect mark."

"His father hired you?"

"No. The foreign minister did. For reasons that should be readily apparent, no one is desirous of an incident that will put us in a bad way with the French. Napoleon is not yet dead a year. Our people are still mourning the death of Queen Caroline, and few members of the parliament expect our king can be effective. He lacked gravitas as prince regent. Naturally there are concerns now. A scandal is to be avoided."

Emma required a moment to comprehend the whole of what she was hearing, but when she did, it was Restell's solemn expression that broke her attempt to remain straight-faced and respectfully concerned. She pushed her face into the pillow to stifle her laughter. Her shoulders shook. Her efforts to restrain herself came to nothing.

A full minute passed before she was able to compose herself and look at him askance. "That is a very good story, Restell, but if you must go to a gaming hell this evening, you should put it before me without elaboration. You lose credibility in the details."

"I do?"

"I'm afraid so, but it is good of you to try so hard. I'm sure it's only a matter of time before the foreign minister *does* approach you with delicate, diplomatic concerns."

Restell chuckled. "I shall remember that. It is invariably the details that trip one up." He finished his drink and rolled the tumbler between his palms as he regarded her sleep-flushed face. "What say you, Emma? There are arrangements that must be made, so it cannot be tonight, but, if you like, you may accompany me to the hell by week's end."

Chapter 12

The hell was not at all what Emma imagined it would be, at least from the outside. Located not far from Covent Garden, the gaming house was a singularly plain gray stone town house, indistinguishable from the houses around it. Emma commented on this as their carriage drew close.

"That is because the other houses are more of the same," he said. "Gaming hells and brothels. Sometimes both. Nightfall and candlelight puts a pretty cloak on the place, fog improves it tenfold. The district has a genteel shabbiness during the day. You would know to stay away from this street if you were out walking, and no reputable hack driver would bring you within a hundred yards of it."

Emma restrained herself from staring out the window. The occasional glimpse she had of the pedestrian traffic revealed gentlemen cut from the same cloth as Restell and women who were most definitely of a certain reputation. She nervously fingered the ends of her sheer rose scarf, drawing it over her bare shoulders.

Restell shook his head, indicating she should lower it again. "You must not flaunt yourself," he told her, "but too much modesty will also attract attention. You should make every effort to be at your ease."

Emma glanced down at the deeply scooped neckline of her bodice. Fearing that her breasts would spill over the top, she had been careful to take only shallow, measured breaths since putting the gown on. "I am almost naked," she whispered.

"And I am painfully aware of that fact." His eyes dropped to her bodice. A rose satin ribbon seemed to be all that was holding her together. "It is not too late to turn back. Whittier will be pleased to take you home. Frankly, I will be pleased to let him."

"Do you want me to go, Restell? I will, if that's what you want."

Restell did not answer immediately. It was not that he regretted asking her to join him, but that he did not know if good would come of it. "I want to be certain this is what you want, Emma. I can be satisfied with that."

The carriage door opened, but neither of them moved.

"Well?" asked Restell.

Emma's chin came up. "You will not leave me in there, will you?"

"I doubt a surgeon will be able to remove me from your side."

"That is all right, then. I will not regret my decision; neither should you."

Restell nodded once, then he alighted from the carriage and held out his hand. If she was transformed by the clothing and accoutrements that Hobbes found for her, then Restell knew himself to be transfixed.

She wore a pale pink gown, several shades lighter than the rose scarf and ribbon. Tiny seed pearls studded the bodice, the hem, and her elbow-length white gloves. She carried a lace fan and wore slippers that matched her gown. It was her red hair, an elaborately coifed wig with pearls and another rose ribbon, that made her seem altogether different in nature. The pink hues that usually colored her complexion were gone, covered by a light application of rice powder and rouge. Henna tinted her eyebrows and a bit of kohl lined her eyelids and lower lashes. The overall effect was not garish, but it was most definitely painted and without question, exotic.

Restell had wanted to take her the moment she stepped out

of the dressing room and again in the carriage. He managed to hold himself in check, but it was a narrow thing, especially because she seemed to be peculiarly naive about her effect on him. He found his thoughts straying to all the ways he might educate her.

They were about to go up the stairs to the house, when Restell tugged on Emma's elbow and drew her to one side to allow another couple to pass. He backed her against the iron fence bordering the sidewalk and sheltered her by holding on to the bars on either side of her shoulders. "You are Miss Jane Warwick," he reminded her. "A courtesan. Do not forget yourself. You must not act in any way ashamed. Gentlemen will stare. Everyone will be curious. You may answer questions as you see fit. If you do not wish to answer, simply change the subject. It will add to your mystery."

Emma's nod was barely perceptible. "Why will they stare? Do I look as if I do not belong?"

"They will stare because you are with me. I am known to many of the patrons, and I've never brought a woman here. Some will know I am recently married. That will elicit comment behind your back." His smile was perfectly wicked as he saw her understand the impossible situation she was willingly stepping into. "You are feeling the double-edged sword, I collect."

She glanced down. His frock coat was a modest covering for the bulge in his trousers. "Is that what you're calling it?"

Restell's shout of laughter actually stopped passersby in their tracks. He pulled her to him, kissed her hard, then drew her quickly up the stairs and into the house. Once they were across the threshold and their voices could not carry over the low hum of all the other patrons, he told her: "They will also stare because you are looking extraordinarily lovely this evening."

"I am *painted*."

He nodded. "Scandalously beautiful."

That description made Emma smile. Her arm tightened in his. Already her eyes were watering a bit from the tobacco smoke that hung in the air. "In the event I forget to tell you later, thank you for bringing me."

Restell bent his head. "Make the most of it, my dear Jane. I don't expect I shall revisit this offer again. Come. This way."

The rooms were crowded but still navigable. Restell escorted her through the sea of patrons, only occasionally stopping to speak to someone. As this necessitated an introduction, Emma preferred it when he merely nodded to an acquaintance and they moved on.

Gentlemen and their occasional companions participated in games of chance or found entertainment in watching others grow lighter in the pockets. Roulette was the most popular game of chance and exquisitely crafted tables were set up in each of the ground-floor rooms. The spinning of the wheel made a distinctive sound, especially as the onlookers typically grew quiet waiting for its revolutions to slow. In contrast to the hush that fell over the roulette tables, the rooms were also occupied by small clutches of gentlemen noisily rolling dice and calling out their wagers on what numbers would appear.

Restell encouraged Emma to place a wager at one of the wheels. "You will not mind if I lose?" she asked. It was Restell's chuckle as well as the laughter from others around the table that made her realize she'd posed a question one did not often hear from a courtesan. Mildly piqued by her misstep, Emma coyly tapped Restell's arm with her closed fan. "And if I win?"

"It's all yours, of course."

She nodded, pleased. "Just so." Turning back to the table, she impulsively made her choice, then waited for all the other wagers to be placed. Several gentlemen placed their markers on the same square she had.

"Why did they do that?" she asked Restell as they climbed the stairs to the upper rooms. "Did they think I was prescient?"

"Hardly. They did it to flatter you and attract your notice. If the wheel had been kind to you, they would have no doubt given you some portion, if not all, of their winnings."

"But I lost."

"Thank God. It cooled their ardor, else they would be trailing after you now like puppies."

At the top of the stairs a footman offered them drinks. Restell chose brandy for himself and a sherry for Emma. He turned her toward the first open doorway in the hall, then steered her away when he recognized the peculiar fragrance of the smoke coming from the room. Feeling the hesitation in Emma's step as her nose wrinkled and she attempted to sniff the air, he answered the question she hadn't yet asked. "Opium. It is an experience you will have to forgo."

"Have you?"

Restell supposed he should have been prepared to answer questions of this nature, but he hadn't given a thought to them. "Used it?" he asked. "Yes. By way of experimentation. And it accounts for the pucker on my backside."

"Oh." Her henna-highlighted eyebrows rose as she regarded him askance. "You truly did aspire to be a rake."

"With a vengeance. Come. We will try another room. One with card play." Restell chose a closed door farther down the hall. "Perhaps we will find Breckenridge here. The owner. He was not belowstairs, and he does not frequent the opium den."

"Lord Breckenridge? Viscount Breckenridge?"

"You know him?"

"I have met him. He commissioned a portrait from Sir Arthur several years ago. Don't concern yourself. He won't recall me."

"God's truth, I hope not. If he sees through your paint and red hair, then he has a better eye for a woman's true beauty than even I suspected."

Emma was not certain what to make of that comment, but it seemed as though there was a pretty compliment for her in it. Smiling over her glass of sherry, she watched Restell's fingers curl around the doorknob. At his questioning glance, she nodded to indicate that she was prepared to face whatever lay ahead.

Her entrance into the room on Restell's arm caused a

momentary hush and suspension of card play at the three tables set up for it. Restell acted as if the notice they attracted was no more than what was due them, and Emma took her cue from him. She smiled coolly and inclined her head as though their attention did not merely flatter her, but honored her.

Restell escorted her to the table closest to the sideboard where silver platters of small cakes, cheese, and fruit were laid out. A young woman wearing a sky blue silk gown with an overlay of lace stood at one end of the sideboard pouring brandy from a crystal decanter. Emma watched her expertly draw back the decanter and stopper it without spilling a drop, then wind her way between the tables to serve the drink to a gentleman who was clearly waiting for her—and easily twice her age. Emma did not miss the sly, knowing smile the woman cast in her direction as she draped her arm around the gentleman's shoulders. It struck Emma then that this woman recognized her as a compatriot of sorts, more sister than rival.

Emma's attention was drawn back to Restell as he was asked to join the table where they were standing. He accepted the invitation and sat. Emma realized she was expected to stand behind him, but slightly to one side as she observed other women in the room were doing. She lay one hand lightly on his shoulder as the player beside him began to shuffle the cards. When it was time to cut the cards, the gentleman did not offer the deck to Restell, but indicated to Emma that she might have the opportunity instead.

"S'il vous plaît," the dealer said. His voice was warm, and his eyes were warmer still.

Emma glanced at Restell. When he nodded, she obliged. "Merci," she said. *"Vous êtes très aimable."* She nudged the deck in his direction.

Looking past her to Restell, the dealer asked, *"Qui est cette demoiselle?"*

Restell made the introduction. "Monsieur Jourdain. Miss Jane Warwick."

"C'est un vrai plaisir, Mademoiselle Warwick." Raising her gloved hand to his lips, he kissed the back of it.

As the rest of those seated at the table took note of this, one of them spoke up. "Have a care, Jourdain. Gardner is credited to be a fine shot and better still with a sword. Even your father will not be able to protect you."

"Qui est votre père?" asked Emma, though she was almost certain now that she knew precisely who his father was.

Jourdain did not have time to respond. Another of the players was all too delighted to answer for him. "The French ambassador."

Emma looked sideways at Restell, her eyes a bit narrowed and accusing. Although others at the table observed her glance, none of them save Restell could divine its meaning. For his part, Restell merely smiled innocently and offered up a thoroughly Gallic shrug.

In lightly accented English, the French ambassador's son invited Emma to sit beside him and view his cards after he dealt them. "I trust you will not give my hand away. These others are like sharks, watching every facial tic for some sign that there is a liar among us. Look especially to the Allworthys." He pointed to the pair of fair gentlemen opposite him. "Messieurs Bennet and William see everything." He waved to a footman to bring over a chair and have it placed closely beside him. Looking past Emma to Restell, he finally had the grace to ask, "You have no objection, Monsieur Gardner?"

"No," Restell said. "I wish you luck of her. She has shared none of it with me tonight." This announcement, taken by some as having an altogether different meaning, raised some chuckles and commiserating smiles.

Emma repressed the urge to pinch Restell and took the chair she was offered instead. The game he had been invited to join was a variation of the old Spanish card game conquian that she had never seen before. Several decks were in use, all of them with the eights, nines, and tens removed. The players— and there were six of them at the table—each played their own hand and were dealt ten cards, five at a time. The deal moved to the right and markers were collected for properly made melds and for being the first player to rid himself of all of his cards.

It was clearly a favorite card game of Monsieur Jourdain's, and Emma observed his friends played with similar gusto, snapping their cards on the table and triumphantly making their final discards. When a hand was won, the markers were gathered with considerable relish. In contrast, Restell's play was restrained. He was more watchful of the cards and the players than he was engaged in the actual game. Occasionally he joined the banter, but mostly he was quiet. Emma also noticed that he was the table's most consistent winner. The markers in front of him grew steadily and eventually his formidable good fortune garnered the attention of others.

As the crowd around their table grew, Emma offered the ambassador's son the opportunity to release her from his side. "You've had little enough luck with me beside you," she pointed out. "Allow me to curse Monsieur Gardner with it instead."

Jourdain would not hear of it. "It is always good luck to be in the company of a beautiful woman. Winning . . . losing . . . it is of no consequence." His thin face was transformed handsomely by his whimsical smile. "But some libation would not be amiss." He pushed his empty tumbler in front of Emma.

"Of course." Thinking nothing of it, Emma started to rise. Restell's firm hand on her wrist stopped her. She sat.

Restell said nothing. Neither did anyone else speak as he slid his own empty glass over so that Jourdain's tumbler was moved out of the way. He released Emma's wrist, making the message very clear indeed.

Emma glanced apologetically at Monsieur Jourdain. *"J'ai regrette."* Rising gracefully, she picked up Restell's glass and went to the sideboard to refill it. Quite remarkably, she thought, her hands did not shake.

The hand was already under way by the time she returned to the table. She did not fail to notice that her chair had been pulled closer to Restell's side. What other messages he might have communicated to the ambassador's son while her back was turned, Emma tried not to think about. She was more mortified by the attention paid her than she was flattered. She might well have been a savory soup bone for two curs to fight over than a woman possessed of any finer feelings.

Restell raked in markers from everyone else at the table in spite of Emma's proximity, then he surprised her by allowing her to take his cards in the next hand. "Go on," he said. "Make your own luck."

She played with more enthusiasm than skill, but did not make a poor showing. On her third round, she won the hand and received congratulations from everyone at the table and polite applause from those around it.

Restell leaned close to her and whispered in her ear. "Is it enough?"

Emma nodded and gathered her markers as Restell excused himself from the play. She had no reticule to carry her winnings and pushed them over to Restell so that he might line his pockets. He took all of them save one. This last marker he palmed and dropped it surreptitiously between her breasts as they stepped away from the table.

Before Emma recovered her wits, Restell was drawing her closer to Lord Breckenridge's table where vingt-et-un was being played. The viscount was watching the dealer, not participating, but when he saw Restell's approach he stepped back from the table altogether.

Breckenridge lifted his chin and shifted his sharp glance to the table that Restell had just vacated. He posed his question in a voice so soft that only Restell and Emma were privy to it. "Are the Allworthys behaving themselves?"

"Didn't you see? I won."

"Yes, but you cheat."

"Only so they don't."

"One would suppose they would learn. They never do. I have nightmares that Jourdain will call one or both of them out."

"Bad for business, that."

"So is bringing one's wife." Breckenridge turned his attention to Emma. "Miss Warwick, I believe." At Emma's surprise, he added, "I overheard Restell make the introduction to

Jourdain." He turned back to Restell. "You, sir, have clearly taken leave of your senses."

"I didn't know you were previously acquainted, else I would not have brought her here. She only told me when I mentioned that it was you that owned the club."

Breckenridge offered a genial, slightly sheepish smile. "You understand, I have great respect for her uncle's work." He took Emma's hand and raised it to his lips as Jourdain had done. "You may depend on my silence, Miss Warwick. You look as if that might be the question uppermost in your mind."

"Indeed it is, my lord."

Restell moved closer to Emma but addressed the viscount. "You are holding Miss Warwick's hand overlong, I think."

Breckenridge inclined his head in agreement. Still, he did not release Emma's hand quickly. His small smile taunted Restell. "It is no more than you deserve."

"Quite possibly true," Restell said. His eyes caught a movement past the viscount's shoulder. "Ah, here is Mrs. Christie, Breckenridge, and she looks in fine humor. One hopes she does not employ a dull knife to cut out your heart." With that parting shot, Restell steered Emma clear of the viscount and moved her toward the hall.

Emma tried to glance back at the inevitable encounter between Mrs. Christie and the viscount, but Restell was relentless in his march toward the exit. "Who is Mrs. Christie?"

"Breckenridge's mistress. That is an introduction that I do not want to make."

"Is your work finished, then?" she asked as he led her down the hallway.

"It will be when I've assured myself that Jourdain's friends do not ask him to share an opium pipe."

"How will you do that?"

"By removing them. It will only require a few minutes." He set her by the doorway and gave her clear instructions to remain exactly where she was. "No one will come this way once it's begun."

Emma had no time to protest his action or even to inquire

what action he meant to take. She stood against the wall and listened to the tinkling sound of glass breaking. The sound was repeated many times and on each occasion she jerked a little, expecting a scuffle or some argument to follow. Neither did. She was further surprised when Restell was the first to step out.

"Now we can go." He took her arm. "It is but a temporary solution, but for tonight at least, the French ambassador's son is safe here. Breckenridge will see that he does not come to mischief in any of the private rooms. Debauched mayhap, but not damaged."

Emma pulled Restell back. "Private rooms?"

"Oh, no." He tugged her toward the stairs just as the first of the opium eaters staggered dreamily out of their smoky den. "Now, Miss Warwick. This way."

She had no choice but to follow. She pressed herself against the stairwell as one of the glassy-eyed gentlemen started down the steps. As soon as he passed, Restell all but picked her up to remove her from the path of the other men that followed. Although they reached the street without mishap, Emma was breathless from the descent. This time when she pulled her scarf about her shoulders, Restell did not advise her against it.

The carriage that Restell had hired for this evening's purpose rolled along the curb. Restell gestured to Whittier to remain where he was and opened the door for Emma himself. He helped her inside and entered right on her heels.

"They looked perfectly respectable," Emma said, staring out the window as two gentlemen from the opium room swung their canes jauntily as they descended from the hell. "One might expect to meet them anywhere."

"And one might," Restell said, tugging her back from the window. "That is why it would be infinitely better if you did not stare. I do not think I can depend on you not to give yourself away if you were to encounter them again. Any one of them might be an art patron."

Emma thought his pointed reference was hardly subtle. "I could not have known Breckenridge owned the house. It is above everything comprehensible that he recognized me. I do not recognize myself."

"He is a man with a keen eye, but I suspect his recognition was prompted by the likelihood that he'd heard I married you and the fact that he'd previously met you."

"So it is not only that he has an eye for a woman's true beauty." Her mouth flattened. "I thought you were flattering me overmuch."

Grinning at her precise accents, Restell wondered why he found the primly set lips so inviting. "Perhaps it is the challenge," he said.

"Pardon?"

Restell had been unaware he'd spoken aloud. He simply shook his head, dismissing her question, and lifted her across the seat until she straddled his lap.

Now it was Emma who shook her head. "Here? I think not."

"A kiss. Nothing more."

She placed her hands over his. They had already risen to her knees, along with the hem of her gown. His thumbs were brushing her bare skin above her stockings. "I suppose you think you are clever or that I am weak." She closed the small distance between their mouths and kissed him with deliberate thoroughness. When she drew back she knew herself to be decidedly overheated. "Perhaps you are clever," she admitted softly. Still, she removed herself from his lap and curled instead on the bench beside him. She smiled contentedly when Restell slipped his arm around her shoulders.

"Will Lord Breckenridge be put out with you for removing his guests?" she asked.

"No. When he bought the establishment it was home to the worst sort of vices. He has been moving steadily toward respectability."

"Respectability?"

"Of a kind."

"What of those private rooms?"

"I couldn't say. They're private." Restell felt Emma nudge him lightly in the ribs. "Breckenridge does not manage a brothel, if that was the bent of your mind, but I think it is safe to suppose there are patrons who use those rooms to entertain their companions."

"You have never been in one?"

"On a matter of political intrigue," he said. "Not for the purposes you are imagining."

"Oh, I was imagining political intrigue," she told him, lying without even a twinge of guilt. "After all, the foreign minister calls upon you to manage such details as would cause distress at the highest levels of government." She lifted her head to look at him. The hack's lamp put his profile in golden relief, and she thought she detected a glimmer of a smile edging the corner of his mouth. "Really, Restell, you might have told me the truth."

"I did."

"Well, you might have made me believe you. You must know that it seemed you were having me on. The French ambassador's son, indeed. He was rather forward, I thought, though you seemed more concerned by the viscount's attentions than Jourdain's."

"Breckenridge is a credible threat. You could manage the other."

"Still, it was rather comforting when you pulled my chair closer to yours. I shouldn't like it if you were so commanding all the time, but just then, well, it made me feel very warm toward you."

Restell said nothing for a moment. "Have a care, Emma, else you will be making a declaration of some finer feeling for me."

Nodding faintly, Emma returned her head to his shoulder. "You'll tell me that the feeling will pass, won't you?"

"If that's what you'd like to hear."

She spoke in hardly more than a whisper. "I think I would, yes."

Restell gave her shoulders a slight squeeze. "I imagine you are yet afraid. You never talk about the man you gave your heart to." He felt her stiffen ever so briefly, then become almost boneless, and he knew his guess had been the correct one. "Was it Neven Charters?"

Emma closed her eyes. "Yes."

"I see." Restell had hoped he was wrong. "Do you love him still?"

Emma's lips parted, then closed. She merely shook her head in response.

"Did he know how you felt?"

"I thought he did. I thought he loved me."

"So you were being disingenuous when I told you my suspicions of that very same thing. You acted as if I couldn't possibly have correctly interpreted what I witnessed when we visited his home."

"He is my cousin's fiancé," she said. "What you observed on that occasion matters not a whit."

"Are you certain?"

"I married you."

"Yes, you did."

Emma's attention was caught by a hint of uncertainty in Restell's voice. She sat up and regarded him with some astonishment. "Do you imagine I entered this marriage to provoke some feeling from Mr. Charters?"

He felt rather foolish admitting it, but he suspected she would see straight through to his soul if he lied. "It occurred to me, yes."

"I am not so small-minded, Restell."

"No, you're not. Forgive me."

"I don't love him."

"I believe you."

"You don't, but it is good of you to pretend." She returned to the curve he made for her with his arm and shoulder. "I think you *want* to believe me."

"You might be right." Restell fell silent for a time. The hack clattered down the cobblestone street, filling the void with its peculiarly comforting rhythm. "Charters is the reason you think love is a temporary condition of the heart."

"It did seem short-lived," she said, then added softly, "On my part as well as his."

It was hearing this last admission, added almost unwillingly, that eased Restell's conscience. He had pressed his suit with some urgency, giving her little time to consider all of the consequences. In spite of that, she'd done well to negotiate the best provisions she could for the short term, but that had never entirely assuaged his guilt. He had had occasion to wonder if she would give him the same answer now that she had given him then. The question hovered on the tip of his tongue, then he called himself a coward when he bit it back.

"Did you say something?" asked Emma.

"What?" Had he spoken aloud? "No. Nothing."

The hack slowed as it approached their town house. Emma picked up the cloak she'd discarded on the opposite seat and allowed Restell to help her put it on. He fastened the frog at her throat and raised the hood over her wig, then looked at her consideringly.

"I have the oddest sense that I am inviting my mistress into my home," he told her. "It is altogether disconcerting."

"I believe the less said on that count, the better."

He grinned, kissed her on the forehead, then opened the door and helped her down. Emma hurried ahead while Restell spoke to Whittier. Once inside, she politely refused Crowley's offer to take her cloak and asked him to send Bettis to her. She went straightaway to her sitting room and waited for Bettis to arrive. She could hear Restell in conversation with the butler in the entrance hall and suspected he was giving her a few moments to collect herself.

Emma threw off her cloak when Bettis entered, then led the way to the dressing room. Catching her reflection in the cheval glass, she stopped. "I look like the veriest tart, Bettis."

"Madam *is* flushed."

Emma regarded herself critically. With her eyes perhaps a bit too bright and her pink complexion finally revealed through the fading rice powder, she looked as if she might be overset, fevered, or excited. Perhaps all three. "That is the very least of it."

"Shall I have a bath drawn for you?"

"Yes." She continued to stare at herself in the glass. The ends of her scarf were looped around her elbows, but the rest of it had fallen across her lower back. Her long white gloves had the odd effect of making her more aware of her naked shoulders and the delicate line of her collarbones. Her breasts had never once climbed above the gown's dipping neckline, but even now, when she took a deep breath they seemed tantalizingly close to doing so. She slipped two fingers between her breasts and removed Restell's marker. Palming it, she smiled.

When she turned away from the mirror, she saw that Bettis had disappeared. There was no movement in the bedroom to indicate that Restell had joined her. She walked back into the sitting room and poured herself a glass of wine while she waited for the maids to bring heated water. It was not long before they were marching to and fro through the bedroom, leaving her in peace while the tub was filled. Puzzled by Restell's continued absence, Emma occasionally ventured as far as the landing to see if he was visible in the entrance hall. She neither saw him nor heard his voice belowstairs.

When she was alone again with Bettis, she inquired after Restell.

"I couldn't say, Mrs. Gardner." Bettis grunted slightly as she pulled the tub off the hardwood floor and onto the area rug. A petite woman with delicate features, Bettis nevertheless could do the heavy lifting of a dockworker. "Don't know why those girls couldn't see this was a problem for themselves," she mumbled. Straightening, she placed her hands on her hips and stretched her back. "I saw Mr. Gardner with Mr. Hobbes and Mr. Crowley, but that was just before I answered your summons. I haven't seen any of them since."

"Curious." Emma waved Bettis aside as the maid came to help her disrobe. "That's all," she said. "You may retire."

"Are you quite certain?"

"Quite." Emma wanted to wait for Restell. She'd thought it

was what he wanted also, but his delay in arriving made her wonder if she'd misunderstood. In the carriage it had seemed he was bent on satisfying certain carnal inclinations. Now that the opportunity was upon him, he'd gone missing. Shaking her head at his perversity, Emma dipped her fingertips into her bathwater and discovered it was satisfactorily hot and infinitely inviting.

Restell found Emma up to her beautiful shoulders in water by the time he reached the dressing room. Her head was tipped back against the rim of the tub and her eyes were closed. She'd scrubbed her complexion clean of rice powder and rouge. Fresh-faced, looking younger than her years, the steamy water lent her skin a lovely pink glow. Tiny beads of moisture dotted the margin above her upper lip and the hollow of her throat. The wig lay on the seat of a ladder-back chair. The rose gown was draped over the back of it. She still wore the sheer scarf, but it was wound loosely around her dark hair to keep it away from her face. In spite of that effort, damp tendrils had managed to escape and curled against her temples.

Restell sighed. She looked thoroughly at peace, even inviolate. His eyes wandered once more to the wig, the gown, then the matching slippers peeping out from under the armoire. She'd shed the skin of the vixen and become the virgin. It was disconcerting to realize that no matter how she came to him, his desire for her defied reason as he understood it and love as he'd practiced it.

Loath to disturb her, Restell started to back out of the doorway.

Emma turned her head slightly and gave him the benefit of one raised, henna-tinted eyebrow. "Do you mean to abandon me again?"

Restell stepped back to the threshold and leaned one shoulder against the doorjamb, folding his arms across his chest. "Is that what you think?" he asked. "That I abandoned you?"

She returned her head to its previous position and kept her eyes closed. "You disappeared. What was I supposed to think?"

"That I was in the garret with Hobbes and Crowley examining a hole in the roof."

"Oh. Well, naturally that immediately occurred to me."

Restell chuckled at her wry tone. The water might be hot, but his wife was decidedly cool. "Is there something I might do to redeem myself?"

"I suppose you are going to suggest scrubbing my back, but I submit that would be more for your pleasure than mine."

"That's because you've only ever had Bettis put a flannel to your skin. If I might be allowed to demonstrate, you will comprehend there is a difference." He watched her mouth purse slightly. Butter wasn't going to warm in it any time soon. He was going to have to be clever. "Mayhap you will permit me to brush your hair."

The thought of it was so tantalizing that Emma thought she might become as liquid as the water she sat in. Still, she managed to sound as though she were granting a boon. "That would be agreeable."

Smiling to himself, Restell picked up Emma's silver-handled hairbrush lying on her vanity and dropped to his knees behind the tub. "Did it distress you that I was watching you from the doorway?"

"No. I suspected you were there. I heard you moving around the bedroom, and when I didn't . . ." She didn't finish her sentence as he tugged the scarf from her hair. One tail of it fluttered across her shoulder before it slipped to the floor. "I'm glad you came back."

Restell applied the brush to her hair. Starting at the crown of her head, he pulled it through the heavy wave of hair that cascaded over the edge of the tub. "I truly never left," he said. "Though I understand it did not seem so to you. I *am* sorry, Emma. Hobbes and Crowley showed regrettable timing."

"So you are committed to your hole-in-the-roof tale."

"I am until something better occurs to me."

"I have always liked it that once you set a course you are not easily moved."

He gave her hair a little tug with the brush. "Stubborn?" he asked. "Is that the meaning I should take?"

"Steady," she said, sinking a bit deeper into the water. "It's very . . . umm . . . comforting."

Restell lifted her hair and dragged the brush through the underside, just caressing the back of her neck with the soft tips of the bristles. Her shiver, he suspected, was not because she was cold of a sudden. He continued brushing, the strokes steady and even, a rhythm that she knew, at least in that part of her consciousness that knew him so intimately. He heard her give up a small sound of satisfaction deep at the back of her throat. Pulling her hair to one side, he held it away from her neck with the brush and leaned forward to kiss the gentle hollow just above her collarbone. He used the tip of his tongue to lick the dew from her skin.

"Do you trust me, Emma?"

She could hardly think what he was asking her. "I . . . I . . . umm, yes . . . mmm, yes, I do."

"Do you trust me with you?"

She turned her head to offer up the sensitive cord of her neck. His lips were warm against her skin, his tongue warmer still. "With me?"

"To do as I like . . . to do *anything* I like."

Emma simply could not think. Restell's voice slid over her like honey: smooth and sweet and thick. He flicked his tongue in the shallow curve behind her ear as if he could taste the words he drizzled on her skin. It seemed to Emma that the water had turned viscous, just like her gray matter.

"Anything I like," he repeated softly. "Do you trust me?"

Emma swallowed. He was pulling the brush through her hair again. Her scalp tingled first, then the rest of her. He let her hair cascade over the back of the tub and lightly dragged the brush across her shoulder. She bit her lower lip. The sound at the back of her throat was a whimper.

Restell withdrew the brush.

Emma waited.

Restell waited longer.

"Yes," she whispered. "Yes."

"Look at me, Emma."

She turned her head. Her lashes fluttered, then opened. His face was not far from hers, his eyes dark and watchful. She

let him study her features and knew he was gauging the truth
of the confession he'd provoked. "I do trust you, Restell."

He nodded slowly. "Give me your hands."

Emma's eyebrows rose slightly, but she lifted her arms out
of the water and presented her hands to him.

"Hold this." He set the brush in her upturned palms.

Emma curled her fingers around the silver-handled brush
while Restell held her wrists together in one hand. Her breath
caught as he showed her what was in his other hand. The sheer
scarf that she'd worn across her shoulders, then in her hair, was
now wound between his fingers and over his forearm. It was not
possible for her to look away as he looped the fine, gossamer
fabric around her wrists. She stared at her hands as if they be-
longed to someone else, but when he stood and tugged on the
tether that bound her to him, she came to her feet as well.

Rivulets of water ran down her arms and dripped from her
bent elbows. Droplets trickled between her breasts; others
clung to her puckered nipples. Her mons glistened. Water fell
in a meandering stream over her flat belly and along the curve
of her hip, but it was the wetness between her slightly parted
thighs that Emma felt most keenly.

The distance separating them closed as Restell made two
small circles with his wrist, shortening the length of the scarf.
Emma's slim frame became a wet imprint on his clothes. Lifting her, he carried her into their bedroom. She still clutched
the brush in her fingers, but when she realized it and made to
drop it, he shook his head.

"I have need of it."

The words were matter-of-fact. It was the husky timbre of
Restell's voice and his darkening look that caused Emma's
knuckles to become nearly bloodless while every other part
of her suffused with color. When he set her sitting up on the
edge of the bed, she didn't move. It was unspoken between
them now that she would take direction from him. She
watched him unwind the scarf from his wrist. The tail slipped
through his fingers, brushed her knees, then fell to the floor.

It lay in a rosy puddle just below where her heels were hitched on the bed rail.

Her eyes fixed on it for a moment, but inevitably they were drawn back to that part of the scarf that was still wound around her own wrists. She looked up at Restell. He was watching her, a faint smile edging his lips.

"You were curious tonight about the hell's private rooms," he said.

Her mouth dry of a sudden, Emma could only nod.

"Shall I satisfy your curiosity, Emma?" He laid one hand over her bound wrists, bent, and whispered in her ear. "Shall I satisfy you?"

Emma's lips never parted, but the tiny moan at the back of her throat was audible to both of them. When Restell lightly squeezed her wrists, she realized it was answer enough.

"Lie back," he said, taking the brush from her nerveless fingers. He set it aside while he positioned her arms above her head and tied off the loose end of the scarf to one of the bedposts. "The private rooms are often used for . . . well, let us say they are often used for the practice of certain singular carnal pleasures." Restell stepped back from the bed as he unfastened the buttons on his frock coat and removed it. He laid it over the back of the wing chair, then loosened his stock and unbuttoned his waistcoat. "You are perhaps wondering how I come to know that to be true."

Frustrated, Emma gave her wrists a little tug, testing the slack in the scarf. The consequence was to tighten the knot just below the ball of her thumbs. Restell's feigned sympathy was maddening.

"Have a care," he said, "else you'll make yourself uncomfortable." He placed his stock over the back of the chair and shrugged out of his waistcoat, then he sat on the arm of the chair to remove his boots and stockings. He pulled on the tails of his shirt, loosening it about his waist, but did not remove it or his trousers. Returning to the bed, he regarded her a moment before he sat. "I won't mind if you decide you'd like to get a little of your own back." He turned, drawing his knee up on the mattress so it nudged the curve of Emma's waist and hip. One corner of his mouth edged upward. The half-grin was meant to nudge her as well. "Forgive me. You made it clear once before that you are not so small-minded."

Emma's tongue was still cleaved to the roof of her dry mouth. Her effort at a rejoinder was further hindered by the warm hand Restell placed over her thigh. "It is an opinion I am prepared to revise," she said hoarsely. His fingertips were sliding toward her inner thigh. When he turned his hand, he made a space for it between her thighs. Emma's own fingers curled around the sheer tether that held her fast to the bed. He was watching her intently now, and she could not look away.

Restell leaned toward the bedside table and picked up Emma's brush. A heavy lock of hair lay across her shoulder. He set the brush against it and dragged it lightly through her hair and over her skin. The path he took led to her breast. He paused, watched her chest heave slightly with a ragged breath, then passed the soft bristles across her nipple. The rosy aureole darkened and her nipple was made invitingly hard. Restell bent and took it into his mouth.

Emma's heels pressed deeply into the bedding. The hand between her thighs held her still, frustrating her efforts to rock her hips. She moaned softly and arched her neck instead as his tongue darted across the swollen bead. He rolled it between his lips and sucked. She tugged harder on the scarf. The bed head groaned with her effort.

Restell heard the groan, raised his head, and checked the binding at her wrists. He slipped one finger between the scarf and her skin, pulling to ease the pressure. He cupped one side of her face, brushing his thumb across her cheek. She turned into the caress. Her lips parted, and the tip of her tongue wet one corner. Restell kissed her and wet the rest.

The sensation of the brush sliding over her ribs was unexpected. The breath she took was Restell's. His mouth was hot on hers, hotter still when he captured her other breast. The brush never stopped its slow descent, gliding over the flat plain of her belly. The bristles dipped in the curve created when her abdomen retracted, then lifted as they grazed her mons.

Emma's soft protest had Restell raising his head. He studied her kiss-swollen mouth, the darkened blue-green eyes, the small vertical crease between her eyebrows, and recognized uncertainty and frustration. He waited. "Shall I stop?" he asked.

Emma closed her eyes. She was a single nerve, pulled taut by not only what he did to her, but by the very sound of his voice. She shook her head.

"Tell me," he said.

"Please," she whispered. "Make me . . ."

He smiled when she didn't finish that thought. She didn't have the word for what she wanted him to do to her. Then she surprised him.

Opening her eyes, she stared at him intently and said, "Make me scream."

Now it was Restell who felt as if he'd been robbed of not only his breath, but his sense. It was her small, satisfied smile that helped him recover both. He might have tied her wrists, but in every way that was important she had bound him to her. Restell lifted his hand and showed her the brush. He gave it a toss, flipping it so that he caught the bristled end. The silver handle rose like a stem from his fist. He saw Emma's eyebrows lift, her lips part, and the certain knowledge of what he meant to do was there in her eyes.

Emma's fingers splayed, then closed, as Restell carefully pushed the handle of the brush inside her. It was warm from the heat of his fist and rigid as only metal could be. He moved it in and out slowly, matching the thrust to her breathing at first, then making her meet the rhythm he set. She watched him; he watched what he was doing to her.

Emma's hips rolled. She was helpless to do otherwise. It was not possible to accept the insistent, intimate penetration without rising up to meet it. Pleasure thrummed through her; every nerve vibrating as though it had been plucked like the string of a bow. She was taut as well: her arms stretched overhead, her shoulders set, the small of her back rising off the bed. All of her was poised on the sharp edge of pleasure, but it was when Restell flung the brush aside and positioned himself between her legs that she knew the moment of crisis was upon her.

The thrust of his body was harder and hotter than what had come before. Emma tried to clutch at Restell's shoulders. The tether thwarted her. She clutched his hips with her knees instead. The soles of her feet pressed the back of his thighs. Every part of her clenched, holding him fast. Her body's contraction moved him to groan, then simply moved him. He ground into her. Rising. Falling.

She was undone.

Restell absorbed her shudder, then held himself still long enough to release her wrists. Turning on his back, he pulled her with him so she was seated on his groin. Now the tempo was hers, and she did get some of her own back, teasing him so artfully that he was made molten.

She pressed him to surrender, to give her his hoarse cry and all of his will, and when he did she was splendidly joyful, laughing at the turnabout in their play. She left him with no strength to deny her this small amusement.

Some minutes passed before Restell said feelingly, "Bloody hell, Emma, but I cannot move."

Since she was lying full length on top of him, the simplest solution was to slip to one side. When she made to do so, he palmed her bottom and kept her just where she was.

"I didn't mean that you should," he whispered. "Not just yet."

This raised Emma's faint smile. She dropped her head back to his chest. "You make me fearless, Restell."

His hands slid up her back, fingertips tracing the length of her spine. He made no reply, closing his eyes instead, hoping that when she realized she could leave him, she would choose to stay.

Chapter 13

Emma alighted from her carriage just as Marisol was arriving in hers. She waved off Whittier knowing that one of Restell's rather unconventional footmen was already close by. She refrained from looking around for this afternoon's guardian. It was a rare moment that she ever spied one of them. Even McCleod, with his shock of red hair and peculiarly elfin features, was able to slip out of sight, seemingly without regard for the properties of solid structures.

Emma stood at Lady Rivendale's gate and waited for Marisol. Her cousin smiled in greeting—a trifle coolly, Emma thought. She understood the cause of it a moment later when Neven Charters climbed out of the carriage. Emma had expected Marisol would be invited to tea, but the presence of her fiancé was very much unwelcome.

"Never fear, Mrs. Gardner," Neven said as he escorted Marisol to the gate. "I have no intention of joining the countess's clutch."

Emma realized that her openly wary expression had bordered on rude. She smiled politely and inclined her head. "It is simply that I had the impression it was to be ladies only."

"And so it is," he said. He released Marisol's arm. "Go on, Marisol. I require but a moment of your cousin's time."

Marisol made a pretty pout, clearly unhappy that she was to be excluded from the conversation. "I don't know why I cannot be privy to it. I know the particulars well enough. And she is *my* cousin."

Neven remained firm, looking pointedly from her to Lady Rivendale's front door. "I will call on you this evening, Marisol."

Emma watched this exchange and called it a draw. Neven had held his position with Marisol, and her cousin had demonstrated remarkable maturity by not flouncing off. Her exit in fact was quite dignified.

When Marisol was out of hearing, Emma turned her attention to Charters. "What can be of such import that you must needs speak to me away from Marisol? She had much to say after I accompanied you to the fountain in the countess's garden, not the least of which was blaming me for your head wound. I can scarce have a conversation with her in which that is not brought to my attention."

"I will speak to her," Neven said.

Emma wondered that he set such store by his influence. She waited for him to explain what he wanted, conscious all the while that somewhere someone was watching and that Restell would know of this encounter by the time she joined him for dinner.

Neven's dark eyes searched Emma's face. He leaned a bit on the brass-tipped walking stick at his side. "There is no easy way to relate this, and I will understand if you do not believe that it pains me to do it, but it must be said."

"Then by all means, say it straightaway." Emma wished Neven had not sent Marisol away. Her cousin would have blurted out the whole of it by now.

"Mr. Gardner has set up a mistress."

Emma's eyes narrowed. Out of patience with him, her whispered rejoinder was harsh. "I cannot countenance this. I will not hear a word spoken against my father-in-law." She turned to go but was stopped by Neven's firm hand on her elbow. She did not attempt to shake him off, merely regarded him coldly.

"Forgive me," he said, pressing on. The look in his eyes

was sympathetic, even a bit rueful. "It is not Sir Geoffrey. I am speaking of Mr. Gardner—your husband."

Emma blinked. She composed herself somewhat stiffly. "My response is still the same, I do not—"

"I *saw* him. With her." Neven snapped his walking stick against the side of his boot. "I did not come to you without consideration. It has been a full fortnight since I observed them together. I could not remain silent, and after I told Marisol, I knew I must tell you."

"You should not have told either one of us. It's not done. I know what's expected of me. I know that I—" She stopped, reining in her tumbling thoughts. "A fortnight past, you said. You've known so long ago as that?"

He nodded. "I'm sorry, it is only that you deserve better than—"

She interrupted him with an impatient, dismissive wave, then raised that hand to her temple. Her head was throbbing now. She stared at Neven's boot, at his walking stick, at the brass tip beating a tattoo against the leather, and she thought her knees might buckle.

"Emmalyn?"

His use of her name, spoken with a certain nuance of intimacy and concern, helped Emma find the last measure of her resolve. *Fearless*. That single word threaded itself around her jangling nerves and steadied the frantic beating of her heart. *Fearless*. Her mouth was too parched to say it aloud, but her lips moved around the word. She stayed upright. Before Neven could reach for her, she pivoted abruptly and hurried up the steps to Lady Rivendale's.

The door opened before Emma knocked. Nelson had been clearly waiting for her arrival. He inquired after her before she had opportunity to compose herself. "I'm all of a piece, Nelson," Emma said, assuring herself as much as the man watching her so closely. She tugged on the ribbons of her ice blue, silk-covered bonnet and swept it off her head. He accepted it without comment and waited for the shawl that loosely draped her shoul-

ders and back. Emma handed it to him, then removed her short
white gloves. "Am I the last to arrive?"

"Indeed." He nodded gravely. "This way, Mrs. Gardner.
They are waiting for you in the music room."

Emma was glad it was to be the music room. She would
think of Restell there, of his proposal and of her protests.
That's what she would remember when Marisol looked at her
with pity in her eyes. She would keep her secret close, knowing that a fortnight ago she had been her husband's mistress.

Lady Rivendale's expression brightened when Emma ap-
peared on the threshold. "Oh, do come in, dear. Thank you,
Nelson, that will be all." She held out her hand and beckoned
Emma closer. "Now we are complete."

Emma walked with more steadiness than she would have
thought possible only minutes earlier. *Fearless*. She made a
curtsy for the countess, then turned to Lady Gardner and offered the same respectful gesture.

"So much ceremony," Lady Gardner said. She proffered
her cheek and tapped it with a forefinger. "All my daughters
kiss me thus. Are you not one of them now?"

Emma dutifully bussed her mother-in-law's cheek. "I wish
to be," she said. Restell's married sisters were standing now,
and they offered hugs before they returned to their seats on
either side of their mother. Emma was reminded of mis-
matched bookends because Wynetta Wellsley and Imogene
Branson were as different as night and day, with Imogene
being the dark one and Wynetta as fair as Restell. Emma's last
greeting was to Marisol. Her cousin was poised prettily on a
Queen Anne chair beside the table set for tea. She offered her
cheek much as Lady Gardner had. Emma bent and kissed her
and was not surprised that her lips found no warmth there.

"Your gown is lovely, Marisol. I do not recall that I've seen
it before."

"Mrs. Wellsley was just complimenting me on the very
same," Marisol said.

Emma realized that she had interrupted that exchange and
quite possibly denied Marisol her full tribute. That was never

wise, and indeed, out of sight of the others Marisol darted a dark look of disapproval in her direction. Emma gave it no heed, much preferring it to the pitying concern she had anticipated. "Well, compliments are deserved. It is lovely, and you are lovelier still."

As quickly as that, Marisol was mollified. "You are kind, Emma, to say so."

Lady Rivendale patted the space beside her on the sofa. "Please sit, my dear, else you will give me a crick in my neck. Miss Vega? Will you be so good as to pour?"

Emma observed that Marisol was glad to be singled out for that privilege. It gave her cousin an opportunity to demonstrate graciousness and grace. For herself, Emma was equally glad she had not been asked. She hadn't Marisol's flair for the task on any occasion and after her encounter with Neven, she suspected her hands would have trembled.

As soon as Emma sat, the countess placed her hand firmly over Emma's forearm as though she expected her to take flight. "It is an age since you have been here," Lady Rivendale said. "I do not believe you have come for tea but once since your marriage. Sir Arthur keeps you too much to himself, I think. That is the observation I have shared with him."

"I hope he told you that I enjoy his company, though that should not be interpreted that I enjoy yours"—Emma extended her glance to include her in-laws and her cousin—"or any of yours, less."

It was Lady Gardner who gave her friend, the countess, a knowing smile. "Did I not say she excels at diplomacy?"

Wynetta looked at her mother askance. "I believe, Mama, that it was Father who made that observation. Is that not so, Imogene?"

"It is."

Lady Gardner dismissed the chiding and confided to the others. "It amuses them to correct me on such small details as this. They cannot know, of course, that while their father might have said it in their presence, I said it first to their father."

Emma did not miss the amused exchange between Lady Gardner's daughters. It raised her own slight and wistful smile. The comfort they shared with each other, and with their mother, was not a point of envy, but one of yearning. She felt Lady Rivendale patting her arm lightly and realized she had given something of herself away.

"It seems of late," Emma said, "that I have spent as much time in your company as my uncle's. Indeed, these past few weeks I have scarcely been at home. With invitations to tea or to accompany one or another of you shopping, I don't believe I've had an afternoon with my husband. Restell has been moved to remark on it."

"Then he has noticed," Lady Gardner said. "That is good. Sometimes I despair of that boy seeing what is in front of his nose."

"There is a difference, Mama," Imogene said, "between Restell seeing what is in front of his nose and being led about by it. Restell is excellent at the former."

"I'm sure I don't know what you mean."

Wynetta chuckled. "There is no sense in baiting her, Imogene. She will not admit that she has never cut our leading strings."

Lady Gardner admonished her daughters. "Hush, girls. You will give Emmalyn fear of me." She accepted the cup of tea that Marisol passed to her. "Thank you, Miss Vega." She chose a small cake from the plate and bit into it delicately. "I wonder if you will play for us later. I am given to understand that you have a fine hand at the pianoforte."

"It will be my pleasure," Marisol said. "If Mrs. Wellsley will turn the sheets for me."

Wynetta agreed. "Of course. I confess, I have been eager to hear you play ever since Lady Rivendale remarked on your talent."

"It is only a modest talent, so I hope her ladyship has not overstated her compliments. I should not like to disappoint."

"I am confident you will not," the countess said. She sipped her tea. "Your father says you have your mother's skill."

"He has told me the same," Marisol said, "but I can't say if it is exactly so. I have no memory of hearing her play."

"Oh, but that is unfortunate. Still, I'm sure your father does not exaggerate. He seems to me to be very cautious in his acclamations."

Marisol returned to her chair when everyone was served. "Would you agree, Emmalyn? Is Father cautious with praise?"

"He is deeply critical of his own work. I have always thought he holds others to a similarly high standard. I would have to agree with her ladyship, Sir Arthur is not easily moved to compliments in regard to one's talent."

Marisol sighed. "It is the same with Mr. Charters, I fear. Is it so with other men?"

Lady Gardner nodded. "I'm afraid so. They pay us pretty compliments for looking fine, but it is only because it reflects well on them to be seen with us. That is a sad truth, I know, but there you have it."

"Lady Gardner is quite correct," the countess said. "If you desire more in the way of notice, you have to train them."

Emma was moved to interject. "But I do not want undeserved admiration. If my talent is mediocre, then it would be a small cruelty for my husband to puff the thing up. It would expose me to the ridicule of others."

"That is unlikely to happen," Marisol said. "You do not play the pianoforte, nor do you sing. You dance only when cornered. What small talent is there to puff up?"

Emma laughed. "If I had one, you have pricked it cleanly. But you are right: I am sadly lacking in accomplishments."

"Do you embroider?" Imogene asked.

"Poorly," Emma said. "I set the threads too tightly. It makes my jaw ache."

"Mine also," Lady Rivendale admitted. "Have you tried your hand at cards? I find it to be a skillful and often rewarding entertainment."

"I recently was introduced to conquian, but I fear I demonstrated no head for the strategy of play."

"Conquian?" Lady Rivendale's expression was at once

suspicious. "That is a game for the hells. Where did you learn it?"

It occurred to Emma to ask the same of the countess, but she was mindful of her place. "Mr. Gardner explained it to me."

Imogene quickly hid her smile behind her hand. It was Wynetta who tittered and earned an admonishing glance from her mother.

Lady Gardner set her cup firmly in her saucer. "Restell is a thorough rascal. As his mother, I am perfectly free to say so."

"And frequently does," Wynetta said under her breath. This comment did not go unnoticed, and she received another reproving sideways look.

"Truly, Emmalyn," Lady Gardner said, "you must not permit him to lead you astray. Playing . . . playing . . . .what is the game again?"

"Conquian." Emma and the countess answered together.

"Precisely. You might have admitted taking instruction in that game to someone who understands its significance."

Emma was fairly certain that's what she had just done, but for reasons that were based in a friendship of many years, Lady Gardner did not mind that the countess knew.

"Someone other than the countess," Lady Gardner said. "She is favored with an excellent, if somewhat eccentric reputation, and no one remarks on her breadth of knowledge of things that polite society does not countenance. Is that not so, Georgia?"

"It is. But I am of an age, you see. One is forgiven certain things when one is of an age. You are not yet there, Emmalyn, and will not be there for some time, so Marianna is quite right to caution you. Restell should have warned you, but then he is a rascal, just as his mother says. We love him, though, don't we, girls?"

In unison Wynetta and Imogene nodded dutifully and gravely while their eyes sparkled with repressed mirth.

"I promise I shall tread more carefully in the future," Emma said.

"And you will deliver Restell a scold, won't you?" Lady Gardner asked.

"I think that is better left to you."

"As if I ever see the boy. He might as well be as far away as Ferrin. Ian is my only son who visits regularly and inquires after my health. Restell avoids me and regularly puts all of my humors at risk."

Emma hardly knew how she might respond. She had a strong urge to defend her husband and an equal desire not to offend her mother-in-law. "He has been occupied of late with affairs of business. Perhaps that explains his absence."

Marisol raised her cup halfway to her mouth. "Affairs of business, Emma? How so?"

There was a certain slyness in her cousin's tone that Emma did not miss but doubted anyone else heard. "I'm not certain what you mean." Emma hoped Marisol had not misjudged her audience. If she thought she could level an unsavory accusation at Restell, then she was sadly out of it. She would only alienate herself. "He has a number of financial interests that require his attention. When I left him today he was deep in the study of a stack of ledgers. I quite felt sorry for him."

"Then he no longer frequents the hells," Marisol said. "That bodes well, I think. I do not heed the gossip, of course, but one hears things whether one wishes to or not."

Emma thought Marisol had done a masterful job of avoiding the family's collective cudgel by crediting gossip. Lady Gardner, she noted, had developed a distinct pallor to her complexion. Perhaps she had not overstated the risk to her humors.

"What have you heard?" Imogene asked.

"It does not bear repeating," Marisol said. "It is certain that the wags have it wrong."

"Still," Wynetta said, "I would like to know how wrong they are."

"Really, I should not like to say it." She set her cup and saucer on the tray beside the teapot and stood. "Shall I play?"

"Please," Lady Rivendale said tautly. She gestured to

Wynetta, encouraging her to join Marisol at the pianoforte. When Marisol and Wynetta turned, she said, "You are looking rather pale, dear. Is there something that can be brought for you?"

It required a moment for Emma to realize that the countess was speaking to her, not Restell's mother. "No, nothing. There is no need—not for me—but perhaps for Lady Gardner."

Lady Rivendale glanced at her friend. "Fan her, Imogene. That will settle her nerves."

Marianna Gardner laid her hand over her daughter's wrist. "What will settle my nerves is not having Restell's name bandied about by the wags. It was very different when Ferrin was the rake. He did not get himself regularly called out, and no one ever shot him. He did not drink himself senseless or become an opium eater. His mistresses were women of breeding, not actresses and opera dancers. Ferrin did not flee every eligible young lady who was presented to him, nor was his wedding a perfectly havey-cavey affair."

"Marianna," Lady Rivendale said sternly. "You are overset and forget yourself."

But Lady Gardner was not finished. "And Ferrin has never come to the attention of the gossips even once since his marriage." The sweet strains of Marisol's playing did not soften Lady Gardner's agitation. It was seeing Emma's stricken face that did that. "Oh, my dear, do you think I blame you? No, goodness no. I blame myself. A mother has little enough influence, I fear, and a wife even less. I recognize Restell's fine hand in whatever has happened that is untoward. It is all very well that he is a rascal to us, but the *ton* is not so kind or forgiving as his family."

"Mother," Imogene said calmly, "you do not even know that he has done anything the least improper. Miss Vega refuses to explain herself."

Emma straightened her shoulders and put a proper lift in her chin. "My husband is a good and kind man, Lady Gardner. There is no cause to reproach yourself. You might, instead, congratulate yourself for any influence that you had in shaping a considerate and compassionate gentleman. He is all of that. A proper Samaritan who asks only what is reasonable in return for his great good deeds. If he has come to the attention of the gossips, then it is as a consequence of doing something that is right, not wrong, and if it reflects on me, or makes me an object of a pitying glance, then I shall accept it because I know the truth. My husband acts on his conscience, and he is in possession of a finely calibrated moral compass. You could ask for no better son, nor I a better companion. We are blessed, both of us."

These last words, spoken as they were with a slight tremor in the timbre, were greeted with complete silence. Even Marisol had stopped playing.

It was the countess who finally stepped into the breach. "Do you see, Marianna? Your fears are groundless. It is much more than affection that she feels for your son. She clearly loves him, and what is more, she respects him. That cannot help but bode well. Now cease fretting that nothing good can—" Lady Rivendale stopped, sighing when she saw tears gathering at the corners of her friend's eyes. "Where is your mother's handkerchief, Imogene? She has been a watering pot of late, and one knows now that it has been for naught."

The countess sighed again, this time with great feeling. "How foolish we are. Embrace it, I say, for there is not the least shame in caring so very deeply." She patted Emma's hand while she glanced over her shoulder at Marisol and Wynetta at the pianoforte. "Continue playing, Marisol. We are endeavoring to recover here."

Emma was lying on the chaise in their suite of rooms when Restell found her. She had a cold compress across her forehead and her eyes were closed. He went immediately to her side. Her eyelids fluttered but did not open. It was enough indication that she was not sleeping.

"Crowley said I would find you here," Restell said. "Are you unwell?"

She hardly knew how to answer that. "Lady Rivendale announced to your mother, your married sisters, and Marisol that I clearly love you. You will not credit it, Restell, but I am certain she's right."

Restell found a space on the chaise where he could sit. He lowered himself somewhat slowly to that spot as he considered his response. "So you came home and prostrated yourself across the chaise. Yes, I can see how that would be the thing to do. The compress makes me think the feeling has not yet passed."

Emma found his hand and slipped hers under it. "You are amused by my condition."

"On the contrary, I am made hopeful by it. How long has it been since Lady Rivendale's epiphany?"

"Several hours, but I have only just arrived home."

"And how long have you suspected that she's right?"

Emma dragged the damp compress over her eyes and laid her free hand on top of it. "It is not a suspicion. I have harbored suspicions for weeks. When I heard her say the thing aloud, I knew it was fact."

"I see."

"I feel as if my heart is being squeezed, Restell."

He understood her discomfort. It was often the same for him. "Does it make you afraid?"

"A little."

"Then I am not the only one. That is good to know."

Emma picked up one corner of the compress and regarded him with a single, wary eye.

"Do you think I'm never afraid, Emma? I hope I am never so foolish as to be without fear. It humbles me. It makes me cautious, and on occasion it makes me clever. Loving you is like that. From the outset. The fear that you would never know the same for me has made me humble, cautious, and—"

Emma removed the compress and placed one finger against his lips. "And very, very clever." She shook her head, marveling at him as her hand fell away. "Have you loved me so long, then?"

"I declared myself in the carriage, remember? You were the one who wanted no part of it."

"You told me you were a romantic, that you fall in love regularly."

"And so I am," he said. "And so I do. I don't fault you for being cautious. I comprehended there was a difference in my feelings for you, but the difference was in *me*. You couldn't have known that then. I'm not certain why you believe it now."

Emma pushed herself up on her elbows. "You invited me to join you when you went to a gaming hell. I don't suppose you can appreciate how dear I hold that memory. Not only the adventure, Restell, but the *invitation*. To be asked to share that small enterprise with you, it was outside all my expectations, yet you proposed it casually, as if there were nothing the least improper or singular about it. You acted as if I were your equal." Her voice became a husky whisper. "As if I were your friend."

Emma sat up the rest of the way. Her face was close to his. "It seemed irrelevant that I was your wife or even that I was a woman. You made it irrelevant to me." Emma cupped his face, smiling sympathetically as Restell's eyes darted to the compress at her side. "Have you need of it?"

"It depends," he said. "On whether you think being a woman—and my wife—is irrelevant now."

Her answer was to kiss him warmly and ardently and invite him to take her to bed.

The window seat in Restell's library was Emma's favorite place for reflection. Even when she was not alone in the room, Restell rarely interrupted her thoughts if she was sitting there. This evening, however, he was making noises behind his paper and on occasion actually giving it a shake. She wondered if perhaps she should not have allowed hunger to draw them from their bed. They might have stayed there and asked for dinner to be brought to them, but she had pressed Restell to dress for dinner and escort her to the dining room.

Her motives were perfectly selfish. She enjoyed looking at him across the table from her. The shallow vase of hothouse flowers did not obstruct her view, and candlelight burnished his pale hair gold. The points of his collar framed the sharp line of his jaw, while the elaborately tied neckcloth softened his beautifully sculpted features. The Viking warrior tamed is what she thought when she watched him take mannered bites and relish the bouquet of his wine. And when he smiled at her over the rim of his glass, even if it was only with his eyes, she was immediately reminded that her warrior's civility could be undone if she gave him the slightest provocation.

Now, listening to him swear softly under his breath, Emma laid down her embroidery hoop and moved the basket of threads out of her way. It was no hardship to put the thing aside. She had been truthful with Lady Rivendale earlier in the day: she had little talent and even less patience for stitchery. She only kept it around so she might have something to busy her hands while her mind was more deeply occupied.

"Is it something you can share?" Emma asked. "Or should I resist asking for the particulars?"

Restell lowered his paper and regarded her with a vague look over the top. "Pardon? Did you say something?"

Emma gave him a pointed stare. "You were growling. I wondered if you wanted to explain those noises."

"Growling? Was I?" He closed the paper, folded it, and set it on the table beside his chair. "It is our good friend Monsieur Jourdain. He is the subject of an unflattering illustration in the *Gazette*. They offer no name, but there is no mistaking the likeness nor the intent to cast him as a wastrel and debaucher. The accompanying article suggests that influences from abroad are corrupting the young gentlemen about town."

"Oh, that *is* unfortunate. What is to be done?"

"The *Gazette* will have to print a retraction."

"You can make them do that?"

Restell shrugged. "We shall see. There are influences that

can be brought to bear. That is but a first step. What to do about the mischief makers, though, that will require some thought. Jourdain calls them his boon companions, but the Allworthy cousins are miscreants of the first water, no better than the Peele brothers, worse, in fact, because they have had opportunities of wealth and privilege denied to fellows like Elliot and Will Peele. They have shown their hand often enough by cheating at cards. It is tempting to throw down the gauntlet."

Emma gave her husband a quelling look.

He chuckled. "Tempting but hardly prudent. It is also less satisfying than a more public set down. I shall have to find some way to impugn their honor."

"Impugn their honor? Is that possible? I believe you called them miscreants a moment ago."

"They are self-important, Emma, and therefore they over-reach. They make themselves vulnerable because of the influential gentlemen they choose as their marks. I wonder if they will accept an invitation to Lytton's."

"The gentleman's club? Not Breckenridge's hell?"

"The club will serve better than any of the hells because the members will not hesitate to come forward. I imagine if I puff the fellows up with their consequence, they will join me in the card room. Father should be there, I think. In fact, he is the better person to extend the invitation. Perhaps some of his friends will join the enterprise. I feel sure the foreign minister will have names to suggest."

"Jourdain's would-be friends are foolish, Restell, not witless. They won't cheat in the company of the minister's friends."

He waved her reasonable point aside. "They don't have to cheat; I only have to make it *seem* that's what they're doing. Oh, but they will hate being caught out at something they haven't done."

"Does it not seem dangerous to you? Are you certain no one will be called to account for it?"

"It's deliciously just, Emma, and no one's been called out

at my father's club in half a century. They plot wars there and the seizing of entire countries. Pistols at dawn do not interest them in the least."

"I must say, you appear to have the thing well in hand. And you have stopped growling. That is most excellently done of you."

He grinned, tipping his head in her direction. "You are my muse."

She raised a single eyebrow. "I am sure you mean to compliment me, but you are planning the certain ruination of reputations. It is just, as you say, but also cold-blooded. Can I not inspire you to write a sonnet?"

"Not a good one."

Emma laughed. "I will choose to believe you have no talent for it, not that I am insufficiently inspiring."

"And you would be correct." Restell stretched out his legs, crossing them at the ankle. His regard was considering. "You have said very little about your visit to Lady Rivendale's, apart from the epiphany, of course. I take it that your afternoon was in all other ways unexceptional?"

Emma did not miss the slight inflection that made Restell's last statement a question. She sighed, knowing very well what he wanted to hear. "I suppose you have spoken to McCleod or Hobbes or—"

"It was McCleod and Shaw this afternoon," Restell said. "For you and Miss Vega. I had the same story from both of them, though neither was close enough to hear the actual exchange between you and Charters."

"Then you know it was brief."

"So I was given to understand. I was also told that the encounter left you agitated."

Emma supposed that was as good a description as any. Still, she flushed, embarrassed that she had not demonstrated more in the way of sangfroid. "I was put off my stride from the moment he alighted from Marisol's carriage. I did not anticipate that he would accompany her."

"I imagine he did so to see you."

She nodded. "He admitted as much. He wanted to tell me that you had taken a mistress."

Emma thought Restell might curse or otherwise take exception to this intelligence. Not so much as an eyelash flickered. He did not blink or shift his weight in the chair. Neither of his eyebrows lifted in the cynical arch he often affected. The corners of his mouth remained as flat as the seam of his lips.

She could not have imagined that such profound stillness could be so threatening. She knew a moment's unease, not for herself, but for Neven Charters. "Restell?"

"Go on," he said. "He is referring to you, of course."

"That's right. He's known for a fortnight. There must be gossip as a consequence of you escorting me to the hell."

Restell's response was dry as dust. "How clever he is to keep his ear to the ground. The only surprise is that he waited so long to bring the news to you."

"You judge him harshly, Restell. He was quite aware that his behavior was beyond the pale. He came to me only after he told Marisol what he'd learned."

"That does not improve my opinion of him. I do not trust his motives, and neither should you. If someone was compelled to tell you, it should have been your cousin."

"She would have announced it publicly. Indeed, she almost did. Recall that tea was with your mother, your sisters, and the countess. She baited me. I would not have been on my guard if not for Mr. Charters."

"I must remind you that Mr. Charters *gave* Miss Vega the bait."

Emma sighed. "I still think you are severe in your judgment."

"Then I freely admit my confusion. If it was not Charters or his announcement that you found disagreeable, what set you off at a run?"

"I do not think I ran."

"McCleod and Shaw would beg to differ, but we will leave them out of it. Tell me the rest, please."

"I cannot like it that you are so bloody single-minded."

Restell was wholly unoffended. The smile he offered her was perfectly genial. "Like a dog with a bone."

"Oh, very well. Mr. Charters was banging his walking stick against his boot. It was unnerving. He has one with a brass tip, and the sound of it against the leather welt over and over simply made my head pound. I remained on the sidewalk as long as I could, but I was afraid I would be sick or faint or begin to scream. Discovering you had a trio of mistresses would have been less distressing than what he was doing with that stick."

Restell was immediately solicitous. He sat up and leaned forward in his chair, resting his forearms on his knees. "I'm sorry that happened to you, Emma. You did well, though, to get away as you did. Not so long ago you couldn't have managed it."

Much struck by this observation, Emma became reflective. "It's true, isn't it? I remember thinking *fearless*. Odd, that, because I wasn't fearless at all. I only pretended that I was. I think I might have fooled myself."

He smiled at that. "Quite effective, is it not?"

"I could not have predicted it." Emma swung her feet onto the window bench and curled comfortably against the pillows in the corner. "Perhaps I will fool myself tomorrow as well. That is worth considering."

"Oh?"

"I am determined to call upon Lady Rivendale on the morrow."

"You are? I thought you would be with Sir Arthur."

"In the afternoon. I want to speak to the countess about one of the paintings in her music room. The Sir Anthony Eden. Do you know it?"

"I'm afraid I don't. Is it a portrait?"

"A seascape. I had opportunity to study it while I was convalescing in her home."

"You wish to purchase it from her?"

"Oh, no. Mr. Charters informed me that it's a copy."

"Really?"

Emma nodded. "He has the original in his home."

"So you mean to tell her ladyship the truth?"

"I haven't decided. Mr. Charters said he would not tell her, but I think she might want to know the truth. I've listened to her discuss her collection with my uncle, and I think it is a point of some pride to her. She owns a Vermeer, you know, and a Reynolds. Even her lesser pieces show that she is particular in her taste. She mentioned that she intends that her paintings should be divided equally between her godson and his sister when she turns up her toes. That is her description of her eventually passing, by the way, not mine."

"I'm sure it is," Restell said. "And I imagine it did not escape your attention that her godson's sister is Ferrin's wife and my sister-in-law."

"No, that was borne home to me. I confess, it caused me to feel a sense of obligation that I had not felt before. When I saw the painting again this afternoon, my curiosity was roused. It is not as fine a copy as I originally supposed. I wish to hear how she came to make the purchase, then I will decide what I must say about it."

"Very well."

"You do not think it's unseemly of me to impose my presence on her? She hasn't invited me."

"I'll send a note around in the morning of your intention to call. She will be intrigued, I think, and quite happy for your attention. I am accounted to be a favorite of hers since I made my proposal to you in her music room, as are you because you had the great good sense to accept it. I imagine that we could not be higher in her estimation short of conceiving our firstborn there."

Emma set her mouth in a parody of prudery. "And I believe, Mr. Gardner, that Mrs. Posey's frequent interruptions were the only thing that gave you pause." Uncurling at the window seat, Emma stood then crossed the room to her husband's side. She took his hand and bid him rise. Her smile was an invitation now. "Come, I know where there is a pianoforte."

* * *

Lady Rivendale reclined comfortably on her chaise and watched her guest study the Eden seascape. "Your expression is very intense, Mrs. Gardner. You will crease your brow permanently with such an aspect."

Listening with just half an ear, Emma simply nodded.

The countess was not deterred. "Sir Arthur has remarked on your earnest nature. I must say that yesterday's spirited defense of your husband did much to confirm that opinion in my mind." Her attention strayed to the painting. She tilted her head to one side and pondered the seascape. "What is it that has piqued your interest? The composition is altogether uninspiring, I think, but I admire the vibrancy of the colors. Eden is very good at capturing the power of the sea. One might expect to touch the painting and come away with wet fingertips."

Stepping closer to the painting and raising her hand, Emma glanced in Lady Rivendale's direction. "May I?" she asked.

"Touch it? Yes, of course."

Emma placed the pad of her index finger at the lower left-hand corner of the painting. She slipped the tip of her nail under the frame and made a scraping, then examined her nail.

"What is it?" asked Lady Rivendale.

"I'm not certain," Emma said. "I truly did not expect to find paint on my nail. This piece is far more than a century old after all. A painting is considered fully dry after sixty or eighty years."

"I must say, I was not thinking you meant to take a poke at the thing."

Emma had the grace to flush. "I beg your forgiveness. I didn't know I meant to do it, either." She dropped her hand to her side and stepped away from the painting to remove further temptation to touch it. "May I know how you acquired this particular work?"

"Goodness. I shall have to think on it." Her brow creased in a way that was not so different than Emma's earlier expression. "I believe it was from the Battenburn estate. Yes. Yes,

I'm certain of it." Her countenance smoothed, becoming thoughtful, not troubled. "It was all very sad about the baron and his wife. They came to a bad end under circumstances that are still not known well. The estate languished for several years in the hands of solicitors while the true heirs were sorted out. Battenburn had a stunning collection of art and artifacts. You might inquire of Mr. Charters. He will know something about it. The evening he was here, he mentioned that he also acquired paintings from the Battenburn heirs."

"Were you discussing the Eden painting at the time?"

Lady Rivendale tapped her cheek with her forefinger. "No, I do not recall that the Eden came up in the course of our discussion."

"Then you have other paintings from that estate?"

The countess shook her head. "I don't. Now that I consider it, I'm not at all sure why he introduced the Battenburns into the conversation."

Emma supposed it was because Neven's mind was occupied by his discovery that the Eden in Lady Rivendale's possession was a copy. "I expect that I shall see Mr. Charters this afternoon. He has business with my uncle."

"Then Sir Arthur will be at home today?"

"Yes. I am going there directly."

"Oh, then I suppose he will be painting."

Emma was careful to temper her smile. Lady Rivendale could hide neither her hopefulness nor her disappointment. "I believe that is his intention, yes, except for the time he spends with Mr. Charters. However, regardless of his plans, I know he would welcome your arrival."

"You know it?" the countess asked cautiously.

"Uncle Arthur has said as much to me."

"He has? Oh, how very good you are to tell me."

Emma was glad of the change of subject and happily encouraged Lady Rivendale's interest in Sir Arthur. She answered her ladyship's questions, amusing her with anecdotes that complimented Sir Arthur's character and underscored his charm. When Emma determined it was appropriate to take her leave, the countess did not inquire about her interest in the Eden, or even seem to recall that it had been the purpose of her visit. In every way, that was to Emma's liking.

Arms braced against the balustrade outside her uncle's studio, Emma watched Marisol step onto the sidewalk and open her parasol. She twirled it as she walked away from the house, her maid following at a discreet distance. Looking around for a few moments longer, Emma finally spied Lewis trudging dutifully after her cousin, though she suspected his real interest was the provocative swing of the maid's skirt.

"Can Covington Street truly be so remarkable?"

Startled, Emma's left hand slipped on the rail, and she had the sensation of falling before she managed to jump back and find her land legs. "I didn't hear you," she said, turning sharply on her heel. She threw out one arm to ward off Neven Charters's approach. "I'm fine. Truly, I have no need of your assistance."

Neven halted his advance. His gaze dropped to her outstretched arm, then lifted to her face. "I suppose you are recalling the mishap at the fountain. At least there is no chance that you will drown here."

Emma had no appreciation for him trying to make light of an awkward moment. "You might have announced yourself on the stairs."

"You are right, of course. It did not occur to me that I wasn't heard. I didn't try to hide my approach."

She did not apologize for her churlishness. Her heart was still thumping hard in her chest, and the air seemed distinctly thin. The balcony rail was at her back, and there was naught but the sidewalk and street below to cushion her fall. The vision of herself sprawled and broken upon it seized her mind and would not be easily put aside.

"Come," Neven said, beckoning her with his fingertips. "You are shaking."

Emma did not accept the hand he held out to her. Instead, she turned sideways and slipped past him, stepping over the sill and into the studio on her own. Without waiting to see if he followed, she reached for an apron and put it on, then began setting out the materials she required to size a new canvas.

"Have I given you disgust of me?" asked Neven. He took up a stool at the end of the table. "Should I have said nothing at all about your husband's mistress?"

"That you insist on mentioning it again does not make you a restful companion."

"Sir Arthur said that you wished to speak to me when my business with him was concluded. Did I misunderstand, or was I misled?"

"Neither, but if I'd been informed that your business was ended, I would have come to you."

"Should I take that to mean you are not comfortable meeting with me here in the studio?"

"You may take any meaning you wish, but my desire was not to inconvenience you."

Neven's narrowed glance revealed his skepticism. "You are cold toward me of a sudden."

"Perhaps I am," Emma said. She made no apology for it. She smoothed the linen over the small, twelve-by-twelve stretcher frame Sir Arthur had chosen. Turning it over, she made certain the fabric was securely tacked. "I visited Lady Rivendale this morning. I wanted to see the Eden painting again."

"You did?"

She nodded, wrinkling her nose slightly as she opened a jar of rabbit skin glue. When she located the brush she wanted in a wooden box on the shelf behind her, she began applying the glue in even strokes onto the stretched linen. "I agree with your assessment of the painting."

"I didn't realize you had ever questioned my opinion. I told you that I own the original, didn't I?"

"Yes," she said. "That's what you told me."

Neven Charters frowned. "I'm not certain I approve of what I hear in your tone, Emmalyn. Do you think I lied?"

"No. Not at all." She finished the first application of glue, set the brush aside, then picked up a bowl of finely ground chalk to spread across the surface. "Lady Rivendale told me she purchased the painting from the Battenburn estate."

"Did she? That is interesting. The heirs have much to account for, then. They, or their representatives, are guilty of perpetuating a fraud."

"You also told me you purchased your Eden there."

"And so I did. Several other pieces as well."

"But you're certain yours is the original."

"Quite certain."

"Mighten it simply be a better copy than the one the countess owns?"

"I don't think so." Neven brushed a dusting of chalk away from the edge of the table before he set his forearm upon it. "You did not find her ladyship's copy well-executed?"

"No, I didn't. It's odd because I do not recall thinking that when I studied it before."

"It was not shown in the best of light, I suspect."

"That probably accounts for it. It was a good deal brighter in the music room this morning." Emma finished layering the linen with chalk dust. As soon as it dried, she would add another layer of glue and then more chalk until she was satisfied the linen was properly sized. This priming would keep the oil paints from making direct contact with the fabric. Out of the corner of her eye she observed Neven was no longer watching her work, rather he seemed deep in his own study. She waited him out, certain he was working up to some question he meant to put to her.

"Would you like to see the Eden in my gallery, Emmalyn? I suspect it would rest your curiosity."

Chapter 14

"You are very pensive," Restell said, watching Emma stare out the window of the carriage. "In point of fact, you've said little this evening. Wynetta remarked on it as we were leaving."

"Did she? I suppose I have not been good company." The expression she turned on Restell was a guilty one. "I do apologize if I've been a bit off."

"Are you sickening for something?"

She shook her head and returned her attention to the view outside her window. Her card play had been abysmal tonight. Wynetta and her husband had trounced her and Restell. For herself she did not mind, but Restell was a good player and did not enjoy losing, especially to his own sister. "I meant to play better," she told him. "I'm sorry I could not follow the cards."

"It did seem as if your mind was elsewhere."

Emma knew it was true.

"Just as it is now," Restell said. "Dare I assume that your call upon Lady Rivendale is what still occupies your thoughts?"

Her head snapped around. "Am I so transparent? How did you know?"

"You haven't said a word about it. Silence is usually a sign."

"Of course," she said softly. "Shall I tell you now?"

"If you like."

"Very well, but I shall tell you the part you will like least first: I spoke to Mr. Charters today—alone—in my uncle's studio."

Restell said nothing for a moment. "I hope you're right, and this is the worst of it."

Emma accounted for her time with Lady Rivendale, then described her exchange with Neven Charters. "I did not expect he would come to the studio," she said afterward. "Certainly it was not my intent that he should. He made it seem that he was doing me a favor by attending me there."

"But you thought otherwise?"

"Yes."

"You are usually charitable in assigning motives to Charters."

"I know." She added somewhat reluctantly. "I was made uneasy by his presence. I cannot describe it better than that."

"That's sufficient." Restell regarded Emma thoughtfully. "What is it that you suspect, Emma? That Charters is also in possession of a copy of the Eden painting?"

"No. I think he has the original in his possession. Do you recall seeing it hanging in his gallery?"

"No, but then neither do I recall noticing Lady Rivendale's work."

"I thought you would say that." She sighed. "Mr. Charters perceived I had some doubts. He invited me to examine his painting."

Restell used his forefinger to tip his hat back so Emma could not mistake the gravity of his expression. "*This* is what I'm liking least."

"I did not accept, Restell. I would not, not without you or Marisol at my side."

"I am very glad to hear it, though I expect you were tempted."

"No, I wasn't. I want to see the painting, but I would rather that Mr. Charters was not present when I do it."

"I'm not certain what you're suggesting."

"Frankly, I am not certain myself. I thought you might conceive an idea."

"If you want to examine the painting outside of Charters's presence, then we shall have to make certain he is gone from home. That is the easiest way. How long will you require?"

"As little as a quarter of an hour."

"Then it is easily arranged. We will arrive at his home on the pretext of an invitation to do so. Since he will be away, there will be some confusion, naturally, on the part of his butler, but we will persevere and insist on being shown to the gallery to wait for Charters. You will make your examination, and we will linger a proper amount of time, then we'll take our leave long before Charters returns home."

"But he will find out later that we were there. I don't think I want him to know. It would be difficult to explain, wouldn't it?"

"Awkward, mayhap, but not difficult. Still, if you would rather there be no awkwardness, then we will endeavor to slip in and out unnoticed."

"We can do that?"

"I can. I do not know if I can do it with you in tow."

"What will happen if we are found out?"

"Now *that* will be awkward. You know Charters better than I. What will he want to do?"

"Well, I don't imagine that he will draw pistols on us."

Restell could not help but wonder if Emma was being hopeful. "That is good to hear," he said. "How soon will you want to make your examination?"

"As soon as it can be arranged."

Restell's eyebrows rose. "What is it you expect to find, Emma? You have not been clear on that count."

"Do you mind if I see the painting first? I shall feel very foolish if I am wrong."

"If that's what you want, then I have no objection."

Emma's smile gently chided him. "I'm sure you have many objections, but your curiosity in every way exceeds my own."

Restell laughed. He could not deny it. When the carriage stopped, he stepped out first, then lifted Emma down. Taking her hand, he led her into the house and straightaway to their bedroom where he satisfied much more than his curiosity.

* * *

Almost a sennight later, Restell and Emma entered Neven Charters's home through a door propped open by one of the kitchen maids. The young woman was in expectation of an assignation with one of Restell's footmen, and when she slipped out to meet McCleod at the appointed hour, Restell and Emma slipped inside.

No one was stirring in the house, but they proceeded cautiously and quietly just the same. "This is perfect madness," Emma whispered as she followed closely in Restell's footsteps.

He stopped under a lighted candle sconce and glanced at her over his shoulder. His look was one of patent disbelief that she was only now arriving at that conclusion.

As the one receiving that incredulous expression, Emma was hard-pressed not to laugh. The response would have been wholly hysterical. Her nerves were stretched so tautly that she imagined plucking one would jangle all the others. She might very well collapse in convulsions. The vision of this did not calm her in the least, and above the hand she'd clamped over her mouth her eyes were stricken with something between fear and excitement.

Restell turned, took her by the shoulders, and pressed his forehead to hers. "Breathe," he said. "Just breathe."

She nodded. Her nostrils pinched as she took a deep breath through her nose.

Afraid she meant to hold it, Restell gently pried her hand away from her mouth. "Let it out slowly. Good." He kissed her puckered lips, then released her shoulders and pressed on.

There was nothing for it but that Emma should follow. She knew what to expect; Restell had explained every part of what they must do. He'd reviewed it with her many times in the days while they were waiting for McCleod to be successful with drawing out the kitchen maid. She'd thought his preparation had been overdone, but now she was glad of it. It eased her mind—as much as it could be eased—that he knew how to negotiate the servants' hall and staircase to bring them to the ground floor. He had remembered a surprising number of details from his previous visit and was careful to avoid bumping the marble-topped table in the hall or shouldering the ornate gilt mirror that reflected their silent passage.

Restell paused at the entrance to the gallery and listened. He nodded to Emma, removed a lighted candle from one of the sconces and held it up as he carefully pushed against one of the pocket doors.

It didn't move.

"What is it?" Emma asked, looking around his bent shoulder.

"It's locked."

Her heart sank. "It never occurred to me."

But it had occurred to Restell. He gave her the candle to hold, encouraging her to be careful not to burn herself, then told her where to keep it to give him the best light. He hunkered in front of the double doors and pulled a palm-sized, soft leather case out of his frock coat. Opening it, Restell examined the four picks and hooks before he made his selection. He inserted the steel pick into the lock, poked a few times, and gave it a twist. When he removed the pick and pushed the doors, they separated almost soundlessly.

A bead of hot wax dripped on the ball of Emma's thumb as she jerked in surprise. The light flickered wildly, but she didn't drop the candle, and she didn't make a sound as dripping wax burned her skin.

She was all admiration as he ushered her inside the gallery. "Did you never aspire to be a thief?" she asked. "I think you have the talent for it."

"Thank you." He closed the doors. "You burned your hand, didn't you?" He took the candle from her and examined her hand, peeling away the flat patch of cold wax.

"I don't know that I even felt it," she said. "I was quite overcome by your skill."

Restell arched one eyebrow. "I look forward to hearing you say so again, but first there is the matter of what brought us

here." He held up the candle. "It is your turn, Emma. Find
the painting."

The gallery was every bit as garish as Emma remembered.
Few of the fine treasures that Neven Charters had amassed
were shown to their best advantage. While the quality of the
pieces was not in doubt, the crowded confines convinced
Emma that Neven cared at least as much for the vastness of
his collection as he did for its value.

Standing at the center of the room, she turned slowly,
eyeing the paintings on the walls. Larger works had been hung
high, their frames only a foot or so below the ceiling. Smaller
paintings, usually the more intimate portraits, were arranged
close together at eye level. The Eden seascape was of a size
that was between the others, and it was not the first painting
to catch her complete attention.

Emma tugged on the sleeve of Restell's frock coat. "Do
you recall our conversation with Mr. Charters in this room?"
She coaxed him toward the north wall and nudged his elbow
higher so candlelight bathed the painting she was studying.
"I spoke to him about a painting he appraised for Mrs. Stuart.
The Tintoretto. Do you remember?"

"I recall your speech quite well. You took Charters to task
for describing Mrs. Stuart as a Philistine."

"Yes." She pointed to the sun-drenched villa depicted in the
painting above her. "That is the Tintoretto we were discussing, the one Mrs. Stuart purchased because the yellows
matched the wall covering in her morning room."

"So Charters bought it from her?" Restell frowned as he
made his own examination of the painting. "Why would he
do that? He knew it was a copy."

"He would not purchase a copy. Not knowingly."

"Then this is the original," Restell said.

Emma nodded. "The question in my mind is whether this
is also the one Mrs. Stuart owned." She tugged on Restell's
frock coat again, moving them away from the wall as she continued her careful appraisal of the gallery's contents. She
stopped suddenly when she faced the south wall. "There it is."

She pointed to the right of the mantel and more than four feet above it. "It's too high, Restell. I can't see it properly from here."

"A moment, Emma." Restell used his candle to light one of the table lamps. He adjusted the wick, then blew out the candle and set it aside. He carried the lamp to the mantel and made room for it among the jade, porcelain, and onyx figurines, then he lifted one of the upholstered Queen Anne chairs away from its conversational setting and placed it beside the fireplace's marble apron. "Come here," he bid Emma, holding out his hand. "The solution is to give you higher footing."

Emma took Restell's hand and supported herself as she climbed onto the chair. The painting was still too high, but before she commented on this fact, Restell was clearing a space for her feet on the mantel. The step she was required to make between the seat of the chair and the mantel was too large for her to negotiate on her own. Restell climbed on the chair behind Emma and placed his hands securely around her waist. He gave her only a moment's warning before he lifted her. She found her footing and grabbed the ornate scrollwork and plaster rosettes that defined the decorative upper reaches of the fireplace.

Now that she was at eye level with the painting, she only needed to lean to one side to make her inspection. "I require the lamp," she told Restell.

He regarded her precarious position, wondering how it might be improved upon, then passed her the lamp before she attempted to reach for it herself. He had an unhappy vision of her setting herself on fire.

Emma thanked him for the lamp, never knowing that she received it only because Restell meant to avert catastrophe. Holding the lamp securely in one hand, Emma gripped one of the rosettes in the other and leaned to the side at a forty-five degree angle. Below her, Restell held up his hands, prepared to catch her.

"It would be better, I think," Emma said, "if you were to

catch the lamp." She smiled when Restell merely grunted. They both fell quiet as she made her examination. Her eyes followed the bold, sweeping brush strokes, the light imagined by the artist on the crest of the waves. She spent several long minutes taking in the whole of the work, just as she had at Lady Rivendale's, and when she finished, she lowered the lamp toward Restell. "You will have to take this now. I need to make a scraping."

Emma did not use her own nail this time. She had a small knife tucked in the pocket of her apron, wrapped in a handkerchief for safety. She fiddled with it, removing it from the handkerchief before she took it from the pocket. Below her, she thought she heard Restell mutter something under his breath. Undaunted, Emma slipped the knife under the edge of the frame, took her scraping, then studied the tip of the blade. The flakes were very different from what she had observed under her nail.

Emma replaced the knife in her pocket and wrapped it as best she could, trying to save the flakes. She pulled herself up so she was standing perpendiular to the mantel, then waited for Restell to put the lamp away so he could help her down. They replaced the chair, relighted their single candle, and extinguished the lamp after putting it back on the table. Restell rearranged the figurines on the mantel, hoping that he approximated their orginal positions so Charters would not immediately notice they had been moved.

He gave the gallery a final survey for signs of their intrusion before he followed Emma into the hall. As she had before, she held the candle while Restell used his pick, this time to lock the pocket doors. They retraced their steps down the hallway and through the servants' quarters, then left by the same door they'd used to enter.

Emma felt the breath rush from her body and only realized when they were safely crossing the street how often she'd held it during their retreat. Whittier was waiting for them two blocks away, driving a nondescript hack that Restell had hired for this foray.

Neither Restell nor Emma spoke until they were inside and the carriage was moving. Emma fanned herself with her hand. "I should not like to do that every evening. I must say, though, I am coming to respect the collective nerve of those who regularly practice a criminal trade."

Restell was compelled to point out, "We didn't steal anything."

"But we could have. Sneaksmen, I have heard them called. Really, it was quite exciting. You are very good to indulge me, Restell."

"I would rather you were satisfied with a string of pearls or a diamond choker."

"Then you should have proposed to Marisol."

He made an uncomplimentary, gutteral sound that communicated perfectly what he thought of Emma's observation. His eyes dropped to the pocket of her apron. Her right hand had disappeared inside, and he could see that she was turning over the knife. "Will you tell me now what it was all in aid of? What did you find on the point of your blade?"

"Proof that it is the original Eden."

"But you already knew that, didn't you?"

"I suspected it, but I wasn't certain that it was the same one that used to hang in Lady Rivendale's music room. Now I am."

"What?" A small vertical crease appeared between Restell's eyebrows. "How can that be?"

"I'm very much afraid that Mr. Charters is a sneaksman," she said. "Moreover, that he is an art forger."

Restell blinked. The truth of it set in slowly, but when it did, Restell threw back his head and gave a shout of laughter. The sound of it was loud enough to startle the horse pulling the hack. The cab rolled jerkily for a moment and Emma was rocked back in her seat.

"Are you quite all right?" asked Emma. "It would perhaps be better if you were somewhat appalled, after all he is a gentleman of your set and he is practically family. You might show some sympathy for Marisol and Uncle Arthur if you have none at all for Mr. Charters."

"Forgive me." Even to his own ears, Restell did not sound contrite. Indeed, the corners of his mouth were still twitching and the lantern light revealed a suspicious moisture on the rim of his eyelashes that could only have been residue of tears of mirth. "It is an interesting turn, is it not?"

"Disappointing," Emma said. "At least to me."

"Yes, I can see how that would be the case. You have listened to him pontificate on any number of occasions as to the value of a particular work of art. He speaks as an expert, and perhaps he is, but he demonstrates the remarkable nerve of the criminals that you admired earlier when he speaks of his contribution in reducing fraud. It seems he has found a perfect venue for perpetuating it."

Emma offered no argument. "I think you are right," she said quietly. "And it gives me no pleasure to have proven it."

Restell was quiet a moment, then he offered gently. "I'm not certain that you *have* proven it."

"What do you mean?"

"Well, you've proven it to your own satisfaction, but if you mean to make a public accusation, you will have to find a way to prove it to others. Then there is the matter of what it is exactly that you will prove. I am not aware that Charters misrepresented the paintings. He told you that they were fakes. Isn't that so?"

"Yes, but—"

"He told you he owned the original Eden, didn't he?"

"Yes, but he—"

"I realize he didn't mention that he owned the Tintoretto, but he could make the point that he did not want to draw attention to it." He saw Emma was about to object. "I don't believe it," he said. "I am merely saying that he could defend himself."

Emma sank back against the hard cushions. "But I know Lady Rivendale owned the painting that was in his gallery. I studied it every day I was there trying to see what caused Mr. Charters to claim it was a copy. I have seen a good many pieces done by Eden. He is an English artist, after all, not like

Tintoretto. I've never seen but two examples of the Italian's work. It is not unusual to find an Eden hanging at the country estates of the same people who patronize my uncle's paintings."

"So you are certain about the Eden," Restell said. "I understand. Is Lady Rivendale, though? Would she know if her painting had been exchanged?"

"She might. She has a good eye if she knows what she's looking for."

"What about Sir Arthur? He should be able to tell the difference."

Emma hesitated. "I don't think he'll want to involve himself. He has a fondness for Mr. Charters."

"Because of Marisol."

"I suspect that's so. He wants to know that she'll be settled well."

"There are any number of young gentlemen that she might choose with pockets as deep as her fiancé's."

"Perhaps, but she's already made her choice. She might lead him about from time to time, but she has no intention of cutting the tether. She would not thank me for telling her what he's done."

"What is it you want to do, Emma?"

"He stole from Lady Rivendale and most probably from Mrs. Stuart. He should have to make that right. That's what I want, Restell. I want him to act honorably and make it right."

Restell made no reply. They finished their ride home in silence and continued in that manner as they readied for bed. He poured Emma a small glass of wine while she sat at the foot of the bed brushing out her hair. She yawned widely as she accepted it. Restell smiled and took the brush from her hand. He chuckled when she regarded him and the brush warily, remembering very well what he had wrought the last time he'd held it.

"Set your mind at ease," he said. "I am all for sleep."

She nodded and sipped her wine.

Restell returned the brush to the dressing room, then crawled into bed. He yanked on his nightshirt when it impeded his progress. The evening was cool but not so much so that a fire was needed, and he slid between the sheets and tugged on the coverlet. Emma continued to sit pensively at his feet.

"You look as if the very weight of the world rests on your shoulders," he said. "Will you not unburden yourself?"

"Perhaps later, when I understand the nature of what I'm feeling. I did not consider this consequence, Restell. I wanted to prove to myself that what I observed was in every sense real. I did that for me. I did not allow myself to think past that to what it would mean or what might come of it."

"Have you considered who is likely to have painted the copies?" asked Restell.

Emma turned her head sharply in Restell's direction. "Mr. Charters painted them. Who else could have done so?"

"Your uncle."

"Is that what you've been thinking? No, Sir Arthur would never do that."

"You are certain?"

She hesitated. "He could not."

"Could not," Restell repeated quietly. "It is curious that you should say it in that manner."

Emma tossed back what remained of her wine. "It is not at all curious. He could not do it; it is not in his nature."

"I don't think that's what you meant. You believe it's no longer in his ability."

Emma stopped rolling the stem of her wineglass between her palms. "Now, *that* is a curious thing to say. What do you mean by it?"

Restell debated the wisdom of telling her what he'd known for almost a month, and in some ways had suspected within a few days of meeting her. Tossing back the covers, he threw his legs over the side of the bed and plucked the wineglass from Emma's hands. "Come with me."

He retrieved his dressing gown and hers from the armoire but ignored their slippers. "Put this on." His tone brooked no interference, and Emma complied without question. She did not even ask where they were going but followed his lead into the hall and then to the end of it where the entrance to the servants' staircase was hidden behind a door. He held a lamp to one side so that Emma's way would be lighted as well as his own. They climbed past the next floor, which held additional bedrooms and what would some day be the nursery, and continued all the way to the top of the house.

"It is not quite finished," Restell said before he opened the door. "But you will recognize the intention." He pushed the door aside but did not enter first. Instead, he inclined his head in Emma's direction and indicated that she should lead the way now.

Emma cast a curious glance at Restell, then stepped over the threshold. The lamp he held out provided a dim glow by which she could make out her surroundings, and what she saw simply seized her breath.

"Restell." She said his name softly, reverently, then spun about to face him.

He saw her lips part again, but she softly pressed the back of her fingers to her mouth, stemming whatever words she meant to say. Her lovely blue-green eyes were luminous. It might have been the lamplight that made them so, but Restell found himself thinking that she lent the light radiance. A tear hovered on the rim of her lower lashes, but her effort to blink it back merely caused it to spill over the edge. He raised his hand and brushed it away with the pad of his thumb.

"I did not mean to make you cry," he told her. "Come, will you not look around and see what is to your liking and what must be changed?"

Emma allowed herself to be turned gently. The studio was very nearly identical to the one Sir Arthur had in his home. She looked up and saw starlight through the glass panes set into the roof. "This is the hole in the roof you told me about," she said, astonished and accusing in the same breath. "Do you recall? The night we came back from the hell, you told me you were—"

Restell stepped around and kissed her. "I remember," he said a moment later. He brushed her lips again when she looked as if she meant to go on regardless of what he'd just told her. When he straightened, he explained the whole of it. "Crowley and Hobbes were overseeing the work while we were away from home. The laborers cut through the roof but were not prepared for us to return as early as we did. At Crowley's insistence they left—secrecy being of paramount importance—but without covering the hole. As we were in expectation of rain that evening, it seemed prudent that something should be done."

"And you arrived home in time to do it."

"I arrived home in time to settle the argument of what was to be done. I was hopeful that my wife was waiting for me in our bedroom, you see, so I was adamantly opposed to doing the work myself."

Blushing, Emma stepped around Restell and stood under the skylight, looking up. "It is perfect." She stared at the starry night for several long moments. Tears welled in her eyes, but it was easier to hold them at bay with her head tipped skyward. "Absolutely perfect," she whispered, awed. She darted a glance at Restell. "And there are four. My uncle has only three skylights."

Emma wandered about the studio, examining the pots and jars on the shelves, the mortars and pestles for mixing the paints, the oils, the stretchers, the bolts of linen for making canvas. There were two easels and two stools, a chaise, an armchair, and a table of such sizeable dimensions that it could only have been built in the room.

"There will be a balcony," Restell said, watching Emma's face as she took it all in. He opened the doors to it and showed her that there was no sill that she must climb over to step outside. "No," he said quickly when she approached. "You can't go out. This is where the work stopped. We all agreed that you could not fail to notice if the house suddenly sprouted a balcony on its uppermost floor." Although the exit was roped off, Restell closed the doors to reduce Emma's temptation to come close to the edge.

"It seems to me that I've failed to notice quite a lot," Emma said, throwing her arms wide. "While you notice everything." She dropped her hands to her sides. "How long have you known?"

"You cannot even say what it is that I know, can you? What if you've mistaken my purpose, you're still thinking. What if I arranged all of this so your uncle could paint here and you would not have to leave home to help him?" Restell shook his head, his smile slight and sympathetic. "Were you compelled to keep the secret by your loyalty to your uncle, or was it that some influence was brought to bear?"

Emma frowned. "I'm not certain what you mean."

"Emma." Restell said her name sternly, expecting more from her than a disingenuous response. "Not only do I know that you paint, but I am fully aware that you've completed a number of paintings for your uncle. The *Fishing Village,* for one." Taking her hand, he drew her to the far side of the studio and raised the lamp to reveal the three sketches that were framed and mounted on the wall. "This is your work, is it not?"

Stunned, Emma made her admission without thinking. "Yes," she said, her voice barely audible. "Yes, they're mine."

"How much of the finished work is yours?" he asked. "I have studied it on several different occasions at my mother's, but I can't tell."

She shrugged and turned away from the sketches. "It doesn't matter. It is my uncle's name that is attached to it."

"Why is that, Emma?"

"For the obvious reason that his paintings command a goodly sum and mine would not fetch a farthing."

"Do you never paint for yourself?"

She was a long time in answering. "The *Fishing Village* was for me," she said quietly. "I presented Uncle Arthur with my sketches and my plan to do a large canvas, larger than anything he'd ever done. He spoke to Mr. Charters about it and was discouraged from doing a painting of that scale. I agreed to begin work on something smaller because we needed the money. My uncle contributed to the painting as best he could. The static backgrounds, the choice of colors, the broad strokes, that is often his work."

"Did you know why there was a need for the money?"

"No, not entirely. I never suspected that he was a gamer. His evenings out were not something that he discussed."

"The gaming was Mr. Charters's influence?"

"I believe so, yes, though it is not fair to lay the whole of it at his feet. My uncle likes to live well, often outside his means, and he indulges Marisol's whims. I had some inkling of that when I was privy to the arrangements made for him by Mr. Johnston, but it was clearer still when I began managing the commissions myself."

Restell placed the lamp on the table and nudged a stool closer to Emma so that she might sit. He spun the other stool around and took his seat. "When did you start painting in his stead?"

"Perhaps three or four months after I arrived in London. It seems to me that I have always had a brush in my hand. My mother and father encouraged my interest. When I was seven they hired a painting master to develop my truly sad but precocious technique, and they spoke often of sending me to London to study with my uncle." She shrugged lightly. "I think it was the estrangement between my mother and Sir Arthur that caused my parents to hesitate. I did not mind for myself, but I saw that it saddened my mother. She believed she was not doing right by denying me the opportunity. After my parents died, well, I really had no choice. My uncle extended the invitation before I wrote to him. He'd learned of their passing before I did, so his letter arrived soon after I came to know the truth. It seemed right that I should come to London."

Emma laid her hands on the tabletop and studied her splayed fingers. "I did very little except paint when I arrived. Sir Arthur allowed me to indulge my grief in his studio, and I stayed up there for the better part of every day—and sometimes the better part of a night—painting until my hands were cramped or I was near fainting with hunger. I painted what was familiar to me about my home: portraits of my parents, landscapes of the countryside, the tenant farmers laboring in the fields, the Peterborough shops and shopkeepers. I surrounded myself with memories, or mayhap it was that I guarded myself with them.

"I was aware of my uncle's interest in my work, just as I was aware of his interest in me."

"Interest in you?" asked Restell. "How so?" Though he posed the question casually, he was aware of a knot in his midsection and a chill slipping under his skin.

"The melancholia," Emma said. "It was finally borne home to me that his willingness to permit such self-indulgent grief was not entirely of benefit to me. I have some money, you see, a trust set up for me by my parents before they sailed to India."

Restell rubbed the underside of his chin with the back of his hand as he regarded Emma's downcast profile. "So you perpetuated a fraud as large my own. You were never the poor relation."

She glanced at him sideways. "I hope you are not imagining that I am an heiress. It is a modest sum, but I might have lived comfortably on it for years, and with some careful planning— and an advisor such as yourself—it might have seen me well into old age. Marriage did not have to be the only choice open to me, and I could have painted at my leisure, perhaps eventually supplementing my income from the trust."

"So Sir Arthur's interest in you may have been of a practical nature."

"It occurred to me, yes. The money will not be mine until I reach my twenty-fifth birthday. My parents were so cautious regarding my future that even marriage does not bring the money under my control. It rests with the solicitors at—"

"Napier and Walpole," Restell finished for her. "Of course. And Mr. Johnston helps manage your funds. That's why you remained adamantly opposed to me speaking to him."

Emma offered a sheepish smile. "It was badly done of me,

though it did not seem so at the time. I should have known he would say nothing about the trust, but I was afraid."

"I did not marry you for your money, Emma."

"I know, but I'd lied to you, and I selfishly did not want to be caught out. I was—I *am*—ashamed."

Restell was infinitely more concerned by the danger presented by her prevarication. "If you had been killed prior to marrying, who would have inherited the trust?"

"Marisol."

It was not the answer Restell had expected to hear, but he thought he understood it. "Your mother did not want it to fall in the hands of your uncle, I take it."

"I suppose that was her reasoning, though he might very well have been able to control it rather than keep it under the purview of the solicitors."

"Did you never think it was important I should know that, Emma? You very nearly died twice before we were married, and Marisol stood to inherit a tidy sum from you."

"Modest," Emma said. "Not tidy. It would not last long whether she or my uncle controlled it."

"Precisely how modest?"

"Eight thousand pounds."

"I do not like to quibble over your adjectives, but it seems to me that 'tidy' rather better describes that sum than 'modest.' I suspect you think of it as the latter because you envisioned it having to last you a lifetime. Others may see it as making a profound difference in their lives if they had a need to, say, pay gaming debts or creditors for gowns and carriages and furbelows they could ill afford."

Restell gave Emma a considering look. "What will you want to do with the money once it is yours?"

"I always thought I should like to have a studio of my own." She reached for his hand and covered it with her own. "I suppose now I will have the means to be as generous to others as you have been to me. It will require reflection. It never occurred to me that I might have choices." She gave his hand a squeeze. "And your suspicions about Sir Arthur are off the mark, Restell. He doesn't know the details of my trust, most certainly not the amount. Neither does Marisol. My uncle believes my parents' debts far outnumbered their profits in investments. It's true that they lost money in the venture that took their lives, but the sale of the house and land was enough to manage the outstanding accounts. Their instructions to the solicitors at Napier and Walpole were most explicit: no information about the trust was to be shared beyond a select few. Mr. Johnston did not become privy to my trust until I suggested he go to the firm after being dismissed by Sir Arthur. When he was hired, I asked him to be charged with investing my money."

Restell offered up a warm, knowing smile. "I am not surprised. I cannot divine if you are naive and lucky or wise and blessed."

"I think it is that I am naive and blessed. Certainly there is an angel on my shoulder." She removed her hand from his and brushed back a tendril of hair that had fallen across her cheek. "Are you angry that I did not tell you about my trust earlier? You do not seem so."

"I can hardly throw stones, can I? No, I'm not angry. I understand that you believe no one else has the particulars regarding your trust. I am more skeptical, but you know that."

"I do." He was the angel on her shoulder, the reason she was so often blessed. She glanced back at the chaise. "Is it as comfortable as it looks?"

"I couldn't say." Somewhat guiltily he admitted, "Crowley chose it."

She chuckled. "Let us hope that he had the sense to sit on it." Tugging on the sleeve of Restell's dressing gown, Emma urged him to stand and follow her to the chaise. "You have done wonderfully well to conceive of the plan. I would not expect that you had time enough to attend to every detail." She curled her fingers around the silk belt at his waist. "How was it all accomplished, Restell? And outside my notice? I am not so inattentive that it could have been easy to achieve."

He watched her eyes but was ever so conscious of her

fingers sliding along his belt. "When you were not engaged
in your uncle's work, I believe you always had an invitation to attend my mother or one of my sisters or even my
father in some endeavor. Lady Rivendale was most eager to
assist me."

"They all knew about this?"

Restell's expression was patently incredulous. "Good God,
no. You would have had the whole of it weeks ago. Have they
impressed you as people who can keep their own counsel?"

"You are too severe, Restell."

"Do not misunderstand. On a matter of life and death, affairs of the crown, or who holds the winning hand at whist,
my family's silence is absolute. In endeavors such as this,
where a surprise is in the offing, they cannot help but surrender every detail."

Emma let Restell's satin belt slide through her fingers. She
parted the dressing gown. His freshly laundered nightshirt
smelled faintly of soap and rainwater. She plucked at the soft
fabric, then laid her hands against his chest. "So what *did* you
tell them?"

"The truth, of course. That I required their cooperation in
making certain no harm came to you."

"Restell!"

He shrugged, unapologetic. "They have not forgotten the
incident at Lady Rivendale's fountain. They don't understand
its full import, but they imagine themselves involved in an intrigue and find it immensely satisfying."

Admonishment warred with admiration as Emma shook
her head. "You have an uncanny talent for engaging others to
serve your interests."

"So I do."

Undone by his perfectly boyish grin, Emma pulled him
down onto the chaise. She had thought seducing him was her
idea, but now she was no longer certain. "I don't suppose it
matters," she whispered against his mouth.

"Hmm?"

The vibration of his lips tickled hers. Emma had not realized she'd spoken aloud. "A wayward thought," she told him. "And wholly unimportant." She looped her arms around his neck and brought some pressure to bear. He fit himself against her as she reclined. The warmth and strength of him did not fail to comfort and calm. Nothing intruded upon her thoughts but thoughts of loving him, and Emma was filled with the sense of the rightness of it all.

Their lovemaking was languorous and lusty by turns and sensual exploration gave way to excitement. They laughed at themselves, tangling and twisting on the chaise, in danger of thudding to the floor as they rolled. Emma's hair spilled over the side as Restell made a feast of her throat and breasts, and when she knelt between his thighs and bent her head, he had to brace himself with one leg to keep from rocking sideways.

Pleasure was in the touch, the fragrance, the sight of his hand on her hip and her fingers buried deep in his hair. It was the sounds he could not hold back and the ones he whispered quite deliberately against her ear. Her skin prickled. The muscles of his back and arms grew taut. They were conscious of their own breathing, of the coursing of their blood, and the sense of friction, tension, and heat as they skimmed the surface of pleasure.

For a while restraint offered reward. The pitch of everything was sweeter, sharper, and more defined, and for all those reasons it could not last. They teased it out as long as was possible, but in the end it was what lay just below the surface that they wanted.

Closing their eyes, they dove headlong into it.

Emma woke with a start. She glanced over her shoulder and saw that Restell was still sleeping beside her. They had managed to fit themselves moderately well onto the narrow chaise by curling like spoons, though she had no memory of how it had been accomplished. Even the memory of drifting off to sleep was unclear. She recalled drowning in pleasure but almost nothing after it. The lack of memory didn't frighten her. She hadn't lost herself in time, merely surrendered to her need for sleep.

Looking up through the skylight overhead, she observed the waning moon. The slender crescent appealed to her. In a flight of fancy she saw a celestial hook, a place where God might hang His nightshirt. One corner of her mouth curled as she considered where He might place His slippers.

Beside her, she sensed Restell stirring. His arm tightened around her waist, then relaxed as he found his bearings. Her hair was pushed aside, then she felt the familiar warmth of his lips on her nape. Her hum of pleasure ended in an abrupt yawn that was wide enough to make her jaw crack.

Restell chuckled. "However long we slept, it wasn't long enough."

She merely nodded. When he didn't move, she didn't, either. She was completely at her ease in the shelter of his arm.

Restell used his dressing gown as a blanket, covering Emma's legs where they were bared below the rucked hem of her shift and robe.

His thoughtfulness touched her. "Thank you." Emma pointed to the overhead skylight. "I've been thinking I'd like to paint that moon. Perhaps a sky at night. It is not as dark as one thinks of it. Have you noticed? So many shades of blue . . . and the light . . . it's brilliant, isn't it? The light is always a challenge. Uncle Arthur has mastered it beautifully in his work. I want to learn more from him in that regard. There is so much that he can teach me."

"Then you are not his indentured servant."

Emma's dark eyebrows lifted in surprise. "I am confounded by your ability to be so deeply skeptical of your fellow man, yet remain confident that goodness will prevail."

"It confounds me as well, but there you have it."

"I am Sir Arthur's student, Restell. He is my teacher, my mentor. It is true that I am useful to him and that he's taken advantage, but painting for him is a privilege, and I do it out of my deep respect for the body of his work. You have seen that his hands are stiff, the knuckles swollen. Some mornings he can barely unfold his fingers. He makes the climb to his studio to preserve the illusion that he is painting, but he often reads and rests while I work."

"And offers criticism."

"When warranted. He cannot only give praise."

Restell suspected there was little enough of that. "He is jealous of your skill, Emma."

"He is mourning the loss of his own. In his place, I don't know if I could be so gracious." Emma carefully turned over so she could face Restell. Her knees bumped his, almost dislodging them both. When they were balanced again, she said, "There is something else, Restell, that you should know. I believe it is worth considering."

"Oh?"

"Time. I have been contemplating time and memory. It's occurred to me that I have no sense of either, or rather I have no sense of either in regard to my abduction to Walthamstow."

Restell considered this. He'd always known her memory of the abduction was incomplete and that what she recalled was suspect. He had not considered the element of time. "Go on."

"I have been plagued with the notion since our wedding night. Or rather, what occurred later in our dressing room. Do you know I never once inquired of the innkeeper or his wife as to the day? I wrote to my uncle, he sent Mr. Charters, and that was the first I knew I had only been gone a few days. I never questioned it. It seemed to me that no time at all had elapsed, and conversely that I had been away from London for much longer. Under Dr. Bettany's care I spent days in a drugged sleep that was not so different from how I recalled my abduction."

Emma propped herself on one elbow. "I think I was gone from London much longer, Restell. Mr. Charters lied to me."

"If you're right, Emma, then he was not the only one. Sir Arthur and Marisol also knew the truth. The length of your absence did not go unremarked once you were returned. I asked questions about it myself."

"I know. I imagine they conspired to protect me, then found they could not back away from the lie."

"Protection? From the truth?"

"Why not? I've been afraid to face it, else why can't I remember everything? It supports their thinking. You might inquire of Dr. Bettany. He could have advised them to do just that."

Somewhat urgently Restell sat up. "It doesn't matter what their motives might have been, it's more important to discover if there was indeed a lie told to you." He stood, put on his dressing gown, and strode toward the staircase, expecting that she would follow.

Emma caught up to him halfway down the stairs. "Where are we going?"

"To find your maid," Restell said. "She is the one person in this house who knows the truth, if you can but convince her to tell you."

It required cajolery and conviction on Emma's part to press Mary Bettis to speak up. The maid was conscious that she had displeased her mistress but clearly afraid to reveal what she knew.

"They told me I shouldn't mention it," Mary said. "And you were so confused, I didn't know I was doing harm."

"No one will know that you told me. I shall say I recalled it on my own."

Mary's dark eyes darted between Emma and Restell. "Sir Arthur sent Mr. Charters and me soon after your missive arrived. My recollection is that you were gone just the two days then. I thought we'd go to Walthamstow and return straightaway, but you were in such a state as broke my heart. I suppose that's why Mr. Charters didn't bring you back as quickly as he might have."

"What do you mean, Mary? We left Walthamstow soon after you arrived."

"Yes, ma'am, but we didn't go far. Mr. Charters set you and

me up in a hostelry south of the village, then he disappeared. I wouldn't let myself think we were abandoned. He promised he would return, and I took him at his word. It was the proper thing to do because he came back right enough and we left the following day.

"Where do you suppose he went?"

"I can't say as to that, but he smelled of spirits on his return. I expect after seeing you he was a man in want of a pint. Lesser of two evils, that."

"What is the other evil?" asked Restell.

Mary Bettis didn't blink. "Murder, sir. Mr. Charters looked as if he could do murder."

Chapter 15

After Emma made her farewell to Mrs. Stuart she waved off Whittier and the carriage in favor of walking. It was not as if she was entirely alone, she realized. It was only a good beginning. Some twenty yards behind her McCleod would be following, and Restell's driver would not abandon her for more than a block at a time.

She opened her parasol and rested the shank against her shoulder while she twirled it absently, her thoughts still on her brief exchange with Mrs. Stuart. The Tintoretto that hung in Mrs. Stuart's morning room was indeed a copy. It was not, however, the painting that Emma had first examined when she encouraged the judge's wife to seek out Mr. Charters for an appraisal. As a copy, it was not a clumsy effort, and even though she was largely unfamiliar with the body of Tintoretto's work, she could recognize certain similarities to the copy that hung in Lady Rivendale's music room. Tintoretto and Sir Anthony Eden painted hundreds of years apart, but their forger was from this century. She had no doubt now that they were done by the same artist.

Emma paused beneath a horse chestnut at one of the entrances to the park. She could leave the sidewalk in favor of the crushed gravel path and take the diagonal route to the park's far side. It was a fair, sunny day and she ached to do what was unexpected. Mr. Whittier would have to take the long way around as this path was too narrow for the carriage, and McCleod could not follow too closely lest he be mistaken for a footpad.

Her stomach turned over as she set her toe over the park's threshold. Her heart jumped once before it settled into a rhythm that was quick but not uncomfortably so. She took a deep breath and released it slowly. The linen canopy of the parasol spun like a top as her nervous fingers twirled the handle.

Decision made, Emma did not permit herself to think better of it. She forged ahead, pausing only when she realized her steps were more in the way of a forced march. She was crossing the green as though she'd begun a military campaign. The image raised a small, tentative smile. She was not yet the young woman she aspired to be, the one who crossed the park in a gusting wind and laughed gaily at the tug on her bonnet and the fluttering of her skirts.

This journey was her Waterloo. Emma set her eyes forward and continued walking, and by the time she reached number Twenty-three Covington, she was flushed with the excitement of victory.

Emma was shown straightaway to the library where her uncle was taking care of correspondence. "It is a glorious day," she said, sweeping into the room. "I was certain I would find you in the studio." She advanced on Sir Arthur's desk and kissed his cheek when he turned to look up at her.

"You are in fine color," he said. "I must say, I approve. It is becoming, Emmalyn."

She smiled warmly. "I came by the park, Uncle. I mean, I walked through it on my own. I should not be so pleased with myself, I suspect, but it has been ever so long." She could not fail to miss her uncle's frown nor the concern in his eyes. "My driver was not far distant, and McCleod did not stray. Still, it was *almost* as if I were alone. Do be happy for me."

"If that's what you want," he said, "then I am."

"Thank you." She glanced at his correspondence. The pile

of letters on the tray was quite high. "Do you require some assistance?" she asked. "I have no objection if you would rather make short work of this rather than paint this afternoon."

"You are good to offer. I would rather paint, but this is pressing me. Marisol has promised to make my replies, but she is invariably occupied elsewhere. The wedding, I think, is much on her mind."

Emma nodded. "Yes, the wedding." She picked up several letters and began to fan through them.

"You have some reservations, I collect. Is it because you had feelings for Mr. Charters?"

Emma almost dropped the correspondence. She set it down carefully and gave Sir Arthur her full attention. "I suppose denials will not serve. I am learning I give my thoughts away too easily." Sighing, she moved away from the desk and sat down on the nearby sofa. She folded her hands in her lap to keep them still. "I didn't realize you knew that I once held Mr. Charters in affection."

"I knew. Marisol knew as well. She set her cap for him anyway. I am sorry for that, Emmalyn, though I wonder if I should be. You seemed to accept his defection rather too stoically for my tastes. Mayhap I was wrong, but I questioned the depth of your feelings that you could surrender him so easily."

"It did not occur that I should fight when clearly his affections were engaged elsewhere. Is that done?"

"If you learned that your husband has a mistress?"

Emma did not hesitate. "I would run her through." She saw him nod, a hint of satisfaction in his eyes, and realized the full import of what he'd said. "You've heard something?"

"Marisol told me. Might I know if it's true?"

"I am comforted you have asked outright. The assumptions of truth are more troubling. No, it is not true, and lest you think I am deluded, I can tell you that I am familiar with the woman who was seen with my husband. She is most definitely not his mistress."

"One of his peculiar enterprises, then."

"Yes," she said. "Something like that. People seek him to redress all manner of things—just as I did."

"He has not found your abductors, though, has he?"

"No. But neither has there been any incident since he began to provide for our protection."

"I seem to recall that you nearly drowned in a fountain. It is more than passing strange that you give it no notice."

"Mr. Charters was the real victim there. What happened to me was a consequence of circumstance, nothing more."

"You are quite certain?"

"I am." She paused as she weighed the points for and against revealing what she knew to her uncle. "I have reason to believe that Mr. Charters participates in activities that might very well cause someone to want to harm him."

Sir Arthur's narrow features took on a decidedly pinched expression. "Have a care, Emmalyn. Your tales are no more welcome to my ears than my own daughter's."

"It's no tale, Uncle, but I'll not say anything else if that's your wish."

"You place me in a difficult position, but then you are clever enough to know that. Whatever it is that you wish to tell me, is it the reason you have reservations about Marisol's wedding?"

"Yes." Emma could have told him it was one of many reservations she held, but her simple response sufficed. "I did not come here today with the intention of sharing this with you. Frankly, I do not know if it is even wise that I do so. You will have to decide if you want to know."

Visibly agitated, Sir Arthur rose stiffly to his feet and paced off the length of the room before he turned on Emma. He crossed his arms in front of him and in a tone that was more challenging than directive, he said, "Go on, then. Tell me what it is you think you know."

Emma was profoundly sorry she had spoken on the matter at all. He'd made it evident that he didn't want to hear her out. "Is it so important that Marisol secure her future now?" she asked. When she observed a bit of deflation in her uncle's puffed-up stance, she realized she'd either hit the mark or was not far off. "That is what concerns you, is it not? If you must revise your high opinion of Mr. Charters you may have no choice but to withdraw your blessing, and I think that is what you do not want to do." Emma lifted her hands in a somewhat imploring gesture. "Marisol is as clever as she is beautiful, Uncle, and more gentlemen step into her path than out of it. Mr. Charters is merely the first to make an offer of marriage. She does not have to settle; neither do you."

"You may sit in judgment of me," Sir Arthur said gravely. "Just as your mother did before you. That is your prerogative. Know only that I will not explain myself to you. That is *my* prerogative."

Emma felt as though she might cry. The joy that had been hers when she entered her uncle's home had vanished, replaced by a sense of futility and disappointment. The weight of it seemed to prevent her from rising to her feet. With effort, she held her chin up and met his narrowed gaze. "Forgive me," she said quietly. "I would not presume to judge you, but I comprehend that you think I have."

He indicated neither acceptance nor rejection of her apology. His nostrils flared slightly as he took a steadying breath. "I would hear what you have to say, Emmalyn."

Emma had refolded her hands in her lap. Now the knuckles were nearly bloodless. "Mr. Charters is forging works of art."

Sir Arthur raised a single eyebrow in skeptical arch. "Forging?"

"Copying, if you prefer."

"I think you are making too much of it. It is done all the time. You know it yourself. Does he suggest the works are his own?"

"No. He examines a painting and pronounces it a copy, then he paints a copy and exchanges it for the authentic piece. Lady Rivendale's Eden seascape is one example. Mrs. Stuart's Tintoretto is another. I cannot say whether there are more."

"Now you are saying he is a thief."

"It pains me to do so," she said. "I mistook his character."

"I suppose you can prove this."

"I believe I have, though that is not to say that I mean to do anything about it. I visited Mrs. Stuart before I came here and saw for myself that the Tintoretto in her possession is not the one I examined when she returned from Italy. It is the same with the Eden work. Do you know the one I mean?"

"In Lady Rivendale's music room. Yes, I know it. And you are certain it is Charters's work?"

"He has her original in his gallery. I studied it there. I know it's the same one she had in her possession."

"I see. And the Tintoretto? It is there also?"

"Yes, and placed there not so very long ago."

Sir Arthur pressed his fist against the underside of his chin. "It is not good news that you have for me, but neither is it the calamity I envisioned. There are things that may yet be done to put it all to right."

Emma thought he sounded a bit like Restell in his belief that situations could be managed. She did not share this with Sir Arthur, doubting that he would find it complimentary in his present frame of mind. "I am glad to hear it," she said, and she was. "Will you tell Marisol?"

"I will speak to Mr. Charters first. As you apparently have not done so, it is only fair to lay it all before him. You appreciated that I made no assumptions upon hearing about your husband and his paramour. I suspect that Mr. Charters will have the same appreciation for allowing him to make his own explanation."

Emma did not offer an argument. There was one serious difference in putting questions before Mr. Charters and putting them before her: She was not the subject of any wrongdoing. That had been leveled against her husband and she had only to defend him. Mr. Charters would be in a position where he would have to defend himself. She could not imagine that it would be a pleasant interview.

Emma glanced at the correspondence on Sir Arthur's desk, then gestured toward it. "Have I put you off this task?"

Sighing heavily, he shook his head. "No. I do not fault you for speaking your conscience, Emmalyn. If I seem angry with you, it is because I am angry with myself." He returned to his desk and sat. "Bring your chair here," he said. "We will attend to this obligation first and then we will paint."

"As to the latter, Uncle, I wondered if you would accept an invitation to my home when we are finished with your correspondence? There is something I'd like you to see that I could not very well bring here."

"Oh?"

"My husband presented me with a very grand gift a few days ago. I've been remiss in mentioning it, but I know now I want to show it to you. I am hoping there will be occasions that we might share it."

Sir Arthur picked up the first letter on the stack and turned it over in his hands. "I confess you have intrigued me," he said, passing it to Emma. "By all means, then, let us be done with this so we might engage in something more pleasant."

Restell regarded his cards without making his disgust evident. He'd hoped for a better hand than the one he'd been dealt. He could not blame the Allworthy cousins for what he had in front of him. These cards were the responsibility of his partner Lord Greenaway. The Allworthys, though, were not blameless for his losses. He'd been wrong to suppose they wouldn't risk cheating at his father's club. They were either too taken with their own skills to believe they would be caught out, or simply moved to foolishness by the challenge Sir Geoffrey's invitation presented.

Restell had spent most of the last three days making arrangements that would eliminate the Allworthys as perpetual nuisances. Swift justice for the pair seemed to be the best revenge. At his insistence, the *Gazette* would print an article on the morrow, one that countered the item blaming French influences for young predators like the Allworthys. There would also be letters critical of the damning illustration, all of them subject to his approval.

Dealing with the publisher of the *Gazette* had been easily done. It was not a matter of calling in an acquired favor, but of making a superior argument and occasionally invoking the name of the foreign minister. The publisher was not entirely immune to coercion, especially since the troublesome story was printed for sensation rather than to reveal some truth.

The more difficult task was bringing the card game about on such short notice. Because he wanted as many witnesses to the Allworthys' fall from grace as possible, Restell decided that three tables of four would generate a sufficient stir in society.

To that end, Restell approached his father first, explaining only those particulars guaranteed to ensure his cooperation, and asked him to invite the Allworthy cousins and two more of his trusted colleagues. The foreign minister was as helpful as Restell had hoped, offering up three gentlemen from his warren of offices to sit at a table. With three places left to fill, Restell turned to his brother Ian, his brother-in-law Porter Wellsley, and finally—for the express purpose of demonstrating what damage could be done to a man's reputation—to Neven Charters.

His father's club was steeped in tradition dating back to the reign of Queen Mary. A protestant stronghold during a time when the papists were in favor, the gentlemen's club had private rooms from which almost no sound escaped. Plotting treason was always a dangerous business. The thick walls covered with burnished walnut paneling allowed men to gather and speak out freely. In the event there was no spy among them, their conversations remained secret.

Leaded windows filtered the dwindling daylight. Polished brass sconces lined the walls at even intervals. Liveried footmen stood at attention on either side of the door and the far wall, ready to offer libation, tobacco, a fresh deck of cards, or assistance to the privy if such was needed.

Restell had chosen this particular room for the illusion of privacy it still afforded, hoping to lull the Allworthys into complacency. He had not anticipated they would arrive in such a state of mind.

Restell made his play. He knew his card would be trumped, but he had no choice. Across the table, Lord Greenaway scowled as Mr. Bennet Allworthy tossed out his card. Restell did not respond to the scowl or the fact that the Allworthys took the trick. Greenaway, he realized, did not understand the Allworthys' manner of communicating their intent. Restell determined that he would have to force some cards on them, something obvious that Greenaway could not fail to notice.

Checking his pocket watch, he saw it was gone nine. He wondered what Emma was doing. He'd left home before she'd awakened. The note he had placed on her pillow gave her the barest outline of his plans for the day, but he had not the least notion of what she meant to do. He wondered if she'd painted in her studio. Perhaps she was there now. Imagining her reclining on the chaise did nothing to improve his concentration at cards.

He checked his pocket watch again just as William Allworthy passed the deck to him to cut.

"You have another engagement?" Bennet Allworthy asked, pointing to Restell's watch. "The divine redhead, perhaps?"

Restell did not deign to comment. At the neighboring tables he saw his father, Ian, and Porter Wellsley all cast a curious glance in his direction. Neven Charters studied his cards, but Restell did not think he imagined the smug smile that hovered about his mouth. "Here," he said, making the cut. "Your cards."

William took back the deck and began to deal. The look of caution he gave his cousin went unheeded.

"She made an impression on Jourdain, I believe," Bennet said. "He spoke of her endlessly after you left. He was persuaded to return to Breckenridge's on three other occasions on the chance that he would see her again." He gathered his cards, squared them off, then fanned them open. "Sadly, it was not to be. You came alone. William remarked that it was churlish of you not to share such a bounty as she was."

Lord Greenaway tapped the center of the table with his index finger. "I should like to start the game," he said. "I come to the club to forgo all conversation hinting of the distaff. This is still a bastion of the masculine, is it not?"

Restell chuckled, grateful for his lordship's intervention. "One hopes that is so, my lord. Let us go on, shall we?"

Greenaway fanned his cards with a flourish and took measure of them. Bennet sulked for a moment, then did the same. Restell studied his cards and waited for William Allworthy to turn over his final card and show them what would be the trump suit.

The round went smoothly for several tricks, then Restell saw Greenaway frown as he glanced at the cards on the table. Restell knew what had happened, but he said nothing. The accusation had to come from someone else. He hoped his father's political ally was up to the task.

Greenaway laid his hand over William Allworthy's as the younger man started to draw the trick into his possession. "I believe that king of clubs has already been played, Mr. William. By your cousin."

William's fair features mottled. "I think your lordship misremembers the cards."

"I have a surprisingly good memory where such things are concerned." He released William's hand and indicated the row of tricks that were lined up in front of him. "Let us have a look, shall we?"

Restell made a gracious protest. "Is that necessary? We're only playing for a few pounds for each trick. It's hardly worth a dust up."

Greenaway shrugged. "Perhaps you're right."

One of the minister's aides offered an aside to the players at his table, "Mr. William might volunteer to show his cards."

"Honorable thing to do," Porter Wellsley agreed.

"No one is questioning Mr. William's honor," Restell said. Out of the corner of his eye he observed that William Allworthy was feeling considerable heat. The area above his upper lip was dotted with perspiration. Opposite him, his cousin fidgeted as if he wished to escape the lick of the flames. "Can we continue?"

As William had taken the last trick, he had to lead the next card. He placed a four of spades on the table. Greenaway followed suit. It was Bennet who had to trump his cousin's play. He put down a jack of clubs. Restell had the card he meant to play already in hand. He began to put it forward when Greenaway pushed back from the table and threw down what was left of his cards.

"That jack has also been in play," he said. "I am of the opinion that the Allworthys do not understand the nature of a gentleman's game. I want to see the cards now."

Conversation at the other tables ceased. The Allworthys looked to Restell, bewilderment warring with suspicion. The pair knew they had not been caught in a cheat of their own design. Their specialty was using small, nearly imperceptible signals to communicate across the table. They were victims of sleight of hand and their silence indicated they were unaware of how it had been accomplished.

"Your tricks," Greenaway said. "Turn them over and fan them out."

Curious, Porter Wellsley left his cards at his own table and walked over to Restell's side. "Perhaps someone neutral should look on." He nodded to William. "Is that acceptable?"

William had no option but to brazen it out. "It is."

Wellsley glanced at the two tricks Restell had taken for his side. "You also, Restell. That seems fair."

"Very well." He flipped the cards he'd collected in the course of the round and spread them in an arc in front of him. There were no doubles among them. "Mr. William? It is your turn."

William Allworthy followed Restell's lead but without the flourish. A pair of kings appeared in the fan of cards, both of them clubs. A jack of clubs was also revealed, the match for the one Bennet had just tried to play. "This is not my doing," William said.

"Nor mine." Bennet held up his hands to demonstrate his innocence.

"Oh, but this is very bad," Sir Geoffrey said, joining Porter at Restell's side. He shook his head as he regarded the cards. "I suspect, Mr. William and Mr. Bennet, that you have little appreciation for the reputation of this club else you would not employ these stratagems to win."

William pushed all of his cards toward Restell's, but he spoke to Sir Geoffrey. "Count them. You will see there are too many in the deck."

"I cannot imagine what that will prove, but I do not mind the exercise."

Restell obligingly gathered up all the cards and started to pass them to his father. Before he gave them over, however, he pushed his chair back, closer to William's side of the table and tapped the deck against his guest's forearm. "It would be better, I think, if someone else did the count. Do you not agree?"

William did. He cleared his throat. "That would be best."

When it was Ian that volunteered, Restell was moved to make the wry observation that it should be someone who was not related to him.

Neven Charters came forward. "I'll do it." The other players who had been prompted out of curiosity to gather closer to the table parted for him. Neven took the cards from Restell and snapped them smartly as he counted out the deck. "Fifty-two," he announced when he finished.

"That's not possible," William said. "There must be more."

Lord Greenaway nodded. "I quite agree. The most obvious place is that they are on your person and that of your cousin."

William countered unwisely. "Perhaps you are carrying them."

Sir Geoffrey held up one hand. "That is quite enough accusations."

"A search, then," Restell said. He went to stand between Charters and Bennet Allworthy and pointed to the deck in Charters's hands. "Since there are fifty-two cards and we know two are duplicates, they must have replaced two others. What cards are we looking for, Mr. Charters?"

Neven tossed cards on the table in separate piles consisting of the four suits. In short order he and everyone else could see that the two and three of hearts were missing. They also found a third set of duplicate cards. An additional six of clubs had been added to replace a missing six of spades. It was clear to all why the trump card William Allworthy had dealt himself had been a club.

"We are looking for three cards, then," Sir Geoffrey said.

Lord Greenaway stepped forward to submit to the first search. He motioned to Ian Gardner. "Have a care with the neckcloth, Mr. Gardner. My valet is most particular that the folds should look flowing, not crisp."

"So that is the secret to a superior stock," Ian said. He completed the search with an economy of motion. "Who will be next? Mr. Bennet?"

"Very well, but it won't be done by you." He gestured to the footman standing at post beside the door. "This man will do."

Restell thought the footman looked as if he wished himself anywhere else. The poor man's hands were shaking as he approached Bennet Allworthy. Restell felt a moment's pity for the hapless servant, but was more concerned that the man's fear would make him ineffective in the search.

Moments later, Restell saw his own concerns were groundless as the footman found the six of spades tucked between Bennet's shirtsleeve and his frock coat. He affected surprise and disappointment. "Not well done of you, Allworthy. Not well done."

Bennet Allworthy stared at the card the footman held up. "That's not possible. He must have put it there."

"Now that would be a neat trick," Greenaway said. "Worth every pound you stole from me this evening if you could but show me how it was done." He waited. When it was clear that Bennet was not up to the challenge, he directed the footman to make a similar search of Bennet's cousin. "I wonder what we'll find," he said to no one in particular. "It would be a decent wager if the answer were not so patently obvious."

His observation was borne out when the footman held up the two and three of hearts. Both cards had been nestled under William's waistcoat and further obscured by his blue cravat. "That's not possible!"

Lord Greenaway was unmoved. "Clearly it is."

William pointed to Restell. "He's responsible."

"I don't much like the sound of that," Restell said.

"Search him," William insisted. "He must submit to a search."

"Would you like to do it, Allworthy? You are perhaps eager to put your hands on me." This last raised several chuckles and further enraged William. Restell shrugged as though he could not have helped himself. "You must please yourself," he told William. "Have at me." He held up his arms, palms out, and gave himself over for a search.

Seething, William Allworthy did not come forward. He jerked his head toward the footman, indicating that he should do it. Allworthy's expression remained unchanged when the footman found nothing.

Sir Geoffrey cleared his throat. "Don't know what you thought would be found, Mr. William. You and your cousin are holding all the cards as it were."

"Naturally you would align yourself to him. He's your son."

"And you are my guest," Sir Geoffrey said. "That trumps blood here. Every courtesy is always extended to our guests, and you have sorely abused my hospitality. It should not surprise, then, that you and Mr. Bennet are no longer welcome here. I imagine you will find yourself similarly barred from other clubs and many of your frequent haunts. Cheats are rarely embraced in society, and never in the society of other cheats." He turned to the footman. "Show them out, Billings. Do not let them persuade you to do differently. I will take responsibility."

The footman handed the three cards he held to Sir Geoffrey and stepped aside to permit the Allworthys to make their exit with a measure of dignity. Sir Geoffrey thoughtfully flicked the cards with his thumbnail. His glance strayed once to Restell. His son looked completely indifferent to the drama. There was not even the smallest indication of satisfaction about the line of his mouth. Sir Geoffrey wondered if he had not perhaps mistaken the matter. Was Restell as wholly innocent as he appeared or simply possessed of more talent for dissembling and subterfuge than anyone had suspected, least of all his own family?

"You will tell the whole of it later," Sir Geoffrey whispered as the other gentlemen dispersed for drink and chatter. "I am depending upon it."

Restell regarded his father with a measure of puzzlement pulling at his brow. "I shall," he said, picking up his glass of whiskey. He sipped, relishing the taste, then the blossoming heat in his stomach. "After someone explains the whole of it to me."

A light rain was falling by the time Restell reached home. He bounded up the steps, exhilarated by his success at the club. The Allworthys were dispatched, the foreign minister was satisfied, and no one present—not even his own father—could assign responsibility for what had occurred to anyone save the cousins. Sir Geoffrey harbored suspicions, but Restell knew they would remain just that. He had no intention of involving his father by telling all.

Handing over his hat and coat at the door, Restell inquired after Emma. "Has Mrs. Gardner retired?"

"She is still gone from home, sir."

"Gone? At this hour? It's after midnight."

"Indeed, sir," Crowley said gravely. "I imagine this means you did not receive her message. She said she would send one round to your father's club, else I would have done so myself. It is her uncle. Miss Vega sent a carriage for her. As best I understand it, Sir Arthur's taken a fall."

Restell nodded. He plucked his hat and coat from the butler just as he heard the familiar sound of Hobbes's peg leg on the staircase. He pivoted to face the valet. "If you're not with my wife, who is?"

"That would be Lewis," said Hobbes. "He managed to throw himself at the carriage as Mrs. Gardner was driving off. I never knew a woman could make herself ready with such speed. Bettis says she threw her gown on over her night-clothes, if you can credit it, sir. She was that anxious to be off."

"As I am," Restell said. "Crowley. Send someone to bring my horse street side. The carriage will take too long." Restell put his hat on and shrugged into his coat. "When did this happen, Hobbes?"

"A few hours ago. About nine, I think. Mrs. Gardner brought Sir Arthur by this afternoon while you were out. Took him up to see the studio."

"Did she?"

Hobbes nodded as he limped toward Restell. He brushed Restell's caped greatcoat with his hands and smoothed the line of it across his shoulders. "I think she was hoping to see you before you went to the club. You didn't return home."

"I changed clothes at Ferrin's. It was merely a convenience. It required rather more time than I allotted to secure the final commitment from one of the guests. Mr. Charters was in no way eager to favor me with his company."

"Understandable." Taking a step back, Hobbes surveyed his work with a critical eye. "I take it the evening went well?"

"Very well. It could have only been more agreeable if I'd thought to have tar and feathers at the ready."

"Humiliating for the Allworthy pups, was it?"

"Quite." Restell looked out the window. "It is taking long enough with my horse. I could have walked to Covington Street by now."

"I'm sure it will be here directly." Hobbes barely had the words out of his mouth when Restell announced he saw the groom. The valet's farewell fell on deaf ears as Restell departed the house in much the same fashion as he had arrived.

Emma heard her husband entering the house and was immediately reassured. She excused herself from her uncle's bedside and hurried into the hallway to greet Restell. She placed a finger to her lips as he came around the landing. He immediately slowed his pace and spoke quietly when he was upon her.

"What happened?" he asked, taking Emma's hands. Her fingers were cold. When he bent to kiss her, he found her cheek and lips were barely warmer.

"He's had a stroke, Restell. I sent for Dr. Bettany earlier, and he confirmed it. It is too early yet to know how he will go on. It is his right side that's been affected, so one can be a bit hopeful, I suppose."

"Hobbes told me there was a fall."

She nodded. "That's what was in Marisol's message. He collapsed on the stairs coming down from his studio. I don't know why he was even there so late." She shook her head as though to dismiss her frustration. "It's not important. Come, Marisol and I have been sitting with him. He mostly sleeps, but when he awakens he is so bewildered that it is painful to look upon."

"Then he is glad of your presence, I'm sure." Restell followed her into Sir Arthur's bedchamber. The large bed dwarfed the artist. Never a robust gentleman, he was made frail and diminutive by the thick bedcovers and ornate bed head. Restell approached the bed a step behind Emma. He nodded to Marisol, but when she did not acknowledge him, he was not at all certain she realized he was in the room. Her blue eyes, usually lambent in their outlook, were without expression. Indeed, she seemed to look through him but without the penetration of a sentient being.

Emma took up her chair again, and Restell drew one away from the fireplace and brought it to her side. The ashen cast of Sir Arthur's face was truly frightening. He possessed little more color than the pillow sham he lay against, and the dark frame of his hair merely emphasized it. He watched Emma slide her hand toward Sir Arthur's and slip her fingers under his palm. Marisol, he noted, sat stiffly in her chair, seemingly incapable of offering comfort for the depth of her own grief.

"When did he last wake?" Restell asked.

"It's been an hour."

"How long ago did Dr. Bettany leave?"

"Just afterward. He examined him one last time and said we should make him comfortable. He can have a bit of bread and broth, though I don't expect he'll want it."

Restell removed the handkerchief from his pocket and rose

to wipe a string of drool that had escaped the right corner of Sir Arthur's mouth.

Her husband's kind attention raised Emma's grateful smile. "Thank you," she said as he sat again. "It is much appreciated. By my uncle most of all. He cares greatly for his dignity."

Restell knew that was true. "Why didn't you send for me? I would have left the club."

Emma regarded him with some surprise. "I did. I merely supposed you couldn't leave." She looked at her cousin. "Marisol? Did you send someone to Lytton's with my note for Mr. Gardner?"

Marisol did not answer immediately. She turned her head slowly in Emma's direction as though moving against an invisible force. "Of course I did." She patted the pockets of her apron, frowning when she heard a light crinkling sound. She reached inside and found the folded note Emma had given her. Her lower lip trembled slightly. "I'm sorry. I didn't—"

"It's all right," Emma said quickly. "He's here now. I merely wondered. I suppose this means Mr. Charters does not know, either."

Marisol's hand returned to her pocket and came away with a second folded note. "I thought he didn't care," she said. There was a clear tremor in her voice.

"Mr. Charters was with me at Lytton's," said Restell. He knew Neven hadn't intended to tell Marisol. "So he wouldn't have received your note at home. Shall I go for him? It is no bother." He was already on his feet when Marisol nodded. Squeezing Emma's shoulder, he said, "It will seem less than a moment that I'm gone."

Emma very much doubted it, but she let him go anyway.

Over the next fortnight, Sir Arthur began to make what the physician called a cautious recovery. What made it cautious, Emma supposed, was that it occurred in increments so small as to be noticeable only to the most vigilant eye. He did not speak in a manner that was understandable to her. Marisol seemed to comprehend him, though, and would snap at the maids to fetch another blanket, pillow, or a damp flannel, depending upon her interpretation of the guttural utterances coming from the left side of her father's mouth.

Emma spent more time at number Twenty-three Covington than she did at home. She rose early and went straightaway to her uncle's, often remaining at his bedside throughout the morning. She read to him from books that she knew he enjoyed and encouraged Marisol to do the same. In the afternoon, Emma made a point to answer Sir Arthur's correspondence. Marisol often looked it over but never offered to assist. Emma did not mind as her cousin was clearly not up to the task. Marisol wandered about the house like a wraith, appearing unexpectedly at odd moments, uncharacteristically silent except for directing the servants.

Lady Rivendale was a frequent visitor. She made certain Dr. Bettany's orders were followed precisely. She oversaw the footmen as they exercised and massaged Sir Arthur's limp arm and leg, and she arrived with food prepared by her own cook to entice Sir Arthur to eat. Emma observed that it mattered very little that Sir Arthur did not try to speak in her presence. Lady Rivendale worked both sides of any conversation and never failed to win her own argument.

Emma returned home each evening increasingly tired, increasingly discouraged, and as Restell noted, increasingly worried. On Sunday night, a full fifteen days since Sir Arthur's stroke, Emma fell into bed beside him and simply lay there unmoving. Restell set aside his book and gave her his full attention, lightly brushing back strands of dark hair that had fallen across her forehead and cheeks. The first evidence that she was still conscious was when she stirred as his fingertips passed over her temples. He shifted his position so she could rest her head in his lap. As he began to massage her temples, he heard her surrender a small, satisfied sigh.

"Will you not stay at home tomorrow?" he asked. "Even Dr. Bettany says that Sir Arthur's recovery is not hastened by you being ever at his bedside."

Emma's eyes remained closed. "I know," she said quietly. "He has said as much to me. I wish I could believe he was right."

That surprised Restell. "Are you so powerful, then? I confess, I hadn't realized."

"No," she said. She shook her head to emphasize the point and winced at the sharp pain the movement caused. Biting her lower lip, she waited for the pain to dull. "Not powerful at all. Most often I feel perfectly helpless, but I'm aware that he rests well in my company. The maids have remarked on it. You have been there on occasion at the end of the day when I am about to take my leave. Can you say you haven't observed his agitation?"

"No," Restell said. "I cannot, but I didn't realize that it occurred every night. You have never said so before."

"I suppose I thought it would pass. Or that I could bear it." Tears slipped beneath her lashes. Before she could brush them away, she felt the soft pad of Restell's thumb doing it for her. "I am afraid for him," she said. "And I think he is afraid for himself."

"Have you spoken to Marisol about this?"

"Several times. I do not think she hears me. She listens, but she doesn't hear. I cannot fathom her mood of late. She had a terrible row with Mr. Charters this afternoon."

"A row? It is hard to believe. I am not certain I've heard her speak more than a few words at a time since Sir Arthur's stroke."

"She uttered a great many more today, most of them at a pitch that can only be described as shrill. It was fortunate they were in the studio, else the exact nature of their argument would surely be known to everyone in the household."

"Do you know?"

"I was reading to Uncle Arthur," she said. "I made it a point to read more loudly. Marisol made no mention of it later."

"Charters?"

"No. He doesn't speak to me outside of Marisol's presence. I quite prefer it that way."

So did Restell, though he wondered if Charters was being circumspect of his own accord or whether Marisol had insisted upon it. "It is odd, don't you think, that they were in the studio?"

"No. There are decisions that must be made about which painting should be made available for sale. Mr. Charters went up to look them over. Marisol followed later."

"You are not painting there, are you?"

"No. The commissioned works that were already begun will have to wait. I cannot finish them for my uncle when all of the *ton* knows he is bedfast. Even if the *ton* didn't know, I would not betray him to Marisol or Mr. Charters. It was a point of pride that neither of them knew how much he suffered with the rheumatism or how it affected his painting. The mornings that he could hardly hold a brush were more than physically painful for him."

"Do you know what painting Charters chose?"

"Yes. *A Windy Day.* It's a perspective of the park."

"I think I know the one you mean, Emma. That isn't your uncle's work. That's yours. All of it. Sir Arthur showed it to me, and I must tell you that the last doubt I had that you painted was removed when I viewed it. I was there, remember, when those two young ladies surrendered their modesty to the wind in favor of securing their bonnets."

Emma was sufficiently moved by this revelation to open one eye and look up at Restell. "Oh. You never said."

"Well, I intended to purchase it for myself. I was unaware that you'd finished it. Now I suppose I will have to meet Charters's stiff price."

"I expect there will be bidding for it," Emma said. "It is all rather ghoulish as Uncle Arthur is merely unwell, not dead. I imagine there is speculation that if he cannot paint again, the value of his work will increase many times over."

"And I imagine that Charters has that sort of thinking very much in his mind." Restell tapped the tip of Emma's nose with his forefinger. "I find it curious that Mr. Charters doesn't realize you've completed any number of paintings for your uncle. That Sir Arthur thought it could be kept a secret from him borders on the ridiculous, and that you seem to believe the same, well, I simply cannot grasp it."

"Sir Arthur and I have been very careful. I told you it was a matter of pride with him that no one knew. You would have only suspicions if not for the fact that I painted a moment in time that was witnessed by the pair of us."

"Is Charters an expert or not? He may not be a superior painter in his own right, but the breadth of his collection indicates that he is not a complete fraud. If he doesn't know for a fact that you've been assisting Sir Arthur in less obvious ways than cleaning his brushes and mixing his paints, then at the very least he must have his suspicions."

Emma laid her hands over Restell's massaging fingers, stilling them for a moment. "Why wouldn't he say anything?"

"For the plain reason that it is to his benefit to remain silent. He is going to marry Miss Vega, today's row notwithstanding, and what will eventually be hers will eventually be his. He is comfortably situated in society and his association with Sir Arthur gives him entry into even higher circles. Given both those things, I doubt that any amount of coercion could compel him to hint at what he suspects or knows."

Releasing Restell's hands, Emma permitted him to begin massaging again. "I don't think I shall ever comprehend the arrangement that exists among them."

"Arrangement?"

"For want of a better word coming to mind at this hour," Emma said. "It has always seemed to me that there existed some . . . *understanding* . . . among them."

"Among them," Restell said, mulling that over. "Not between them? You are including your cousin in the arrangement, then. It is three, not two."

"Yes, I suppose I am. It's always been a triangle."

Restell made no comment. He looked down at Emma and saw that her eyes were closed again, the shadows beneath them evident in the flickering candlelight. She looked weary beyond measure, yet he knew she would rise early and attend to her uncle on the morrow. She would give her uncle comfort that he did not find in the presence of his daughter. Emma had not said that was the case, but Restell had observed it. Sir Arthur's agitation did not merely occur when Emma left him of an evening, but when she left him alone with Marisol.

Restell wasn't certain that Emma had made the connection herself, and he was loath to put it before her. She was better able to share her fears about Sir Arthur than she was able to say anything at all about her cousin. Some of what he knew he had seen firsthand; the remainder came to him from Lady Rivendale. The countess had her own reasons of the heart to be concerned.

Marisol Vega fingered the keys on the pianoforte but produced no sound. She played the tune in her head, neither humming nor carrying the melody in her sweet soprano. She knew every note, every measure, having played it on many occasions for her father. She could not recall if she'd ever played it for Neven. He'd always said he enjoyed her talent on the pianoforte, but he rarely requested that she play for him except when there were others around to remark on her skill as well. His appreciation of her talent, she suspected, was greater when it reflected well on him.

Marisol appreciated the practicality of his position. She was of a similar mind where he was concerned. Neven always looked better to her when he was surrounded by his admirers. Knowing that he was sought out for his cleverness never failed to warm her. How clever she must appear to others, she reasoned, for having caught the attention of such a man. Cleverer still, for having secured his interest when they seemed to have been fixed on Emmalyn.

Marisol spread her fingers across the keys, and she struck a strident chord hard. When the notes faded to nothing, she picked up the threads of another melody in her mind and began to play it without accompaniment.

"I thought I heard you here," Emma said, slipping into the

drawing room. "It was just the one chord, though. Won't you play something? I believe your father would like that."

"It won't disturb him?"

"No. On the contrary. It will give him peace and soften Lady Rivendale's chatter."

Marisol winced. "She does go on, doesn't she?" Her grim smile vanished as quickly as it appeared. She began to play, this time with her fingers fully depressing the keys. "You heard the argument yesterday, didn't you? No, there is no need to pretend otherwise. I shouldn't wonder that all of Covington Street heard me. I was shamefully rude to Neven." Marisol bowed her head and lowered her voice so she was barely audible above the pianoforte. "I think he is going to end our engagement, Emmalyn."

"Oh, surely not. Did he say so?"

Marisol didn't answer the question. Instead, she lifted her face and blinked back tears. "Will you speak to him? Please, Emmalyn. He will listen to you. He thinks you are sensible. If you tell him that it is my father's illness that has made me unreasonable, he will understand. I could not bear it if he leaves me."

"Marisol. I'm sure you're—"

Marisol stopped playing and swiveled to face Emma, effectively interrupting her. "Could you bear it if Mr. Gardner left you? You couldn't, could you? I can see it in your face. Please. Won't you go to Neven? I know you can persuade him to do what is right by me. You can take my carriage since you sent your own driver off."

"Now?" asked Emma. "You want me to go now?"

"You must. He left here yesterday with nothing resolved between us. You must know that every moment since then has been a torture. Say you will, Emmalyn. Say you will do it."

Emma was certain she meant to refuse. Her lips had parted in anticipation of doing just that, so it was difficult to know if she or Marisol was more surprised when what they heard was *yes*.

Chapter 16

Emma looked around for Jamie McCleod before she stepped into the carriage. She wished the man was not so very good at disappearing. Now that she had given Marisol her word, all the reasons that she should not have done so were coming to her mind. Emma suspected it would unravel the knot in her stomach if she saw that McCleod was close by.

Turning back to the house, Emma observed Marisol watching from one of the windows. The distance separating them was not so great that Emma couldn't make out Marisol's anxious expression. Indecision held Emma still for another moment. At her side she sensed the driver's impatience. The man had begun beating a hard tattoo against his leg with the braided leather handle of his whip. The steady percussion accelerated her heartbeat and within moments her head was thumping with the same rhythm.

Gritting her teeth, Emma spun on her heel and faced the driver. The lowered brim of his hat made it impossible for her to catch his eye. He was oblivious to what she hoped would be a quelling glance, and the drumming continued unabated.

Emma startled the driver even more than herself when she made a grab for his whip. He jumped back, knocking his shoulder into the carriage and causing him to lose his balance. Emma seized the whip as he stumbled and made no move to help him when his foot was wrenched between the curb and the carriage wheel. He went down hard, grunting in pain. His hat tipped sideways, then slipped from his head altogether.

Emma's skin crawled for reasons she did not understand, but she gave the driver no more of her attention. It was the sound she'd heard from inside the carriage that caught her notice. She sidled closer to investigate just as the driver was starting to rise. He'd placed his hand in the opening of the door to pull himself to his feet. Emma didn't hesitate. She slammed the door hard on his fingers, then threw herself against it. The driver bellowed, but it was the person inside the carriage trying to get out that cursed his bloody misfortune.

Emma knew she couldn't hope to keep the door closed, so she didn't try. In anticipation of the next push from the inside, she spun sideways. The door flew open, and the man that tumbled out sprawled belly down on the sidewalk. When he started to rise, Emma plunged the toe of her slipper into his ribs. He swore again, this time cursing her. She gave him the other foot in his soft side, harder than before. Then did it again. And again. And . . .

Jamie McCleod lifted Emma by the waist and set her more than a leg's length away. Lewis was attending to the driver, helping the man up from the street so he could shove him to the sidewalk beside his accomplice.

"Is she uninjured?" Lewis asked McCleod. "You know he'll have our guts for garters if there's been so much as a hair harmed."

McCleod appraised Emma. He still had an arm flung sideways to keep her at bay. She looked in every way prepared to trample the men on the ground if he lowered his guard. "She's in fighting fettle."

"Perhaps you should take the whip," Lewis said. "Before she uses it."

McCleod's appraising look turned wary. "Mrs. Gardner? Might I have the whip?"

Emma set the whip handle squarely in McCleod's large palm. "Use it to lash them to the carriage wheel."

"Ma'am?"

"Lash them to the carriage wheel," she said. "Make certain they're secure, then one of you go and fetch my husband. Tell him you have captured Elliot and Will Poole. That will save your guts."

McCleod flushed to the roots of his red hair, while Lewis stared at her, slack jawed. The pair watched her sweep calmly past them and through the gate, her bearing unruffled, even regal in profile.

"D'ye suppose that's who we have here?" Lewis asked. "The Poole brothers?"

"I'm inclined to believe her," McCleod said. He hunkered down beside one of the men and roughly grabbed him by the hair, jerking his head up. "Will or Elliot?" he asked. When the man merely spat at him, McCleod gave his head a smart bounce off the pavement. "Suppose I just call you a bad piece of work and not bother with introductions. Mr. Gardner will have it from you, just see if he don't."

Mr. Gardner had it first from his wife. When Restell arrived at number Twenty-three Covington a small crowd had gathered in front of the house to observe what was toward. They parted for Restell so he could advance on the gate, then closed ranks as McCleod joined Lewis in watching over the spitting, snarling pair tethered to the carriage wheel. No one had emerged from the house to separate the matched grays from the carriage. The animals were restless, made more so by the jostling of the spectators. Occasionally the carriage would lurch forward, making the awkwardly held positions of the captives even more unbearable.

Restell noted all of this as he passed, but gave no order that would have improved their lot. Whatever indignities they suffered in the street were nothing to what they would endure on the transport ship. He was of a mind to prepare them for their voyage.

He was shown immediately to Sir Arthur's library where

Emma was sitting with Lady Rivendale on the sofa. His first thought was that his wife was infinitely more composed than the countess. Indeed, it seemed to him that Emma was giving comfort rather than receiving it. She had her ladyship's hand between her own and was alternately squeezing, then patting it.

Restell was in no wise prepared to accommodate Lady Rivendale's nerves. "May I speak to my wife alone?" he asked without preamble.

"Lady Rivendale is overset," Emma said.

Restell said nothing. His stare was pointed.

Now it was the countess who offered Emma a measure of comfort. "It's all right, my dear. I believe your husband is more overset than I am."

Emma released Lady Rivendale's hand and went to Restell's side. "Are you, Restell? You can see for yourself that I'm all of a piece. McCleod and Lewis were quite heroic. They dispatched the brothers with admirable efficiency."

He arched an eyebrow. "That is not precisely how it was related to me."

"Oh."

"Hmm." Over Emma's shoulder, Restell watched Lady Rivendale rise from the sofa and begin to take her leave. "I don't suppose you were a witness to what happened."

"I was not." The countess paused. "I will be with Sir Arthur if either of you have need of me." She left the room quickly before Restell could press more questions on her.

When she was gone, Restell took Emma by the shoulders and regarded her from head to toe. She was in fine color and thoroughly settled. "I am suspicious of so much serenity, Mrs. Gardner."

"I should be concerned if you were not. That is very much your nature."

"Lady Rivendale may not have been a witness, but she knows what happened."

"As I do. You must ask me."

"I trust McCleod told me the truth," he said. "And heroic is not a word he used to describe his intervention." He nudged her toward the sofa and bade her sit. "Where are Sir Arthur's driver and groom? McCleod didn't know what had happened to them."

"Cook found them unconscious and trussed like geese for baking in the carriage house. They never saw their attackers, but we can safely assume they are the pair amusing our neighbors right now."

Restell's lower jaw jutted forward as he slowly blew out a breath. "God's truth, what were you thinking when you left this house with no escort?"

"I was thinking someone would be close by. Someone always is."

"Yes, when they know you're coming and going. Lewis saw the carriage and thought your cousin was leaving the house. McCleod told me that Lewis then discovered that the carriage wasn't brought around for Miss Vega but for Lady Rivendale." Restell glimpsed a frown briefly darken Emma's expression. "When they realized that it was you that meant to take the carriage, they both converged at the front of the house." His tone turned wry. "Apparently you had the miscreants well in hand by then."

Emma's slight frown returned; she nodded absently.

"Where were you going?" asked Restell. "McCleod didn't know."

"I think you must have interrogated poor Mr. McCleod on the way here."

"I might have. At least he arrived with his skin intact."

"Lewis said you would have their guts for garters."

"And so I might if you do not answer my question. Did you think I hadn't noticed?"

Emma sighed. "I was going to Mr. Charters's home." The fact that Restell simply stared at her moved Emma to expand her answer. "As a favor to Marisol. She thinks Mr. Charters intends to end their engagement. She asked me to speak to him."

"Of course she did. Did you even hesitate?"

"I meant to," she said, somewhat defensively. "But I didn't, not really. Not until I was outside. It was my fear that held me back. You were right, Restell, about fear making one cautious and sometimes clever."

In other circumstances this would have raised his smile, but not now. "And then?"

"Then the driver grew impatient and started slapping the butt of his whip against his leg, and I knew. *I knew,* Restell. That was the sound. Exactly. The rhythm, precisely. And he was the man, without question. I never saw his face, either, when he took his turn beating me or when he waited his turn, but I knew him. There was no other thought in my mind except that I must needs take the whip from him." Her voice held a little of the awe she still felt at her own audacity. "So I did. Can you credit, Restell? I took it from him."

Restell thought he could credit it more easily than she could. "It does not surprise, no. You are altogether fierce when you set your mind to it."

Emma was encouraged to go on. "He fell against the carriage. I think that's when he jostled the person inside, or at least that's the first I was aware that someone else was present, and I knew at once who it must be, even though I'd never set eyes on him before. Somehow he spilled out onto the walk and—"

Restell cleared his throat lightly, interrupting her. "Mc-Cleod said it was as if the man was catapulted from the carriage."

"Did he? I didn't realize he was outside then."

"Running down the steps, I believe, with Lewis on his heels. You didn't start to kick the man until McCleod had cleared the gate. He told me you never heard him calling your name."

Emma was much struck by that. "He's right. I didn't hear anything for the pounding in my head. The first I knew he was there was when he was restraining me from delivering another blow."

"That was unkind of him."

Emma was not entirely certain that he wasn't serious. "What is to be done with them, Restell? They are Billy

Poole's cousins, you know. Did you notice their resemblance to the sketches Sir Arthur made?"

"I noticed their resemblance to the sketches *you* made." He saw she was about to deny it. "No, Emma, do not dissemble. Not now. There were four sketches, but I don't think they were all your uncle's work. There were two that the innkeeper told me did not do justice to Peele. Those were the ones Marisol and Charters picked as most like the man. The one Mr. Broadstreet and his wife chose was the one you said bore the best resemblance to Peele. *That* was your work. You did it on your own when the others did not satisfy. Am I wrong?"

Emma looked down at her hands. "No," she said. "You're not wrong."

"Bloody hell, Emma, even you must suspect what is happening here."

She shook her head because she was helpless to do otherwise. "Please, don't make me say it. I can't." Tears came to her eyes. "I just can't."

He nodded. "Where's Marisol?"

"She went to sit with Sir Arthur."

"All right. Collect your things, Emma. McCleod will take you home. There are details I must attend here, not the least of which is sending for the runners. I won't be long. We'll sort it out." He drew her close, pressed a kiss against her temple, and held her until her breathing quieted. One of the things she collected before she left the house was herself.

The runners arrived with all due speed at Restell's summons. It helped, he supposed, to have persons of importance in the household such as Sir Arthur, and most particularly the countess, for he had never known the authorities to respond with alacrity. He was glad he'd thought to mention their presence in the note he sent to Bow Street.

The runners made short work of sorting out the accounts of the witnesses, the information that Restell gave them, and the tales that Will and Elliot Peele interjected to portray themselves

as wholly innocent. While the story the Peele brothers spun was
true relative to the incident in front of number Twenty-three
Covington, it did not account for the driver and groom who had
been rendered unconscious or the oddity of Elliot Peele being
inside the carriage. One by one witnesses stepped forward to
make their statements. Restell doubted so many people had
seen what happened, but never questioned that they wanted to
come to Emma's aide.

These were the same inhabitants of Covington Street that
she observed from the balcony: the lads from Sir Harold
Wembley's home that waited for the milk wagon of a morning, the Harveys' kitchen maid and the footman she flirted
with from the Ford house, the Allens' cook who often had occasion to argue with the tinker. Emma had pointed them out
to Restell, though not from the balcony. They were all recognizable to him because she'd sketched, then carefully painted
every one of them into the *Fishing Village*.

Restell's own account was brief but bore considerable
weight with the runners. He made it clear at the outset that his
wife would not be made available for their questions but that
he would answer for her. This seemed to suit them admirably
as they confided they had no wish to further overset Mrs.
Gardner.

Once the runners had the story in hand, Lewis unlashed
Will and Elliot Peele from the carriage wheel and gave them
over. The pair was frog-marched along Covington Street amid
cheers and jeers, and the youngest lads left the crowd in favor
of trailing after the Peeles and throwing bits of muck at their
hapless heads.

The gathering dispersed as soon as the runners and their
charges disappeared around the corner onto Appley Way.
Restell and Lewis watched them go before they stepped
inside the house. Lewis went to inquire after the groom and
driver, while Restell set himself the task of making inquiries
above stairs.

He found Lady Rivendale at Sir Arthur's bedside. She had

managed to calm herself, though he suspected she'd had little choice because Sir Arthur was so clearly overwrought.

"How can I help?" asked Restell as he came abreast of the bed.

"You can assure him that Emmalyn is well. I don't think he believes me."

Restell masked his surprise. It hadn't occurred to him that Lady Rivendale would inform Sir Arthur of any part of the incident. The artist's agitation could have been anticipated, and it did nothing to improve his speech. Sir Arthur was wholly unintelligible when he was in such a state.

Restell looked down at Sir Arthur and could sense the man imploring him, though what it was in aid of was less clear. "Emma is already home," he said. "No doubt she is having tea in her studio by now. It is her sanctuary, Sir Arthur, modeled after the one you gave her here. I know she took you to see it. Think of her there, and it will give you peace of mind."

Sir Arthur shook his head vehemently and used his good arm to flail at Restell. His fingers caught Restell's hand; he gripped it hard and tugged. He spoke slowly, enunciating every word. None of it was understandable.

Restell looked to Lady Rivendale. "Has he tried pen and paper again?"

She nodded. "He can make letters that are recognizable to my eyes, but the words are incomprehensible. Whatever he thinks he is telling us is not what is writ on the page."

"Where is Miss Vega? Emma says that she seems to be able to understand her father." Restell felt his hand being jerked hard again. "I'll bring her here, Sir Arthur. I have need to speak to her also." When Sir Arthur shook his head, Restell was moved to ask, "Do you want your daughter here?" This time Sir Arthur nodded. "Very well," said Restell. "Then I shall find her." Sir Arthur responded by shaking his head as hard as he had before, prompting Restell to glance helplessly in Lady Rivendale's direction.

"I cannot make sense of it, either," she said. "Perhaps it is because Miss Vega is the one who told him what happened."

"She did?"

Lady Rivendale took umbrage. "Why, you thought I was the one who told tales out of school. That is rarely the way of it, Restell. I heard some commotion and went downstairs to see what was toward. Miss Vega was at the window looking out on the street and gave me only enough of the particulars as to keep me there. When I returned to Sir Arthur it was to discover Miss Vega was at the end of making a more thorough explanation to him. He was in such a state of nerves that I shooed her out."

"So when I saw you with Emma later, it was Sir Arthur's turn that had upset you."

"Yes. Your wife was generous to offer her sympathies when she had just had a bad turn herself."

A bad turn was rather understating Emma's confrontation with the Peele brothers, but Restell did not point this out to Lady Rivendale. Emma was recovered from her encounter, while Sir Arthur was still greatly disturbed by it.

"Where is Miss Vega?" he asked the countess.

Her mouth flattened momentarily as she considered the question. "I'm not certain that I know." She glanced at Sir Arthur. He was gripping the sleeve of Restell's frock coat now and tugging on it with renewed urgency. "Oh dear, we have made ourselves disagreeable again. Go on, Restell. I will stay here while you look for Miss Vega."

Restell eased himself from Sir Arthur's grasp, apologizing for the distress he'd caused. He bussed Lady Rivendale's cheek before he left her side and whispered that all would be made well.

Restell sought one of the maids to show him to Marisol's bedchamber. She waited beside him as he knocked, then showed him in when there was no answer. Since he had expected to find Marisol prostrated across her bed, he was taken back to discover she was not in the room. The maid showed him her dressing room and it was similarly vacant.

"Where did you last see her?" he asked the woman.

"Coming out of her father's room, sir. It was that long ago. I couldn't say where she is now."

Restell was on the point of asking the maid to make a search of the downstairs when Lady Rivendale stepped out of Sir Arthur's room. The countess gestured for him to join her. He asked the maid to wait, then went to her ladyship's side. He arrived with a question in his eyes.

"I believe she may have gone up to the studio," Lady Rivendale said. "At least I think that's what Sir Arthur is trying to tell me. It cannot hurt to look."

Restell nodded, thanking her. He told the maid to remain where she was while he let himself into the stairwell leading up to the studio. He called up before he began his climb. "Miss Vega? Are you up there?" Restell was not deterred by the silence that greeted him, though he was disappointed. He mounted the steps quickly and was only two thirds of the way up when he had his first unhappy glimpse of what he would find at the top.

The studio was in complete disarray. Jars of ground cobalt and sulfur had been opened and upended. Chalk dusted the table and the floor around it. The canvases that had been neatly stacked against every wall of the room were tipped on their backs and lay scattered across the carpet. Slender threads of rabbit glue had been drizzled across some of them. Hog's bristle and miniver brushes littered the area beneath the shelves. The aprons had been removed from their pegs and tossed through the balcony window. One empty easel lay on its side; the other remained squarely under one of the skylights, the painting it held still shrouded in linen.

Stepping over a cracked mortar and around an overturned stool, Restell approached the standing easel, almost certain what he would find beneath the cloth. He grasped one corner of the fabric and tugged, letting it slide over the stretched canvas and fall almost silently to the floor.

Marisol—and Restell had no doubt that it was she who had laid siege to her father's studio—had employed a palette knife to savage Emma's painting. *A Windy Day* had been violently shredded with dozens of slash marks. Restell recoiled from the rage that had produced this violation, for he could think of it in no other terms. What had been done here was so intensely personal that it was painful to look upon.

He closed his eyes, and when he opened them again the colors blurred on the canvas. The brush strokes no longer seemed so well-defined. He blinked back tears until even the shredded threads of the canvas came into focus.

"Bloody hell," he said under his breath. "Bloody, bloody hell."

"Miss Vega's not here," Restell told Lady Rivendale. They had stepped into the hallway again to keep from upsetting Sir Arthur. "No one saw her below stairs. She must have left by the trade entrance."

The countess held her chin, pondering this last. "I was so certain you would find her in the studio."

"She was there. I think Sir Arthur must have known. Perhaps she told him, I can't say, but it would explain his agitation."

"What do you mean?"

"Later," he said. "I think I know where she's gone. Emma told me that Miss Vega suspected Mr. Charters meant to end their engagement. If there is but a scintilla of truth there, then it's likely she means to end it herself—on her own terms, I fear." It was an impoverished explanation at best, raising more questions than it answered. Restell took his leave before the countess demanded something more substantial from him.

Neven Charters was nursing a hangover with the hair of the dog when his butler announced that Restell Gardner wished to see him. "By all means," he said, setting his glass of whiskey aside. "Show him in." Neven rose from his chair in anticipation of Restell's entry into the drawing room. He was mildly amused at the speed of Restell's approach until he saw the dark expression that accompanied him.

Neven was instantly alert to a host of possibilities that could give rise to such a countenance. "What's happened?" he asked without preamble.

"Is she here?"

Frowning deeply, Neven was genuinely bewildered. "I don't know who you mean, but it doesn't matter. I'm here alone."

"Miss Vega," Restell said. He removed his hat and placed it in the crook of his elbow. "Has she been here?"

"No. Has something happened to Sir Arthur?" He felt Restell's narrowed gaze settle on him and was hard-pressed to remain rooted under it. "You will have to say something, Gardner. State your purpose or go."

Restell advanced. He grabbed Charters by the neckcloth, twisted, and pushed him hard into the chair he'd recently vacated. "What's your game, Charters? Did you arrange Emma's near abduction this afternoon?"

Neven's head snapped up. "What has she done?"

"Emma? Nothing at all to deserve the end you and Marisol planned for her."

"No, not Emma. Marisol. I'm speaking of Marisol." Neven struggled to his feet, an action that put him toe-to-toe with Restell. He held his stance and demanded again, "What has she done now?"

Emma sat at the table in her studio idly fingering the brushes she'd arranged in front of her. A gentle breeze from the open French doors ruffled her loosely pinned hair. A pair of wrens settled on the rope slung midway across the entrance to the nonexistent balcony. Occasionally they nudged each other, but mostly they seemed content to preen.

Emma picked up one of the round brushes and regarded the pointed tip, imagining the fine detail work she would be able to accomplish with it. The bright brushes, those with the broad ends, could apply a swath of bold color to the sky or sea or a young lady's debut gown. She manipulated the brush through her fingers in much the same manner she'd seen Restell manipulate cards. It was a meditative exercise, she realized, requiring no thought for the task and allowing her mind to wander at will.

It wandered again and again to the Peele brothers. They would have killed her this time, she was certain of it. Perhaps they would have done so before if not for her escape from the cottage. She couldn't know. The confrontation at number Twenty-three Covington hadn't returned her memory, but she no longer felt a need to press for recollection. If it never came back, she could still be satisfied. Mr. Jonathan Kincaid—ambitious Billy Peele of Walthamstow—was dead, probably at Neven Charters's hands, and she knew that Restell would see that Billy's cousins were not long for true English soil, not unless they found a resting place beneath it.

The why of it remained unknown to her, but she was not in the dark about the who. She hadn't been able to say it aloud to Restell, nor even yet to herself, but that didn't mean she didn't know the truth of it. It sat uncomfortably with her, an ugly worm of a thought insinuating itself deep in her gray matter.

Emma chuckled softly, mockingly. The image in her mind's eye was not a pleasant one. She dropped the brush and nudged her drawing tablet closer. There were perhaps a dozen sketches in it, all of them of her husband. Restell grinning boyishly. Restell arching an eyebrow. Restell looking every bit the Viking warrior.

Emma picked up a pencil and began to draw. She started with an almost perfect oval and worked on a three-quarter profile. It required surprisingly few lines to give the face its doll-like perfection and only a few more to cast that same countenance in a more sly, clever light. Emma made the bottom lip of the bow mouth a shade fuller so that it thrust forward in an artful pout. A bit of shading about the eyes changed their guileless slant and revealed their cunning.

Emma added more strokes to suggest ebon hair and a few fine lines to show the delicate wisps that often fluttered near the temple. The confusion that sometimes set these features awry was absent. The young woman staring back at Emma knew precisely what she wanted. Emma realized now that she always had.

"Marisol," Emma said, recognizing the light tread on the stairs. She closed her sketch book and turned on her stool to face her cousin. "I didn't expect that you would come here, though perhaps it's just as well. It would be difficult to speak frankly in your father's presence."

Marisol unbuttoned her pelisse, then plucked at the strings of her bonnet as she surveyed the studio. "Father told me about this place. It is impressive what Mr. Gardner has done for you." Removing her bonnet, she tossed it on a chair, then she slipped out of her pelisse and placed it over the back. "You don't mind that your housekeeper told me you were here, do you? She offered to announce me, but I assured her we do not stand on such ceremony. I found my way."

Emma realized she had not successfully captured Marisol's over bright blue eyes in her sketch, nor the fine edge to her expression. "I didn't imagine that Sir Arthur would mention my studio to you. To anyone, for that matter."

"Why? Because you didn't want anyone to know you paint?"

"It was your father's wish that no one knew."

Marisol gave her head a small toss so that her hair tumbled back over her shoulders. She spread her arms wide to indicate the whole of the studio. "This worried him, though I doubt you realized it when you brought him here. That's why he told me about what you'd been doing for him. He didn't know what to do if you no longer finished his paintings. The fine work was no longer possible for him, he told me. He was afraid you would abandon him. Can you imagine? He was fearful that you meant to paint for yourself and not for him."

"I didn't know," Emma said softly.

"Of course not. Didn't I say as much? I acquit you of being cruel, Emmalyn. I know you didn't set out to worry Father.

That is not your way, although it made no difference to the outcome. I have come to realize, quite recently in fact, that one's intentions do not always shape the consequences." There was a hint of regret in Marisol's brief smile. She began a tour of the studio, stepping first in the direction of the chaise longue, walking her fingers over the brushed velvet arm as she passed. "If intentions were all that mattered, well, I would not be talking to you now, would I?"

Emma followed Marisol's slow progress about the room. "I was never a threat to you, Marisol."

"I expect you believe that. It speaks to your naiveté, I suppose. Father and I managed quite well for years on our own, but with your arrival I became an afterthought."

"That's not true. You were everything to him. If I made myself useful it's because I had no place in his heart as you did."

"So you became his arms and his legs. It serves nothing to shake your head at me, Emmalyn. You cannot deny what I saw with my own eyes. You were always doing whatever he wished, whenever he wished it. It seemed to me that he no longer had to ask for anything aloud. You anticipated what he wanted. You even encouraged his connection with Lady Rivendale. You must have known I had no use for the woman, yet you welcomed and encouraged her and ignored every one of my concerns."

Emma frowned deeply. She had not comprehended the depth of Marisol's jealousy. "Sir Arthur enjoys her ladyship's company. Would you deny him that?"

"She will ruin what little you have left untouched. She will take his heart as you have not been able to do. I cannot allow her to have the place left to me by my mother. Can you possibly appreciate that?"

"I don't think I can," Emma said carefully. She slowly turned on her stool to better follow Marisol's circuitous examination of the studio. Her cousin was idly tracing the top of a lacquered box with mother-of-pearl inlay. Emma held her breath as Marisol picked up this small treasure, a gift from her own parents. It required considerable effort of will not to leave her perch at the table and seize the box.

Marisol allowed the box to teeter between her hands, but her attention was all for Emma. One corner of her mouth curled. "You still do not fully understand. I can see that you don't." She shrugged as if it were of no account.

Emma's stomach was knotted with dread for all the things that Marisol was *almost* saying. "Are the countess and I truly such a threat? You can't have forgotten that you will be married to Mr. Charters soon. Is he not enough for you, Marisol?"

"Because he dotes on me? That is what you think, isn't it?"

"He *does* dote on you."

"He is my *keeper*." Marisol set the box down hard. The small end table wobbled with the force of it. "What he and I have is by arrangement. For all that I would have the *ton* believe otherwise, there is no love match. He is still in love with you."

"You're wrong."

"You'd like to think so, but I know differently. Why else would he have killed Jonathan? I have the truth from Jonathan's own cousins. They barely escaped themselves. They say Neven was enraged. He brought you back to London, right enough, but not before he found and murdered my poor Jonathan."

Emma felt as if her throat was closing. "There is no Jonathan Kincaid, Marisol. There was only ever Billy Peele, and he betrayed you by keeping me alive."

Marisol's short laugh held no humor. "So you are not without some sense of what happened. I have wondered these many weeks what you had come to remember or what manner of things Mr. Gardner discovered. You have shared very little with me of late. It quite put me out of patience with you."

"I shall be disappointed to hear if that is why you set the Peele brothers in my path again." Emma held the threads of her composure together and managed a wry smile. "You might have just asked me."

Marisol blinked as though startled. "Oh, you are teasing. I have always admired your self-possession, Emmalyn. I don't suppose I shall ever master it for myself. Things are such a muddle for me at times. I think I know what I want." She shrugged. "Then I don't. It is all very confusing. Now, for instance, I am finding that I like you immensely."

Emma noted that Marisol did not sound as if she was pleased to realize it. "I like you, too."

"I know you do." Marisol moved past the table toward open doors. The pair of fluttering wrens took flight. Marisol stopped, turned in Emma's direction, and folded her arms under her bodice. "Did you know our grandmother, Emmalyn?"

"No. She died when I was an infant."

"Did she? Father never said. I always had the impression she lived much longer. She was mad, you know, and confined to Bellefaire."

"Mother said she was melancholic."

"Father says it was snits and fits." Marisol sighed heavily. "I do not think I should like Bellefaire. As Father is of a similar opinion, he arranged my marriage to Neven. In the event that something should happen to him—as indeed it has—he wanted to be certain I was settled. I like Neven well enough, I suppose, but he wears on my nerves. I liked Jonathan ever so much more. We had such plans, Emma." Marisol's perfectly symmetrical features were set awry when she drew her mouth to one side in disgust. "He disappointed in the end, though, and now I have come to wonder if that's not always the way."

"He never met me at Madame Chabrier's, did he?"

"He was there. You must believe I didn't mean that you should suffer, Emmalyn. I was most specific that it should end quickly. That's what Jonathan promised. Instead, he watched. That is what his cousins told me, that he liked to watch. Odd, that he could observe such grisly fare as your face being pummeled. A man who could choose a Barcelona silk handkerchief seemed to possess finer sensibilities. Did I not say he disappointed?"

Emma could not suppress a shiver.

"They shouldn't have taken you to Walthamstow. That was

an annoyance, really. I could not imagine what had become of you."

"My body, you mean."

"Well, yes, but as you're right here before me, it seems impolite to speak in such a manner." Marisol unfolded her arms and let them fall to her side. "Father had the whole of it from me before your letter arrived. You will know that I have never been able to keep a secret from him, though I have had occasion to keep secrets *with* him. You will comprehend that is altogether different."

Emma did not comment on this last. She was acutely aware of the distance that separated her from Marisol. Her cousin still stood framed by the open doorway, and sunlight cast a halo about her dark hair, lending it a blue-black sheen. That otherworldly appearance was at odds with Marisol's cold, implacable smile. "Tell me about the evening when I almost drowned in Lady Rivendale's fountain, Marisol. I should like to hear how that came about."

"The merest happenstance. Neven should not have accompanied you to the garden. I have always made it clear that I would not countenance him trifling with you."

Emma could not keep the incredulity out of her voice. "You struck him?"

"It was but the passion of a moment."

"But Hobbes was there."

"So he was, and he misjudged the view he had. You and Neven were occupied with each other. Some things are not so difficult to accomplish as they would appear in the aftermath. And truly, it was unexpected that Neven's fall would trap you."

"But not unwelcome," said Emma.

"No," Marisol agreed. "It was not unwelcome."

"Do your father and Mr. Charters know what you did?"

"If they do, they have never said a word about it. It is difficult for them, given what I know."

"You are speaking of the forgeries now, I suspect."

"How clever you are at times. I told Father and Neven they

could not hope to keep it from you forever. They were content to wait, though. I didn't understand it until I realized that you were finishing paintings for Father. His poor hands were stiff from attending to the master works that Neven required him to complete. There were many nights he did not come to bed. I wondered at his stamina to paint during the day as well, but that was my error. He was not painting then, was he? Or at least he was not painting as often. You were doing it for him, thinking all the while that it was his rheumatism that kept him away from the easel."

Emma was glad for the stool under her. She had been so certain it was Neven Charters who'd made the copies. "But why would Sir Arthur do it?" she asked. "Why would he risk his—" Emma stopped. Marisol was advancing on her. She quickly slid off the stool and put it between them. "He did it for you, is that it? It was what Mr. Charters demanded in return for the promise of marrying you?"

"For the promise of *keeping* me," Marisol said. "Father could not do to me what he did to his own mother, though perhaps he has had cause to regret that decision. I cannot say."

Emma's hand flew to her mouth. Above her fingertips, her eyes widened, and her voice did not break a whisper. "Oh, my God, Marisol. There was no accident before your father's stroke. He fell because you pushed him." Emma watched tears well in Marisol's eyes and for a moment it seemed that her cousin was lost.

"Do not blame me, Emmalyn. You musn't. He was so distraught that he might lose you. Have I not already told you that? Should I have been glad of it? He wanted *you*. Not me. He was giving me away. I was the one being abandoned, and he refused to see it." Her voice began to rise steadily. "He should not have treated me so shabbily, not when I've done everything he asked. I am the image of my mother, am I not? Am I not the image of his beloved wife?"

The sharp pitch of Marisol's voice made Emma wince. She took a step backward just as Marisol lunged and made a grab for the stool. Emma feinted right and dove left, catching her hip on the corner of the table. Marisol swung the stool at her head and shoulders, and one of the legs caught Emma's upper arm. She stumbled, trapped the hem of her day dress under her shoe, and nearly fell. Marisol spun with the momentum of the stool and came at her again.

This time Emma had no chance to get away. She hunched like a hedgehog, hoping to take the worst of it on her back. The blow flattened her and robbed her of breath, but she still managed to kick out hard when she felt Marisol take her right leg by the ankle. Marisol was able to drag her only a few inches before Emma forced a release. Emma turned on her back and kicked again, catching Marisol in the midriff as she bent over. Marisol was thrown against one of the French doors. It slammed shut, forcing Marisol to pedal backward to keep her balance. The crown of her head thudded off the door frame. She cried out softly as Emma scrambled to her feet.

Emma kicked aside the stool and retreated to the stairwell, never once taking her eyes from Marisol. She was out of reach, most likely out of danger, and Marisol was no longer regarding her as if she meant to attack. Her attention in fact was wandering to the view through the single open doorway.

"Marisol?" Emma gripped the top of the handrail. "Step away from there. You can see there's no balcony."

"Indeed," Marisol said, turning. She inched closer to the opening and placed one hand on the slack length of rope that comprised the flimsy barrier to the outside. "Do you know what else I see, Emmalyn?"

"I don't, but come here and tell me."

Marisol glanced at Emma over her shoulder. Her smile was edged with regret. "Mr. Gardner has just arrived," she said quietly. "And Neven is with him. I do not think that can bode well. Neven is out of patience with me, and your husband never had any."

Emma wondered what reassurances she might offer and could find none.

Marisol's slim smile was tinged with regret. "There is

nothing left to say, is there? Even you realize there is nothing left to say."

Emma refused to give in as easily as that. She released the handrail and tentatively took a few steps toward Marisol. She extended one arm, palm up. "Please," she said. "Come away. Come here."

"You would save me? That is what you're thinking, isn't it? You mean to save me. Even now it does not occur that I might take you by the hand and fling you away. It might be lovely, you know. To fly. Can you see yourself taking flight?"

Emma could. Contrary to what Marisol said, Emma was ever conscious of her outstretched arm, of Marisol's planted feet, of the breeze beating hard now against their skirts. She thought suddenly of the pair of young women in the park, the choices offered, the decisions made. The whip of the wind. The threatening rain. A bonnet lifted into the air and the impulsive leap to save it.

Emma made that impulsive leap, launching herself into the air in the very moment that Marisol did the same. The perfect coordination of the flight might have been planned save for the direction each one of them took. Marisol dove for the street; Emma dove for Marisol.

Emma heard the rent of fabric as her fingers curled tightly in Marisol's skirts. Her shoulders were wrenched by the pull of Marisol's weight, and she struggled to find better purchase without letting go. Marisol was struggling also, but her intentions ran counter to Emma's. She flailed at the air and tried to wriggle from under Emma's grasp, more than half of her body already dangling free over the threshold.

Emma closed her ears to Marisol's pleas and closed her eyes to the view of the street below. She held on, grimacing with the effort, tasting blood on her lip. She could feel Marisol successfully inching her way farther over the edge, dragging her along. The rope drooped a foot above her at its lowest point, but Emma knew if she reached for it with one hand, she would lose Marisol with the other. She pushed her hip against the door that was closed, seeking to slow Marisol's steady creeping. The door shuddered, and for a moment Emma thought it might give way, but it held, even when she didn't.

The hands that suddenly gripped her waist caused Emma to sob with relief.

"Hold on!" Restell was on his knees slipping one arm under Emma's torso. "Charters is going to open the other door."

Beneath her, Emma could feel Marisol squirming harder. There was little left of her that was not twisting in the wind. The door scraped her hip and thigh as Neven yanked it open. Emma hardly felt it. Instead, she was aware of Neven dropping to the floor beside her and pushing himself over the lip. He extended his arms but could not reach Marisol's flailing ones.

"Pull me back, Restell," Emma shouted. "I can hold her a little longer. Pull me so Neven can reach her."

Restell was loath to alter his grip on Emma's waist. He tugged, but their position did not lend itself to creeping backward. He had to let go and reach over her taut shoulders to take her forearms in his hands, then he pulled as hard as he could, raising Emma, then raising Marisol.

Neven leaned even farther out the opening, this time catching Marisol by the back of her dress just below her neck. "Take my hand, Marisol! For the love of God, take my hand!"

"No!" It was Emma who cried out, not Marisol. "Don't let her do that!"

But Neven was already thrusting his other hand out, and Marisol reached back to grasp it. "I've got her!"

"She has you!" Emma shouted. "She has your wrist!" There was another rending of fabric. Emma felt Marisol literally being torn from her hands. Restell was still pulling on her arms; his last effort was hard enough to yank her back into the studio. She twisted out from under him and rolled away. Scrambling to her knees, she saw that Restell was already moving to help Neven. Emma leaned her head out the opening. Marisol was no longer dangling headlong above the street. Her entire position had changed when she grabbed her fiancé and Emma had let go. Now she was swinging upright from Neven's arm. "You have to grab her!" Emma told them. "Take *her* wrist!"

Marisol looked up. She caught Emma's eye and their glances held. The moment was infinitesimal. The moment was an eternity.

And then she let go.

Epilogue

Lady Gardner rose to her knees on the quilt spread out beneath her and attempted to secure her husband's attention by calling his name. As she was not confident he would respond to this overture, she also used expansive arm gestures, alternately waving him over, then pointing to the space on the blanket beside her.

Sir Geoffrey glanced back at this wife, observed her comically urgent gesticulations, then looked somewhat longingly in the direction of the stream. A trout cleared the surface of the water in the exact spot he had hoped to make his first cast. Sighing, he hefted his rod and slew it over his shoulder, then with the joy of a man condemned, began dutifully trudging toward his wife.

Emma observed Sir Geoffrey's slow climb away from the stream and found herself smiling. She ducked behind her easel so no one save her husband saw her amusement.

"Your mother is insistent that we should be left alone," she said.

Restell was lying back in the grass, resting on his elbows. His legs were crossed casually at the ankles and his frock coat was unbuttoned. Sunlight glanced off his pale hair. "That's because she knows perfectly well that I have designs upon your person." Lest Emma be in doubt regarding those designs, he raised an eyebrow and added a look that suggested all manner of licentious behavior.

Emma merely rolled her eyes. "It is because she fears that your father's fly fishing will interfere with my composition. I think she will be disappointed to see how little I have accomplished this afternoon." She set her brush down and eyed her work critically. "I do not think I have the skill to capture the industry of your family, Restell. They are not at all peaceful, you know."

Restell glanced over his shoulder. The patchwork of colorful blankets on the knoll behind him was all but invisible for the bodies sprawled across them. In various states of sated repose were Wynetta and Porter, the twins and their spouses, and Ferrin and Cybelline. Sir Geoffrey was already dropping to his knees beside his wife and in moments would be dreaming of all the trout he hadn't caught. Hannah and Portia had managed to herd their younger nieces and nephews onto the largest quilt, but even they were napping or amusing themselves quietly.

Restell's mouth twitched. To his way of thinking the inhabitants of an opium den were more inclined to industry than his family. Like successive doses of laudanum, the picnic repast, trickling stream, cloudless autumn sky, and warm sunshine had a soporific layering effect. His father had tried to break away, but had surrendered to forces of nature that included his lady wife.

He looked up at Emma. She was no longer regarding her painting, but regarding him instead. Her eyes were amused, and her lips twitched in a way that mirrored his. He liked these moments when they shared a thought without a word passing between them. The fact that they occurred more frequently of late was encouraging.

She looked quite lovely. More importantly, she looked rested. Marisol's suicide—and there were no illusions it was anything but that—had left Emma as battered as anything the Peele brothers had done to her. Having learned beyond a doubt that it was Marisol that wanted her dead was a blow like no fist could ever deliver.

Restell observed that Emma's response to the figurative beating was different than her reaction to the literal one. Where her fears had confined her before, in the aftermath of Marisol's death they drove her relentlessly from the house. She went to the park almost daily and made a point of calling upon his mother and sisters several times each week. She accepted what invitations she decently could, preferring to be out of their home rather that in it. She attended Sir Arthur every morning and again in the evening, but never stayed above an hour on any visit, and as it became evident that his grief at Marisol's passing would not impede his recovery, she visited even less. That behavior confounded Restell until Emma, at a point of utter exhaustion, had revealed the particulars of her last conversation with Marisol.

Restell understood it was unlikely they would ever know the exact nature of the relationship Marisol had with her father, but he was inclined to believe that Marisol had not twisted the truth in the end. For Emma, her cousin's final, damning confession made it impossible for her to be at rest in Sir Arthur's presence. Her admiration for her uncle's talent and appreciation for his instruction were not diminished, but in every other way her feeling for him was altered. Lady Rivendale also carefully disengaged herself from Sir Arthur's side, raising the question in Restell's mind of what she had come to suspect at the end. Perhaps, Restell thought, there would come a time when he would ask Sir Arthur if he'd forced his daughter to perform the intimate duties of a wife, but as he only expected a denial, he wondered what would be served by posing the question.

What he decided to do instead was draw Emma away from London and applied to his brother for help. Ferrin was happy to oblige with an invitation to call upon him and Cybelline in the country. As often was the case with the Gardners, an invitation to one was somehow transformed into an invitation to all. For himself, Restell did not mind—Ferrin's country estate had almost as many rooms as Buckingham Palace—but he had a twinge of sympathy for Ferrin who would be compelled to act the gracious host while the peace and dignity of his home was regularly assaulted.

Recalling that the earl was stretched comfortably on a blanket with his dear wife curled beside him, Restell decided that for the nonce peace and dignity had the upper hand.

"May I see your work?" he asked, darting a glance at Emma's painting. She'd purposely kept it angled away from him. A sketchbook lay in the grass at her feet, and she'd finally chosen one drawing she liked well enough to render in ink and watercolor. The heavy paper was clipped to a wood panel that rested on the easel.

Emma wiped her hands on her apron. Her fingers were stained with splotches of watercolor from splashing the contents of the rinsing cup when she washed her brushes. "It's not finished, you understand." She gave it a second study, then shrugged, dismissing caution. She lifted the wood panel and turned it so Restell could view her painting.

Restell's grin surfaced immediately. Emma had a keen eye for the humor of a moment and the talent to put it to paper. This was no serene portrait of his family. Indeed, they could never be truly captured in that static state. What Emma put before him was his family at their most familiar: Imogene challenging Ian and their spouses to a foot race up the knoll, his father hooking his mother's skirts with the fishing rod, Hannah juggling oranges from an overturned picnic basket, Portia regarding her reflection in the water as she danced about, Wynetta and Porter swinging a child between them while another hopped on one foot demanding a turn. Ferrin was laughing at something his wife said; she seemed within a heartbeat of doing the same. Children darted between the adults, catching a skirt here, a trouser leg there. And in the lower left corner, Emma had captured him saving her airborne bonnet from a certain soaking by snagging it with the point of his walking stick.

For a long moment Restell could find no words, then he

managed to work them past the constriction in his throat to pronounce the painting perfect.

Emma felt her cheeks grow warm. "I think that is rather too—"

He shook his head. "I cannot say how others might view it, Emma, but to me, it is perfect."

"Thank you." She set the panel back on the easel. "You were also thinking of the other painting, weren't you? The one that Marisol destroyed."

Restell admitted that he was. "It was extraordinary. I think I regret its loss more than you do."

Her smile was bittersweet. "I don't know if that's possible, but I have the advantage of knowing that I'll paint the like of it again."

With the evidence of her watercolor before him and the confidence in her voice, Restell realized he could believe Emma's assertion. Had she said the same when they were yet in London, he would have considered she said it to set his mind at ease, not because she believed it herself.

"Ferrin's spoken to me about the London house," Restell said.

"Our house?" she asked. "Or his?"

"Both actually. He's expressed an interest in selling his home and wondered if I might like to purchase it."

Emma's response was a careful, "I see."

"What do you think of it?"

"I think I detect your fine hand at work. Am I right?"

He sighed. "I would tell you otherwise, but you'll know it for a lie. Yes, I put the idea before him. You may ask him yourself, though, he required no convincing, and he is perfectly capable of saying no."

"No one says no to you, Restell. Least of all your family."

There was too much truth to it for Restell to do anything but offer up a sheepish grin. "This is a bit different. Something more in the way of a favor. After all, I did him the service of returning the real Eden seascape to Lady Rivendale, thus ensuring that his wife will inherit the original. That was accomplished at some risk, I might add, as Lady Rivendale's home was infinitely more difficult to enter than others I have attempted."

"But Mr. Charters gave you the Eden to return to the countess, didn't he?"

"He did." Restell had brought the thing about with very little in the way of coercion. The fact that Neven Charters had run Jonathan Kincaid to ground in Walthamstow and killed him for what he and his cousins had done to Emma was a point in his favor as far as Restell was concerned. That he had failed to offer this information, however, was perhaps understandable but ultimately unforgivable.

Only slightly less damning was Charters scheme to ingratiate himself to Sir Arthur by discrediting Mr. Johnston. Every price that Charters's friends swore they paid for paintings was inflated so that it appeared Johnston had recorded too little and kept the difference. The real cost, though, of Charters's perfidy was that it put him squarely in Marisol's path. Sir Arthur saw the advantages at once and encouraged the pair. When Charters became wary of Marisol's uncertain moods and would have sought Emma out again, Sir Arthur revealed he knew the precise nature of the trick Charters had played on the hapless Johnston. Neatly caught out, it was not long before Charters and Sir Arthur engaged in a contract for their mutual benefit. Once they conspired on the forgeries, neither of them could call retreat, but it was clever Marisol who came to hold the upper hand. The unpredictability of her behavior caused her father and Neven Charters to tread carefully around her when she was of a certain temper.

"And he also surrendered the Tintoretto belonging to Mrs. Stuart," Restell said. "Though that pained him mightily."

Emma was not surprised to learn of it. "Then I am compelled to point out that Ferrin would not know about the Eden forgery if you had not apprised him of it."

"A mere detail. He is quite happy to extend the favor. It's not as if he's presenting me his home without recompense. We are working out the financial particulars."

"I am not fooled, Restell. You are doing this for me. I know you've been aware that I haven't been able to use the studio. I am sorry for that. It was such a splendid gift you gave me, but to go there . . ." Her voice trailed off, and she simply shook her head.

"I am contemplating the move for us, Emma. Ferrin's town home has a conservatory that I believe you will find most excellent for painting. If that pleases you, then I am pleased as well. You would not see me miserable, would you?"

She shook her head again, this time with a modicum of restrained humor. "The bent of your mind is most peculiar."

"Mother says I am an original thinker."

"She was being kind, I fear."

Chuckling, Restell pushed himself upright. He reached for Emma, taking her hand so that he could get to his feet, then draw her up also. When they were standing toe-to-toe, he kissed her. "Come. I know where there is a lovely clearing where we may take our own rest."

Emma darted a look past his shoulder. No one was yet stirring on the blankets. "If it was rest you had in mind, we would be joining the others." Before he could acknowledge it as fact, Emma began pulling him toward the wood. "It is this way, I believe."

Restell thought it indecent to ask how she came by that intelligence. If it was a place used by Ferrin and Cybelline, or any other member of his family for that matter, he did not want to know it.

Slim beams of sunshine were filtered by the canopy of pine boughs. A thick bed of needles made a fine, soft spot for them to lay upon, though Restell sacrificed his frock coat as well. The occasional breeze struck down a dried leaf from the nearby chestnuts, then lowered it gently to the ground.

That was how Restell lowered Emma, cradling her so carefully she barely felt his fingertips against her back. He lay on his side, fit closely to her, and sifted her silky hair with his fingertips. Her smile was soft, a bit dreamy, but her blue-green eyes were clear and focused. She slipped one hand around the back of his neck and applied the slightest pressure.

"I'm always willing to take direction," he whispered. Then he kissed her. Her mouth was sweet and warm. He touched his tongue to her lips and tasted a hint of the apple cider that was another of autumn's pleasures.

Their lovemaking was unhurried. Sunshine dappled their bodies; the breeze lifted the fragrances of tall grass and fecund earth. The rush of water in the distance was a steady thrum, first in their ears, then in their veins. They exchanged only a few words, yet nothing was left unsaid. A touch, a glance, the shift of a shoulder, the fine edge of a smile, all of it had purpose, all of it had meaning.

Healing was behind them; what remained was hunger. Peripherally conscious of an audience they might attract, they nevertheless indulged their healthy appetite. Restell kissed Emma's open mouth when she would have cried out, and he buried his face against her neck when he would have done the same.

Replete, they lay unmoving long enough to steady their heartbeats, then set about righting their clothes so they might make a more modest presentation when they returned to the picnic. Restell plucked pine needles from Emma's hair. She straightened his stock. Eventually they pronounced each other fit, though neither made to leave the clearing. The exchange of glances that had worked so well for them when making love, demonstrated that it had wider application as they simply lay back on Restell's frock coat.

"I don't suppose they'll be trekking to the house any time soon," Emma said. Her head rested comfortably in the crook of Restell's shoulder. "We shall have to face them sooner rather than later."

"You are rather slow coming to that epiphany."

"I came to it earlier. I am only speaking of it now."

Restell was not proof against her tart tongue. He pressed his smile in the crown of her dark hair. As a consequence, Emma was perfectly agreeable to nestling closer.

"It occurs to me, Restell, that you have yet to secure the favor I owe you."

"Perhaps if there had been a more satisfactory resolution, but under the circumstances, no, there is no favor owed."

Emma understood his reluctance. "You used a favor on my behalf," she said. "There should be some exchange for that."

Curious, Restell asked, "What do you know about it?"

"I know Neven Charters has removed himself to Paris. Although, as I think on it, it may be that he was removed. I have it on good authority that he was accompanied—or escorted—by Monsieur Jourdain and his ambassador father. It seems Mr. Charters has acquired a position authenticating certain antiquities acquired by the government during the Napoleonic wars. He has also surrendered his treasures to the Royal museum."

"You know all that, do you?" Restell couldn't quite see Emma's smile, but he imagined it was smug. "I suppose you had it from my father."

"In his defense, he didn't understand the import of what he was telling me. I imagine it was all arranged because you brought the influence of the foreign minister to bear."

"Perhaps."

"You will not admit to it?"

"I don't think so, no. There should be some mystery. A rogue would cultivate a sense of mystery, don't you agree?"

Emma turned so that he could not miss the superior arch of her eyebrow, then settled back in the cradle of his shoulder.

Restell waited until his chuckle faded before he spoke. "There is a favor I would have from you, though."

"Truly?"

"Truly." A slight smile edged Restell's mouth as he felt Emma hold her breath in anticipation of what he would say. "Breathe, Emma. It is not a Herculean task I am going to place before you. I merely want you to release me from my promise."

"Promise? What promise is that?"

"The one you made me swear to before you would marry me. Do not say you don't remember."

Now that he put it before her in plainer terms, she did recall it. "I made you promise that you would divorce me if I asked."

"Yes. I want you to release me from it."

"Very well. I release you."

He blinked. "What? There is to be no argument? No negotiation for other terms?"

"As I have no intention of releasing you from your vows, arguing is entirely disagreeable."

Restell considered this for a long moment. "It occurs of a sudden—and I do not find it at all objectionable—that I am to be made a kept man."

Emma turned and raised herself up so that she might look at him and that he might have the same advantage. "A kept man," she repeatedly softly. "Yes, I suppose that's so."

Restell drew her hand close to his chest so that it rested just above his heart. "As you are a kept woman." He squeezed her fingers. "Here. Always here."

Emma kissed him warmly on the mouth. Some truths could be communicated in just such a fashion, and Emma's truth was this: If her home was in his heart, it didn't matter where she lived.

About the Author

JO GOODMAN lives with with her family in Colliers, West Virginia. She is currently working on her newest Zebra historical romance, once again set in the Regency period. Look for it in 2008! Jo loves hearing from readers, and you may write to her c/o Zebra Books. Please include a self-addressed envelope if you would like a response. Or you can visit her website at www.jogoodman.com.